New
CRIMES
3

New CRIMES 3

edited by Maxim Jakubowski

Carroll & Graf
Publishers Inc.

New York

First published in Great Britain 1991
First Carroll & Graf edition 1991

Carroll & Graf Publishers, Inc.
260 Fifth Avenue
New York
NY 10001

ISBN: 0–88184–737–2

Printed in Great Britain.

Contents

CONTENTS

Acknowledgements

"Last Kiss" by Norman Partridge. © 1991 by Norman Partridge.

"Baz" by Julian Rathbone. © 1991 by Julian Rathbone.

"Hijack" by William Schoell. © 1991 by William Schoell.

"The Absolute and Utter Impossibility of the Facts in the Case of the Vanishing of Henning Vok (a.k.a. the Amazing Blitzen) (r.n.Jack Ralph Cole)" by Jack Adrian. © 1991 by Jack Adrian.

"Blast from the Past" by Gabrielle Kraft. © 1991 by Gabrielle Kraft.

"Natural Powers" by Margaret Lewis. © 1991 by Margaret Lewis.

"Boogie Dead Men" by W.R. Philbrick. © 1991 by W.R. Philbrick.

"Souls Burning" by Bill Pronzini. © 1991 by Bill Pronzini.

"Dry Run" by Gary Lovisi. © 1991 by Gary Lovisi.

"Death in the Ditch" by Del Marston. © 1948 by Del Marston; renewed 1991 by Richard A. Lupoff, executor for the estate of Del Marston.

"The Monk's Tale" by PC. Doherty. © 1991 by P.C. Doherty.

"What Goes Around . . ." by Mark Schorr. © 1991 by Mark Schorr.

"Star" by Molly Brown. © 1991 by Molly Brown.

"The Persian Apothecary" by Cay Van Ash. © 1991 by Cay Van Ash.

"Too Late Blues" by Mark Timlin. © 1991 by Mark Timlin.

"Until I Do" by Robert Lopresti. © 1991 by Robert Lopresti.

"Lord Peter and the Butter Boy" by Mike Ripley. © 1991 by Mike Ripley.

"Squeezer" by Steve Rasnic Tem. © 1991 by Steve Rasnic Tem.

"Surrogate" by Robert B. Parker. © 1982 by Robert B. Parker. First published in a limited edition chapbook by Lord John Press, Northridge, California.

"Jukebox Jungle" by John D. MacDonald. © 1950 by John D. MacDonald. First published in *Black Mask*, December 1950.

"Another Glass, Watson!" by John Dickson Carr. © 1957 by John Dickson Carr. First published in the catalogue of the Sherlock Holmes collection of the Sherlock Holmes public house, London.

Introduction

A lready our third cornucopia of crime, and once again a most varied bunch of stories from our contributors in Britain, the USA and Japan (where Cay Van Ash currently resides).

The response to the *New Crimes* anthologies has been most positive from readers and critics (apart from the anonymous *Publishers Weekly* reviewer who felt my own story in the second volume bordered on the pornographic) and it was particularly heartening to see Ed Gorman's story in our opening volume, *Prisoners*, nominated for the Edgar best short story award and John Conquest winning the non-fiction Edgar for his definitive study of Private Eyes, "Trouble is their Business", an excerpt of which was also featured in the first *New Crimes*. Congratulations to both Ed and John who will hopefully be in future volumes of *New Crimes* again.

The aim of this series is basically to feature the best in new crime and mystery writing from all over the world, regardless of theme, sex or sub-genre. Because of my own reputation, it is often assumed that *New Crimes* is predominantly hardboiled. It ain't necessarily so, as the song goes. Unlike other anthologies, I blend material from both Britain and the USA, to demonstrate the sheer breadth of talent there is around and, if all goes well, hope to present one or two foreign language stories in translation in years to come, to make *New Crimes* even more representative.

So, who's on board the mystery train on this year's journey?

Norman Partridge is the first to open fire and hails from Lafayette in California. His story "Last Kiss" is a beautifully understated shocker. He has previously sold stories to various fantasy and horror anthologies including Charles L. Grant's *Final Shadows* and Joe Lansdale's *Dark at Heart*.

Julian Rathbone, on the other hand, is a veteran mystery writer who has spent much of the past few years writing some greatly underrated thrillers like *The Pandora Option* and *The Crystal Contract*. His mischievous story "Baz" is the first in a series featuring a modern couple of sleuths more than inspired by Holmes and Watson. I have read the first five and know you have a treat in store.

The author of suspense novels like *Late at Night, Shivers, The Dragon, The Pact* and *Fatal Beauty*, **William Schoell** is a New Yorker who has also penned one of the first books on the slasher film phenomenon, *Stay out of the Shower*. His contribution, "Hijack" will ring bells with many of us who live in large cities and often have to depend on the vagaries of public transport.

Edgar nominee **Jack Adrian** lives in rural Worcestershire and is a specialist of British post-war pulp and comics and a keen appreciator of locked room mysteries. His latest book is an anthology of impossible murders, *The Art of the Impossible*, co-edited with Robert Adey. His story spins another, tongue-in-cheek, variation on the ever-fascinating theme of the locked room murder.

Gabrielle Kraft's first Jerry Zalman novel, *Bullshot* was also nominated for an Edgar, and has since been followed by three more, *Screwdriver, Bloody Mary* and *Let's Rob Roy*. Gaby lives in Portland, Oregon and her story "Blast from the Past" is part of a series of Hollywood-inspired tales of the underbelly of the film world.

Margaret Lewis has just published the authorised biography of golden age author Ngaio Marsh. This is her first published crime story, with an academic background that will come as no surprise in view of her work for the Open University and the University of Newcastle upon Tyne.

Born in Boston, but now living in Maine, **W.R.** (Rod) **Philbrick** is the author of the popular J.D. Hawkins mysteries, of which *Walk on the Water* is the latest, and other hardboiled series. He has twice been nominated for the Shamus award.

What would *New Crimes* be without a **Bill Pronzini** story? Bill makes it three out of three with a new case for his classic character, Nameless. The last novel in the series was *Breakdown*, the new one will be *Quarry* and Bill is presently working on the next, to be titled *Kinsmen*.

INTRODUCTION

Gary Lovisi is the intrepid editor and publisher of *Paperback Parade*, the indispensable magazine for all of us collectors of vintage paperbacks with lurid but wonderfully nostalgic covers, as well as *Hardboiled Detective*. He lives in Brooklyn and his story, "Dry Run" has a nice gritty feel to it.

"Death in the Ditch" was written in 1948 by **Del Marston**, then the greatest rival to Ellery Queen, but now a sadly forgotten figure from a time when crime writing in America was not as violent as it is today. This unpublished story was found by Richard A. Lupoff during the course of research for an article on Marston for Gary Lovisi's *Paperback Parade* and appears to be the opening for an unfinished novel that heralds the hard-boiled blood and guts school of a Mickey Spillane.

P.C. Doherty is fast becoming the prince-in-waiting of the medieval mystery field made so popular by Ellis Peters. A school headmaster outside London, he has also begun a new historical series as Paul Harding.

Mark Schorr is another member of the Portland writing gang (as is Gabrielle Kraft). It's such a nice place that it's no wonder so many authors now live there. Here's to hoping for future *New Crimes* stories from K.W. Jeter and Robert Sheckley, other Portland acolytes. In the meantime, Mark's story spins a yarn that will warm the heart of many a writer.

In *New Crimes 2*, I introduced **Molly Brown** as an erstwhile cabaret artist. Being American, she pointed out to me this made her sound like a burlesque or strip-tease performer. Mea culpa. What I meant was her previous career as a stand-up comic. Somewhat more respectable, I'm sure you'll agree. Molly has, since our last volume, begun selling her stories quite widely elsewhere, confirming our predictions. "Star" is a damn good chiller.

Cay Van Ash wrote the definitive biography of Fu Manchu creator Sax Rohmer (in collaboration with his daughter Elizabeth) and is also the literary executor for Rohmer's estate. His offering takes place in days of old in Cairo and is a splendid example of classical mystery storytelling.

South London's **Mark Timlin** is part of Britain's new wave of realistic crime writers. His character Nick Sharman patrols London's mean streets with dubious confidence and charm in four novels already. His story of a bungled heist has a disquietening ring of truth.

Robert Lopresti has edited *Thurber on Crime*, a collection of James Thurber's ruminations on villainy. He has also published stories in *Alfred Hitchcock's Mystery Magazine*.

Mike Ripley is the creator of the popular, humorous Angel series and also the driving force behind Fresh Blood, a group of British crime writers for the year 2000, i.e. somewhat more realistic in manner and execution than Christie and cohorts. His story offers an unusual angle on Lord Peter Wimsey.

"Squeezer" by **Steve Rasnic Tem** is another American slice of death with a gently twisted twist. Steve, who lives in Colorado is known for his work in the fantasy and horror field and contributed to one of my own fantasy collections, *Lands of Never*, some years back before I became a (literary) criminal.

With past nuggets from David Goodis, Ed McBain, Charles Willeford and Cornell Woolrich, our Vintage Corner, where we uncover previously uncollected stories from some genuine masters of crime and mystery, has proven a popular feature with readers and this volume's rediscoveries are as exciting as any. To the best of my knowledge, "Surrogate" by **Robert B. Parker** is the only known Spenser short story, a cynical tale of rape and revenge, previously only available in a small, limited chapbook edition. Travis McGee creator **John D. MacDonald** was a prolific contributor to the pulp magazines before fame beckoned; "Jukebox Jungle" first appeared in the legendary *Black Mask*.

An appetizing menu of misdeeds both clever and crude, I'm sure you'll agree.

Maxim Jakubowski

Last Kiss

by Norman Partridge

I f you're like me, there are things you need to tell people, but
you can't get the words out. You want to, but you can't. The
machinery just won't work, and everything gets all jammed up,
churning in your guts long after those people are gone from your
life.

You're stuck with them, and they stay inside you forever.

The things you wanted to say. And, in a way, in memory, the
people you wanted to say them to.

All together, stuck inside you forever, and there's no way to get
them out. You can write about them—like I'm doing now—scribble
from A to Z and back again, but they're still with you when you're
done, because writing starts and ends in your guts.

And that's kind of funny, isn't it? All that stuff churning inside
you, all those people you remember and all those things that you
wanted to tell them. . . it's funny how it never comes together. I
mean, it's all in there, catalogued and nicely filed, and somehow
it seems like you should be able to put it together. After all, you
remember the person and you sure as hell remember what you
wanted to say. It's like you should be able to figure out what would
have happened had you only said it.

How your life would be different.

How the lives of those other people would be different.

That's my problem. I keep on trying to figure out what might
have been.

1

Maybe that's why I still have those dead people stuck inside me.

Maybe that's why I still have Anelle Carney stuck inside me, too.

We met in high school, of course. Isn't that where all great American romances start? We shared two classes during our sophomore year, and because my last name is Carter, which is just three letters short of Carney, I sat behind Anelle in both of them.

I was hooked right from the start. She always had a smile for me, Anelle did, and her smile made me feel like someone special. That smile was a toothpaste advertiser's wet dream—gleaming white teeth surrounded by perfect lips that were somehow just short of inviting. And when Anelle parted those lips and teeth and you heard her voice. . . Well, it wasn't the kind of voice you'd expect a teenager to have. It was quiet, but not in a shy way. Kind of sleepy, too—Anelle always talked slowly, like she had all the time in the world, like she thought a lot about the things she said. She didn't jabber. She considered every word.

That was the same way I talked, back then. Someone told me once that people listen closely to a person who isn't blabbing all the time. I guess that was part of the reason that I was so quiet.

The other part, the biggest part, was fear.

Anyway, I get nervous and expectant just thinking about the way Anelle made me feel, even now. What was that old Carly Simon song? "Anticipation," or something like that? Back then, that could have been my theme song. I still remember the funny rush that crept up my spine every time she entered the classroom.

Summer was the worst time, of course. It was hard to keep in touch with her when school was out. No more than three blocks separated our houses, but Anelle's house stood at the end of a court that was bordered by a dead end street and a cemetery. One way in and one way out—that was her joke. I didn't know any of Anelle's neighbors, and I didn't have any relatives in the boneyard, so it was tough for me to find an excuse to walk by and try to catch a glimpse of her.

I tracked Anelle like I was a bounty hunter. That wasn't hard, because her dad bought her a brand new Pontiac for her birthday (June 12th, if you care). So I knew her car and I looked for it everywhere, cruising the streets in a bruised Dodge that was *my* first car. I don't particularly have any fond memories of that Dodge, apart from the fact that it was the car I drove when I hunted for Anelle.

2

Anyway, Anelle always used the same gas station, and I hung out there with a buddy, Pete Hatcher, who worked the pumps. Pete didn't mind my company. He was always fixing up some junker in hopes of making a big resale profit, and I was pretty handy with cars. The guy who owned the station let us use the equipment when the main mechanic wasn't busy with it, so Pete had a really good deal going in more ways then one.

So the price of seeing Anelle was a little free work. That was okay with me. I didn't begrudge Pete my labor, because Anelle gassed up that Pontiac pretty often. She never let the gauge fall beneath three-quarters full, like she had some phobia about running out of gas. I'd fill her up myself if Pete was busy. Believe it or not, I even got a rise out of doing that little thing for Anelle. It was nothing compared to the other things I did for her, but it made me feel good in a tingly way I can't put words to.

That summer I learned a lot about Anelle Carney: where she bought her cheeseburgers (no onions, extra mayo), where she shopped for clothes (jeans and loose blouses, never skirts), which swimming pool she liked to hang out at on hot days (she used Coppertone, and I still dream about rubbing it on her). Damn, I remember spending whole afternoons working on a suntan, just because Anelle always had a deep tan and I figured she'd find that attractive.

She liked to go to the library, too. It was easy to figure out when she'd show up there—all I had to do was count three weeks from the day of her last visit, because that's when her books came due. On due day, I'd hang around reading until she came in. Anelle thought that I was a real bookworm, and I guess I was, though I stuck to Westerns and didn't sample the glitzy romances that she liked to read.

The best place to catch her was the movie theatre. She had a job there—nights, except for Wednesdays and Thursdays—working behind the candy counter. The deal with her old man was that she had to pay for her own gas and insurance since he'd popped for the new car. One of those lessons in responsibility, I guess.

It was kind of a drag, that job. Anelle didn't like the people she worked with. The cashier was a bore and the projectionist was always trying to peek down the front of her usherette uniform. So she didn't like it much, and I didn't either, though for me her job had its good points.

It was good because I knew exactly where she was most nights, but it was bad because the movie only changed once a week (this was pre-multiplex), so I couldn't actually see her that often. And on top of that there were bad pictures that summer. Real turkeys.

3

I sat through at least two Robbie Benson movies, endless disaster epics, even some junk about a mule that played football.

I always went on Tuesday night, because the crowd was pretty thin and I knew I'd get a chance to talk to Anelle.

Tuesday night—my big night of the week. Was then. Is now.

It was on a Tuesday night that I kissed Anelle Carney for the first time.

I can't remember the name of the picture they were showing that night. That's not so strange, because I only saw about twenty minutes of it. All I remember is that it starred Doug McClure and a pack of rubber dinosaurs.

Anyway, I watched the coming attractions, not wanting to seem too eager about hitting the candy counter. I always liked to wait until the picture got started before I went for popcorn. By then the lobby was clear, leaving Anelle with plenty of time to chat.

It wasn't long before I lost patience with Doug and his sad rubber pals. I left my seat and headed for the lobby. I remember all that like it was yesterday. Where I sat, what I was wearing. Christ, I even remember checking to see if my fly was zipped before I pushed open the padded doors.

I stepped into the lobby slow and cool, smiling like I knew the movie was a big joke.

No one appreciated my little act.

The lobby was empty.

I walked up to the counter, figuring that Anelle was crouching behind it, stocking paper cups or napkins or something. But she wasn't there. I turned and glanced at the glassed-in box office, which was a closed booth outside the lobby, thinking that maybe the cashier got sick and Anelle was pulling double duty. But a chunky girl sat there, hunched over the same paperback she'd been reading when I bought my ticket.

I stood there, glancing from the counter to the door of the ladies' john. No Anelle. Popcorn popped in a big glass case. Hot dogs revolved on little chromed rollers, tanning themselves under orange heat lamps.

No Anelle.

And then I heard her scream.

I dodged around the counter just as an angry roar eclipsed Anelle's scream. Pure male. Pure rage. There was a narrow doorway between the soda machine and the popcorn popper. Gold letters on the door spelled out MANAGER. I grabbed the knob.

The door was locked.

A muffled voice came from behind the door, pleading. Another voice shouted down the first. "I'll teach you, you little—"

I kicked the door. The bottom half flexed, giving everywhere but around the knob and hinges. Something thudded against the other side. The knob moved, and the door opened an inch. I got a glimpse of a green eye, chestnut hair. Then thick fingers tangled in the hair and pulled the face away.

I pushed through the door.

The projectionist stared at me. He had his forearm around Anelle's neck. Her blue and red usherette blouse was unzipped. Her skin was scratched where he'd ripped off her bra, and the button of her jeans was undone.

I didn't want to look at those things. I looked into Anelle's eyes. They were wide open and wilder than eyes should be.

"Close the door, boy," the projectionist hissed. "I've seen the way you look at this little tease. Take a good look now, buddy. There's enough here for the both of us."

His right hand kneaded her breast, and I noticed a red crescent where she'd bitten the soft flesh at the base of his thumb. For a second I wondered how much a wound like that would hurt, and then my hands balled into fists.

Anelle's lips parted. Her teeth parted.

She said my name, and then her perfect teeth sank into the projectionist's hairy forearm.

He howled and I sprang. The three of us hit the floor together. I could feel Anelle's breasts pressing against my chest. I could smell her hair and her breath, and her breath did smell like toothpaste.

She rolled away and my fists were flying. The projectionist's howls became little mewling sounds, then petered out altogether. His face had gone pasty white, and I stopped punching.

Anelle pulled me off him. I realized that I was crying, and I knew that she saw my tears, saw the confusion in my eyes, but I didn't even care because there was confusion in her eyes, too. Her arms went around me. Again I felt her breasts pressing against my chest.

There was nothing between us but my thin cotton T-shirt.

Anelle Carney kissed me then.

Not a lover's kiss. Not the kiss I'd dreamed of. But it was Anelle's kiss. And it was for me.

I closed my eyes. We didn't do anything but hold each other. When Anelle pulled away, I was ready to tell her everything.

I opened my eyes. Saw a little smear of blood on her chin and wondered if it was hers or the projectionist's. It rattled me for a second, but it wasn't going to stop me.

I swallowed. Opened my mouth.

Then the cashier stepped into the room, one finger jammed in her paperback so she wouldn't lose her place. "I already called the cops." She gasped, staring down at the projectionist. "Oh, Jesus. I'd better call an ambulance. . ."

The district attorney went hard. The projectionist had quite a record, including a rape conviction, so there wasn't much trouble about it, especially after he lost his head and threatened Anelle right in front of the judge. Anyway, the guy went off to prison. Fairly quickly, fairly quietly.

Anelle and I were minors, so our names were kept out of the papers. The little word that did leak out enhanced my reputation. Some girls saw me as a knight in shining armor. Pete and the other guys I hung out with thought I was a *número uno* badass.

Personally, I think the projectionist would have had that heart attack even if I hadn't touched him. After Anelle bit him the second time, it was pretty obvious that he was going to have to fight the both of us.

I think that scared the shit out of him.

After it was over, I figured things would work out just fine with Anelle. Sure, I hadn't had a chance to tell her how I felt in the heat of the moment, and I wasn't seeing much of her now because she'd quit her job at the theatre, but I figured that I'd have plenty of opportunities to set things right once school started.

My folks dragged me off on a two week vacation. Then it was September. The Jerry Lewis telethon came and went. I bought some new jeans and hit the books once again.

Anelle wasn't in any of my classes. Pretty soon I discovered that she wasn't in school at all. I didn't ask anyone what had become of her, because I was afraid of the answer I might get.

I didn't want to hear that Anelle's mind had caved in.

I wanted to call her. I sat down and made a big list of things I wanted to ask her, and things she might reply, and things I could say after that. But none of it seemed real. Like I said, writing things down doesn't work.

So I tried to pick up her trail. I spent a solid week of afternoons working on an old Chevy at the gas station. Anelle didn't show, and Pete felt so guilty about me single-handedly rebuilding the Chevy's engine that he actually paid me forty bucks. I spent my evenings at the library, practically sitting on top of the romance paperback rack.

No Anelle.

One night her mother showed up at the library. She was picking out nonfiction, mostly school assignment stuff. I worked up the courage to reintroduce myself—we'd met briefly at the projectionist's trial. Trying not to seem overly anxious, I asked how Anelle was doing.

"As well as can be expected," she said. "There's been a lot of strain, both for Anelle and for the family."

I asked when Anelle was coming back to school.

"She is in school. She transferred to the Catholic Academy. We thought a girls' school would be better for Anelle, at least for the time being."

I could tell that Mrs. Carney didn't want to say more, so I left it at that.

The next day I cut class and waited for Anelle outside the Catholic Academy.

Funny. It was a Tuesday. Another big one.

The Tuesday I walked Anelle Carney home from school.

She came down the stairs and I started out like I always did, talking about music and movies and books, but that wasn't what Anelle wanted to talk about.

She opened up to me that day, but looking back on it I think that she would have opened up to any familiar face. She said that she felt like she was the one who'd done something wrong. Her parents, especially her father, had turned into overprotective watchdogs. He'd insisted that she transfer to a girls' school, and he'd taken her Pontiac away, too.

"Look at me," she said, pointing at her plaid dress and knee socks. "He's trying to turn me into a little girl. I'm not a little girl. It's time for me to start cutting ties, and he's just tying them tighter."

In my head, I tried to twist that into some kind of opening, but everything I came up with seemed clichéd. We were cutting through the cemetery, and I knew I had to say something soon if I was going to say anything at all.

I slowed my step as we approached her door. My mind slipped into neutral.

"Thanks for walking me home," she said. "I really needed to talk to someone, and you're such a good listener."

I looked up, trying to smile, ready to tell her that she could talk to me any old time, but then I saw the thing rooted on the freshly mown lawn. A "FOR SALE" sign.

That night I followed the red Pontiac, but this time I was following Anelle's father.

Even though I'd never met Mr. Carney, I'd always figured that he was a pretty steady guy. He had a good family, a nice house, and a job that allowed him to buy a new car for his daughter on her sixteenth birthday. So it surprised me, how many bars Anelle's dad hit that night. Not olive and onion bars, either—these were nasty joints out on the highway.

I didn't know what to make of that. Maybe Mr. Carney had always been a drinker. Or maybe what had happened to Anelle was breaking him up inside.

Either way, the chances of me talking him out of moving seemed ridiculously long. After all, I was a sixteen-year-old kid. I couldn't just belly up to the bar and buy the old boy a brew, now could I?

So I sat there in the Dodge, and I wrote Mr. Carney a letter. I told him how I felt about his daughter. It was eloquent stuff. I practically asked him for her hand, his blessing. Yep, I got it all down in writing.

It wasn't hard to get into the Pontiac. Mr. Carney hadn't locked the door. I figured I'd leave my letter on the dash, where he'd see it real easy.

There was only one problem with that.

Another letter lay on the dashboard.

It was from Mr. Carney's boss, and it said that his transfer to the east coast was "a rock solid, incontrovertible, done deal."

All my carefully considered words were nothing compared to that one-paragraph bombshell. I balled up my useless letter and shoved it into the pocket of my new jeans.

An hour later I was safe at home, cleaning brake fluid from under my fingernails.

I guess Anelle could handle her mom pretty well, because things got back to normal after her dad's funeral. The red Pontiac had been wrapped around a telephone pole along with Mr. Carney, of course, but the insurance money bought Anelle a nice, sensible Volkswagen. The "FOR SALE" sign came down a week after Mr. Carney was laid to rest in the cemetery across the street—another good Tuesday for me—and I remember feeling that destiny was finally on my side.

Not that things were perfect. Even though Anelle had transferred back to public school, she still wasn't in any of my classes. And I couldn't hang out at the gas station anymore, because Pete had been fired.

I didn't feel good about that, because it was my fault. Just two weeks before the crash, Pete had serviced Mr. Carney's Pontiac. The brake fluid had been changed—Mrs. Carney had a receipt

8

which showed that clearly. Pete was low man on the totem pole, and the owner was tired of him using so much time to work on his junkers, so Pete took the heat.

So I had a tough time keeping up with Anelle. She didn't show at any of the usual places. Her life was changing fast, and I knew that I had to do something dramatic unless I wanted to be remembered only as part of a bad experience. I remembered what she'd said about "cutting ties," and I started to get the crazy notion that she'd been talking about me. I thought about her lips and the time that I'd kissed her, and I knew that I'd made too much of it. That kiss had been more like a handshake than a kiss that passes between lovers.

But I couldn't stop thinking about kissing her. I'd picture her closing her eyes, opening her mouth to mine as I pulled her close. . . I knew I had to make it happen, and soon.

So I spent more and more time at the library, waiting. It seemed pretty futile, because lately Anelle wasn't reading romances at her usual clip. I kept thinking about that line in the old Beach Boys tune: *See she forgot all about the library like she told her old man now. . .*

One night I got involved in an exciting Western written by a guy named Ray Slater. I wasn't really expecting Anelle to show up anymore, so I paid more attention to the book than usual, and I finished it just as the librarian started flicking the lights to signal closing time.

I shelved the Western and headed outside, walking on pins and needles because my left foot had gone to sleep while I was reading. As I shuffled through the doorway, I looked up the street and saw a girl walking toward the library. The dull glow of a streetlight shone on her long chestnut hair.

The girl looked a lot like Anelle.

She passed into the shadows that lay between the streetlights, which were set at each corner. Her stride was slow and unhurried, and even in the shadows I could tell that the girl was Anelle. I'd seen that walk of hers in enough dreams to have it memorized.

A car turned the corner and paced her, lagging a few feet behind, its bright lights turning Anelle into a silhouette. I couldn't tell for sure what make it was—it looked kind of like a Chrysler—only that it had a bad muffler that coughed smoke.

I started down the stairs, my eyes on the car, and I tripped.

My sleepy foot went out from under me. I hit the stairs, hard.

I was up in a second, but the car was gone.

So was Anelle.

All of a sudden I was thinking about the projectionist and the threats he'd screamed at Anelle. I imagined a prison break, a guy dressed in orange con clothes hot-wiring an old Chrysler. Crazy with fear, not feeling the pain of the ankle I'd twisted on the stairs, I half ran, half hopped to my Dodge and peeled rubber, certain that I could catch the other car.

Three blocks later, looking up and down the main drag, I knew I'd lost it. My forehead was damp with sweat. I tried to calm down. I drove straight to Anelle's house, hoping to put my fears to rest, praying that I'd see her waving to a friend as she opened the front door. But the house was quiet and dark. Even Anelle's bedroom window was black; her frilly white shades were wide open.

I knew that she wasn't there, that her room was empty.

I palmed the wheel and came to a stop at the mouth of the court, thinking that I should call the cops.

Something red flashed in the cemetery across the street.

Tail-lights.

I rolled down the window and smelled heavy exhaust. Burned oil. It was a long shot, but I didn't have much else. Killing the headlights, I pulled to the curb.

I took a tire iron from under the seat.

I'd guessed correctly. The car was a Chrysler. There were two people in the front seat, chest to chest. They leaned back as one, against the passenger door.

Anelle and Pete Hatcher.

If I would have given it a chance, it might have seemed funny.

All Anelle's not-so-subtle visits to the gas station, filling a gas tank that was three-quarters full, chatting up Pete the same way I chatted her up at the movies.

All those romance novels that were going unread in the presence of the real thing.

All that free labor I did for good buddy Pete, my unknown rival.

All those kisses he was getting in the front seat of his latest junker.

All those kisses I was missing.

I don't remember opening the car door, but I remember what I did with the tire iron, and I remember the way Pete whimpered.

And I remember catching up to Anelle on her front lawn after Pete was dead. I grabbed her and held her close on the same spot where the "FOR SALE" sign had stood, thinking about all those things I wanted to tell her and the way I wanted to kiss her and the way I'd seen her kiss Pete.

10

My fingers locked around her biceps. Panic swam in her green eyes. Her lips trembled.

I said, "There's something that I've wanted to tell you for a long time."

Those were the last words I ever said.

Anelle's lips parted.

Her teeth gleamed in the glow of the porch light. Toothpaste advertiser's wet dreams, every one.

She started to scream then, and I jammed my mouth against hers because I knew this would be my last chance for that special kind of kiss that only lovers share.

I did kiss her, and it was a lover's kiss.

I held her tight, my mouth to hers, not letting her breathe.

When it was over, I fainted.

They tell me that Anelle passed out at the same time, just a few seconds after she'd swallowed my tongue.

Baz

by Julian Rathbone

olmes and I met under circumstances which can only be described as absurd and I use the word in its fullest sense—not as a synonym for the ludicrous or laughable, but intending to imply a higher sort of comedy, a theatrical surreality. The occasion was a party given two years ago to celebrate the opening of Murder One, a shop which claimed to be the first in London that sold nothing but crime fiction. It is to be found in Denmark Street off the top end of Charing Cross Road, in the shadow of Centre Point. My presence there was a joke. My name is Watson, I am a doctor—of psychology, not medicine. The boy friend of the moment was a nasty yuppy with what for a time I took to be a sense of humour—anyone who wants to go to bed with me probably has to have a sense of humour since I am thirteen stone, five feet ten inches tall. . . .

Yes, well. Since I seem to have launched on a description of myself I'd better go on with it and get that out of the way. Apart from being grossly fat and rather tall for a woman, I am thirty-five going on forty. I start the day in contact lenses and end it in National Health circa 1960 plastic frames. These were my mother's and are more comfortable than the expensively prescribed lenses. I have a deepish voice and I don't often whisper. When out professionally or socially, I wear mannish clothes – black jacket, striped trousers, waistcoat, a black homburg. It's what my colleagues in the same line of business wear—so why

12

shouldn't I? It saves having to make up one's mind two or three times a day about what to put on next, and with the jacket generously cut and the trousers supported by braces rather than a constricting belt it is more comfortable and more flattering to a figure like mine than any female gear other than kaftans and so on. I do wear kaftans at home. . . but that's enough about me.

Marchers, everyone who knows him calls Marchmain "Marchers", had inveigled me along so that he could go around introducing me as Dr. Watson, which he thought was the height of wit at a party given to celebrate not only the opening of a new shop but the crime novel as well. The joke went even better when an out of work actor appeared in the guise of the original Sherlock Holmes. That there should be not only a tall, thin, dark-haired man with a large boney nose (nose-putty actually), dressed in tweeds with a deer-stalker, who claimed to be the greatest detective of all time, but also a comically fat woman in mannish clothes who actually was Dr. Watson, was a source of mirth indeed.

I laughed along with the rest—publishers and literary agents for the most part each with two or three deferential writers at heel or on a leash, clutched my glass of dry white and choked on vol au vents made with animal fat. I soon got bored, and Marchers discovered a female writer, thin and wispy, whose work he claimed to have admired for years. I tried to do what I have always found difficult in an interior smaller than St Paul's, that is, melt into the background, only to find that my distaste for the whole business was in fact shared by another person, whose appearance was in fact but in very different ways indeed, as eccentric as my own. He, I felt sure it was a he though one could not help remarking an epicene quality, also found it difficult to melt.

The person in question was about my height, or a little less, had very jet black hair cut short but stylishly swept back off a domed forehead that narrowed at the temples to frame an authentically boney nose that the first Duke of Wellington would have been proud to claim. It was this conk that made one sure the person was a male—any female with a bob or two to spare would have had a nose job done. The lips were thin but sensitive, and just then curled into an expression of almost sinister disdain—they were painted but in a flesh-coloured reddish ochre. Most striking were the eyes—dark violet, the pupils slightly dilated beyond what one would expect under those bright lights, and that made them seem darker than they perhaps actually were.

He wore a long thin tube, something between a high-collared long coat and a dress, faintly reminiscent of the sort of garment notable brahmins wear, made of bronze silk, over white linen trousers.

More curious than striking were long fingers whose nails were long and claw-like on the right hand, trimmed almost down to the quick on the left.

"You are wondering at the disparity between the nails of my right hand and those of my left."

The voice was deep like mine, but mellifluous, the delivery drawled, but not lazily so, the accent perfect—educated but classless.

I gulped.

"Yes," I said.

"I play the guitar." The obvious but unspoken words hung in the air between us—Elementary, my dear Watson.

"Professionally?" I offered. But the question was not taken up, and I sensed it had been impertinent. This was a person whose intelligence and gifts were such that to be a professional anything, or even several things, was unnecessary and out of the question.

"This is a silly business, is it not?"

I concurred.

"And doubly so for you. . . I mean that you should be Watson, and a doctor. But not I think a doctor of medicine?"

"No," I agreed, "Not of medicine. Of. . . ."

"Oh something in the social sciences, I imagine. But one of the more disciplined branches, I suspect. I would hazard a guess that you offered your thesis to the social psychology department of a third generation university and that the subject was group and individual inter-reaction, that sort of thing. . ."

"Actually yes," I answered, more than a little put-out, "but how did you. . . .?"

At this moment what I later learnt to be a most rare but rewarding occurrence took place—a smile. It expressed delight and humour that were totally unfalse, the real soul shining through, a soul that delights in all that is ironic, absurd, unusual, and is profoundly bored when nothing is around to excite it.

"Because, my dear Watson, your hat does not have a bulge in one side of it. If you were a practising doctor it would have, because that of course is where you would keep your stethoscope, as for the rest, well. . . never mind. Would you care to dine with me at home? It requires no great gifts of observation to be sure that you are less than enchanted with your escort."

Finger tips, cool, almost icy, rested briefly on the back of my podgy hand, brooked no refusal.

"You have the advantage of me," I murmured.

"My name?"

I assented but felt a moment of absurd anxiety, almost of foreboding, for I knew even before the answer came that the next words would change my life utterly.

"Holmes, of course."

"Of course". But I was gasping for air, as if I had been winded by a punch to the solar plexus.

Out in Charing Cross Road, still broad daylight since we were in the middle of June, Holmes produced from quite where I do not know, for he carried no bag and his garments had no visible pockets, what looked like a miniaturised radio-phone, but it merely required prolonged pressure on its one button to procure us an empty cab in less than two minutes, at a time of day when most were bespoken for early diners and theatre goers.

The surprise was compounded when the driver, leaning into the rear space to release the passenger door, merely said: "Barbican?" and on receiving a brief nod in reply said no more. No money changed hands at the end of the trip.

"You have forsaken Baker Street, then?" I asked somewhat archly.

"Indeed yes." Holmes took my question at face-value. "A noisy brash area now, with nothing to recommend it. And the sort of problems, cases if you like, that are worth one's attention are now rather more common in the City than elsewhere in London."

"I take it," Holmes continued, "you run a small private clinic, expensive but efficacious, where under the guise of 'counselling' you offer therapy and solace to the troubled souls of the well-to-do?"

"Well, yes, but I also –"

"You also work free or for a pittance in the social services department of one of the less fashionable but left-wing boroughs, Lambeth perhaps, where you offer a rather more brusque version of your skills to street-crazed mothers who batter their children, or unruly adolescents given to vandalism and drug procurement."

I felt piqued but could not at the same time restrain my admiration.

"This, I suppose, is where I am meant to say—Holmes, how do you do it?"

Cold dark eyes held mine for a moment and this time not a trace of a smile softened their gaze or twitched the corners of the thin lips.

"Why not? Ah. We're nearly there. I should warn you I have a man, Hudson, who appears a trifle louche to some, but he is I assure you, quite harmless."

Thus began a relationship which has often been irritating, sometimes acerbic, but always rewarding.

Several times Holmes sorted out problems for the City and Wessex Bank, and now they pay a considerable retainer. The first of these I was instrumental in bringing to Holmes's attention.

Not long after our acquaintance began, Mrs. Kayte Hatchard became one of my clients. This incidentally is the correct term—I am not a medical practitioner and I do not have patients. Patience either, come to that. Kayte Hatchard, thin, svelte, and tough, claimed to be in marital trouble. Her husband, Robert, was the boss of Citee-Wex, the subsidiary of City and Wessex which trades in commodities, futures, bonds, stocks and shares and has brand new offices on Blackfriars Wharf. One of the first things I told her was that any wife married to a man like Hatchard—tall, silver-hair, good family, one of the top City jobs, and contrived to have marital problems, was an idiot. Either that or she had a very considerable fortune of her own. She disclaimed the fortune, somewhat disingenuously as it turned out, but claimed a lover, Jack Cassell, some ten or so years younger than Kayte (who had just turned forty) and who was employed by Citee-Wex as a commodity trader. . .

"You know what that means?" Kayte asked.

I replied that of course I did. He was one of these persons you occasionally see on television, sitting with thirty or so clones, in front of VDTs, buying and selling other people's property or even such notional things as property other people might own in six months time, for huge sums of money. They wear broadly striped shirts, loose ties and no jackets, make a lot of money in commissions, and burn out by the time they're thirty.

"He's thirty. And no longer very good at it," she added dryly, stubbing out a half finished Dunhill on the ashtray I allow clients to use no more than twice per session. "Electronic trading I mean. At the other thing he's rather a whizz. I mean in bed, you know?"

"I rather thought he might be. . ." Show me a pikestaff and I'm as good as Holmes at spotting the obvious.

It went on like that for three or four sessions—the trouble seemed plain enough—she didn't want to give up young Jack, but was terrified Robert would find out about it, and she didn't want to give Robert up though Jack urged her to. Robert had a bit on the side now and then with Ms Sara Ponsonby who was, like Jack, a dealer for Citee-Wex. In the meantime she needed someone professionally discreet to talk to—it's often the case with my clients.

The fourth session she came in bubbling with excitement, laughter even, and that afternoon, almost as soon as she had left, I went over to the Barbican and told Holmes all about it.

By then I was a fairly frequent visitor to the Barbican flat, and had already been of some assistance in two minor cases. This time I felt I had stumbled on a problem worthy of Holmes's skills.

Roc released the multiple locks in answer to my ring and showed me into the presence. Dear me. Any literary person who bothers to read these pages will already have detected that I am a novice at narration, and it just now occurs to me that I did not after all, as I had intended, describe "Roc" Hudson, Holmes's man, when he was mentioned a page or so back.

Roc, I have to say I rather like. He is tall enough to make me feel normal, black as the ace of spades, lean, long-limbed with long feet and long hands. Indeed he is so uncannily like a Mapplethorpe model that I suspect he also has a long dick. Which is not something I am ever likely to, um, substantiate, since Roc is also of course as gay as Paree and as camp as Brownsea Island. Holmes picked him out of the gutter up West where he was luding out and bleeding heavily from the back passage.

"Why? Because Roc is precisely what the decor of my flat required."

Holmes's flat is seeringly, abrasively modern—done out in white and primary colours—mostly reds. There is a lot of edgy bright glass, and laminates as hard and cold as marble but unblemished by pattern natural or designed. The only two things in it with warmth are the guitar and Roc.

Roc took my hat, the homburg, and as he always did perched it on the top of his head, tilted it over his eyes and posed. Then he gave it back, so it was me who had to put it on the hall chair. That's Roc for you.

"God," he said, "is in the computer room, but not busy, just having a tinkle."

The door was open. Holmes was sitting on a tall, black, hard, high-backed armless chair, feet perched on a bottom rung, knees spread, head bent over the guitar, fingers flickering, knitting together a pattern of sound that I later learnt was a three part invention by Sor. Apart from the magic of the music the room was filled with savage melancholy—the blinds were closed against the sun, the four VDTs were blank, the keyboards shrouded. On the table top, white as a slab in a morgue, just one glass of still Malvern water. . . and three acid blue capsules.

The music finished and Holmes looked up at me with eyes more dilated than ever from a face pasty and shiny with a slight film of sweat.

"Watson, I hope you have something for me, for I am as bored as hell." There was desperation, unemphasised but there, in the voice.

"Well, I should jolly well think I have." I was determined to buck my friend up a bit, if nothing else. "You know I have a client whose husband and lover both work for Citee-Wex, well Citee-Wex has a problem. This very morning one of their dealers, a girl called Sara Ponsonby, had just concluded a deal buying copper futures for the Shah of Khazee, when an unbidden message appeared on her screen, which was then showing the Shah's metal account. It read to this effect: I am a virus. Please use EFT to transfer £100,000 to account number 1234567890 in the Banco de Santa Margarita, Panama. Failure will result in the loss of all electronically stored data in the Shah's account. You have one hour. . .

"You can imagine the shock, the horror. My client's husband, the director, Hatchard is his name, ordered the back-ups to be run. They were half an hour behind, and when they got to the same page as Sara had been reading the deal she had just struck was not there—however the virus was, with a suitably sardonic tag to its original message. . . ."

"Hard copies?" Holmes interrupted and I was pleased to see this glimmer of interest. "I imagine the volume of dealing is such that the paper work at Citee-Wex is at least thirty-six hours in arrears –"

"Forty-eight, my client said."

"And how much is out on the Shah's account in the last forty-eight hours?"

"Six million."

"And no question of going to the second parties in the deals and asking for their records—Citee-Wex would lose all its market-place credibility."

"Precisely."

"The sum asked for is insignificant, of course, so they paid."

"Immediately."

"But the virus will strike again. And again."

That same afternoon, an hour or so later, following a crisis meeting in the Fenchurch Square headquarters of City and Wessex which Sir Alec Greene himself chaired, Citee-Wex made a discreet approach to Holmes, enlisting his aid. Kayte Hatchard, who was well acquainted with Sir Alec, had already made a private phonecall to him, recommending my new friend. Imagine my consternation then when the very next morning, while I was still brushing out my hair, and with Marchers still snoring in the bed beside me, the phone rang.

"Watson? Holmes here. Listen I've decided not to handle that Citee-Wex business after all. It too silly, just plainly too boring. But I have an acquaintance who is good with this sort of thing, and he could use a break. He's agreed to take it on, but, well, I'd like a first hand account of how he makes out so I wondered if you'd meet him and take him round to Citee-Wex for me. . .? His name is Conran Dial, and he's Irish. He'll be outside Blackfriars tube in about half an hour. Can you make it? Of course you can."

In half an hour? But Holmes had rung off. I gave it a moment's thought, but no more. Marchers, who sometimes wakes up randy enough to do it without giggling at the floppiness of my bum, was not going to wake up until noon. I had no client until eleven, and he was expendable. Moreover, I felt I owed it to Kayte, to whom I had confided that I could persuade Holmes to take on the job, to pick up the pieces if this Conran Dial character turned out as naf as he sounded. I mean whoever heard of an Irishman any good with computers?

Dial turned out to be every bit as awful as I expected. He was a short, slim, sharp, young man. He had red hair that flopped over his brow, and a cute little yellow moustache, beneath a nose like a parrot's beak. His eyes were a sort of weak golden brown. He wore one of those floppy dark suits that pretend to be silk and from Milan, but this one was polyester off the peg in Whitechapel. His tie was a kipper of blotches orange on blue or vice-versa. Co-respondent shoes in blue and white. He carried a hard document case bound in ridged aluminium strips, with brassy combination locks. There was a Dan-Air label on it.

"Hi there," he called, when I was still on the centre island crossing the road to meet him, and only five minutes late. "You must be Dr. Julia Watson – you fit in every last detail Baz's description of you."

"Baz?"

His face clouded

"Baz Holmes. Who else, for Jasus' sake? Don't you be telling me now I've approached the wrong person. There can't be two like you in the Great Wen."

Baz? Until now my new acquaintance had been Holmes, nothing else. Dial went on: "Do we need a cab, or can we hoof it?"

"We can walk. It's not far."

Yet in five minutes he told me he was a graduate of computer sciences from Dublin University, had ploughed his doctorate when his supervisor said it was too original, and still found time to tell me the worst Irish joke I've ever heard. It seems two Paddys were sitting on a bench in Phoenix Park, shooting up with second hand needles, when along came a nun and said, sure could you not be catching the dreaded aids like that, come along to my rehabilitation centre and oi'll fix you up wit' new ones. To which they both replied, sure sister, and isn't that the very t'oughtful person you are, but we're quite safe, we're both wearing condoms. I hadn't heard it before and Dial had to save me from falling under the wheels of a 78 bus—I'm afraid I over-react to bad taste jokes.

Inside the Citee-Wex building we first had to cross marbled halls with rubber plants. Dial's shoes squeaked. Then a Hitler, one of those burly ex-coppers with a cinema commissionaire's uniform, asked to see inside Dial's case.

"Impossible," he said, "for haven't I just misremembered the combination on the locks?"

The Hitler shook it.

"I shouldn't do that, sor. It's filled with Semtex."

The Hitler kept his cool.

"It feels very light, sir."

"Of course it does. It's as empty as a bottle of Jameison's on the eighteenth of March. I only carry it for show. You can be arrested for walking the streets of the City without a document case, did you know that?"

The dealers' room was big, with an acoustic ceiling, about thirty consoles of VDTs, telephones and keyboards, a coffee machine, and enough static about to lift the hair on the back of your neck. The centre of attention was again Sara Ponsonby's corner. She, blonde, silk blouse, opaque but no bra so it might just as well have been transparent, tailored navy skirt with a pin-stripe, was wailing: "What shall I do, what shall I do?"

On one of her screens the Duke of Belfont's sugar account was overlaid with a message asking for a mere £50,000. Well, Dukes don't carry the same clout as Shahs these days, do they? Hatchard, and a burly ex-rugby player running to fat whom I guessed, rightly, must be Cassell, were behind her, and behind them anyone who could tear themselves away from the accounts they were handling, or the markets they were dealing in. Quite a crowd. I used my shoulders a bit and got us through.

"Let me handle this," said Dial, and Sara gracefully surrendered her position.

Dial attacked the keys for three and a half minutes and got this message back: "Okay, you're good, but not that good. Now pay up and sod off, or everything this terminal has ever handled gets erased."

"Shit," said Dial, and without further ado made the Eft to account 1234567890 in the Banco de Santa Margarita, Panama.

"You're fired," said Hatchard.

"Hang on a jiffy," said Dial.

He swung his chair round, cracked his knuckles and played an arpeggio or two on a different keyboard. Presently script scrolled down. Account of Conran Dial, in the Bank of Ireland, Dublin. Credit: £50,000 transferred from the Banco de Santa Margarita, account number. . . .

As the minions behind Hatchard and Cassell applauded, he pulled out a cheque book, made out a cheque for forty thousand pounds payable to Citee-Wex and handed it to Hatchard.

"Don't worry," he said, "my account in Dublin is hacker proof, I've seen to that. All that remains for me to work out is where your man is working from, for you see this is not a real virus you're coping with here, he just pretends to be to frighten you. What you have is a hacker, a good one, but I'll nail him, sure I will."

All of this was done in less than an hour. Outside the Blackfriars tube I refused Dial's offer of a pint of stout and got back home in time to receive my eleven o'clock client after all. The rest of the day unravelled in a routine way until six o'clock when I felt free to go round to the Barbican and report the morning's events to Holmes. Roc opened the door.

"God," he said, "is in, in the computer room, and not to be disturbed."

"Tinkling?"

"No."

"Smashed?"

Roc spread his long hands.

"I think not," he said. "God has been very busy, has drunk three pots of strong Ceylon, and has left a message for you and a present—a tin of Diet Coke."

"Ho, ho," I said, "I suppose that's meant to be funny."

I am a little too ready to assume comment about my weight where none has been intended.

"May be. But why not read the note?"

It was printout on perforated listing paper, just one sheet. But Holmes's swanky machine had done it in Gill Perpetua Italic, which is probably beyond the abilities of my publisher's technology, so you will just have to imagine it.

Dear Watson

I am sorry I shall not be able to communicate with you personally this evening, but I am unfortunately involved in another affair that requires all my attention. However, I am sure you and Dial, who has already reported to me his achievements of earlier today, will be able to tie up the loose ends of the Citee-Wex affair without further help from me.

Here is what I would like you to do. Tomorrow morning, at eleven, I should like you to be at the Healthy Bit. I am indebted to you for telling me about this place—I think it will be an ideal setting for the finale of the affair. Dial will be there a little behind you and will shortly be joined by at least one of the culprits in this case. They will probably proposition him to keep his mouth shut. When he refuses they may seek to do him some mischief.

Please take with you the device Roc will give you. It is a directional eavesdropper and recorder of extraordinary efficiency. Simply you must place the end with the ring-pull on against the wall or door of the room you wish to eavesdrop on and activate the mechanism by pressing the small protuberance on the bottom of the "can". Pressing the same protuberance a second time will turn off the recording mechanism.

If it is at all possible you should also place your ear against the base of the can while it is operating—you will then gain first hand experience of what it is recording. Thus you will not only satisfy your own curiosity as to what is going on, you will also be able to detect if Dial is in any danger from the person or persons who are with him.

Yours

B. Holmes.

"Roc," I asked, "What does the B stand for? It cannot be Baz, can it?"

His face assumed an expression of infuriating inscrutability.

"God will reveal all, when the time is ripe. Okay, Jewel?"

My own first name, as I think I have already revealed, is Julia. It is typical of Roc that he should so quickly have hit on the abbreviation that my intimates cannot resist using, and which infuriates me most.

I followed Holmes's directions to the letter. The Healthy Bit is much what you would expect—a small complex of squash courts, iron-pumping room, sauna baths, and so on, with a small licensed bar off the foyer where one can wait for one's friends. The site was previously occupied by a two-floor sex shop and a Bangladeshi grocery store.

It is not a club. It relies on its very inflated prices and the glossy smartness of its decor to deter riff-raff, these and the presence of Wild Bill Macleish. Wild Bill was once a heavyweight all-in wrestler of some standing in that under-rated sport. Contrary to received opinion on the subject by no means all the bouts are fixed, indeed the championship ones are often contested with great seriousness and ferocity. . . I know Wild Bill because I counselled him for some six months following the death of his aged mother, of whom he was inordinately fond. After she died he took to breaking up public bars, sometimes as many as three in a night, and it was a condition of his probation that he should receive qualified counselling. It occurs to me now that Holmes knew of this, I had mentioned Wild Bill on that first occasion we dined together, and that was how he knew not only of the Healthy Bit but was also aware that I had an ally on the premises.

Wild Bill was of course surprised to see me and then disappointed to learn that I had not come to sample any of the premise's facilities, assuring me that a beginner's course with the weights would do marvels for my muscle tone. However, he drew me a pint of mild and accepted without demur that I was there to meet an acquaintance. He pulled a large diary towards him and his large finger tracked down the morning's bookings.

"This time of day is very slack, doesn't really begin to pick up until half twelve. Would it be a Mr. Cassell you are going to meet? His is the only court booking before midday." Wild Bill's voice is very high-pitched, squeaky even, a fact which, if his attention is drawn to it by someone he doesn't much like, can lead to broken bones.

Cassell? Mr. Jack Cassell? This could not be a coincidence. Clearly I should make sure that he did not see me since he would be sure to guess I was there to spy if he was indeed one of the culprits. I turned to the bar, and watched the entrance in the mosaic of mirrors beneath the spirit bottles and disclaimed any knowledge at all of Cassell. Wild Bill polished glasses and went into a eulogy of his sainted mother I had heard many times before, but always previously at the expense of Lambeth Council's probationary service.

Presently the street doors swung open and shut and Dial and Cassell came in together. Cassell carried a duffel-bag from which protruded the handle of a squash racquet, but Dial, oddly enough, was already kitted out in sweater, sports shirt, shorts and training shoes. They went straight past the bar, with never a glance in my direction, disappearing into the inner sanctuaries. I gave the matter a moment's thought, then drank up.

"Bill," I said, "it doesn't look as if my friend is going to come after all. But before I go I'll just cast an eye over what you have here—you never know, but I might make some use of it after all."

"Feel free. Do you want me to show you around? I'm not meant to leave the bar until the help comes at twelve, but I can make an exception for you."

Of course I refused this well-meant offer.

A short passage led into a wider area. On one side there were changing rooms, male and female, the weights room and three saunas labelled male, female, and mixed; on the other side four squash courts—and here of course was the first unforeseen problem—they were the modern sort with the outer wall, the one with the door in, made out of plexi-glass and quite transparent. However, the side walls were traditionally opaque and a moment's thought told me what I had to do. I entered the women's changing room, which was well appointed with free eau de toilette dispensers and so on, and waited with the door ajar. Presently Dial and Cassell came out of the men's changing room, and took the court opposite. There was still a moment of risk: Cassell might turn and see me as I crossed the open space. But soon both players were knocking up with some intensity and concentration and I got into the court next door without being observed by either of them.

It needed only a moment now to station myself against the dividing wall with one end of the Diet-Coke "tin" pressed to my ear, the other, ring-pull end, to the wall.

The device was amazingly efficient but my comprehension of their conversation was limited by the inherent noisiness of the game, and later by Cassell's puffing and grunting. One thing became very clear—Dial might be slight of build, even frail compared with the ex-Rugby player, but had the advantage of being a far better squash player. Cassell lost the first game and was already three points to two down in the second when he raised the real matter that had brought them there. I transcribe.

24

Cassell: Plop, thwack, bang, damn—you know you play like a woman relying like that on drop shots all the time. Never mind, it's doing me good stretching the odd muscle. Thwack plop, damn, five two? Are you sure? Shit. Look, I expect you've guessed, this is not merely a social occasion, nor are we really here to. . .Thwack, plop, thwack, plop, bang, oh bugger this, can't we stop for a moment? Pant, puff, pant. Look, I'll not beat about the bush, you are a bloody clever little man, too clever by half, and I and my colleagues have come to the conclusion, that there are two alternatives open to us.

Dial (very cool): A pony gets you only five to guess right what they are.

Cassell: Eh? What?

Dial: I am proposing to myself that I can guess what those alternatives are. Still my serve I think.

Cassell: Plop, thwack, bang, shit. Actually, it's not like a woman's, your game, I mean, it's like that of those Paki twins who were so bloody good a few years back.

Dial: Ismael coached me actually. Still my serve then. Plop.

Cassell: Shit. Look Dial. You're a clever little prick. With a box and on the squash court. I grant you that. But never forget that you're a prick, and a Paddy to boot. Horrible mixture. So just you listen to me. Fifty grand, on the nail, and you give up, tell Sir Alec it's beyond you.

Dial: Or?

Cassell: Or, and nasty little man that you are it'll be a pleasure to lay it on, we arrange for you to be cut up into small bits and distributed around the Home Counties. Do I make myself clear?

Dial: Fifty grand is a paltry sort of sum, now, for what you're suggesting.

Cassell: Yes, but it's the sum we've been quoted by certain people who specialise in cutting nasty little schemers up into small bits. . . So, really not much call to go higher, is there?

Dial: My serve still. Plop, thwack, plop, crash! My game, and first set.

Cassell: Puff, pant. You horrid little man! You've made me break my racquet. Listen. I've had enough of your squash. Pant, puff, pant. But I think there's still some more talking to be done. In the sauna perhaps, I think I could use a sauna. And in there we could talk of ways of raising the ante without actually obliterating you.

What, of course, this transcript fails to record is what was going on outside court number one. Very little actually. All that happened was this. Robert Hatchard arrived. He went into the men's changing room shortly after Dial and Cassell started their game. Came out two minutes or so later in a voluminous white towelling bathwrap and entered the male sauna. That was all. He was joined there fifteen minutes later by both Dial and Cassell—both similarly attired. It was with me the work of a moment to leave court number two and station myself ouside the sauna with my Diet Coke "tin" once again in place. There was a moment's doubt. During the move had I stopped the recording mechanism by pressing the small protuberant area on the base of the can? Or hadn't I? Was I now turning it off or on? Probably I was turning it off—but it didn't matter. The conversation, as much of it as I stayed to hear, was brief and memorable.

Hatchard: Ah. Here you are then. How's it gone, Jack? Dial being as sensible and co-operative as a sensible laddie would be?

Cassell: Not exactly. Nasty little runt wants more than fifty grand.

Dial: That's not exactly what I said. . .

Hatchard: You told him the alternative?

Cassell: Certainly. He didn't seem too impressed. In fact I don't think he believed me.

Hatchard: Well then. How can we convince him we mean it?

Cassell: We could start by pulling his balls off.

Hatchard: What a good idea!

Sounds of scuffling. Cassell shouts with pain.

Hatchard: Good God.

Cassell: Fucking cunt bit me.

Hatchard: Good God. He hasn't got balls at all. It's a bint!

At which point I banged on the door with the Diet Coke tin, doing the mechanism inside terminal damage, much to Holmes's annoyance, tried all my weight against the locked door to no avail, and ran—or at any rate moved as speedily as I am able, back to the bar.

"Bill," I cried, "There are two men molesting a woman in the sauna."

"You here still?" he replied. "In the mixed is it? It happens all the time."

"No. In the men only."

"Ah. That's a different matter then. That is OTT, and out of order. They know that. They should know better. Plenty of our clientele would be most upset to think they might come across a person of the female sex in the men's. They go to the men's because they expect to meet men. If you follow my drift."

26

As he said all this he raised the bar-flap and set off through the bar and down the corridor, all at a steady pace, quite a lot slower even than mine. At the door to the men's sauna he didn't pause, but put his shoulder to it. On the first push the hinges began to crack from the wood, he stood back, prepared himself for a second charge.

A voice, one familiar but not Irish or definitively male, cried out: "Hang on a sec, no need for that!"

But too late. Wild Bill's charge was already under way and could not be deflected any more readily than if he had been a London bus. The door crashed down, hinges and lock going together.

Holmes rose from the stooped position she (and at last I could be sure that "she" was the correct pronoun) was in—one white hand seeking to recover her robe, the other looking for "Dial's" red wig. On one side of her, Cassell sat on the floor against a wall and nursed a bloody nose, on the other Hatchard rolled in agony clutching what he had and "Dial" had not.

One odd thing about Holmes at this point was that she had one violet-blue eye, and one pale hazel. We spent twenty minutes looking for the lost and pigmented lens before I trod on it.

There is not much more to tell. Certainly I have no intention of revealing, even if I could, just how Holmes had used her computer prowess to discover who had got into Citee-Wex's knickers and how. But it did, she informed me, during one of several post-mortems on the case, turn on the fact that she quickly realised that there was no virus, and then there was not, in the proper sense of the word a hacker on the outside. It was, she soon realised, an inside job.

Let Kayte Hatchard explain. She kept her last appointment with me, which was civil of her since the aura of radiant well-being she now carried round with her was much at odds with the lean, hungry, neurotic person I had met when she first arrived in my waiting room. Clearly she was no longer in need of counselling.

"Sara Ponsonby," she said, "was Robert's mistress. And he wanted a divorce. In the meantime he encouraged me to take a lover, and since I was bored, frightened that I had lost my ability to attract men, feeling generally insecure, I did so—that lout Jack Cassell. I gave the divorce side of it a lot of thought and finally agreed—but only on condition that Robert first made over to me all his capital assets. Although he had no money in the bank, indeed he had an overdraft, the assets were considerable—the house in Hampstead, the farm in Brittany, the villa in Marbella. A large Mercedes, a new Volvo estate, and two or three smaller cars. And of course the Hockney double portrait we had done when we got married. And lots of smaller bits and bobs too, the silver, you know? The porcelain. Altogether it's valued at over three million, so I shall not be pauperised. And of course there is no question of the court sequestrating any of this because the hand-over was made before he embarked on a life of crime.

"Poor Jack thought he would marry me once the divorce was through, and also marry this small fortune. Sara, however, was not too pleased with the arrangement—she had supposed that she was bedding a properly rich person, rather than a bank lacquey, albeit one on three hundred grand a year. She has a coke habit to maintain, and in spite of his three hundred grand Robert was in fact getting quite seriously into debt. She and Robert concocted the plot to milk Citee-Wex—the idea was to to take a few small lumps, a hundred grand here and there, and then offer to be bought off for a million or so. But they lacked the expertise and facilities and approached Jack for assistance. I imagine the conversation went like this. . ."

Here, she adopted a laid-back, mannish, public school sort of voice, all clipped and done with a motionless upper lip.

" 'I say, Jack old chap. You want to marry Kayte I know, but you can't without an awful untidy fuss unless I go along with it, so be a good chap and lend us a hand with this frightfully clever wheeze Sara and I have thought up. . .' "

"Actually," I interrupted, "it was a fearfully clumsy business according to Holmes. It was the sheer naivety of it that baffled, oh, for several hours."

"That does not surprise me at all," she reassumed her normal voice, "I mean that the plot was clumsy. I have long since discovered that the arrogance, the conceit of the English upper class male is almost always a mask for obstinate stupidity. But that Holmes might have been baffled by it was not not something I had reckoned on. . . . Ah, I have surprised you and perhaps let a cat out of the bag. My dear Julia, I did indeed value your counselling, but I have to confess that when I realised this evil trio were up to something at the Bank, I felt sure Holmes was the person to approach. However, he, or is it she? No-one seems to know, is notoriously unapproachable. However, you are not, and so I took the liberty. . ."

I hope I concealed a mild wave of chagrin—I really had believed I had done a good job as Kayte's counsellor; moreover, I really had believed until that moment that it was I who was instrumental in bringing Holmes into the case off my own bat, rather than as an unwitting intermediary. . . never mind. I congratulated her on her finesse and the successful outcome of her endeavours. She stubbed out her second Dunhill, and wrote out a cheque for what she owed me. We parted on the most cordial terms. I could not resist looking out of the window when she went, and was rewarded to see her driven off in a Ferrari by that young Spaniard who was such a sensation at last year's Wimbledon.

One question still bothered me.

"Holmes." I said that evening as Roc served me a spicy okra stew, delicious, while he and Holmes dined on curried goat, "what is this Baz business?"

She dabbed the corner of her mouth with a napkin, sipped the Jamaican Red Stripe lager Roc always serves when he cooks West Indian.

"My father," she said, "was the son of Myron Holmes, Sherlock's brother. Sherlock is therefore my great uncle. My father expected me to be male and had already decided on a first name—Basil. He refused to countenance my failure to be a boy, and insisted I be christened Basilia. He was determined I should be Basil in some form or other."

"Why?"

Her violet eyes took on the cold look I have come to expect when I have failed to appreciate the obvious.

"After the greatest impersonator of my great uncle."

I was still at a loss. Roc filled me in.

"Come off it, darling. Basil Rathbone of course."

Hijack

by William Schoell

T his sure didn't look like Petersburg.

Ronald Forest looked at his watch and took out his schedule again. It was 3:15; according to the time table they should have been passing through Petersburg, but either the bus was very late or the driver had for some reason switched to another route. Odd.

Forest scratched his head and stared out the window at the unfamiliar countryside rolling by. Lots of trees and leafy branches. Occasionally a gas station or convenience shop. The road looked just like the road they usually took, a two lane blacktop that stretched from one dismal town to another. But he had taken this bus from New York to Cloverdale so often that he knew all of those dreary little hamlets by heart. So what the hell had happened to Petersburg?

The trouble was he hadn't been paying attention. The driver must have gone to an alternate route at some point, but Ronald's nose had been buried in a dog-earred library copy of *The Iliad*. True, he had been engrossed, but not *so* absorbed that he would have missed an announcement over the driver's public address system. Well, that's what happened when they put new drivers on a route. Even though they would go through a trainee stage, travel with the regular driver once or twice to become familiar with the circuit, some of them were so dumb they took odd detours, or wound up in the wrong place at the wrong time. Ronald hoped this

30

wouldn't add up to a lengthy delay.

If only he'd been paying attention; if only he'd known just *when* the bus had gone off the route. He considered asking some of his fellow passengers, but they seemed distant and preoccupied—books, magazines, those silly cassettes with head-phones that some of them wore—and besides, Ronald was too shy to willingly call attention to himself or to the problem: they were going the wrong way.

Ronald thought back to when he'd first seen their driver, back at the Port Authority bus terminal in Manhattan. They'd renovated the entire terminal, adding new sections with layers of bright paint, and attractive shops and concessions— but they hadn't been able to keep out the people: weird-eyed panhandlers, obnoxious drunks, sullen youths who jabbered menacingly in foreign tongues—these and others paraded around the building as if they owned it, and Ronald lived in terror of the day that one of them would address him. No, that was not the word, *attack* him; that's what he was afraid of. He'd heard so many stories—innocent people surrounded by muggers, travellers reaching to pay for their precious tickets and discovering their wallets gone, people being knifed in the men's room. The Port Authority had thrown a glossy coat of paint and polish over the whole building, but the improvements were only cosmetic. The sleazy underbelly still remained.

Ronald could have sworn when he first saw the driver that he was one of the pack rats who haunted the terminal. His hair was too long, curling up unattractively in the back. His face was not freshly shaven, and his clothes were rather tattered. The blue bus company jacket hung too large on his slender, almost emaciated frame, and his tie was poorly knotted. Had it not been for the jacket Ronald could have imagined the man roaming the building hour after hour panhandling or striking up "conversations" with terrified strangers. There was something about the eyes. Hungry, threatening. *Diseased.*

Ronald had settled on assuming that the man was merely a porter, perhaps a mechanic, for Mercury Bus Lines, when he later discovered to his dismay that the fellow was literally in the driver's seat. The man had stood at the door leading from the lower concourse out to where the bus was parked and taken their tickets as they moved through the gate. Still Ronald had been busy denying: *the driver's getting a last minute cup of coffee, letting this creature collect the tickets for him.* And when Forest saw the greasy n'er do well pick up his suitcase and put it with the others in the luggage compartment beneath the bus he was convinced the fellow had to be just a workman. But then Forest was in the bus and in his seat halfway up the aisle on the right—where he always sat—and he could only watch with dismay as the man climbed up into the vehicle and sat down behind the wheel.

Oh, well, you can't judge by appearances, Ronald thought. *Perhaps the man is a very good, very competent and safe, driver.* That was all that really mattered.

And the ride had been smooth. No bumps, no near-misses, no problems of any kind. The new driver, while not especially friendly or polite, seemed adequate enough. Some of the other regular riders had asked him where Joe, the usual man for the one o'clock Saturday run, was, but the new driver had merely shrugged and said, "He's off." His glaring, terrible eyes discouraged further conversation or questioning.

But now Ronald thought that perhaps something was wrong. How did any of them know that this man was really the driver? What a bunch of gullible, middle-aged fools they were, complacently getting on the bus with this strange-looking man and assuming that all was well with the world. How *did* they really know? This fellow could be *anyone*, he could have gotten the jacket from anywhere—it didn't even fit him—and would the bus company have been likely to hire somebody so scruffy in appearance? But who would ever have thought such a thing could happen?

Now that Ronald thought about it, he realized that it wouldn't be all that difficult to actually hijack the bus. After waiting until both the driver and porter were off getting coffee or something, a man could go up to any gate and easily convince everyone waiting in line that *he* was their driver. Why would anyone think otherwise, especially if the man were calm and confident? He wouldn't even need the distinctive blue jacket of the bus company; all he'd have to do was dispose of his own jacket, and everyone would assume he had left the company jacket on the bus.

Ronald chided himself. His imagination was running away with him! There had to be a logical explanation for the change in route. And perhaps the man's appearance could be explained by a recent illness or even mental stress.

Mental stress—how well Ronald understood *that*. His publishing firm had been taken over by another one that specialized in religious material, and suddenly Ronald found himself being given directives that ordered all contracts to be cancelled for books whose "moral values" did not coincide with the larger firm's. Good books, fine books, had to be returned because they were full of "wrong" words and characters and attitudes. Such censorship after 22 years in the business had almost given him an ulcer. But what could he say? He'd been with the firm for so long. He had to accept, to compromise. Ronald Forest had never been a fighter.

Once a week he took the bus trip to see his mother in Cloverdale; a trip he did not really wish to make. He and his mother had never gotten along, but he had to do his duty, that's how he'd been raised. His mother had not approved of his late wife, Linda, had not ever—not *once*—expressed regret or dismay over the woman's untimely death. When Linda was alive they'd had a car, and she had done all the driving. Ronald hated to drive, had hated it since the night his father had driven him home from high school, caused an accident, and died; since Ronald himself had acquired the scars on his legs, the memories of all that painful surgery. *Since Linda had died in an automobile crash.* He sometimes thought that taking the bus was worse than driving. At least in his own car he would have had some control. Now his life—the lives of all the other passengers—was in the hands of a total stranger.

And—God help them—the man looked as if he drank or took drugs.

Ronald checked the schedule again and looked out the window. Another twenty minutes had gone by. They should have gone through Westfield and Pennington by now. Instead they were travelling along a narrow river on a completely alien highway. Where on earth was this fool taking them?

Ronald knew this route by heart. Engrossed in his book he might have missed some towns, but others were too distinctive to ignore. Chesterton, for instance; or West Barrows with its factories; the huge shopping mall where the bus picked up and discharged passengers in Lynnville. And then Southby, Hemington, and Cotterfield Lake. The bus had not gone through *any* of them. Was he on the wrong bus? No, he recognized many of his fellow travellers, and knew the bus *always* left from gate 27. He had been at gate 27, he was sure of it.

Besides, now some of the other passengers were murmuring amongst themselves; he was not the only one to notice it. The girl in the aisle across from him, one of those intense types with long dull hair and bony features, headphones across the hair, looked at him querulously and said "Do you know where we are?"

Ronald shook his head. "Haven't the faintest idea. He's either taking a different route or has completely lost his way."

The girl sighed and brushed the hair out of her eyes, then turned back to look out her window. Ronald looked around the bus, hoping someone would get up and ask the driver what was happening. Most of the other passengers were sitting behind him; the only ones up ahead were two elderly ladies and a mildly retarded girl who travelled to Cloverdale as he did every weekend. Wasn't *any*one going to get up and do something?

He knew that his fellow travellers were as compliant and tired as he was, too weary and unobservant to notice or particularly care as the bus rattled through unfamiliar terrain, refusing to accept or believe that there might not be a sensible explanation for the detour. Even those who were suddenly alarmed had been previously accepting their fate with a queasy resignation. Clearly none of the passengers had had to get off at any of the towns the bus had skipped or someone would have then certainly made a ruckus. Perhaps *that* was it; perhaps the driver, after checking the tickets, had realized he could bypass all of the earlier towns.

But then that would have stranded all those passengers who'd intended *to board* at those places.

Something was wrong. Ronald steeled himself, took a deep breath, and went down the aisle to the driver's seat.

To get the man's attention, he coughed.

"Are we taking a new route?" he asked meekly, appalled at how weak and high his voice had sounded.

His lips turned down disdainfully, the driver kept his eyes on the road. "Yeah. It's a new route."

Ronald tried to deepen his voice. "Will we still get to Cloverdale at the same time?"

"Oh, sure." There was an awkward pause. "Roadblocks," the driver explained when he saw that Ronald was still standing there. "Highway construction crews. Had to go a different way today. It's an *express* run," he added quickly. "No local stops."

Ronald felt relieved in spite of the fact that he was sure the man had been laughing at him, at all of them. *Nonsense!* he told himself. *Cut the paranoia and relax*. He went back to the others and told those who bothered to come over what the story was. All accepted it without qualm, though none of them looked too happy.

Ronald opened his copy of *The Iliad*.

In two hours he would be seeing mother again.

It was 5:30, the bus was almost an hour late, and Ronald had still not seen a familiar landmark. The girl across the aisle had fallen asleep. A few others in back were murmuring again, their whispers shrill and troubled, but no one was challenging the driver or lodging any protests. This was wrong, very wrong. How much "road-work" could there be? The driver had turned up a radio and was bouncing in his seat to some insane, gibbering music. They were driving on a narrow country lane past ramshackle houses and ponds full of children and mosquitoes. Backwoods;

off-the-beaten-track. Ronald debated, questioned, agonized. *This is not right*—but *why* would the man have stolen the bus, pretended to be the driver? It wasn't logical. Perhaps this detour merely took *longer* than the usual route. He looked out the window again at the shacks and lily ponds. *This is not right.* Ronald sat for another twenty minutes hating himself and his inability to confront, to take action.

Finally, he braced himself for the ordeal. He got up unsteadily and slowly approached the driver.

"Sir, I must ask—*where* are we going? It's nearly six o'clock. I haven't seen hide nor hair of a single town on the timetable, and I'm getting sick of sitting on this bus. When are we getting back on the route? *When* are we arriving at Cloverdale?" Ronald's anger was even surprising to him.

The driver turned and gave him a withering, hate-filled grimace. "Maybe never," he said.

Ronald went pale. *It was true. God, it was true. This maniac was not the real driver, this was not a detour, and they were all in terrible danger.*

But such things didn't happen, they just didn't happen to everyday people and everyday buses, did they?

"*Why?*" asked Ronald. Breathlessly, he spewed out his suspicions. "You don't even work for the bus company, do you? *Do you?*"

The driver's answer was to reach into a paper bag at his side and lift out a huge, sharpened butcher knife. "Get back in your seat," he said. "Or I'll cut you up into tiny little pieces and feed you to the fishes. Ha." The mad eyes glinted with evil. "Or would you like me to drive the bus into a nice, big tree?"

Ronald gasped. "You'd kill *yourself* that way, too."

The man chuckled.

"*Where are you taking us*? I insist—"

The man glared at him and bellowed: "GET BACK IN YOUR SEAT!"

Shaking, *quivering*, Ronald walked back down the aisle and collapsed into the chair. God—this could not be happening! What was going to become of them? *Damn you, mother. I'm on this bus because of you and now I'm going to die before you do.*

The girl with the headphones was awake now. She leaned across the aisle and cupped her hands over her mouth. "Are we—in trouble?" she asked. Obviously she'd heard part of his conversation with the driver.

35

Ronald had to swallow twice before he could answer. "The driver. . . . he's not the real driver. . . . he's crazy. . . . has a knife."

Some of the others—none of whom were strong and beefy, not at all heroic in their own minds or anyone else's—came down to Ronald's seat and asked him what the driver had been shouting about. Upon hearing, they put out a hue and cry, expressed outrage and retaliation. A chubby fellow of fifty with swollen cheeks and a waddling walk went forward to confront the driver. Ronald tried to warn him. "Don't go! He—He's crazy!"

The man was determined. "Crazy or not, we're not putting up with *this*."

It was over in thirty seconds.

The fat man's bellows. The driver's snarls. Then: the flash of a blade—quick, sharp, definite. The fat man's collapse and outcry. The hands over the protruding belly, the blood running through the fingers. The driver's cackle, the dripping knife in his hand. So smooth that the bus had not even slowed or swerved a fraction. A mere thirty seconds and it was over.

The fat man sprawled across the steps at the front of the bus, breathing heavily, bleeding. The driver held up the knife and hollered:

"Stay in your seats. Anyone who comes near him gets it."

And they all knew that he meant it.

All his life Ronald had been afraid of them, the maniacs, the street animals who preyed on the slower and the weaker. All his life he had avoided them as best he could. But once a week in the terminal, once a week he would have to stand in line at gate 27 and hope the creatures would not approach or bother him. And now, like sheep, like docile fattened lambs to the slaughter, he and the other dozen or so passengers had passively gotten on a bus and allowed one of those animals to drive them straight to nowhere.

"What do we do?" someone, a woman, was asking. They were looking to Ronald for the answer. Ronald, the first one who had approached the maniac and lived to tell of it. A man was dying up front and they, in a different way, were dying in the back of the bus, and he, the reluctant leader, was suffering the most terrible death of all. The death of hope and survival, the death of his faith in himself, the long, unflagging belief that if put to the test, he really could rise to the occasion. But here he was, put to the test, in the middle of a bus piloted by a crazy armed with a knife, and all he could do was moan and sob and shiver.

The bus began to bounce and shudder. They were driving down a rutted lane, over rocks and holes. *Where* was he taking them? What was he going to do? Ronald felt utterly helpless. He was not a cop with a gun and a nightstick, a trained partner by his side. Neither were any of his fellow passengers. He looked at them: elderly women, a retarded girl, men as flabby and frightened and out-of-shape as he was. There was no one on the bus who could save them.

Ronald tried to think of the "logistics" of the situation through his panic, tried to formulate a plan while the bus swerved and rocked and rattled.

Problem one: disarm the driver. Problem two: get control of the bus without causing an accident. At this speed, on this road, the bus could overturn, kill or injure them all. He wasn't just confronted with a man with a knife, but a man with a knife who was *in control of a bus*. If you could call the bumpy ride he was giving them as being "in control."

Ronald sat back in his seat and held on for dear life. If only the shaking would stop; the shaking of the bus, the trembling of his body. If only the bus would stop moving.

The driver was shouting maniacally, at last explaining what was happening: how he'd been fired from his job at the bus firm, knocked out the real driver and taken his jacket, how he'd pretended to be the driver and no one had even challenged him. Beyond that, he seemed to have no plan, no definite destination in mind. He was merely getting even with the bus company. That made it worse. Did he simply want to screw up one bus trip, or did he want to wreck the bus and kill the passengers, casting a pall of negative publicity over the firm and its entire operation?

Something had to be done. The driver, the bus, had to be stopped.—without killing them all. Making it worse was that the driver seemed psychotic enough to commit harakiri and take all of them along for the ride.

Suddenly the bus swerved to the right with a jarring thud that almost knocked the passengers out of their seats.

The bus was shooting across a field of tall grass. In the distance, Ronald could see a lake; smooth, silent, silvery.

The driver was heading for the lake.

The passengers were screaming. Someone had fallen out into the aisle and was struggling to get up. The girl across the way had her face against the glass and was crying.

Ronald jumped to his feet. Whipping off his jacket as he ran, he dashed up the aisle grabbing each seat to steady himself as he passed.

37

The driver's foot rammed down on the gas pedal. The lake was looming larger and larger in the gigantic windshield at the front of the bus.

The driver turned, sensed Ronald approaching, then looked up and saw him in his mirror. One hand steered the bus while the other got out his knife.

Ronald's jacket dropped down over the hand with the blade in it. He twisted and tightened the jacket, pulling the man's arm behind him.

Ronald leaned over the driver, grabbed at the steering wheel. He had to get at the brake!

The driver tried to cut his way through the jacket, to push Ronald off his lap.

Ronald got a good grip on the wheel. He began to wrench it to the right—

Sssplashhh!

Too late. The lake was filling up the windshield; water was climbing up the glass like scrabbling liquid fingers.

The bus was weaving from side to side but coming to a stop. Ronald's jacket lay in shreds on the floor. He pounded the driver in the face with two upraised fists—leaving the man's eyes and lips and nose all red and bloody. He didn't stop until the man was practically unconscious. He had to give them time. The bus had stopped before it had reached deep water, but still the lake would pour in through a dozen different entries until it finally reached its own level.

Ronald saw someone trying to open a window. "Stop! You'll just let the water in faster!" While the driver was dazed, he grabbed the semi-conscious stabbing victim and dragged him up to the middle of the bus. Better to make his injuries worse than to leave him there to drown.

After all his trips on this bus, Ronald knew the way out in an emergency. "We'll go out the roof," he told the others. He climbed up on top of a nearby seat and steadied himself. He followed the instructions—"Pull the handle all the way down, then push the panel upwards"—and felt the cool air coming in through the trapdoor. With assistance, he raised the fat man to safety, then stepped down.

He directed the others to hurriedly climb up and out onto the top of the bus where the water could not reach them. It was streaming in by the gallons. He stood aside and helped the first few through.

Unnoticed by anyone, the driver had recovered from the reign of blows Ronald had given him, and was advancing unseen up the aisle, knife in hand. The streams of water gushing into the bus would not deter him.

The last passenger was on the roof of the bus. Ronald was just about to climb out when he turned toward the front of the bus and saw the driver approaching.

Quickly, desperately, he pulled himself partway up through the opening in the roof—he knew he'd never be able to get all the way out before the driver could reach him—and started swinging his feet back and forth. God, it *hurt*. His scrawny arms were not built for such athletics.

The driver lunged out with the knife.

Ronald's feet made contact, hitting the bony wrist of the man and sending the knife flying. Another foot flew out and bashed the man repeatedly in the face, sprawling him onto the floor of the aisle. He sunk out of sight below the frothing water that had filled the bus and was now at waist level.

Ronald couldn't let the man die. He dropped down into the water and started searching for his body with his hands. Suddenly the driver jumped out of the water with a maddened howl and wrapped his dripping hands around Ronald's neck.

They grappled together under the hole in the roof as the water rose higher and higher. The maniac was incredibly strong and sinewy. While his hands tried to crush Ronald's windpipe, he was slowly pushing Ronald's head below the water. Ronald tried to break free, to pull away, to rise up and get away from his assailant, but he was much too weak and dizzy. He started losing consciousness, felt water touch his lips. *To have come this far and survived so much. . . .*

Crash! A bottle of soda pop flew down from the hole and cracked apart on the maniac's forehead. Blood mingled with water. He released his hold on Ronald and fell back, disappearing into the swirling miniature lake inside the bus.

Ronald looked up. The girl with the headphones smiled down at him and raised her fist in victory.

The water had stopped rising, but it was nearly at Ronald's neck. With the girl's help, he pulled his drenched and aching body out of the bus. He had no intention of trying to save the driver a second time.

Later, after their rescue, Ronald was so numb and shaken he could barely feel the congratulatory pats of the passengers on his back, or hear their words of thanks in his ear.

"You must feel like a real he-man," someone said.

Ronald shook his head. "I just feel tired, nervous, and more than a little scared for all of us."

Ronald walked into the Port Authority Terminal from the IND subway and made his way past the drifters, derelicts and bag ladies with stony assurance. They didn't bother him anymore; nothing bothered him. Now that he had laid hands upon, kicked in the face, beaten with his fists, one of the animals, he found them more pitiful than dangerous.

It had been three weeks since the incident, three weeks since he'd spoken to police and reporters, three weeks since he'd called his mother from a pay phone in the town of North Plains, Ma.—that crazy man's hometown—and told her that he would be late because the bus had been hijacked. After that weekend, after he'd hired a taxi to drive him all the way to his mother's house, he had told the old woman not to expect him for at least three weeks, that he was only coming up maybe once a month instead of every week from now on, that she would have to be satisfied with that.

He knew the bus companies had not increased their security in spite of the incident three weeks ago. Why should they? They had simply assumed it had been a freak occurrence, a once-in-a-lifetime mishap. Someone taking the place of the driver?—it was too absurd for words. No one would ever dare try it again, so what was the use of worrying, what was the point of taking precautions?

Oh, how he hated the thought of going to mother's. He'd rather go to Florida, somewhere south, somewhere warm. How he hated the thought of being one of those docile creatures in the lines, those who put their fate, forever put their lives, in somebody else's hands. How he wished he could be one of the rulers instead of the sheep. Normally he would have stood there beside the railing at gate 27 and waited in his usual taut, frightened manner, terrified lest some bit of human debris approach him. Now, now that he was no longer scared of them. . . .

He had decided. Today was the day. He'd been planning it ever since the hijacking. . . .

The woman at gate 38 to Florida stepped through the doorway and smiled at the nice man standing beside the bus. He smiled back—such a pleasant fellow—and held out a slender hand.

"Tickets, please," said Ronald.

The Absolute and Utter Impossibility of the Facts in the Case of the Vanishing of Henning Vok

(a.k.a. The Amazing Blitzen)
(r.n. Jack Ralph Cole)

by Jack Adrian

The facts were these: in the bath-tub, shifting gently under eighteen inches of rust-coloured water, lay the fully-clothed (even down to his overcoat and Oxfords) corpse of Herman Jediah Klauss, the Moriarty of Manhattan, a large ornamental ice-pick sunk in his skull. Never personable (especially in the matter of nasal hair) he now gave the impression of a dead dugong.

That (that he was unequivocally dead) was one fact. A second fact was that his murderer was not in the bathroom with him. A third was that he ought to have been.

There were other facts. The apartment was in a building in the

41

low West 70s, a spit from the Park, half a spit from the Dakota. It was on the 11th floor. It was b-i-g. It had been built at a time (maybe the 1900s) when architects had grandiose dreams and clients with money to fuel them. To Commings, the bathroom looked about as spacious as a side-chapel in St. Patrick's. The bath itself was a vast boxed-in affair, fake (or maybe not) ivory with a dark mahogany trim. The toilet, next to it, could easily have doubled as a throne. You could almost certainly have bathed a Doberman in the bidet.

Over by the door, which was at least three inches thick and might well have withstood the full blast of an RPG-7 anti-personnel rocket, Trask bellowed, "*It's impossible!*"

Which, of course, it was.

Commings thought through the sequence of events for what seemed like the fiftieth time.

Klauss had entered the apartment closely followed by patrolmen O'Mahoney and Schwaab (flagged down outside the building and invited in because, in Klauss's words, "There's a guy up there wants to ice me"). They were met by an English butler (hired for the evening, it now transpired) and a black maid (idem). They were escorted up the long hallway, past shelfloads of books (mainly mystery fiction: Carolyn Wells, H.H. Holmes, Carter Dickson, Hake Talbot, Clayton Rawson, Edward D. Hoch, Joel Townsley Rogers, a raft of others), past cabinets full of rare Golden Age comicbooks (mainly from the Quality group: *Police Comics, Smash Comics, Plastic Man, The Spirit, National Comics, Doll Man*, many more), and past a series of framed posters featuring a preternaturally rangy man clad in, first, evening dress ("The Amazing Blitzen: Unparalleled Feats of Legerdemain and Prestidigitation!"), second, vaguely Arabian robes ("The Sultan of Stretch, the Emir of Elongation—see the many-jointed Blitzen zip himself into a carpet-bag!"), and, third, a skin-tight black costume akin to what bathers wore two generations back ("Blitzen! Illusionist *extraordinaire!*"). Smaller bills showed him peering out from a cannon's mouth ("The Shell Man!"), being lowered into a swimming-pool by a gantry with what looked to be a half ton of ship's cable cocooning him ("The Man With the Iron Lungs!"), and chained spread-eagle to a vast target ("Can he escape before the crossbow bolt pierces his heart?!").

Henning Vok (or, as his real name now seemed to be, J.R. Cole) had emerged from a doorway at the far end ("skinny as a beanpole," as Schwaab said later, "but looking kind of flushed. . .like he'd been running") and welcomed, in open-armed fashion, his visitor, who'd turned to the two cops and warned,

42

"Don't trust the sucker an inch."

Vok/Cole had laughed distractedly and said, "You want the cards or not, dammit?", gesturing at the half-open door. Klauss had walked in and said, "This is a bathroom." Vok/Cole said, "You catch on fast", and then, reaching behind the door, had produced the ice-pick, with which, to the consternation of the witnesses, he had proceeded to poleaxe Klauss, Klauss toppling into the tub (full) and sending a tidal-wave of displaced water spraying over Vok/Cole, the toilet, the oxygen-machine next to the bidet and the floor. Vok/Cole had then jumped for the door, slamming it shut and locking it.

It took the two patrolmen (not having an RPG-7 launcher) twenty minutes to break down the door. When they finally entered, the room was empty. Apart, of course, from the now defunct Herman Jediah Klauss.

"Im-poss-i-*bul*!" said Trask now, through clenched teeth. "And bull's the operative word." He clutched at a straw. "What if they were all in it?"

Commings said, "The butler and the maid, maybe. And could be Schwaab's on the take. But hell, Lieutenant," his voice rose a notch or two, "O'Mahoney?"

"The Prize Prepuce of the Precinct House," groaned Trask. "The only totally honest man on the roster. *God!*"

This last profanity was spat out not only on account of O'Mahoney's notorious incorruptibility, which hinted at stupidity on a serious scale, but because, at that moment, a figure of surpassing bulk, clad in a fur-coat and brandishing an unsheathed swordstick in a hamhock-sized fist, came barrelling into the apartment.

"Trask!" bawled the newcomer. "The Commissioner called me! It's a demented dwarf, depend on it!"

Trask shot him a look that could have split an atom.

"Now see here. . ."

"Don't interrupt! Show Professor Stanislaus Befz an Impossible Crime and he'll show you a deranged midget with an ice-pick. They never alter their *modus operandi*, the little devils." He surged through the hall like a resuscitated Golem, cutting a swathe through cops, photogs, morgue-men in white coats, and only coming to a halt at the bathroom door. Here he yelped triumphantly. "William Howard Taft! An ice-pick! What did I say!" He jabbed the swordstick at the corpse, the blade parting Comming's hair as the detective ducked to the floor. "You've already snapped the gyves on the hunchback, I take it?"

"Professor, there *is* no hunchback. . ."

"Balderdash! Out of the three thousand thirty three Miracle

Problems I've investigated, analysed and catalogued over the past quarter century, crazed mannikins hidden in the false humps of ersatz hunchbacks account for well over half." He glanced down at Commings. "What are you doing down there?"

Trask was snapping his fingers urgently as the behemothesque Befz, not waiting for a reply, strode towards the tub. Commings scrambled to his feet and handed to his chief the packet of antacid tablets kept for times like this. He wondered miserably why amateur detectives specialising in Miracle Problems were invariably fat. And loud. And. . .and *eccentric*.

"Aaron Burr!" oathed the man-mountain, jowls quivering like a turkey's wattles. "Herman Jediah Klauss, the Moriarty of Manhattan!" He spun—or, rather, lurched—round, the swordstick scattering various detectives. "So where's the hunchie?"

Trask was holding his stomach and wincing.

He muttered, "Tell him."

Commings explained about the lack of counterfeit hunchbacks in this particular case. This took some time owing to Befz's innumerable interruptions. Commings finished, "In any case, there were four witnesses who saw Vok, or Cole, do it."

"Mass-hypnosis!" thundered Befz. "The oldest trick in the book! I have three hundred forty-eight cases in my records, of which probably the most illuminating was the Great Hollywood Bowl Pickpocket Scam. This Vok, or Cole, undoubtedly flapdoodled the witnesses into thinking he was skinny then flipped open his false hump and let the demoniacal pixie out to do its fell business. The man was clearly a master-mesmerist."

"The butler and the maid, sure," agreed Commings. "And Schwaab, too. But," his voice pitched up, "O'Mahoney?"

Befz glanced at the patrolman. "You may have a point there," he grudged. "Well, there are plenty of other Impossible Murder Methods to choose from. . ."

"Sweet galloping Jesus!" screeched Trask. "The murder method is not in question! We know how he did it! The guy even admits to it himself!" He gulped down three or four more antacid tablets. "Show him the note, Commings."

The note read:

Dear guys,
    I have decided to retire on my well-gotten gains, which over the years (due to judicious investment) have made me a millionaire many times over.
    Before I go, however, I believe I can do you a couple favours.
    Primus*: Attached is a list of robberies which should feature*

44

heavily in your "Unsolved" files. Strike 'em. I plead guilty on all counts;

Secundus*: I also plead guilty to the expunging of Herman Jediah Klauss, murderer, shylock, fence (who invariably paid bottom-dollar: hence my hatred of him) extortioner, blackmailer, procurer, rabid collector and generally worthless scoundrel. Having inveigled him here on the pretence of selling him a rare set of 'Woozy Winks' bubble-gum cards (circa 1948), I split his head with an ice-pick.*

I mourn the fact that I leave behind my vast collection of interesting artefacts.

That's a lie. Where I'm going, I have duplicate copies of everything.

Hasta la vista!

Henning Vok, a.k.a. The Great Blitzen

(r.n. Jack Ralph Cole)

P.S. There are plenty clues.

"Hmmm," larynxed Befz. "So the problem is how he escaped from the bathroom. That shouldn't prove too tricky. As you probably know if you've read my *magnum opus* on the subject, there are precisely one thousand three hundred fifty-two ways of getting out of a locked room, only seven hundred eighty-six of which depend on a reel of cotton. And out of that, only one hundred thirty-five need a new pin and split paper-match. Walls?"

"Solid brick," Trask grated.

"Ceiling?"

"Same."

"Window?"

"Hasn't been opened in fifty years."

"Floor?"

"Forget it."

"Oh."

Befz absently tapped the blade of his swordstick on the oxygen-machine next to the bidet. It made a tanging sound. His eye was caught by the large old-fashioned air-extractor fixed into the wall, high up.

"John Quincy Adams! The fan!"

"To get up there," growled Trask, "you'd need to be able to fly."

"*Precisely!*" Befz triumphantly whacked the swordstick against one of the oxygen cylinders. The blade shattered into several shards. "Damn! That's the one hundred twenty-eighth this year. The blessed things cost a fortune too. Never mind. Vok, or Cole, inflated himself with oxygen and floated up to the fan, where. . ."

"Where he'd slice himself up in the extractor blades, yeah. You're losing your touch, Befz. I might just as well ask O'Mahoney if he's got any bright ideas."

"Oh sure," said O'Mahoney. "I mean, it's transparently obvious, Lieutenant."

Numerous pairs of eyes focussed on him. He hitched up his gun-belt self-consciously and began to walk around the room, slapping the tip of his nightstick into the open (gloved) palm of his left hand.

"It's an interesting problem sure enough, Professor. Uh . . .and Lieutenant. Oh, and. . ." he glanced at Commings ". . .Sergeant. But there's really only one exit. Although, as Vok/Cole pointed out, there are plenty clues. See, I asked myself, why the bath? But we'll get to that later. I'd like you all to follow me."

Numerous pairs of shoes and boots tramped after him into the hallway. He gestured at the posters.

"It's all there. He was a contortionist. Skinny as a rake. This is an old building. Way back, they built things bigger. Follow me."

They followed him. Back into the bathroom.

"You very nearly hit it, Professor. The oxygen-machine was crucial to his plan. Possibly not many of you know that in 1959 a technician in California hyperventilated on oxygen and then created a world record for remaining underwater for thirteen minutes forty-two seconds. Vok/Cole, as we know, had 'iron lungs', but the oxygen gave him that extra edge. As you'll recall, my partner described him as looking flushed, as though he'd been running. Fact was, he seemed semi-hysterical. But like I said, it was the bathwater that tipped me. Way I figured it, water splashed from the tub would hide the tell-tale subsequent splashes of water from quite another source."

He used the nightstick as a pointer. Numerous pairs of eyes swivelled towards the mighty throne-like structure next to the tub.

"That's right," said O'Mahoney. "He flushed himself down the toilet."

Blast from the Past

by Gabrielle Kraft

T he trouble with living a stable life is that people from your
past always know where to find you. I've lived on the top
floor of this West Hollywood fourplex for twenty years and
in LA, twenty years is a lifetime. Once widowed, once divorced,
I bought the building in the 70's, right before real estate shot into
hyperspace. Could have sold out ten times over and made a killing,
but I'm an LA baby and I love this town.

This is what you need to know about me: I used to live on the
edge, I used to be somebody else. But after my divorce ten years
ago I realized I had to settle down, grab hold of a chunk of reality
before it was too late. So I transformed myself from a woman on
the edge to a woman in the middle. Now I live off the income
from the building and teach bonehead darkroom technique three
nights a week at UCLA. I have friends, boyfriends from time to
time. Hell, I even have a dog. But cops never give me the fish
eye, my bills are paid, I'm a solid citizen. It's a dull routine,
but it's predictable and that's the way I want it. I've had enough
excitement to last me a lifetime.

So when there was a knock at the door late one night, I got a bad
feeling. I keep a .38 by the bed and one by the front door and I

know how to shoot so I wasn't scared, but I didn't like the pleasant routine of my smooth, even life disrupted. That's the only thing a midnight knock can mean to someone like me.

Knock knock again, soft and insistent. I got the gun, went to the door and looked out the barred peephole. It was Charlie. I lowered the gun to my side and opened the door, staring at him in the glow of the porch light. He looked better than the last time I saw him, ten years ago. Tan even though the dead ghost look is fashionable in LA, leaner, grayer, but aren't we all?

"I love a woman with a gun in her hand," he said as he bent to kiss me hello. "So 90's."

His cheek was rough; he always complained he had a tough beard, but he smelled the same, a French cologne he used. I remember it came in a rectangular bottle with a blue label and cost too much. But then, a lot of things about Charlie cost too much. He moved past me and went through to the living room.

"Looks better," he said, pointing at the low, overstuffed couches and the big glass topped coffee table. "Looks like you finally spent some money on yourself. Any of it mine?"

This, I ignored. I put the gun down on the table and the cold click of metal on glass sounded like a page turning. "Scotch?"

"What're you drinking?"

"Lillet."

"Expensive tastes, chickadee."

"I'm a bloodsucking landlord living off the wages of the working class. I can afford it." I went into the kitchen.

"I'll take scotch," he said. He sighed and stretched out full length on the couch, kicking his loafers to the floor. "God, this feels good. Tina, can I stay a few days? I'm tapped."

"We're not married anymore, Charlie," I called mildly.

"Too damn bad too. Can I? I'm working on something."

"Christ, you were working on something the day we got married, you were working on something the day we got divorced." I tried to keep the old anger out of my voice.

He took the glass of scotch I offered him and drank it off. "C'mon, don't give me that Little Miss Moral act, you loved it. What're you now, a retired maiden lady with a thousand cats?"

"One dog," I said, sounding as defensive as I felt.

"I don't hear any barking."

"He's at the vets overnight, getting his teeth cleaned."

Charlie burst out laughing. "Another drink. With ice."

"Jesus, Charlie. . ." But I took his glass and went back to the kitchen to get his ice. I used to crush it with a hammer when we were married.

You see, Charlie and I were a team. We were married, but we were way more than husband and wife, we were bookends, an unbroken pair. As I broke out the ice cubes I had one of those stunning middle-aged moments of revelation that sneak up on me more and more frequently of late. My past is more vivid than my present. My present is safe but bland; my past is where I live. People from the past know you because there's an intimate story lying between every snippet of history like a paperback novel face down on a rumpled sheet. And Charlie and I had a hundred stories together. I thought about having another Lillet—it's a tony French aperitif wine my last boyfriend liked—but switched to scotch. As I poured the pale golden liquid into a stemmed glass, I wondered what Charlie was working on.

"So what's the deal?" I asked as I went back to the living room, conspicuously rattling the ice in his glass.

"Interest? Do I detect interest? My my sugarplum, I thought you gave up the wild life."

"I have." Defensive again. "I'm just curious."

He patted the couch next to him. "Listen my dear and you shall hear, there's bucks to be made if you have no fear."

"Champagne Charlie. You haven't changed." It was true. He hadn't, but I had. I was dull, safe and secure, but that was the choice I'd made, right?

"Oh yes I have," he said, very serious. "I want to make a killing, settle down. Like you."

"You? Quit? C'mon. . ." I drained my glass and tucked my feet under me on the couch.

Charlie shook his head and I saw the old vigor and impatience oozing across his face. All that speed and anger I used to love, the barely controlled violence that he kept in check always excited me and as I watched his fervor recede I remembered how much fun we used to have. God, I used to be crazy for Charlie. I had a weird physical flashback, Charlie's hands sliding down my back one night as we waited in a parked car above the Strip for some jerk to drop off our end of a score, adrenaline pumping like an oil well. . .

"Another drink," he told me.

I went back to the kitchen. "So what do you have?" I called.

"Letters, I've got letters," he chirped. Very perky, our Charlie.

"Letters? How Victorian," I said as I bent down to put our fresh drinks on the table. I looked up and caught him staring down my shirt.

He shrugged. "You're still gorgeous."

"Never mind the sweet talk, tell mama the story."

"OK, here's the deal. Long time ago, the Dark Ages of the Sixties, young struggling actor has a crazy girlfriend, he likes to write her weird letters, she reads 'em out loud, then they do the stuff in the letters."

"Like what?"

"Oh God, the usual. Dress up like a schoolgirl who forgot to wear knickers, bend over and give the boys a thrill. Suck my lollipop. Nobody ever comes up with anything original."

"Slave girl and the warrior king? Miss Maple the mean old governess?"

"Exactly so. Dissolve. He's now a big daytime TV star with a homey flair, she's still got the letters and wonders if he wouldn't be willing to pay for the privilege of getting 'em back."

"And now you have the letters?"

"Well, not exactly. She's got the letters and I've got her." He looked decidedly uncomfortable. "Look, it's just a hustle. Alison's not my type."

"But you're willing to make her your type. Temporarily."

"It's just a hustle," he said again. "Women like me."

Funny thing was, I felt a rush of jealousy but I kept it to myself. "How tidy. What's my part in this happy scenario?"

"You sell him the letters."

"Why me? Why not you?"

"I thought it would be a nice touch if we played it like we used to. You know, I've got the letters, then you double cross me, sell 'em to him a little cheaper. He isn't burned too bad, thinks he's getting a bargain, doesn't call the police. Christ, we've done it a thousand times."

"That was another life, Charlie. What's in it for me?"

Something flickered across his face, a shiver on glass. "Nothing."

"What a guy," I said. It didn't quite have the ironic insouciance I'd hoped to achieve.

"Tina, I need you to help me with this. When you left me, my luck ran out. Oh, I've made some good scores in the past ten years. . ."

Yeah, I thought, so good you come around waiting to crash on your ex-wife's couch. But I didn't say anything. It's tough to see the man you loved down on his luck, scrabbling for crumbs.

". . .some good scores," he went on. "But things get too close when you work solo. You always watched my back. Now I need a stake and I'm asking you to help me. Look at it this way," he gave a wicked grin. "The damn recession's hit everybody and this town's tightened up."

I knew I was going to give in. When we broke up I walked away with most of our cash and I figured I owed him. Plus, I felt sorry for him. Took him *so* long to figure it out. He's forty years old and he's finally realized he can't slide by on a smile and a hustle, a bit of blackmail here, some smalltime extortion, the occasional bit of thievery. God, Hollywood was an easy town for a while. . .

"OK, Charlie. I'll think about it."

"Let me show you the set-up in the morning. You're going to love this one, Tina," he said. "It's a beauty. Besides, aren't you bored? Doesn't all this cotton wool bore the crap out of you?"

"You get what you want, you get the box it comes in. Can't have everything."

"Why? We used to." he said. "We can again."

I felt the pull of the past, the tie that still bound me to the life I used to live. If you want to kill passionate love, you have to cut off its head and jam a stake in its heart. Otherwise, it lives inside you forever.

"Just a looksee," I said.

We finished our drinks and I made Charlie a bed on the couch, not because I was a prude but I didn't want to make life too easy for him. Not yet.

The next morning we tossed Charlie's briefcase and my camera bag into my Mustang and drove out to the beach with the top down while he roughed out his plan. "I'm a writer from Vanity Fair and you're my assistant." Charlie said this very casually as he checked his look in the rearview.

"You're a writer?" Incredulity *bigtime*. "He believes that?"

Charlie grinned, that sureness of his spreading over me like a riptide. "He's an actor, of course he believes it. Listen, the guy's so ego-damaged he'd do an interview for the Physician's Desk Reference. This is just the cute-meet. If you like it, we'll figure out the rest later. Just follow my lead and you won't go wrong."

I nodded. It was a postcard California day, blue sky with puffy white Maxfield Parrish clouds, gentle sunshine, wind in your hair. . . oh yeah, life can be a dream. That's what a good day in LA can do, make you feel like you're on the edge of a precipice about to jump into a warm pool of luck.

As we pulled into a circular driveway in front of a low ranch house crouching on the side of a hill Charlie reached into his briefcase and pulled out a yellow legal pad. "Props," he said. "Take your camera."

I grabbed my huge Nikon out of my camera bag. My weapon of choice is a thirty year old Leica that almost fits in the palm of my hand but people believe an impressive camera with a fat lens makes you a better photographer. I took the Nikon.

We walked up a herringbone brick pathway edged with moss toward a white front door with a pair of brass lamps on either side that could easily illuminate Versailles. There was lots of flagstone, probably no more than six-seven bedrooms, pool, tennis court, maybe an ice rink. You get the picture.

Bill Coffey himself opened the door and I was disappointed. I'd hoped for some servile groveling from one of his flunkies. I have to admit, he was a shock. I'd seen him on TV, he had a syndicated chat show called "The Coffey Club" that was heavily weighted with advice for the happy homemaker. Sort of show that puts you to sleep when you've got the flu. But when you see a real live personality—or maybe he was a celebrity—they look so familiar, you think you've known them for years.

But Coffey looked bigger, coarser. Big head, big features, rough skin on the pockmarked side which I guess they smooth over with make-up on TV. "Who's this?" he said.

I smiled and looked demure, clutching my legal pad.

Charlie's mood changed. No one else would have noticed but when you've been married, worked and hustled together, you learn to read the details flickering in the half light. He'd slipped on his own version of the coat of many colors and he exuded power and respectability; he was now a man of parts. "Ginger is my assistant," he said. "She's been with me for years, haven't you Ginge?"

Ginger. I could have killed him.

Coffey led us into the living room, we all sat down and I pulled out my pad and made notes as Coffey filled Charlie in on the thrilling details of his high school drama class in Kansas City. The early afternoon sun was glistening on the pool, a blue jay shrieked on the patio and it was déja vu all over again.

All the years I'd spent teaching my little classes and collecting my rents and making sure the faucets weren't dripping were erased like chalk on a blackboard as I watched Charlie play Coffey's narcissism like Miles Davis plays his golden horn. Sure, I had my safe, quiet life, but boredom is the flip side of stability and as I realized how tired I was of my stale life my careful equilibrium snapped like a taut string. I guess we're never as sure of our choices as we like to pretend.

Besides, everybody has a dirty little secret and mine is that I like to work people. Manipulate them. That's why Charlie and I made such a great team—he'd set 'em up and I'd knock 'em down. Pull on the strings, baby, and watch 'em jump. I sat and listened to Coffey drone on about his big break in showbiz and I knew I was dying to do it again, dying to take the TV star and run him ragged. Even if there was nothing in it for me.

I crossed my legs and watched his eyes reflexively slide up my skirt. He didn't mean anything by it, but I filed his look away for future use. Idly, I wondered what the inside of a star's bedroom at the beach looked like and if his predilection for sex games had died with the other dreams of the Sixties.

After an hour of interviewing, Charlie and I left. "Well?" he said as we pulled away from Coffey's house. "It's a snap, right? We do more interviews and in a few days you tell him I've got the letters and I'm planning to publish. But you can get them away from me—for a better price. C'mon, it's money from home. No fuss, no muss."

"It looks good," I said as I watched Sunset Boulevard uncoil across the windshield. "How much were you thinking of asking?"

"Two hundred."

"And I ask a hundred?"

"Sure. Maybe one fifty to start."

It was a hot afternoon, a bright sun washed out all the shadows and the street looked clean and new. We parked in my driveway, went into the apartment in silence, walked down the hall to the bedroom without talking. I'd drawn the blinds in the morning against the afternoon sun but sharp streaks of light shone through the slats, throwing a pattern of stripes across the cabbage rose bedspread. A zebra lost in a hothouse, I thought inadvertently, as Charlie began to undress me.

"I've missed you," he said as he unbuttoned my blouse.

"The hell you have." His hands were still familiar and a deep calm invaded me, as if all the nervous excitement of the day had drained away and only warm syrup remained.

"I've thought about you." We fell on the bed wrapped together in a knot of flesh striped by the sun.

"I've thought about you, too," I admitted. What's past is prologue, a voice reminded me as Charlie's mouth covered mine. Prologue.

It was early evening when I got out of bed and went into the kitchen for a drink of water. Charlie was still asleep. As I stood at the sink looking out the window at the palm fronds scraping the side of the house across the way I realized I'd forgotten to pick up Dee, the dog. I called the vet and left a message on her machine saying I'd get him tomorrow. I'd forgotten how different it is when you live your life for two. Isolation has an unexpected result; the isolate craves more and more of the precious drug and eventually begins to seek it everywhere. There's a delicious component to solitude, wandering alone through crowded shopping malls, the midnight ride with the radio blasting, the table for one and it's a hard habit to kick. But for Charlie, it was worth it. Ten years had vanished and we were a pair again.

So, Charlie and I spent the nights making love, a honeymoon that made me feel there were still possibilities ahead and during the day, we'd meet with Bill Coffey. Twice at his house, twice at his office in Century City, twice for lunch and by that time we knew the man up and down. On the seventh day we rested and Charlie announced that Coffey was ready for my pitch. The next morning I drove out to Coffey's house alone. Another diamond day.

My hibernation of the past few years was over. Charlie had persuaded me to shed my stale snake's skin and I'd emerged fresh and new for my encounter with Bill Coffey. I didn't have all the details but one thing I knew for sure; life on the edge is life worth living.

"Where's Charlie?" he asked when he met me at the front door. His eyes flicked over my shoulder, across the driveway.

"I'm here by myself," I said. "I want to talk to you."

"Oh." Coffey closed the door behind me. His tone was non-committal. "Let's have a drink outside."

He led me out to the pool, a blue gash in the landscape that was far bluer than the ocean in the distance and he seated me at a slab of glass resting on a sheared-off tree trunk.

"Mr. Coffey. . . Bill. . ." I began, hesitancy playing across my voice. "I have to tell you something."

Coffey was making drinks at a rolling tea cart that served as an outdoor bar. "What, Ginger?" he asked as he sat down and slid a spritzer in front of me.

Ginger. I winced. Damn Charlie anyway.

"When I took this job. . ." I started slowly, wondering if he was bright enough to pick up the cue.

He was. "I thought you'd worked for Charlie for years," he frowned.

"That's part of it," I said, letting a patina of helplessness creep over my face. "Mr. Coffey, I haven't been with him for years and I'm not his secretary."

Coffey's frown dug deeper. "I don't understand."

"And my name's not Ginger," I said. "It's Jackie."

Coffey hitched his chair closer to mine and I felt the tension rising like steam. "Why don't you tell me what this is all about, honey." His voice was harder, his genial act was fading.

I didn't balk, didn't give in but leaned closer to him, close enough to smell his lemony aftershave.

"He's got some letters of yours, Bill."

I could see his mind clicking through his past like an abacus.

"Kind of . . . dirty letters," I prodded. "You wrote them a long time ago. To a girl."

"A long time ago?" He still didn't get it then, bam! It all fell into place. "Letters." His voice was dull.

"About ten of them." I was winging it; I hadn't even read his damn letters. I mean, who cares about some pathetic TV star's 20 year old sex games? Only the star himself, only Bill Coffey who believed he was the hub of the whirring world. Certainly not me.

Coffey sighed and leaned back in his chair. "And what's your part in this, Jackie? Is that really your name?"

"Oh yes," I lied. "He hired me two weeks ago and told me if he could get an interview with you it'll make his career. He wanted to play it up big, that's why he brought me along."

"He's not from Vanity Fair." Coffey was resigned.

"He's not from anywhere. He's not even a real writer."

Coffey closed his eyes and held his face up to the sun like a sacrifice. "Not from Vanity Fair. Not a writer. So, he's got the letters. Something tells me he wants to sell them. How much?"

"200,000."

"200 K? Christ, woman," he laughed. "I can't raise that much cash. Are you insane?"

"I'm not involved with him, Bill." Yeah, right. You've got to believe me. "You've got to believe me." I said it straight at him without blinking and he went for it.

"I believe you, honey." He patted me on the hand. "You're a sweet kid."

"At first I thought he was sincere, really a writer, but when I found out. . . I can help you, Bill. But I have to live too." Jesus. Next week, *East Lynne*.

The thing was, it felt so good, powerful and strong. For those few brief seconds my voice hung in the air every word I spoke was sincere. I believed—momentarily. And that's what made it work just like a crystal clock ticking in a silent room.

He raised his eyebrows, rubbing his pockmarked face. "How? How can you help me, honey?"

"I can get the letters, Bill. For a better price." I said it softly, moist lower lip trembling so, so slightly.

"Ahhhh. . ." he exhaled like a burst tire. "How much better?"

"Half of what Charlie wants."

"100 K. It's a better price," he mused. "Let me think a minute." Coffey got up and paced back and forth along the lip of the pool, his brain flipping through an endless sequence of possibilities.

"Tomorrow," I prodded.

He sighed and nodded his agreement. "It won't be easy, but I'll pay," Coffey said slowly. "I *have* to have them back. Honey, you'll help me, won't you?" His voice was strained, his big hands shook as he reached for me. "I've got a career to think about. You don't know what those letters are worth. . ."

I went back to the apartment; Charlie was propped up in bed watching the Lakers game, Dee the dog was hanging off the foot like a vulture.

"How'd it go?" Charlie asked, eyes on the screen.

"Perfect. He'll go the hundred."

"And happy to have the deal, I bet."

"Sure," I said as I stripped off my clothes and turned on the shower. "Coffey thinks he's getting a bargain."

"I'm the one who's getting the bargain," he said, patting the bed. "C'mere."

Charlie didn't know it but his hustle shot new blood into my petrified soul and it was pushing through my veins like sap in springtime. With Charlie, the boredom I'd taken for stability was gone and Coffey's hundred grand would provide the foundation for our new life together. No more cash poor boredom, no dripping faucets to fix, the past was alive and the future was bright as steel.

First thing in the morning I put my .38 in the briefcase for insurance and trotted over to the Kopee Kat on Melrose to copy the letters. More insurance. Then I put the copies in my safe deposit box and drove out to Coffey's.

The housekeeper said Coffey was on his way and as I sat in the lobby that passed as his living room and admired the view, I felt the expanse of sky and water in front of me sinking into my brain and I felt invulnerable. A .38 makes you feel that way.

Coffey came in a few minutes later, an oxblood briefcase in his hand. Stuffed with money for our new life, I thought happily.

He sat down across from me, all business. "You've got the letters?"

I nodded, patting my own briefcase. "You've got the money?"

He handed me his oxblood case without speaking.

I opened my briefcase and handed him the packet of letters. I left the briefcase open beside me, my hand resting on the .38. Just in case.

Coffey glanced at one of the letters and smiled, happy as a toddler. "This is great. Better than I thought."

There was a cheerful note in his voice that seemed out of place. I felt like knocking it out of him. "Bill? I lied. I have copies."

He smiled at me, very relaxed. "Darling, I don't care. I've got what I want."

My composure, while not shattered, was cracked. "Charlie'll sell them to . . ."

"Give it up, Jackie, or whatever your name is. I figured it was you and Charlie all along. But you're the captain of this little ship, not Charlie. Want a drink?"

"Sure," I said, playing for time. I was confused.

He went behind the built-in bar by the fireplace. "You know what your problem is?" he asked.

"I bet you're going to tell me."

"Darling, if you're gonna try to hustle in Hollywood, you ought to learn the rules of the game. You think I'm a big star and if these letters get around, I'll be horsemeat. Not true, darling. I'm a zero, a zombie trapped in the limbo of daytime TV and for three years I've been a half-dead relic lying in the bottom of a well, staring up at the stars a thousand feet over my head. But you've given me a way out."

I took the drink he handed me. It was gin but what the hell. "Tell me more," I said.

"Darling, I'm going to write a book chronicling my wicked youth. I've already lined up a ghostwriter. You see, Americans love a reformed villain and I'm about to be publicly rehabilitated. I'll even swear off drugs—I don't take drugs but I'll swear off all the same. With my book in hand I can tour the talk shows, the important ones, not this jerkwater garbage I do. Get it? With the letters, I'm hot, I'm sexy, I can revitalize my career. Without them, I'm just another half-dead personality."

Not what I expected. "You don't care if we sell the copies to a scandal rag?"

"Nope." Very pleased with himself. "Sleazier the better. More publicity when I deny it first time around," he said wisely. "Darling, let this be a lesson to you. A hundred thou is cheap cheap cheap. You should have played this one straight. Gone to my agent, asked for a half a mil, maybe tried to get a percentage deal. That's the way it works in this town." Coffey smiled like a self-satisfied python. "Next time, do your homework."

"Charlie?"

He was in the kitchen, fixing hash and eggs.

"Good news, bad news," I said. "I've got the money but Coffey says he would have paid lots more. He thinks it's a great career move if he's revealed as a onetime sex freak."

Charlie sat down at the kitchen table, his food neatly arranged on his plate like a still life. I told him the whole story.

When I was through, he simply shrugged. "Bastard. But there's nothing wrong with a hundred grand and it's so much easier this way."

I heard a new note, a wash of complacency in his voice that wasn't there a week ago, and I had a glaring premonition of a dark, streaked future. When he'd walked in he was all desperation and raw nerves; now he was scuttling around my kitchen, playing gracious gourmet while I took the risks and did the work.

He pushed back his plate, got up, snapped open the briefcase and looked at the money. "LA. Who can figure it?" He changed again, another moody switchback passed over his face, he shrugged off his old personality and became yet another Charlie. Chameleon Charlie. All business, he took the money out of the open briefcase and headed down the hall to the bedroom. Dee ambled after him.

I looked at the littered plate on the table and took a bite from the toast he'd left there. I heard noises in the bedroom and five minutes later he came out carrying his suitcase.

"Charlie. . ."

"Tina, don't make it tough, OK? You knew it was just for fun, like the old days, huh? You helped me out and I appreciate it. But I can't live like this and you can't turn around. You're not tough enough, honey. You've lost your edge. Ten years of living like a square is too long."

"Is Alison a square?" I asked him.

He shrugged. "She's easy, Tina. You're always a problem."

A problem. I watched him walk through the living room and followed him to the door.

Outside, the sprinklers were hissing and spitting like angry snakes and the narrow sidewalk in front of my building was shining with water. A deep, thick calm spread over the street like honey.

"Charlie," I called softly.

He didn't stop walking.

"Charlie .." I called again, the gun I keep by the front door in my hand.

He turned. He froze. "Wait a minute, wait a minute," he said. He was holding up his hand as if the soft flesh of his hand could stop a bullet.

58

I raised the gun at him, the sun glinting off the barrel.

He began to run but he was moving very, very slowly, feet trapped in the honey coating the cement as he swam through the warm afternoon air.

I got off four rounds and two of them connected. He never made it to the car.

Natural Powers

by Margaret Lewis

W hen visiting professor Helmut Schmidt collapsed and died in the cafeteria of the Staff Club one lunch-time, sliding under the table in an undignified slurry of chicken à la king and caramel custard, the general opinion was that the elderly German chemist had suffered a heart attack. He was already past retiring age, but had been brought over from Munich by an old friend; the university old-boy network throughout the world keeping itself going on little treats arranged by elder statesmen for each other.

A group of high-powered medics who were dining rather more sumptuously in the private room next door were summoned to the scene, but nothing, it appeared, could be done to revive the distinguished academician. A silence fell on the Staff Club as the ambulance men removed what was obviously a corpse from the floor, and several portly middle-aged lecturers went off to think seriously about purchasing an exercise bicycle. No one took any notice of a small, faded snapshot of a young boy that had fallen from the table when Professor Schmidt collapsed.

The inquest, and the post-mortem that followed, did not however, give any support to those wives who were nagging their sedentary husbands about the need for more activity and less steak and kidney pie. Professor Schmidt had, it appeared, been poisoned, with a very rare toxin that could only have emerged from a very sophisticated laboratory, like, for instance, a university department of chemistry.

Professor Thomas, head of the Chemistry Department, was highly indignant that such a suggestion should be made. To the interested men of the press he had nothing to say, and he instructed his staff to do likewise. He sat drumming his desk in fury as forensic scientists investigated his laboratories and as detectives questioned his staff. Unfailingly polite, Chief Inspector Franklin was thorough and unflappable. One after another he interviewed lecturers, research assistants and secretaries. No one appeared to have any motive whatsoever to kill Helmut Schmidt; in fact, most of them hadn't even noticed that he was around. After several days of irritating police activity, the department was left in peace for a while.

Inspector Franklin was definitely puzzled by the poison that had been used to dispatch Professor Schmidt. Brucine was extremely difficult to synthesize, requiring a great deal of time and equipment.

"There is one thing, though," said Dr. Hall of Forensic as he was pulling on his coat after calling round to discuss some evidence involved in other cases, "you can get this poison very easily from a rainforest plant. Have you thought of looking up in the greenhouses?"

The greenhouses. Deadly poisons of the Amazon. It smacked of Sherlock Holmes and murders in the conservatory. All the same, he remembered the case of the Bulgarian broadcaster who was killed with a similar kind of natural poison, ricin, a few years ago.

"George, get the car will you. Any good on house plants?"

"House plants, sir? No, I leave those to the wife. She's always spending money on them. I stick to my leeks."

The university botany department was a gentle backwater on the quiet fringes of the university. An elderly professor and an unambitious staff had minded their own business for several years, pondering the primula and cultivating dandelions. New developments under a recently-appointed younger professor had disturbed the status quo, and a large new glasshouse had been completed a year ago. One of the prize exhibits, Inspector Franklin was interested to see, was an extensive collection of rainforest plants, gathered over the years by an eccentric botanist who spent every possible vacation tramping through the jungle with a striped umbrella.

"Poisonous plants?" The professor of botany laughed as he showed Inspector Franklin round. "Virtually everything here is poisonous. Although in tiny doses many are highly therapeutic." He launched into a long monologue on the pharmaceutical reserves of the rainforests, and how this great resource was being lost by ruthless felling.

Inspector Franklin listened politely for a few moments, but then his patience began to crack a little. He nodded his head and seized a moment to ask, "What I really want to know is if you have a plant here that would be as poisonous as ricin?"

"Ricin? You mean the poison that the KGB add to umbrellas?"

"That's the kind of thing."

"I'll get our tropical plant expert up for you. He's been analysing these things for years." He looked down the length of the glasshouse and shouted into an apparently empty section.

"Joseph? Can you spare a moment? Police Inspector would like a few words. No, not a parking ticket." He laughed jovially. "About your plants."

A white-haired, wiry shape disentangled itself from some creepers and dusted off a deposit of bark from his shoulders.

"Yes indeed, Professor Dent. What can I do to assist?" He pocketed a large folding knife with care and wiped his hands on a white handkerchief. Joseph Lang had been working in the department for as long as anyone could remember, but no one knew him well. His hair, which surrounded a rather bony face, had been white for many years. He was intensely private, lived alone, and devoted himself entirely to his plants.

"Inspector Franklin is investigating Professor Schmidt's death, Joseph. You'll have heard about it, I'm sure. They are wondering now if someone used a tropical poison to assassinate him. I've told him the whole idea is preposterous."

Franklin studied Joseph's face carefully.

"What do you think, Dr. Lang? How difficult is it to isolate these poisons?"

Lang spoke with great precision, as though English was not his native language.

"The knowledge of poisons is not difficult to acquire, Inspector Franklin. Any reference library can supply the information. And as I am sure you know, even green potatoes can be hazardous."

"Is there anyone up here who might have had contact with the victim?"

"Certainly not on a departmental level," said the professor. "We keep to ourselves up here."

"I see. Oh, just one thing. Were all your staff at work on the day that Professor Schmidt was killed?"

"I'm sure they were, but I'll ask my secretary to check. We have very little absenteeism up here. We are all hard workers."

Joseph nodded in agreement.

"Yes, we are all hard workers up here."

Franklin ran a Home Office check on Joseph Lang as soon as he got back to the office. As Josef Lange he had been just 17 when he was released from Birkenau by the American troops. His family dead, he had been brought back to life in a series of camps that led him westward to the British Zone. Ultimately he was admitted to Britain and the support of other Jewish refugees. His university career was one of thorough achievement rather than brilliant flair. Once graduated, he had never moved from his present post.

When Inspector Franklin made his second visit to the glasshouses Joseph was waiting for him.

"You wish to know the story, Inspector. I shall tell you what you want to know. You may already have guessed the reasons why I wanted to murder the man who called himself Helmut Schmidt, even so many years too late."

They strolled together in the clammy air of the subtropical house, with the spicy scents of warm rainforests implausibly wafting up against the snow flurries hissing on the glass panes above.

Schmidt, whose real name was Lothar Heine, had been in charge of Joseph's hut in the camp. He had personally beaten to death Joseph's younger brother, laughing as he did so. Joseph had never expected to have the pleasure of killing him, but he knew that if the chance came he would take it.

Even forty-four years on he recognised those cold grey eyes and the loose, rather feminine mouth. It was the simplest thing in the world to edge up behind him in the cafeteria queue, to reach across his tray for a dessert, and to release a few drops of carefully distilled liquid. A rather pretty plant, strychnos ignati, conveniently produced the toxin which mimicked the symptoms of a heart attack. As the forensic scientist had noted, the compound, brucine, was readily available from the plants in his glasshouse display. Schmidt had died quickly; his distillation had been perfect. The photo of Joseph's younger brother had been delivered to him through the internal post that morning.

"So now what do you wish me to do?" Joseph paused, put his hands in his pockets, and turned to face the inspector. Behind him, strychnos ignati bloomed innocently against its splendid display of glossy leaves. "At my age, I really don't mind."

"I'm afraid you'll have to come with us, Dr. Lange. I don't know at this stage what the charge will be."

"So. I understand. But I can assure you that my charge is now over. There is a certain justice in using the products of the natural world to destroy such an unnatural power, is there not?"

He picked a hibiscus flower from the nearest plant, stuck it in his buttonhole, and walked out steadily into the swirling snow.

Boogie Dead Men

by W.R.Philbrick

1

Miami Beach. Say it with your eyes closed and you'll see miles of pearl white sand, gin clear water, and smiling sunshine. Depending on your age and inclinations, you may connect the place with Groucho Marx and Jackie Gleason, or Meyer Lansky and Murph the Surf.

Comedians and gangsters: the *real* essence of Miami Beach.

Unswamped and revamped, hustled by postcard, paved over, Art Deco-ed, sold and resold, it remains what it always was: an air-conditioned dreamer with a slight limp and a straw hat.

And traffic jams, in November yet. They were tearing up Collins Avenue, hefting jack-hammers like submachine guns, creating automotive gridlock, and generally irritating the hell out of a freelance claims investigator who was there to do a favor for a friend.

"Hey buddy," I said to the back of the flag man, who was slouching against the hood of my car, "how long before the lane opens?"

The flag man shrugged without turning around and planted himself more firmly on the hood. Grinding lime dust into the paint. I stepped on the brake, shifted into reverse, and popped the brake off. The flag man staggered, lost his balance, and sat

64

down on his butt. He got up, shook his road flag at me, and questioned my sanity, sexual proclivities, and paternity, in that order, and in three words.

"Only on Tuesdays," I replied.

"Lookit, pal, I could call a cop."

"Go ahead. Let's see how long it takes 'em to get through this mess."

The flag man's walkie-talkie squawked, signaling the All Clear. He had to wave me through or risk the wrath of a hundred Cadillac owners revving their ac units behind me.

At which point I finally realized I was going north on a one-way section of the avenue, with my destination well to the south. Reminding me of the middle part of the name, rarely mentioned on the palm-treed postcards:

Miami goddam Beach.

It was my first experience with the Crystal Sands. Often referred to as "The Incredible Crystal". I could see why. There's a chandelier in the lobby that looks like the mother ship in a Spielberg sci-fi movie, enough marble to tombstone the entire state of Arizona, and a clientele out of Central Casting. Latin American businessmen wearing Hong Kong suits, Bahamian bankers, Japanese tourists in weird tropical shirts, Hassidic Jews, deposed dictators, those posing as deposed dictators, and those planning to depose dictators. All strewn over a gaudily landscaped boardwalk that looked, to my born-in-Brooklyn eyes, like Coney Island without the hotdogs.

"Excuse me," I said to a clerk at the reservation desk, "is it true this place was designed by Walt Disney on acid?"

"I don't know, sir," the clerk replied, deadpan. "I could check."

"Never mind. Which way to Loco Charley's?"

"Through the lobby, down the stairs, first exit to your left. Then follow the signs."

Just going down the grand staircase was a trip. Ahead of me a willowy teenager with short, chemically enhanced red hair and a blond bikini was debating the stock market with her mother, similarly attired, except with the colors reversed: blond hair, red bikini.

"I don't care *what* Daddy thinks," the girl was saying, "IBEX at twenty-nine is a chump deal. I'm optioning Vandox at forty-one, and the rest of you can just chill out."

"Yes, dear," Mother sighed. "It's your money."

"Hold that thought," daughter dear replied.

I touched Mother's elbow and said, "Disown it now, while you still have power of attorney."

"Get away from him, Ma. I'll call security."

"Chill out," I said, patting the lump under my jacket. "I *am* security."

A blatant untruth, but I was out the door and blending with the big-finned palm trees before they could react. The concealed weapons under my jacket were a Nikon 2020 and a mini-cassette recorder. Tools of the trade, useful for photographing whiplash victims when they're frolicking on the golf course, or, as the case may be, recording daughters of Mafia dons who have run away to Miami Beach.

Loco Charley's was a jumped-up tiki bar set in a little grove of Royal Jamaican palms, shaded from the boardwalk by canvas windscreens that looked, in the late afternoon light, like billowing sails on a ship that had long since run aground. I moseyed up to the bar and found an empty stool between two yarmulkes and a Stetson cowboy hat.

"Beer, please."

"Draft or can?" a deeply-tanned bartender asked. He indicated a row of beer cans arranged above the coolers.

"No bottles?"

The bartender blinked wearily. "Bottles break."

"So do eggs," I said. "They don't put eggs in cans at the Crystal Sands. Or do they?"

"You want eggs, try the café."

I settled for a plastic cup of beer.

"When's the band play?" I asked, indicating the empty stage under the striped canvas tent.

"They're on a break."

I sighed. Conversation with bartenders is getting increasingly difficult. My last conversation with a bartender—a retired cop—had resulted in my present situation, i.e. sidled up to a sucker's bar in Miami Beach at an hour when I should have been heading home to Key Largo for a barbeque dinner with Maria and the kids.

"They should be back in in ten minutes or so," the Stetson offered. "Really good band. What I heard, they're breaking out. Album, major promotion, the whole shootin' match. This set they're playing here is what they call a teaser for the main show tonight. Club Cabana. Which is, by the way, already sold out."

"What part of Texas you from?" I asked.

"New Jersey."

"New Jersey, Texas?"

"New Jersey New Jersey," the Stetson said. "I've never been to Texas. I got the hat at a shop right here in the hotel. Same with the boots."

I looked down. He had on snakeskin cowboy boots. "No spurs?"

"They get hooked on the chair rungs."

I nodded. Spurs were an inconvenience in Miami Beach. Like poverty, ethics, or a wedding ring. I sipped the beer, being careful not to accidently crush the flimsy cup, and squinted at the thick tropical foliage behind the tiki bar. You could almost see the billion dollar beach through the bougainvilleas.

"They're back," the Stetson said happily. He raised his plastic margarita. "Bad News!"

2

I'd been expecting to find a standard gloss-and-glitter show and was surprised to discover that Bad News was an urban, art-rock quintet, of a type rarely seen in the Miami area, or in daylight anywhere, for that matter.

The male lead singer seemed to be a skinny kid with long, rat-brown hair and rubbery lips. He had young moves and a youthful, questing voice, but after a bit of studying you could see the years imprinted: he was too old to play shortstop in the major leagues, which is one way to judge the shelf life of youth. My age, more or less. Although he was playing competently, the guitar in his hands seemed to be more a prop than a musical necessity.

The real licks, tight and sassy, were the work of a hyper kid wearing a dirty-looking trenchcoat. He was bare chested and barefoot and as scrawny as a vegetarian drug addict, but oh my yes, he could make the strings talk.

When you hear the real thing you know what the jazz junkies mean when they say bad is bad. And this kid was *baaaad*.

someone who
in the dead of night
someone who
can love you

The two women singers were an interesting contrast. The one blonde and ethereal, floating over her keyboards and blending her voice into the chorus, the other dark and big busted, a hip shaker and a strutter who belted out the songs with a voice that could shape itself around corners in the music.

"I'm in love," the Jersey cowboy said, breathing a toxic combination of breath mints and beer fumes.

"That's nice," I said. "Anyone special?"

The cowboy sighed. "That pretty little blonde. Name of Carla Dee."

"A word of caution," I said. "Her father is a Mafia hoodlum."

"Seriously?"

"An icepick in the heart is serious."

The cowboy gulped his beer. "She's not *that* beautiful."

She was, though. Carla, with her cool, creamy-pale complexion, had an unearthly elegance that seemed alien to this sun-drenched place. She slinked and swayed at the keyboard with a kind of quirky confidence, cocking her slim hips, aware of her power.

She had the moves. Big time moves.

No, the young lady who called herself Carla Dee didn't look like a killer, but then, who does?

I strolled along the boardwalk, waiting for the set to finish. Half expecting to be accosted by the teenage stock manipulator in the blond bikini. No such luck. The leggy little brat was probably inside, faxing instructions to her broker.

The crushed beer cup went into a trash bucket masquerading as a planter. No littering at the Crystal Sands. And not much swimming in the cobalt sea. Most of the bathers were lounging by the enormous swimming pool. Tiles on the bottom formed the hotel logo. Seen from the air the pool must have looked like a pastel hanky with a cheap monogram.

I leaned against the boardwalk rail smoking a Tampa cigar and listened to the music drifting through the bougainvilleas toward the sea. Bad News had a pretty nice island rhythm going. White man's reggae, soothing and cool. A sexy beat without the dreadlocks.

> Ride me a slow train
> on a tropical isle
> Feelin' no pain
> Caribbean smile

The salt air must have done something to my head, because I flashed on a beach from another time and place: the beach where my late wife and I had taken our last vacation. Not that we knew it then. There had been a good bar overlooking the sea, and a great band, and a barefoot stroll through the surf that ended with lovemaking in the dunes. Storybook stuff. Too good to last.

I blinked my eyes, flicked the cigar butt into a receptacle, and went back to the tacky tiki bar.

68

feelin' no pain
Caribbean smile

The girl with the black bangs was shaking her shapely butt and crashing a tambourine into her hip. I found a molded plastic chair a few yards from the little dance area under the tent and watched a number of eager couples prove that white people can't dance, at least not while attired in clashing plaids. My friend the New Jersey cowboy gave it a shot but the new boots must have been pinching his toes, because he moved like a man under attack from fire ants.

Two tunes later the set was over. It was, as the cowboy had said, a teaser for the big evening show in the Club Cabana. Bad News walked off the stage, carrying such instruments as could be carried. I followed. Had to jog to catch up—they weren't exactly eager for an encore.

"Excuse me, miss?"

The blonde turned, hesitated, resumed her quick march.

"Miss DiMonte? Could I have a word? I've got a message from your family."

That stopped her.

"Not here," she whispered. "In the lobby."

That was fine by me. I played caboose to their little train, following through the lush, overdone landscape and on into the opulent hush of the Crystal's cakebox interior. Under the assumption that Carla DiMonte, aka Carla Dee, would deign to speak to me, as promised.

What she did was slip through the brushed bronze elevator doors just as they sealed shut. I was left listening to the ding ding ding as the car ascended.

A wiser man would have turned on his heel and left it at that. Wisdom not being my strong suit, I sauntered over to the reservation desk.

"Jack Dempsey, KO Productions, to see the band."

"Excuse me?"

"The recording artists. Going by the name Bad News at the moment. We may change that," I added grandly.

"Oh," the clerk said. "That band. Do you have a number?"

"I've got lots of numbers," I said, grinning. "I do a great Gene Kelly, if it's raining."

The polite blankness of the clerk's expression convinced me she'd never heard of Jack Dempsey or Gene Kelly. In the late 20th century fame only endures if you do beer commercials.

"Thing of it is, I took the red eye from L.A.," I said. "Must have left my briefcase on the plane. The memo was in my briefcase."

The clerk raised her eyebrows, or what remained of them after plucking.

"The memo with the room number on it," I explained, casually removing a pair of mirrored sunglasses from my breast pocket. "I'm *sure* they want to see me."

The clerk tapped a few keys on her computer, glanced at the screen.

"I can dial the room phone for you," she offered. "We're not allowed to give out numbers."

"Dial away," I said, placing the sunglasses on the counter.

As she rang the room I contrived to knock the sunglasses onto her computer desk. Grinning sheepishly, I picked them up, held the twin mirrors at an angle to the screen, and picked off the room numbers for Bad News.

The clerk said "Call from Mr. Jack Dumpster, hold please," and handed me the phone.

I cleared my throat. "Dempsey here, KO Productions. Could you put Ms. Carla Dee on the line?"

A husky male voice growled, "Another flake," and the line went dead.

I said: "Yeah, sure, I'll be right up. No, no, that'll be fine. Hey kid, relax already, okay? We love you, baby. Ciao."

The clerk had one of those secret smiles, like who was kidding who? Maybe she was bored and figured it might be interesting to see how long I lasted before the hotel dicks launched me into the purple fountains.

The answer to that was: less than an hour.

The premise of the Crystal Sands is that there are no rooms without a view. The more pricey suites face the Atlantic, of course, and the rising sun. The only slightly less expensive rooms face Indian Creek and Biscayne Bay, where the Cigaret boats cut white spray lines through the blue water. Beyond that is the emerging skyline of Miami, as jagged and modern as a set of spaceage dentures.

Bad News had two connected suites on the bayside, seventh floor. Getting in was easy. I knocked, waited until the door swung open, and put my foot against the jam.

The singer with the rat-brown hair and the rubbery lips glanced down at my intruding foot and said, "What's this?"

"Miss DiMonte is expecting me," I said. "We had a little problem with the elevator doors but I never hold a grudge."

"Hey Pockets!" he said. "Call the cops!"

A voice from behind the door said, "Like hell. Are you nuts, Mick? The *cops?*" He said 'cops' the way some people say 'black death' or 'bubonic plague'.

"No need for the cops," I said, trying to sound reasonable. "I just need to give Miss DiMonte a message."

Mick made a face. Close up every day of his life showed. "Miss DiMonte isn't taking messages today, dude."

"Maybe I could leave it on the bathroom mirror. In lipstick."

Mick laughed and rolled his eyes. He opened the door. "What the hell. Come in and join the party. It was just a matter of time before Mr. Mike tried again."

"Mr. Mike?"

"You know," he said. "Michael Murphy. The dude who sent you."

"Don't know any Michaels," I said. "Is Carla here?"

"What do you think, Pockets?" Mick said. "Is this guy for real?"

Pockets turned out to be the scrawny kid who'd been twitching such mean licks from the lead guitar. He squinted at me from behind steel-rimmed glasses, the kind John Lennon was wearing when that psychopathic cretin gunned him down. "He looks like a cop," he said, sipping thoughtfully from a bottle of beer.

"We all have crosses to bear. Is Carla here?"

Pockets just smiled.

Behind me Mick sighed deeply. "This is getting old. You're a private investigator, right? Just like Mr. Mike said *he* was. Until he turned up phony."

"Would you like to see my credentials?"

Mick shrugged, as if to say the truth didn't really matter. "You see Mr. Mike, tell 'em we all think he's a cute act. Except for Carla. The message from Carla to Michael is go directly to hell, do not pass go."

"Okay," I said. "If I ever meet a Michael, I'll give him the message. Now when do I get to see Carla?"

Pockets flashed a nervous grin and said, "When you tell us what you want with her."

"That's easy. I want to do her a favor, if possible."

The two of them were exchanging glances. The old eyebrow semaphore routine. I got the impression they thought 'favor' was a code word for something illegal.

Patience, I thought, remember you are dealing with rock musicians: their hearing may be damaged.

"You have a gun?" Mick wanted to know.

"Not at the moment."

"Well, I do. So keep that in mind, okay?"

"Okay," I said.

A pudgy, naked man walked out of the bathroom, dripping water from the shower. There were soap bubbles in his beard. "Oh shit," he said. "Is this a bust?"

"Who's he?" I asked.

"Terry the Pirate," Pockets said. "Our drummer."

"I didn't notice a drummer," I said.

The naked man turned on his heel and stomped back into the bathroom. His moist feet made soft plopping noises. Wet bongo drums.

"He's the sensitive type," Pockets explained.

"This sure is a wild party," I said, surveying the room. "Where are the groupies?"

Pockets thought I was a very funny guy. He laughed soundlessly, gulping for air. I started to like him. Laugh at my jokes and you're a friend for life.

"Carla doesn't want to see you," Mick said. "She doesn't want to see Michael. She doesn't want to see anybody connected to her. . .family."

I winked at Mick. "I'm not connected to her. . .family."

Mick rolled his eyes. He thought I was fibbing. Say what you want about long-haired rockers with rubbery lips, this one had *very* expressive eyes.

"Look, dude," Mick said. "The last few weeks have been like very stressful, okay? Your buddy Michael made a pest of himself and poor Carla has been the focus of, uhm—how would you put it, Pockets?"

"Unwanted attention," Pockets responded immediately. "The sticky kind."

"Sticky?"

"Gumshoes," Pockets explained. "Heavy duty low lifes."

"Sticks and stones," I said.

Pockets turned to Mick and shrugged. "He doesn't really *act* like a cop. And he talks funny."

I wasn't finished talking funny. I walked to the closed double doors that connected the two suites, knocked, and said, "I'll huff and I'll puff and I'll—"

One of the doors swung open.

"Nobody's blowin' nothin' down," Carla said.

She was pointing a gun. At me.

3

"Tell Michael to drop dead. And if you work for my father, tell *him* to go to hell."

Things got pretty shaky. Her hand was shaking. The gun, a small caliber revolver with a short barrel, was shaking. And my head was shaking. As in, no no no, you don't want to pull that trigger, lady. I was willing to go a long way for Sal Carlucci, but getting gutshot was not in the game plan.

"You've got it all wrong," I said. "I don't work for Michael, whoever he is, and I certainly don't work for your father."

Behind me Pockets was giggling.

"Come on Carla," he said. "Chill out. Put the pop gun away."

"Shut up, you geek."

"I dare you," he said tauntingly. "Shoot me instead."

"Who are you?" she said, ignoring the scrawny, crazy boy and trying to concentrate on me. "What do you want?"

"My name is Tony Mack. I'm an insurance claims investigator. A retired cop from Brooklyn asked me to look in on you. Said you'd been having trouble. Something about a pending murder rap."

Behind me Pockets was laughing out loud. "This is *so* excellent," he hooted. "This is *totally* radical. Never a dull moment with Carla Dee."

He was trying to rattle her and it was working. Her lovely, startled eyes were flicking from me to him.

"Oh Pockets," she said plaintively, "how can you be so *mean*?"

"Come on, Carla. Shoot me. I never been shot before."

The hand was wavering now, the small black eye of the barrel shifting away from my abdomen. And I could feel Pockets moving up beside me, making himself a target.

"Pretty please?" he said.

Guitarists have quick hands, as he was about to demonstrate. I saw the flash of his fingers gripping the little pistol, heard a small, cold click as he twisted it away from her. Grinning, he touched the barrel to his nose and clicked the trigger again. And again.

"Bingo bango," he said. "I borrowed your bullets, Carla. Guess I forgot to mention that, huh?"

Then Carla was weeping hysterically and the crazy kid was wrapping his spindly arms around her and making a cooing noise as he grinned over her shoulder at me.

"Maybe you better split," he suggested.

The idea appealed to me. I had places to go, people to meet. Food to eat. Mick the middle-aged boy stopped me at the door.

"She's not usually like that," he said. "You really interested in helping?"

"Not when guns are pointed at me."

Mick shrugged. "It was no big deal. An unloaded gun, right?" He looped an arm around my shoulder, very buddy buddy, and walked me out into the hall. "The fact is we got a mess here," he said, keeping his voice low. "No thanks to that goombah family of Carla's. Right when we're on the verge of breaking through, you dig?"

"Not if I can help it."

"I'm talking about the *band*, man. This is our chance. You don't get many chances in this business. Believe me, I know. And everything is breaking right. The contract, the tour, the songs we're writing, everything is clicking. Except Carla." He paused, flashed an exasperated expression. "Tell you the truth, man, I'd ditch that crazy kid only it would upset the chemistry and that's like fatal at a time like this. Absolutely fatal."

The word fatal has a certain resonance. It tends to focus the attention. For instance contact with the DiMonte crime family has been, for many individuals, fatal. Dealing with them is like tip-toeing through a minefield without a map. At night, wearing a blindfold.

"Can I ask you a question?" I said.

He shrugged. The guy was a world class shrugger. "Sure," he said. "Why not?"

"Has Carla killed anybody lately?"

"Hey man, that little gun wasn't even loaded—"

"I'm serious. The word is that she's involved in a murder."

"Rumors, man. Somebody out to hurt us."

"Any idea who's circulating the rumors?"

"Beats me," Mick said. "All I know is, strange things keep happening."

"Such as?"

"Isn't that for you to find out?"

I gave him my card. "Check it out," I suggested. "Call the Detective Division of the Metro Police, if you don't believe the insurance company. I'm licensed, bonded. I don't know if I can do anything for Carla, but I'm willing to try."

"Hey, dude, we're cool," Mick said. He tried giving me a rock 'n roll handshake, which apparently involved something complicated with the wrist and thumb. I got it wrong, but he didn't seem to mind. "I got to go back in there, try to unfrazzle the little lady," he explained. "We have a sound check at the Cabana in less than two hours and I want her playing in the right key, you dig?"

"Anything you say."

"Come by after the show, man. Just give the stage manager your name."

He waved, did a little moonwalk back into the suite, and closed the door.

Waiting for the elevator, I took several deep breaths and tried to clear my head. So far dealing with Bad News was like jumping into an Abbot and Costello routine when you have no idea who's on first. I did know who was in the bleachers, though.

The entire DiMonte crime family.

4

Two pieces of Miami Beach beefcake were waiting for me in the lobby. Both wearing lime green blazers with shoulders that didn't need padding.

"Scuze us, Mr. Dempsey. Right this way please."

I found myself doing a bookend act. Biff and Billy Bob, pinning my elbows and "walking" me to the reservation desk. Where the teenager with the tinted hair was chewing gum and reading the Wall Street Journal. Wearing, in place of the bikini, white shorts and a halter top.

"Miss? Is this the gentleman who accosted you and your mother?"

"That's him," the girl said.

The Crystal security boys have a cute little trick with the revolving glass door. What they do is shove you in, lock the spindle and amble around to the exit side, where you are ejected like a plug of tobacco, propelled by the force of humanity.

"Don't you want to hear my side of the story?" I asked.

"No."

"I'm with the band," I said, dragging my heels. "Bad News."

"Bad news for you, pal."

On the way out to the street they dipped me in the famous fountain. Kind of a baptism.

"Next time we'll hold you under. Get it?"

"Thanks," I said, blinking away the water. "That was refreshing."

"Dempsey," one of the guards said. "We'll remember that name. Now go away."

"And stay away," his partner said.

The miracle was, my cigars didn't get wet. There is a God who watches over children, fools, and private investigators. And He smokes.

The Eden Roc was a few million dollars to the north. I walked over to their lobby and used a pay phone to call Maria, who answered on the fourteenth ring.

"Anything wrong?" I asked.

She caught her breath. "Jorge got up in the tree. He was dropping coconuts on Roberto and Eddie. I had to break up the fight."

Jorge was four, and a handful. The youngest of the seven children. Three of her own and the four cousins adopted after Maria's husband and his brother were killed. I hadn't been able to prevent their deaths, something I had promised to do when hired, so I did the next best thing. I married the widow.

And never, ever regretted it.

"I'll be late for supper," I said.

"You already called to say you'd be late, *mi amante*."

"Yes, well, I'm going to be later."

Maria clicked her tongue. After three years the sound still makes me shiver. "I will have something waiting," she promised. "Very especial."

That put a spring in my step. I walked along Collins Avenue until I found a little shopping district in the shadow of the giant towers that line the beach. I left dressed in a Banlon shirt, bermuda shorts imprinted with palm trees, rope sandals, and a Mets baseball cap. And sunglasses, of course. My mother wouldn't have recognized me, or if she had, would have pretended otherwise.

No paste-on mustache. I draw the line at paste-on mustaches.

The sun went down. The street lights came on. I bought take-out cheeseburgers and black coffee and treated myself to supper on a bus stop bench across the avenue from the Crystal Sands. After which I smoked a cigar in peace, with no complaints from the maitre d'. Buses came, buses went. I waved at all the drivers, who soon learned to ignore the screwball in the Mets cap. He wasn't going anywhere.

It was a balmy night. The hotel was lit up like a ship at sea, but it wasn't going anywhere, either. Limos began to arrive. When the time came I stubbed out the cigar, adjusted my new hat, and crossed the avenue.

It was showtime.

Club Cabana is the big room at the Crystal. For years, the Cabana relied on Las Vegas-style acts to fill its twelve hundred plushly upholstered seats. Times have changed. Inspired by the recent success of clubs in the Art Deco district, the hotel now bills the Cabana as a showcase for "emerging bands". It was obvious that Carla Dee and her pals were emerging in a big way. The show was sold out.

The stage door was on an alley that dead-ended at the beach. More limos, parked bumper to bumper. Cocaine cabs, rented by the hour.

Back here the security guards wore muscle shirts.

"Wait right there, sir. We'll check the list."

I wondered what the odds were that old Mick had followed through on his promise.

"Could we see some I.D., sir?" the muscle asked, after consulting his clip board.

I complied and was given a laminated pass. Good old Mick.

There were at least a hundred others with similar passes. Roadies, media-types, kids who'd won prizes in a concert promotion. It was a far cry from the laid-back scene at the tiki bar.

I asked one of the roadies about that. He was keeping an eye on a stack of wheeled equipment cases stenciled with the name of the band.

"Man, the tiki bar was like a freebie for the hotel guests. I guess what happened, originally we were booked for just the tiki gig, but when the band started taking off, management rewrote the paperwork, gave us the Cabana. Which has like this incredible history. Elvis used to play this room, man."

I tried to act amazed and impressed. Actually, I was. There was a buzz going around, an electric feeling that transcended the music. Bad News was happening. It took a while to work my way around to where I could get a glimpse of the stage area.

Under the lights Mick looked young and vibrant. Singing an up tempo ballad with the black-haired beauty. The boy called Pockets was jerking around like he'd been plugged in, rather than his guitar. Carla remained cool and blonde and distant. A woman you couldn't get close to unless she had a gun in her hand.

"Howdy partner!"

It was the New Jersey cowboy. There was a laminated pass clipped to the brim of his Stetson.

"Cost me a hundred to get back here," he said proudly. "You think she'll talk to me?"

"Who?"

77

"Wendy Wilson," he said, indicating the female lead. "My new love."

"What happened to Carla Dee?"

He gave me a Howdy Doody grin. "Changed my mind. How come you're dressed so, um, *casual*?" he asked, eyeing the palm trees on my shorts.

"It's the new me," I said.

"I just *knew* you were going to go nuts for this band. And for Carla Dee, am I right? Come on, man, I saw you trying to pick her up."

I grinned sheepishly and confessed to being an autograph hound.

"Is that a fact?" For the first time the cowboy's eyes slitted suspiciously. "Well then, I guess you must know about Mick Dunston."

"Mick is a friend of mine," I said grandly, indicating the back stage pass.

"Yeah? Did you know him back then?"

"Uh, when exactly?"

"When he was with The Gnats, man. 'Boogie Dead Men'. And I guess my favorite cut off that first album was 'Go Come Back'."

It was "Go Come Back" that made it click for me. I'd been a rookie patrolman when the song hit big. If anybody asked I could have whistled the hook line, the "go. . .no no come back", although I might not have remembered the name of the band. The Gnats. Modeled—it was coming back now—modeled on the Beatles. Like so many other bands from that era. And "Boogie Dead Men"—damn straight, that had been a favorite party cut. Dancing drunk and stoned.

Everybody boogie. Mom and dad boogie. Chil-dren boogie. Dead men boogie. *Every* body boogie.

Oh yes, that relentless, long-playing boogie riff repeated end-lessly. The song was associated forever in my mind with the first time I smelled burning cannabis. And nearly freaked because in those days marijuana was a very big deal and just the *rumor* that a young cop was at a pot party was enough to warrant review and possible suspension.

Of course all that anxiety dissolved when I met the girl who was holding the joint, her nose wrinkled up and tears streaming from her eyes. Carole. The way she said: "It tastes like socks".

Hell, we probably *danced* to "Boogie Dead Men" that night. Definitely we slow danced to "Go Come Back". What a rush *that* was. First dance, first kiss with Carole.

And I owed it all to Mick Dunstan and The Gnats.

Bad News played for nearly an hour, one new tune segueing into the next. Mick spoke to the crowd a few times, thanking them for their attention, encouraging the kids to push back the tables and dance, if that was okay with the management (it wasn't) but he never once mentioned The Gnats and it was doubtful that many of the new fans were even born when "Go Come Back" hit the charts.

During the break—they were playing two sets—the band was hustled into dressing rooms. Which were off limits to everybody, even those who held the prestigious back stage passes. Maybe there was a back-back stage pass that got you through to them, but I didn't see any point in pushing my luck.

What I needed was fresh air and a stale cigar. The alley that dead-ended on the beach was still jammed with limos and now the limos were jammed with people. Back stage types huddling behind locked doors and yards of tinted glass, doing lines and inflating egos that could only be vented by endless, empty chatter.

Me me me. Mine mine mine.

Cocaine has to be the noisiest drug of all. More rap per gram than methedrine, the old speed freak's yakkety-yak. I sincerely hoped that Carla DiMonte's problems were not drug related. I have a low tolerance for junkies and coke freaks; when a druggie wants a favor I just say no.

I was finishing up the cigar and thinking about going back inside to catch the second set when someone tapped me on the shoulder. I turned. The only thing I saw was fist.

5

I was never completely out. There were hands patting me down, I remember that much. And a black, sick feeling in the pit of my stomach. A salty taste in my mouth. After a while I was able to roll over on my back and see stars. Real stars. Wobbly, but real.

Sucker punched. Mugged. Slam bam to the chin, pockets emptied.

Tried sitting up. Laid back down and studied the stars again. A rectangle of sky visible between the concrete towers of the Crystal Sands. How nice. And there was a gentle sea breeze blowing in from the beach. Very comfy there, on my back in the alley. Why not make a night of it? Why expend all that effort to stand up? When chances are you'd fall back down again.

Take a snoozer, Tony. When you wake up maybe your jaw won't feel unhinged. Maybe your lower front teeth won't feel loose, and your tongue won't be bleeding.

Nap time. It was so tempting. I conjured up an image of Maria waiting for me in Key Largo. Maria got blurred with Carole but that's okay. What the hell, I'd taken a blast to the chin. Even the great Ali got wobbly when Frazier caught him on the button.

I rolled over, got on my knees. Laced my fingers in the chain link fence that ran along the beach. Good old fence, my pal. Pulled myself up. Knees misplaced somewhere. Looked at the ground. My but I'd come a long way. Miles.

Limo doors were opening. Youngsters with glittering eyes and dusty noses were heading for the stage door. Chattering like magpies.

"Hey!" I said. "Wait up!"

They looked right through me. I was a geek with his bermuda shorts pockets turned out. Staggering like a wino with the jim jams. I checked the top of my head, found something missing, went back for the Mets cap. Major effort reaching down to get that cap. Worth it. Good old Mets. Marvelous Marv Throneberry had taken a few in the chin, when he'd forgotten to get his glove up for the throw. And people cheered. How come they didn't cheer for Tony Mack when he got mugged?

The muscle boy at the door put his hand on my chest. "You're gonna puke, do it out there," he said.

"I'm not a puker," I protested. "Smell my breath."

The boy made a face. "No thanks, mister."

"Go ahead. I'm not drunk. I've been mugged."

He looked me over, condescended to sniff my breath. "I guess so," he said. "You want to call the cops, file a complaint?"

"Waste of time." Also I didn't want to endure the ribbing sure to follow when certain Metro detectives heard Tony Mack had been done like a little old lady. Hell, your average little old lady puts up a better fight.

"You better sit down, mister."

I almost missed the chair. Amazing what one solid shot to the chin will do to your sense of balance. Muscle boy gave me a cup of coffee. Not a bad kid, really, for a bouncer. The coffee burned the cuts in my mouth but the caffeine helped.

As my head cleared I started to get mad.

My wallet had been lifted, damn it. Two hundred or so in cash. Various credit cards. My p.i. license, concealed weapon permit, and bonding certificate. Hours of telephoning would be required to cancel, explain, replace. The pain I was feeling now was nothing to the pain in the ass of dealing with all *that*.

Three years of working some of the meanest streets in Dade County and I'd never been mugged. Was it the tourist outfit? Had that made me a target?

Or was it, maybe, the DiMonte connection? I make contact, however briefly, with the don's daughter and a few hours later I've been laid out, my name rank and serial number taken. Coincidence?

Sure. Just like it was a coincidence that the DiMonte crime family spent more time in court than F. Lee Bailey.

The final set lasted about thirty minutes. Then Bad News went back for an encore. The song sounded familiar but different, if you know what I mean. It was a stanza or so before I caught on.

I want you to go
no no
come back

A white reggae version of that certified golden oldie, 'Go Come Back'. So Mick Dunstan hadn't forgotten his roots afterall.

Maybe it was the blood crusting on my chin, or the look in my eye, but I didn't have any trouble working my way through the backstage crowd, or getting within hailing distance of the band as they trooped back to the dressing room.

"Mick!"

At first he looked right through me. Then he did a little double take and crooked his finger, inviting me to come along. A bouncer tried to intercede but Mick muttered something and the bouncer backed off.

"What happened to you, man?" he hissed. The stage sweat made him shine and glow.

"Dental work," I said. "I've got this orthodontist who won't take no for an answer."

The after-show celebration was already underway. A fruit-and-cheesey type of buffet had been set up in the dressing room. There were cases of Gator beer on ice, and champagne, and as many glittery, grabby people as could fit into the place. I got the impression that very few of them were actually acquainted with the band. More likely most were cronies of the Club Cabana management.

I wondered if any of them had sore knuckles.

"You checked out okay," Mick said, keeping his voice down as he handed me a sweating cold bottle of Gator beer. "More than okay. Carla said she'll talk. Doesn't think it'll do any good, but she'll talk."

"Great. Where is she?" I looked around, hoping to catch a glimpse of translucent white.

"Not here, man. Carla hates the after-gig scene. She'll see you tomorrow for breakfast. Ten o'clock."

"I need to see her now. Tonight."

"Can't be done," Mick said. "Come on. Relax, have a few beers. Who the hell was that dentist anyway?"

I didn't stay long. Mick politely refused to discuss Carla's "problem", other than to allude to the family connection—no surprise there—and we ended up conversing about his favorite subject: Mick Dunstan, his life, his loves, his career.

"Man, I had an eighteenth birthday party like you wouldn't believe. The first album was going gold, we were booked into a stadium tour with The Dave Clark Five, and we were lining up material for a second album. I figured, you know, it would just keep getting better."

He laughed bitterly when I asked him what happened.

"We got old, man. I don't mean age either—that happened later. The *sound* got old. The second album was a reworking of the first—the label insisted on that, assigned us a producer who could've been a Marine drill sergeant."

"I remember that album," I said. "There was good stuff on it."

Mick reached out and squeezed my hand. "Thanks, man. And it's true, we had some good tunes. But we weren't *evolving* and the scene then was if you didn't change and surprise, there were like fifty new bands each month competing for air time. The label and the producers wanted us to sound like the good old Beatles, but the Beatles were already into this new sound. We died out there, man. Released two more albums that just sat there in the bins and then the label refused to renew—I had new material, new ideas, but they didn't want to hear it. Nobody wanted to hear it."

Although no longer a heart throb for *Teen Beat*, Mick had stayed active in the business. Writing tunes for other bands, doing studio work, back up singing. Whatever made a buck and kept him near the periphery of the scene, clinging to the edge.

"I must have done a thousand demos, man. Trying to interest a major label. The new Mick Dunstan, right? They'd go to me, kid—and I was thirty something at the time—kid, if you could sound just a little bit like Jackson Brown, or Warren Zevon, or Randy Newman, or whoever was hot at the moment. That was always my exit cue. I mean I'd *been* there, okay? And I *knew* the clone thing was a nowhere scene."

Then Carla DiMonte had come into his life. He and Wendy Wilson were collaborating on some pretty good tunes, figuring maybe a demo, sell the material to a name band. Wendy, he explained, had a similar history. Early success followed by years of not quite getting back into the mainstream. Mick and Wendy decided to get real, concentrate on song writing for other, more successful performers.

"It was just going to be a demo, man. Carla was this chick who came in to help with the back-up vocals. And she like fell in *love* with the songs. Said we were crazy to shop the stuff around, we ought to form a band, go to a major label. The rap I'd been hearing for years. So I try to set her straight, how there's no way to make it work unless we get a real push, unless some twenty-year-old marketing specialist decides we fit into that slot marked success."

"So what happened?"

"What happened is that Carla was connected. She knew somebody in the business. The business end of the business, right? And she gave this somebody our demo tape and I don't know what else she might have said or done, but the next day his company signed us to a major deal. We got the big push and it's working, man. Mick Dunstan has finally risen from the ashes."

"Thanks to Carla?"

He nodded. "Absolutely. Without her connection this never would have happened."

I was deciding on how best to break into my own car—the thief had taken my keys along with the wallet—when a sporty new convertible with an Avis bumpersticker pulled up to the curb.

"Need a hand, Mr. Mack?"

"Who the hell are you?"

Not very polite, but it was late and my jaw still ached like hell and the idea of a stranger knowing my name gave me ugly ideas. The stranger was a slim youth in his mid-twenties. Short blond hair, neatly dressed. He got out of the ragtop and tried to shake my hand.

I backed away.

"You *are* Tony Mack, right? The private investigator? If you're not I'm sorry, I made a mistake. I'll still give you a lift, if you want."

"You haven't answered *my* question," I said.

"Huh?" He kept looking down at his hand, as if incredulous that I wouldn't shake it.

"Who are you, pal, and how do you know my name?"

"Oh, sorry. I'm Michael Murphy. I'm an investigator, too." He pulled a wallet from his crisply ironed slacks, carefully removed a card. It was new and engraved. Very classy.

"You're licensed in Stony Brook, New York? This is a long way from Long Island, Murphy, in case you haven't noticed. And you still haven't explained how you know my name."

It was hard to detect a blush under the streetlights, but I got the impression Murphy was painfully embarrassed. He cleared his throat, pointed to my license plate. "I, uhm, noticed you at the tiki bar, so I took the liberty of checking your registration. This *is* your car?"

Then it clicked. "Wait a minute," I said, "are you the Michael who's been bothering Miss DiMonte?"

He seemed to lose about two inches in height as he sagged against the door of his rented car. "Carla said that? That I was *bothering* her?"

I didn't have the heart to tell him that she had been a little more specific, as in 'tell him to drop dead'. The anguished, smitten look said it all: Michael Murphy, the engraved investigator, was carrying a major league torch for Carla Dee.

"Maybe I got it wrong," I said.

"No, no. I messed up. I blew it," he said, slapping his hands against the car door in frustration. "I was trying to help and somehow she got the idea that I work for that bastard father of hers. Which is, if you knew, I mean it's *totally* ridiculous. Just *totally*."

I tugged the Met cap and sighed. It had been a long night and it was going to get longer.

"What's your interest in Carla?" I leaned against his rented fender and waited while he sighed and looked at his nails and generally fidgeted.

"Rad Records," he said. "That's how it all started. I was doing some freelance work for the company, just a normal computer security check, nothing very exciting. Happened to be in the office when Bad News came in with their demo. I saw Carla and you know, it just clicked for me. Boom."

"Boom?"

"What can I say? I felt like I'd known her all my life, you know? This weird, wonderful feeling? So I made sure I was there for the studio session, while they were recording, and it seemed like we were hitting it off pretty good. Carla and me."

"What happened?"

He shrugged. A shrug not quite in Mick Dunstan's class, but close. "What happened is that just before the tour kicked off she started getting these threatening phone calls."

"Can you be more specific?"

He gave me a funny look. Like he wasn't sure he could trust me. "She hired you, didn't she? Look, I'll tell you everything I know if you'll let me work with you on this. I'll stay in the background. Carla doesn't have to know. Not unless you think she *should* know."

I gave him a good long look and said, "Tell me what you've got. Maybe we can work something out and maybe we can't. No promises."

While he thought it over I fished out my last cigar. Like me it was somewhat bruised and battered. By the time I got it fired up Michael Murphy was baring his soul.

6

There was a hairy brown thing in my face when the alarm went off. I jumped awake. "What the hell is *that*."

Maria rested her chin on my shoulder and said, "That's a coconut."

"I can see it's a coconut. Why is it staring at me? What's it doing on my pillow?"

Maria laughed. A prettier melody has yet to be written. "Jorge bring it in. He make you a present, *comprendez?*"

"I guess."

"These coconuts he likes to carry around, they are, how you say it? A phrase?"

"Phase," I said. "He's going through a phase."

I hauled myself away from the sweetness of that bed, stood under a tepid shower, and doused myself with a large mug of thick Cuban coffee that contained enough caffeine to jump start an elephant. The ache in my lower teeth remained, but the swelling in my jaw was down. I looked as normal as I get.

"You're leaving me to have breakfast with a beautiful young girl?"

"Quit batting your eyelashes," I said. "It's just business."

"O.K. Just remember, *mi amante*, you mess around, how they say it? I scramble your eggs."

"Right," I said. "That's how they say it."

I jumped in the car, cried "Ouch!" and jumped right out again. Little Jorge had left a coconut on the front seat.

Driving away I figured I was probably the only man in South Florida who had been jumped twice by coconuts before getting out of the driveway.

Apparently the green blazer brigade was occupied elsewhere, because I was able to get through the hotel lobby without incident. The door to the suite was answered by Wendy Wilson, she of the glossy dark hair and the slam bang hips. She didn't seem the least embarrassed to be found in a black silk peignoir that showed a lot of very lookable leg.

"Are you breakfast?" she asked, trailing fingernails over the door jam. "No bermuda shorts today? Too bad. You had such sweet little dimples in your knees."

"I think Miss DiMonte is expecting me."

"I guess you want her autograph, huh? Or maybe she wants yours."

"Something like that."

Miss DiMonte was late. I waited out on the balcony, stealing glances at the breakfast trolley and thumbing through the complimentary copy of USA Today. Did you know that fifty-three percent of us consume eighty-five percent of all the breakfast foods manufactured in twenty-two percent of the states? And that a wopping two-thirds prefer butter over margarine? Or that a shocking seventy-eight percent of the readers think that ninety-five percent of the USA Today statistics are a hundred percent baloney?

I get cranky on an empty stomach. Twenty minutes of thumb twiddling. Ten more admiring the gaudy yachts parading through the Indian Creek waterway. Give it another five and I was going to open the trolley covers and start without Carla. Maybe even polish off *her* breakfast.

"Oh, hi." Miss DiMonte wandered on to the balcony, yawning. No silk peignoir for the don's daughter; a simple cotton beach wrap and a large pair of dark glasses. "What's your name again?"

"Tony Mack," I said. "But you can call me anything but late to breakfast."

"Help yourself," she said, her voice husky and low. "I never touch the stuff."

Carla drank two glasses of fresh squeezed orange juice while I worked on the slightly stale bagels and thin tasting coffee. The dark glasses made it tough to interpret her expression. I concentrated on her mouth and chin, trying to read the inflections there.

"First thing, okay? This is a favor to Mick."

"What favor is that?" I asked innocently.

"You know."

"I don't, really."

"You. You're the favor."

"Oh," I said, keeping it amiable. "You think you don't need any help."

"Correct. Why should I need help?"

I smiled. "I had a long talk with Michael Murphy last night, Miss DiMonte. He told me about the anonymous calls you received at the recording studio, just prior to the tour. Calls threatening to implicate you in a murder unless you left the band."

"You *talked* to Michael?"

I nodded. "He gave me his card. Not a lot of licensed investigators have engraved cards. I was impressed."

"I'll bet. Michael Murphy is a pest."

"I had a different four letter word in mind, Miss DiMonte."

"Oh cut the DiMonte crap. I hate that name, that's why I changed it to Carla Dee. And what four letter word are you talking about?"

"L-O-V-E, Carla. That's Murphy's problem."

The sunglasses slipped off the end of her nose. Her eyes were red from weeping. "Well that's his problem, okay? I can't help it. Everything was going just fine until *he* came along."

"Okay," I said. "Forget for a minute that the boy is infatuated with you. The fact is you did get threats. And when Murphy tried to investigate, you were told to get him removed from the case or your recording career would be over. Do I have that right?"

The dark lenses were back in place, forming a partial mask. "Not quite," she said. "I guess he didn't mention about him getting fired, huh?"

"Fired by you?"

"By the studio. Rad Records. That was the first thing happened. *Before* the phone calls started. So, do you get it now?"

I shook my head. I could sooner spin my head like an screech owl than follow Carla's inverted logic. She made an impatient sound. "Can't you see? Rad Records fired Michael. I don't know why, exactly, but I guess they had their reasons. Which meant he didn't have any excuse to be hanging around the studio, pestering me. A couple days later I get this muffled voice on the phone with some crazy story about me and a murder. And then, surprise, cute little Michael pops into my life again."

"You think *he* made the threats? As a way of getting next to you?"

She shrugged. "It occurred to me. Not right away. For a while I let him check things out. You know, he came along on the tour. Or followed us, sort of. Doing his undercover thing. Appearing in a lot of silly disguises. It was all very mysterious. And finally I could see he didn't want it to stop. That's when *I* fired him. And guess what? No more phone calls."

As always, when several versions of a story are being presented by various participants, none of them unbiased, sorting out the truth can be like chasing a heat mirage down a long, long highway. Sometimes the best tactic is to start lobbing verbal grenades, see if that clears the air.

"Michael says you think he works for your father," I said, pulling the pin. "Do you? Does he?"

"Dunno," she said, fiddling with the dark glasses. "Don't care."

A dud. Nothing to do but rear back and try again.

"How about the guy you *did* kill, Carla? Your mother's boyfriend. Is that what this is all about?"

Direct hit. Her pale chin was trembling.

"That was an. . . accident. Self defense." Her voice became small and faint, as if someone was turning down the volume. "A long time ago."

"Eight years isn't forever," I said. "There's no statute of limitations on murder. And as I understand it, the indictment was dropped when you agreed to undergo psychiatric treatment."

"How can you be so *mean*?" A flood of tears began leaking from under the dark glasses.

That's the trouble with grenades. You never know which way the shrapnel will go, or how deep it will strike.

"Look, Carla. I'm not here to cause you grief, honest."

"Then why *are* you here," she said. "Why can't it just be *over*."

Now it was my turn to sigh. The pretty morning was starting to turn ugly. Even the gaudy, harmless yachts navigating the waterway began to appear menacing, bristling with antenna whips and sharp edges.

"Okay, Carla," I reached out, tried to pat her hand. She snatched it away. "I'm here because an extortionist is threatening to reveal information that will result in your arrest unless your father pays a million to shut him up."

The lovely chin stopped trembling. An edge came into her voice. "So you *do* work for my father."

"Indirectly," I admitted. "I don't like it any better than you do. Frankly, I'd like to see your old man put away for the rest of his life. He and his kind have caused more misery in Brooklyn than the last three wars combined."

"Then why are you here?" she asked, puzzled.

"Doing a favor for a friend. And because a young woman might be in serious trouble through no fault of her own. Anymore than she's to blame for the fact that her father is a psychopath in a silk suit."

Carla stood up, went to the balcony rail. For a fleeting moment I thought she intended to leap and I came out of my chair a little too fast, startling her.

"Excuse me," I said. "I thought. . ."

"I don't care what you think. I'm the only one who knows what happened. I never meant—he was, uhm, hurting me, but I never meant to kill him."

"That isn't the point Carla. What happened then, happened. You can't change it."

"What *is* the point?"

"To make sure you don't get hurt now."

She was shivering in the eighty degree shade. Ordinarily I have shoulders big enough to cry on, but there was something about the way Carla Dee carried herself that warned me away. Extremely fragile. Do not handle. Do not touch.

"It's not *fair*," she sobbed. "We're so close. They'll all hate me."

She was talking about the band. Bad News. I persuaded her to sit down, suggested she try eating some of the breakfast. She picked up a slice of pineapple and began to chew it methodically.

"Don't worry about the band," I said. "You won't like it when the press comes sniffing around, but nobody is going to stop playing the music because of what you did or did not do eight years ago. You defended yourself against rape, right? There's no shame in that."

I didn't mention what might happen if she was arrested. If my reading on Mick Dunstan was correct, his loyalty was in inverse proportion to any risk that was the result of keeping a member on board. For now Carla was fine, because he didn't want to damage the "chemistry" of the ensemble. If the chemistry turned sour—watch out.

"Will my father pay the money?"

"I've no way of knowing. I doubt it. You're old man is smart enough to know that blackmailers are like junkies. They always need another fix."

I didn't add that anyone attempting to blackmail a Mafia godfather was more than a little crazy. And there were at least a couple of things that drove people crazy. Like love and murder.

Wendy Wilson was modeling a peek-a-boo swimsuit as Carla walked me through the suite to the door.

"Whattaya think?" she asked, snapping the elastic. "I feel like I'm hanging out all over the place."

"You are," Carla said.

"What do *you* think?" she said, pointedly asking my opinion.

"If you can't let it all hang out in Miami Beach, where can you?"

Where indeed? I had the feeling though, that public exposure was going to go well beyond swimsuits. That was intuition. I had no way of knowing I would be the one who got hung out to dry.

7

Michael Murphy was wearing holes in the pavement, pacing next to my car.

"Well?" he demanded. "What did she say about me?"

I twisted the key in my lock, opened the door, stood back to let the heat rush out. It was noontime and the tar was sticking to my shoes and I wasn't sure I wanted to deal with a lovesick man-boy from Stony Brook, Long Island.

"You hungry?" I asked.

He looked blank, then brightened. "You'll tell me over lunch? Gee thanks, Tony. This means a lot."

"Stop squirming and get in the car. I'll drop you back here later."

Silly me. I'd forgotten all about Collins Avenue being ripped up. Ten minutes turned into sixty. Stale bagels masquerading as breakfast had put me into a mood for crab claws at Joe's and I was too bullheaded to pull off the avenue and find another, closer restaurant. As a result I heard all about Michael Murphy's charmed life, from childhood on.

"I was adopted," he said, "which was for me this lucky thing. See, my adoptive parents are these two really great people. Dad's a lawyer, he's retired now, and Mom has always been involved in charities. People make fun of it, her social set, but they do a lot of good."

"In Stony Brook?"

"Yeah, in Stony Brook and all over. Does a lot of work for the Catholic Charities which is, you know, how they got me."

"Ever been tempted to find your natural parents?" I asked.

Murphy stared out the window. "Nah," he said. "Why dig it up?"

"You decided to be a detective," I said. "That's what detectives do."

"Yeah, but not for myself. For other people."

"How long have you been a licensed investigator?" I asked.

There was an uncomfortable silence. "Not long," he mumbled. "Actually, the gig with Rad Records was my first job."

"What?"

"Well, it's like this. I was going to law school—going to be an attorney like Dad. Then, you know, with one thing and the other I sort of dropped out. Or what I did, transferred to a graduate course in criminal justice. Except I never finished, not exactly."

"And you went direct from school drop-out to setting up in business?"

He nodded meekly. And no wonder. An investigator with absolutely no practical experience is not exactly a credit to the profession.

"Tell me something," I asked, tapping the wheel as we waited to clear through the diverted lane. "How'd you ever get a client?"

"I'm not sure," he said. "I assume it was through my Dad. Someone he knew in business. All I know is this record company called, asked me to check out their security system. They had this problem with unshielded phones, and a computer system that was wide open to hackers. So I was checking it all out, getting ready to write my report, make a few suggestions. And then, what happened, I met Carla."

"And Rad Records fired you."

He cleared his throat, scratched his nose. "That was later," he said. "I guess I got sort of fixated on Carla. Neglected my job."

"Uh huh. I guess you wanted to be a hero for Carla."

"What's that supposed to mean?" he asked with an edge of suspicion.

"Just talking here, Michael, while we wait for traffic to clear. You know, idle speculation. For instance we could speculate that if a guy wanted to be a hero, say to impress a girl, he might be tempted to invent a problem and then solve it."

Murphy squinted. "What are you saying?"

"Just speculating." I tapped the wheel, whistled "Boogie Dead Men", and waited for him to react. He was slow on the uptake.

"That's a dirty lie!" he finally exploded. "Whoever said that, it's a dirty lie."

"Loosen your necktie," I advised. "Your face is getting all purple."

"You really think I'd do something like that? Threaten Carla? Maybe screw up her career? Is that what Carla thinks?"

"Never mind what Carla thinks. Just tell me what happened."

"I've been telling you, Tony. It happened just like I said."

I accelerated as we were finally cleared through a barricade. Joe's was finally in sight. My stomach growled in happy anticipation of stone crab claws smothered in dijonaise sauce. Maybe a cold beer. Definitely a cold beer.

"I mention this, Michael, because whoever is messing with Don Carlo DiMonte is way, way over his head. DiMonte kills people who annoy him, and he's very annoyed at whoever is demanding a million dollars to maintain his daughter's reputation."

"*What?*" He looked not merely surprised, but astounded.

"You didn't know about that?" I said with feigned casualness.

Murphy grabbed my arm, very nearly wrenching the wheel from my hands. We rolled over an orange divider cone and were soundly cursed by the road crew. Murphy never even noticed.

"Somebody contacted Carla's father? But that's impossible. Impossible!"

I managed to peel off his clutching fingers as we drifted, more or less in control, into the restaurant parking lot. I turned the key, opened the window.

"Really?" I asked. "Care to tell me why you know it's impossible that whoever threatened Carla at the record company wouldn't threaten her father?"

Murphy had gone pale. He had a foggy, furtive look in his eye. "I mean crazy," he said finally. "It would be crazy to threaten her old man. Not, I guess, impossible."

"But you said impossible, Michael."

"Well, you know, I was excited, I said the wrong word. What's the big deal? Hey come on, I'll buy you lunch."

He bolted from the car. I followed.

Inside it was, as usual, packed. Quality food at a reasonable price is such an obvious formula for success it's surprising how few restaurants try it. Although my appetite had not diminished, my interest in cracking crab claws was now equalled by a desire to crack Michael Murphy, engraved investigator, champion of the weak.

"Hey, this is great," he said when we were shown to a table overlooking the water. "Has kind of a picnic feel, am I right?"

"Except no ants," I said.

He laughed, avoided looking at me, and immediately seized the menu. "What do you recommend?"

I smiled. "The truth, Michael. I always recommend the truth."

He laughed again. Big joke. It went like that for most of the meal, with me prodding, prying, encouraging him to come clean. All I got out of him was a nervous laugh and the sense that he couldn't wait to be rid of me. Finally I gave up and concentrated on the food.

It was along in there, after the last beer but before the iced tea, that the cowboy galloped in without his hat.

"Hey Tony! Hey, what a small world, huh?"

His hand grabbed mine, shook it before I had a chance to react. Thus the dijonaise stain on my shirt pocket.

"Hey, lookit who I got with me here. Can you believe it?"

Wendy Wilson smiled tentatively. Looking more than a little uncomfortable. As if regretting, perhaps, an impulsive decision.

"Wendy here was lounging at the pool in this outrageous outfit," the New Jersey cowboy said. "I just *had* to introduce myself. Again. You know what? She said she didn't recognize me without my hat!"

"Hello Wendy," I said.

"Er, hi. This is supposed to be a great place. Is it?"

I nodded. "Care to join us?"

She eyed Murphy. He was an alarming shade of pink. They really teach 'em how to blush in Stony Brook, Long Island.

"I better not," she said. "Carla might get the wrong idea."

They walked on. Wendy trying to keep her distance from the grabby cowboy and not quite succeeding.

"You think she'll tell Carla she saw me with you?" Murphy wanted to know.

"Does it matter?"

"Well, yeah. 'Cause then she'll know we're working together on this."

I patted my lips with a paper napkin and reached for the bill. "No she won't," I said.

"How do you know?"

"Because we're not working together."

I got up, turned my back, and walked out. On the way I passed the cowboy's table. He was talking a mile a minute, trying to make himself sound like the last of the urban Romeos. Wendy, for her part, looked like she was undergoing painful dental surgery.

Ain't love grand?

The folks at South Florida Mutual Life were not expecting a visit from their favorite freelance investigator.

"Tony? Tony, you son of a bitch, I been leaving messages on your machine for two days. Then I get through to your wife, she tells me you joined a rock band."

"You rather I joined the circus, Ralph?"

Ralph is Rolf Hamsun, Investigations Coordinator. Gets on his nerves when I call him Ralph, but then it gets on my nerves when he bypasses my business number and calls Maria direct.

"We're swamped here, Tony. We got three more whips just yesterday and this morning we picked up a major spine which, if I don't get the paperwork, the L.D. is going to fry my ass."

Translation: The Law Division had requested investigations on three pending whiplash claims and a spinal injury case. Rolf wanted me to handle surveillance on all four cases. Normally that would be cause for celebration. I hadn't established myself as a reliable freelance investigator by turning down work. An early pension from the NYPD helped, but it wasn't nearly enough to keep seven kids in coconuts.

"Just one more day," I said. "The band leaves tomorrow."

Rolf's jaw dropped. "You really *are* joining up with a band?"

"Sure," I said. "And the pope's hired on to play bongos. What I'm saying, Rolf, is that after tomorrow I'll be back on the job, okay? I'll get the work done. I'll keep your butt out of the bacon grease."

Rolf nodded uncertainly. Still trying to figure out what I meant, exactly, about the pope playing bongos.

"I need a terminal," I said. "And a phone."

"For your own case? You know that's against the regs."

"Bacon fat, Rolf. Hot and bubbly."

He sighed. "Use my office. I'm going to go home and drink Maalox."

"Tomorrow, Rolf. Your worries will be over."

"Yeah, sure."

"Trust me," I said.

"I do," he said, snapping shut his briefcase. "That's how I got the ulcer."

You ever want to know anything about anyone, no matter how private or personal, consult an insurance company computer system. The electronic tentacles reach everywhere. Into crannies you've forgotten, under rocks you never thought could be disturbed. Into company files, bank files, police files, court files, school and university files, church files (truth, I swear) credit card files, state files, local files, military files (if you know the

94

right codes) insurance files (the great brotherhood of insurance carriers) magazine subscription files, video rental files, library files, newspaper files (open to the public), and, if you have friends in low places, the F.B.I. files.

You're covered, pal. Forget privacy. Forget keeping a secret. All an inquisitive snoop has to do is start massaging the microchips, key into the right circuits, courtesy of your favorite long distance carrier, and everything you never wanted anyone to know is printed out at high speed, in slightly fuzzy dot matrix.

Rape of the Data, a modern tragicomedy in three acts: Search, Retrieve, and Print.

The local carrier in Stony Brook had pages of data on Lawrence and Antonia Murphy of Stony Brook, Long Island, adoptive parents of Michael. I used it to pry open other files in other places. Lawrence, born in Queens, was still a registered attorney, nominally retired but remaining on the masthead of a firm that specialized in tax problems. Wife Toni, née Petrazio, born in Brooklyn, was indeed active in charities and on the Long Island social circuit. According to Suffolk County court records, Michael, now twenty-six years of age, had been legally adopted at one month of age in a transaction that did not mention the Catholic Charities or any other adoptive organization.

Maybe he'd been found on a doorstep.

The boy had an unremarkable school record. Several prep schools had tried to foster a willingness to "pursue academic excellence" and failed. Michael spent a leisurely six years as an undergraduate on two campuses. He'd left law school (Lawrence Murphy's alma mater), prior to being expelled for a low grade average and re-enroled in a criminal justice grad course before again dropping out two years later.

He had never been arrested. He lived at home, or that was his legal address.

Using two different access codes to various license bureau files I found a Michael J. Murphy licensed as a private investigator with the State of New York. Murphy was fifty-two, a former Westchester police officer, and he happened to be black. There was no other Michael J. Murphy listed.

So my Michael Murphy wasn't actually licensed as an investigator. Despite the fact that he was listed in the Stony Brook yellow pages under Confidential Inquiries. Young Murphy had a lifelong habit of not following through—maybe he just hadn't bothered to fill out the application. Maybe he lacked the fee, or a stamp for the envelope.

"Onward and upward," I said to the computer screen. "Cherchez la femme."

(Hey, I'm not the only one who talks to computers. I heard Rolf telling his terminal a joke one day, and he seemed genuinely disappointed when it didn't get the punchline)

The first femme I searched was Carla DiMonte. Found reams of data. I found, for instance, exactly what she spend on lingerie at Bloomingdales before the tour departed. Eighty-six dollars and fifty-two cents, in case you're interested. I was able to dredge up her parochial school records through the diocese insurance carrier and discovered a very bright little girl with a gift for music. Later, a somewhat troubled or troublesome adolescent who still had a gift for music. No surprise there. Divorce proceedings between her parents were likewise unremarkable. Carla was given in custody to her mother and Don Carlo agreed to pay hefty alimony and child support. Division of property awarded a house and motor vehicle to the mother.

Running down the death of Jerry Berg, her mother's lover, proved more difficult. The record on Carla's initial arrest had been expunged by order of the court, following dismissal of the charges. Autopsy reports were sealed. Newspaper coverage was scanty at best, and smacked of being compiled from police reports, rather than direct coverage. There was an impression that Berg was a minor hoodlum, but no details.

I was left with the insurance angle. Payments had been made from Don Carlo's account to a psychiatric hospital in New Jersey, for Carla's treatment following Berg's death, but I was unable to gain access to the actual psychiatric files. Quite possibly they'd never been entered into a computer and I wasn't prepared to visit New Jersey, not even for the fun of breaking into a shrink's office.

So I back-tracked and in a lucky hit discovered a file that listed Rad Records as a risk for fire and theft coverage because, as the investigating agent reported: "company has in past been under federal investigation as possible money laundering front for New York area crime families". Unquote.

Well well. What a small world. Mick Dunstan was righter than he knew; Carla and Rad Records *were* connected. By blood. Whether it was her father's blood or her own was a question that remained, for now, unanswered. Maybe she'd merely asked a favor of her father's associates, who were, from what I could determine, at least as interested in selling records as they were in laundering cash. And Bad News was a good bet, irregardless of what strings had been pulled to sign the initial contract.

Did someone at Rad Records have it in for the Godfather's

daughter? A power struggle inside the family? Would they be going to the mattresses over the royalties sure to accrue from the latest version of "Boogie Dead Men"? And why was it so important that Michael Murphy be kept away from Carla DiMonte?

"Stay tuned," I said. The computer screen obligingly remained on.

Having exhausted possibilities in the present, I went back, back, *way* back. Digging up roots in the family tree. Don Carlo, as a boy of ten, had been sent to a reform school following the unexplained death of a neighborhood boy, aged fourteen, from a rival gangland family.

Interesting, in a bleak kind of way, but did a fifty-year-old crime have any connection to the current blackmail attempt?

I followed Don Carlo up till the tender age of twenty-two, by which time he had been arrested or suspected in a wide range of felonies. Assault, rape, murder, burglary, mail fraud. The Don was a one man crime wave. In the end I gave up. Most of the local population was either victimized by him or worked for him, often both. If I wanted to know who might have it in for Don Carlos DiMonte I simply had to pick up the Brooklyn phone book and select a name at random.

I picked Francesca DiMonte, née Gaetti, his former spouse and Carla's mother. And discovered that unlike her future husband, Francesca's life had centered around the church. Nuns and priests in the family. Parochial school. The same school, I noticed, that her daughter would attend some twenty years later. A tradition in the family.

I was running through the list of Francesca Gaetti's classmates when one of the names clicked. I backed up the scroll. Oh yes, there it was, plain as day. Antonia Petrazio. Michael's stepmother. Who later adopted a child outside the normal channels.

Suddenly a lot of things made a lot of sense.

8

You can't actually see the sunset from the beach at the Crystal Sands. The million dollar beach faces dead east and the enormous structure of the hotel blocks the view to the west. What you see, if you're there at the crucial moment, is a dark monolith tinged with crimson along the edges. The shadow of the building extends far out into the sea and if there happens to be an offshore breeze it can be, as I discovered, downright chilly.

Or, as George "Pockets" Bates would have it: "I'm freezing my nuts off, man."

"You mean you've chilled out?" I said.

Pockets smirked, wrinkling his nose up. "Beyond chill, man. I thought it was against the law or something, it goes below eighty degrees here."

"You could try wearing a shirt."

"Ruin my image," he said.

We crossed the boardwalk, found a place to sit behind the canvas wind barriers where heat was still rising from the terrazzo tiles. Much better.

"You were telling me about Michael Murphy," I said, prodding gently.

"Yeah, Mr. Mike. What a trip he is."

"How so?"

"This an interrogation?" Pockets asked. He didn't seem disturbed by the idea. But then he was used to having hot lights shined in his face, and staying up till all hours.

"This is merely a conversation," I said.

Pockets guffawed. "Man, nothing is merely a conversation with you. No offense."

"None taken."

Pockets had a finger hooked around the rim of a beer bottle. Imported from private stock, since the tiki bar dealt only in plastic cups. He peered into the nearly empty bottle, blew a note across the top.

"That's a B-flat, in case you wondered."

"Mostly I've been wondering about—"

"Yeah, yeah. Mr. Mike." He upended the bottle, burped, and announced that the burp was in D-minor. "Like Beethoven's Ninth, man."

"You know Beethoven's music?"

"I'm a musician. I listen to all kinds of music. Read it, too."

"So," I said. "What's you're reading on Mr. Mike?"

"I told you, man. He's a trip. One of these cats, everything is a fantasy. He's living inside his own movie. Like this thing with him being a private eye."

"You don't think he's really an investigator?"

Pockets shook his head, thumbed his glasses back. "I mean, its not like I know any real detectives. Except, I guess, *you* are, right?"

"I like to think so."

"Yeah, well Mr. Mike would like to think so, too. But with him its all pretend. Just posing. Talking tough, disguising himself, pestering people. One of the cats from Rad, he told me it was all a game. They didn't really need a detective. They like hired Mr. Mike as a favor to a friend or something."

"The friend have a name?"

"I'm sure he does, but I don't know it."

I happened to glance at the pool area. A teenager was dropping her robe, kicking off her sandals, and diving into the aqua-blue water. My little nemesis, the girl with the red-tinted hair. I shifted in my seat, putting my back to the pool.

"What about romance," I asked. "Was there a serious thing going between Michael and Carla?"

"No way, man. Mr. Mike thought there was, but like I say, that dude is living his own movie. He decided Carla was going to be his leading lady before he even *talked* to her. Said they were soulmates and fate had drawn them together and all those kind of grotty old lines he borrowed from the flicks. And Carla, she like was reading from a different script."

"She doesn't like Michael?"

Pockets made a face, considered the question. "He makes her nervous, is what it is. I don't think Carla's ever had time to find out if she likes him or not. Mr. Mike never gave her a chance."

I peeked over my shoulder. The teenager was swimming laps with strong confident strokes, her ankles flashing.

"Did Carla have him fired?" I asked, turning back.

Pockets was fidgeting, his pick hand scratching the air. "He tell you that? Well it's not true. We're just a band, man. One of many Rad has under contract. And we don't swing that kind of weight, not yet. The word came down, they canned his ass. Carla had nothing to do with it."

"You've been a big help," I said.

"I have?" He laughed, shaking his head. "Does that mean I can be a detective, too?"

"You've already got the trenchcoat."

There was a flat, splatting sound. Wet feet running on the terrazzo. I saw her coming and steeled myself for an unpleasant confrontation.

"'Scuze me! I mean, I'm sorry, but are you Pockets? I mean the Bad News Pockets? Georgie Bates?"

Miss Wall Street was dripping chlorinated water and shivering. Her eyes were big and wet and focused utterly on the guitarist. He nodded and the girl quickly turned and ran away.

"This happen to you all the time?" I asked.

"More lately," he said. Not unpleased with himself but not, from what I could see, particularly impressed with his emerging celebrity. The girl returned moments later, toweling herself dry and still shivering from excitement.

"You guys were so excellent last night," she babbled, teeth chattering. "I mean *really really* excellent. I haven't got an autograph book but could you like sign me or something?"

There was, I noticed, a felt tip pen clutched in her fist. Pockets shrugged and said why not and signed his name where indicated, on her flat young belly.

"Make it big," she exclaimed. "What I'll do is have a picture taken and then I'll always have the picture even if this comes off in the shower."

With that she pranced away, buoyant with joy. In the whole transaction she'd never once glanced my way. The glow from Pockets made me cease to exist.

Maybe Maria had the right idea. Maybe I *should* run away to join a rock band.

In the lobby my name was being taken in vain. The green jackets, not the same pair who had evicted me, were slipping armlocks around Michael Murphy, hustling him out of there.

"Come on pal. We got our orders. You're gone."

"You don't understand," Murphy said, peddling futilely as they picked him up. "There's been a mistake. I'm a private investigator. I'm on a case!"

"It's easier if you don't fight us, pal."

"I work for Tony Mack! Don't tell me you never heard of Tony Mack."

"Never heard of him, pal."

"He's been retained by the band and I'm working for him and this is all a big misunderstanding."

They had him to the revolving door by then. The ejection went according to plan: Michael popped out the door like a peanut from a shell. I trailed behind, keeping my distance, and saluted the green jackets as they strutted back inside, mighty pleased with themselves.

Michael crawled to the edge of the fountain. I helped him out and checked to be sure there were no fish in his pockets.

"All I did was try and talk with Carla," he said, forlorn and drenched.

"I guess she didn't want to talk," I said. "Maybe you should take the hint. Go back to Stony Brook and find another girl to worship."

"She's got the wrong idea about me," he said. "If I can just talk to her I can make her understand."

This I doubted. Carla clearly didn't want to be included in Murphy's fantasies, however romantic. Maybe she was running on instinct, reacting in a way that was, to her, natural.

"Go home," I said, wringing water from his tie, tucking the soggy end in his pocket. "The crap is going to hit the fan and you'll just be in the way."

"Don't insult me, Tony."

I patted his cheek. "Nobody can insult you, Michael. You just tune it out. Now try and listen to me for a minute, okay?"

He nodded. His eyes seemed more or less focused on me. A good sign. Maybe the soaking had sobered him up; there's nothing more intoxicating than a fantasy life.

"You didn't mean to, Michael, but you've set certain events in motion. An irresistible force is about to collide with an immovable object."

"You mean Carla's father?"

I nodded. "And her mother."

"What's her mother got to do with this?"

I stood up, shaking the dampness from my hands. "That's what I'm going to find out. And you're going to help me by going back to Stony Brook on the next available flight."

Getting Michael J. Murphy airborne wasn't just a job, it was an adventure. Intent on speeding up the departure, I agreed to return his rental car later, after his flight had embarked. This made Michael nervous.

"You know," he said uneasily. "I'm responsible. It could go on my credit card, if anything happens."

"Nothing is going to happen. Forget the car. Worry about Don Carlos."

"I never met the guy."

"Then consider yourself lucky. And pray that he doesn't think *you're* the one who's trying to rip him off for a cool million."

It was typical that a credit rating worried him more than the prospect of ending life in a trunk—a favorite gangland ploy—or as filler in a sausage factory. Michael still didn't get it. He didn't know why I wanted him to go home and ask his mother a simple but crucial question.

"I could always phone," he said.

"If you phoned you'd still be here," I said. "And then you might convince yourself only magic bullets can kill you."

"Even if she *knows,* Mom won't tell me."

101

His flight was departing from a gate on the lower level of the main terminal. We were quick-stepping through the crowd of passengers who, in largely Hispanic Miami, are accompanied by large extended families.

Michael kept stopping to take in the sights. A Bolivian childrens' choir, got up in uniform, singing in sweet voices to a flock of nuns. A family of six sleeping in a large cardboard box, scrawled with the words FLIGHT DELAY! A Guatemalan soccer team that looked like an intermural death squad. All in all, a fairly typical sampling of Miami International Airport.

"Michael, can I have your attention?"

"Sure."

"I want you to tell your mother all about Carla, okay? What her real name is, how you feel about her. Who her father is. Everything."

"You really think I should?"

I sighed. Those who think uranium is the densest thing on earth, think again. The flight, by some miracle, left on time, and I exited the airport with a not-so-vague sense of guilt. It was true that I wanted Michael out of the way for his own protection. It was also true that I didn't want to be around when his crazy dream turned into a nightmare.

I was extra careful returning the rented convertible, though. So his credit rating was safe, if not his psyche.

9

I could hear the music, clear as a boom box, even before the elevator doors opened. They were playing my song. At high volume and with enough bass to tickle your feet.

I want you to
No no, come back

The good old Gnats. Accent, sad to say, on old. But as I walked down the hallway in that gaudy, bad dream hotel, years began to fade. The youthful sense of electric, party-time excitement returned: loud rock music, the promise of interesting strangers, pretty girls, a pungent whiff of marijuana.

Tony Mack, party animal.

The bass line resonated in the handle as I opened the door to the suite and pushed my way inside.

No no, come back

I'd had in mind an intimate conversation with Carla DiMonte, concerning events that had happened before she was born. Right away that plan was aborted. Intimacy here was the sweaty kind, where you bump into strangers and grin. Walking was impossible. You had to dance.

I boogied through the tangle of twitching limbs, heading for a place where Mick Dunstan's face had bobbed up, just for a moment. Mick had been smiling, so apparently he wasn't being trampled to death. I was beginning to think he'd been swept along into the adjoining suite when he surfaced just behind me.

"Tony!" he shouted. "You made it!"

The song ended just as he spoke and the last phrase filled a moment of relative silence before the next tune wiped out conversation. Mick had a girl attached to each hip, both young enough to be daughters. I wondered if Little Miss Wall Street had been invited; she could get the whole band to autograph her body.

"What's the occasion!" I shouted.

"Big Apple!" he responded. "We're headed back tomorrow!"

I asked for Carla. He suggested I check the adjoining suite.

Getting there was no easy task. I boogalooed, did head and shoulder fakes. This was burning off more calories than a Hanoi Jane workout. The last time I'd approached the adjoining suite Carla had emerged with gun in hand. Now the warning was slightly more subtle. A hand-lettered notice thumb-tacked to the door:

This door to be kept locked. Please do not enter.

I tried knocking. It was like whispering in a hurricane. Out of frustration I tried the handle and felt the latch slip. So much for the sign; the suite was unlocked.

I timed the next dance surge, waited until the moment was right, and slipped inside, locking the door behind me. The noise was diminished by about half, which meant it was slightly less than deafening. From somewhere in the darkened suite came the bright tinkle of female laughter.

"Carla?"

The laughter ceased abruptly. There was a murmur with a masculine undertone. A door opened, spilling a rectangle of light into the room. Wendy Wilson and the Jersey cowboy stumbled out of the bathroom. Both were glassy-eyed and sniffling. Wendy's blouse was buttoned up wrong and the cowboy was having trouble with his zipper.

103

"Uhm, who's there?" Wendy said.

"J. Edgar Hoover," I said. "Put your hands up and don't sneeze."

"Huh? Who *are* you?"

How soon they forget. Twelve hours ago she'd been modeling a bathing suit for me. Now I was just another bruiser crashing her party-within-a-party. I mentioned my name, said I needed to speak to Carla on an urgent matter.

"Hey man," the cowboy said thickly, with a slight air of menace. "That was pretty funny about J.Edgar Hoover."

Wendy had recovered her poise. She straightened out her blouse, cleared her throat—that steady drip of whatever the coke had been cut with—and informed me that Carla wasn't in a visiting type of mood.

"She's into this alone thing," Wendy said. "Come back to-morrow."

"You'll be gone tomorrow," I reminded her.

"I promised her I wouldn't tell."

"What if I say somebody's life may depend on my speaking to her?"

"Are you serious?" Wendy looked sceptical.

"Heavy duty, man," the cowboy said, shaking a finger at me. "You better lighten up. This a *party*."

Wendy took him in tow, heading for the bedroom area. He was just meat, her action implied, but meat in an interesting package. Passing me, she winked and mouthed the word 'balcony'.

The drapes had been drawn across the sliding glass door. I pulled the stiff material to one side and looked out into the night beyond. Miami was etched in lights. Cars sped along Collins Avenue, as if chasing speed boats on the parallel waterway. And Carla DiMonte was huddled in a canvas deck chair with her back to me.

I tapped on the glass. Carla jerked in the chair and I saw the whites of her eyes, like a wild thing caught in a beam of light. I tapped again, very gently, and she seemed to recognize me. I pointed to the handle. Slowly, as if moving under water, she got up from the chair and unlocked the slider.

"You scared me," she said, trembling.

"Sorry," I said. "I wanted you to know I put Michael Murphy on a plane. Back home to his mother."

"Right. Good," she said. "That's good."

She was too distracted or frightened to really comprehend. If I'd said the hotel was about to drop into a sinkhole, her response would have been the same. The more I looked at her the more I saw pure, unadulterated fear.

"What happened, Carla? Have you been threatened again?"

She allowed me to help her sit down. It was a warm, sultry night and the balcony was sheltered from any errant sea breezes, so it wasn't the weather that was making her shiver. I pulled up a chair, took her cold hands in mine.

"Maybe I can help," I said.

"There's nothing anyone can do."

"I'll try."

"He'll kill Michael."

"Who will?" I squeezed her hands, urging her to respond. "Carla, tell me who wants to kill Michael."

"My father," she said bitterly. "I'm supposed to call him, tell him to pay the money or I'll make trouble, but it won't do any good."

She looked directly into my eyes. Showing me her naked fear.

"Who told you to put pressure on your father?"

"The man on the phone."

"He called you here? When?"

"An hour ago," she said. "Right after the show."

"A familiar voice?"

She shook her head. "Just a whisper. It could have been anybody. He said it was my turn now, that if my father didn't pay the money, he'd make it look like Michael was behind the blackmail scheme. And that would be the end of Michael."

As well it might. And for more reasons than a simple, stupid attempt to extort money from a gangland boss.

"What have they got on you, Carla?" I asked gently.

"Not on me," she whispered. "On my father. It was him, always it was him."

Then it came spilling out. The stainless steel horror of that night eight years before, when her mother's lover had died.

"It was all my fault," Carla said. "If I hadn't been wearing that skimpy little night dress, I don't think my father would have killed him. At least not right then and there. What happened is I'd been fighting with my Mom. I don't even remember what it was about, isn't that dumb? Just the kind of argument a bratty teenage girl gets into with her mother. Jerry Berg was over—he and Mom were seeing a lot of each other at the time. I guess they'd been friends even before my mother got married, and now she was getting divorced they could be friends again. Does that make sense?"

"All kinds of sense," I said.

"I got ready for bed. Then I decided I was going to play my stereo real loud. Just to make her suffer."

"Your mother?"

She nodded. "So Jerry knocks on the door. I turn down the stereo—I wasn't mad at him, okay? We got along pretty good. Fact is, he treated me more like a daughter than my bastard father ever did. Anyhow, I started to cry and Jerry hugged me and patted my head and then we just sat there, the two of us on my bed, and we talked. About my mother and the strain she was under and how she just wanted the best for me and Jerry wanted the best for all of us, because he intended to marry my mother. He said we'd get out of Brooklyn, as far away from my father as we could get."

There were paper napkins on the table, left over from breakfast. I handed one to Carla and she daubed away her tears. After a sigh that shook her from head to toe, she continued.

"Jerry had, like, his arm around me okay? Just reassuring me, trying to make me believe everything would be fine. And that's when my father burst in. He saw me in that silly little night dress and Jerry sitting on the bed with his arm around me and he just went completely crazy. That's when I knew he really was a killer, like they'd been saying in the papers. The look in his eye! Like he was this animal that needed to kill, that just wanted an excuse. And Jerry was all the excuse he needed.

"Jerry knew it, too. He tried to get out of the room but my father picked up a bookend—it was heavy, lead or bronze or something—and he smashed Jerry in the side of the head."

All Carla's assurances that Jerry had not been molesting her went unheeded. Then, standing over the body, her father had turned on her. She had been leading Jerry on, he decided, tempting him, and he, her father, had only been trying to protect her.

"He said he hadn't meant to kill Jerry, only hurt him a little. And now my little temptress act with the nightdress was going to cost him the rest of his life in jail."

Don Carlos had told his daughter that he and Jerry had once been associated in "business" and that they'd had a falling out years before. Before Carla was born. Threats had been made at the time and now it would look like Don Carlos had finally carried out the threat and killed his old rival. In which case he'd be indicted for first degree murder.

"He told me to tell the police that Jerry had been trying to molest me and that I picked up the bookend and hit him."

"And you agreed?" I asked.

She shook her head. "Not then. I was in shock. I couldn't believe any of it had happened. I went way deep inside myself. To that soft, dark place where no one can touch you. I wouldn't talk to anyone. Not my mother, not the police, not anyone."

"Your mother knew what really happened?"

106

"Of course. She was right there in the next room. Heard every word. But she didn't dare say anything. She knew my father. What he was capable of. She went along with it."

"With committing you for psychiatric care?" I said, suppressing a shudder.

"They called it 'observation', like that made it okay. And my father's lawyers said they could fix everything. All I had to do was say Jerry tried to rape me."

Eventually, afraid for her own sanity in the cloistered world of the insane, she had agreed to cooperate. Charges were dropped, the case was buried, and Carla returned home.

"My mother and I never talk about it. Not ever. Like it never happened. But I know what she thinks. If her spoiled little girl hadn't thrown a tantrum, demanded attention, then Jerry would still be alive. None of it would have happened. Except for me."

I shook my head. Guilt is such a sticky thing and it always seems to be sticking to the wrong person. "Try giving yourself a break, Carla. If what you say is true, your father killed a man, not you. And then he compounded the crime by making his own daughter take the blame."

Carla was hugging her knees, rocking quietly in the chair. Getting distant and numb as she relived the past. I wanted to snap her out of it, make her see that she had to learn to live in the present, one day at a time. Maybe that explains why I told her more than I intended. More than was good for her, or for anyone caught in the web of Don Carlo's deceit.

"Don't worry too much about Michael Murphy, okay? I think we can clear him with the Don."

Carla looked up, radiating an expression of doubt and disbelief. "You can do that?"

"I'll try. First I have to find out who took over from Michael, who targeted your father for blackmail."

"What are you saying?"

"I'm almost certain Michael was the source of the first threats, those directed toward you rather than your father. Rad Records was pressured into firing him, just as they'd been pressured into hiring him in the first place. So Michael invented a reason to be your hero. He wanted to be near you, he wanted to impress you. So he invents a threat, then knights himself in your defense."

"I don't understand," she said.

"About Michael and his fantasies?"

"No, not about him. About the record company."

Her confusion seemed utterly geniune. I believed the lady, and that's another reason I told her more than she needed to know.

107

"Rad Records is a front, Carla. A cash laundry for the mob. One of hundreds of businesses used for that purpose."

She appeared to be stunned. "Rad isn't a real record company?"

"They're real enough. They sign musicians, release records, promote their acts. But when the mob says dance, Rad Records says 'what tune?'."

She covered her face with her hands. "Oh God. I should have known. I knew the president of the company owed my father a favor. I didn't know my father *owned* them."

"Not just your father. Other crime families use Rad Records to dry clean their loot. Like a private branch bank. If my little theory is correct, someone connected to one of those families used his or her influence to get Michael Murphy his first job as an investigator. And then made sure he was fired when he developed a crush on you."

"His or *her*?"

I nodded. "Your mother, Carla. She wanted to help Michael get started in business. Or maybe it was Michael's stepmother. Take your pick. Doesn't make much difference."

Carla had the look of someone who has been falling for a long time, and who just now has glimpsed the ground rushing up to meet her. I thought she was going to faint and then something hardened inside her and she straightened up.

"My mother," she said. "Michael's mother."

"That's right," I said. "One and the same person. He's your brother, Carla."

10

The glass door slid open. The cowboy emerged.

"Howdy, folks. And yes, it's loaded," he said, displaying the gun in his hand, "and yes I'll kill you both if you don't do exactly what I say."

"Nobody asked," I said.

"That's the idea. I do the talking, you do the listening. Tony, you dumb schmuck, get down and hug the floor."

I had to admit it, the dumb schmuck part was absolutely right on. He'd played me for a fool by convincing me *he* was the fool. And now he had me belly down with a 9mm Beretta jammed in the back of my head. The Jersey cowboy was obviously experienced in this kind of thing—he had my belt off and my hands cinched behind my back in about as much time as it takes to hogtie a calf.

I could see Carla staring in shock as he patted me down and found my old police issue .38 snub nestled in an ankle holster. He checked the cylinder, snick-snick, and slipped it into his belt.

"What do you want?" Carla asked him.

He laughed. "Only a million bucks. And I happen to know your old man keeps that much in a paper bag taped under the pool table in that goombah social club of his. Just for walking around money. All I gotta do, convince him to hand it over."

It's hard to be taken seriously when you've been trussed up with your own belt, but I couldn't help myself. "He'll give you the money," I said. "Then he'll kill you."

"Nope. The way I'm gonna do it, he'll give me the money and then go after pretty boy Mike. That was the plan all along. Now I'm making a few modifications. On account of schmucko here."

He kicked me, just to make sure Carla knew who schmucko was.

"Guy is so dumb he carries real I.D. in his wallet."

Another mystery solved. It was nice to know I'd been K.O.'d and robbed by a professional.

"What's going to happen, we're all leaving here very quiet. Then we're going to a little place I know where we'll make a few phone calls. And Carla, honey, you're going to say exactly what I tell you or you and your retarded friend are fucking canceled, capisci?"

Carla looked at me, looked at the Beretta. "Anything you say," she said.

"You're a smart kid. A quick learner, just like your mama said."

Carla's chin jerked up. "What's my mother got to do with this?"

"Oh, not much," he said, chuckling. "She asked me a favor and I obliged. Now I'm doing a favor for myself."

"You're a liar," Carla said.

I thought he might shoot her for that, or me. He laughed instead. Under the circumstances I'd rather have heard fingernails on slate.

"Everybody is a liar, honey. The difference is I'm gonna get paid for it. I'm known on the streets as a fixer, a problem solver, capisci? Your mother, a very sweet lady, came to me with her troubles. A boy was bothering her darling daughter and could I do something about that? Without hurting the boy, of course. I figure, this sweet lady is the Don's ex, how can I use this to my advantage? Imagine my surprise when I discover the dirty little secret. The sweet lady gave an illegitimate kid up for adoption so she could marry the Don. And now the kid has the hots for his own sister."

"Everything flowed from there," he said, marveling at his own genius. "One dirty little secret led to another. Your Mom felt the need to confide. So I knew about the Don offing Jerry Berg and the way I figure, if his daughter threatens to testify, he'll pay up."

He reached over and jerked on my belt. Pain shot through my shoulder blades. I got to my knees, struggling to keep my arms from dislocating.

"You'll never pull it off," I said, panting. "The DiMonte organization is too big."

"They'll never know who hit 'em," he sneered. "Now. Time to move on. Ladies first."

He marched us through the darkened bedroom. Wendy sat up in bed, her voice thick with sleep. "Is that you, Tex?"

He was quick. Viciously quick. Before I could react he slugged her unconscious. I could see him grinning in the dark. Just his white teeth and the glint of the gun barrel. He yanked a pillow case off the bed, slipped it over the Beretta.

"Be good," he said softly.

Outside in the hall the party noise was winding down. Tex waited until a few stragglers went by, heading for the elevator, and then motioned us across the corridor and into the stairwell.

We'd like to think, in this kinder and gentler nation, that it would be impossible for a criminal to march two victims out of a large resort hotel at gunpoint. Or that any hotel guest who happened to notice a grinning psychopath with a pillowcase wrapped around his fist might go a few steps out of his or her way and notify the authorities.

Never happened. I felt like the invisible man. Claude Rains version or Ralph Ellison, take your pick. Now and then we would pass a someone coming up the stairs and Tex would say "Howdy folks," and folks would mumble or nod and avoid making eye contact. We had been cautioned that a plea for help would mean an automatic death sentence for all involved, which tended to put me on good behavior. No mugging or winking or mouthing words of alarm.

I believed in Tex. He was a problem solver and we were a problem who wanted to avoid being solved for as long as possible.

"This is what they call improvisation," he informed us. "You got to react, go with your instincts. My instincts say the Don will start to panic, he hears his looney daughter wants to sing to the cops. He'll come after her, with the money as bait."

Prodding a viper with a short twig was not my idea of improvisation. But then Tex was full of surprises. Hired to quietly discourage Michael Murphy, he'd discovered the blood connection, then borrowed the boy's dumb little scheme of making empty threats and turned it to his own purpose, leaving Michael exposed. Tex had nerve, if not smarts. He'd managed to camouflage himself as just another noisy male tourist, perfectly positioned to observe Carla and overhear anything cogent to his extortion plan.

As a disease, Tex would be an insidious viral infection, reacting quickly to the body's natural defenses. As a human being he was scary as hell. And I didn't know if he was working alone or had confederates or if we would live to find out.

"Where are we going?" I asked. It was a lame question; I just wanted to hear my own voice.

"You'll find out when we get there. Keep moving."

Carla appeared to be sleepwalking. Going deep inside herself to that soft dark place where no one could touch her. I wondered if she could hear music there; a choir of angels, maybe.

Celestial music. It was a nice thought. I wanted to carry it with me into my own impregnable place. Tex had the tombstone look. He was going to use us and kill us, not necessarily in that order.

"That door," he said.

We had arrived at the ground floor. He herded us through the exit, into the parking lot. Three acres of motor vehicles, sparsely illuminated by argon lights. I was afraid of that parking lot, not so much for Carla's immediate safety—she was an integral part of the extortion scheme—but for my own. I was excess baggage and Tex had the attitude of a man who liked to travel light.

"All the way over," Tex said. "That dark corner there."

We never got to that dark corner. Headlights veered around a row of cars, hesitated, then slowly converged on us. I couldn't see much beyond the glare. A car door opening, a male figure emerging. The cowboy cursed and hissed at me not to move.

"Carla?" A voice spoke. "Carla, is that you? I've got the most incredible news! Are you ready?"

Michael left the car idling and strolled into the beams of light. From the way he was rattling on I knew he hadn't quite taken it all in. Maybe he thought we were out for an evening stroll, just me and Carla and a tough looking guy with his fist wrapped in linen.

"Soon as we took off I called my mom. My stepmom. I told her about you and who your father was and then I asked her about my birth mother. And she told me, Carla! My real mom is *your* mom! Isn't that wild?"

111

There was an ugly noise behind me. After a heartbeat or two I recognized it: Tex was laughing. You can tell a lot about a man from the way he laughs. Tex sounded like a death rattle.

"Mr. Mike," he said. "Hey, welcome to the party."

"Excuse me?"

"We're doing this improv thing here," Tex said, waving his fist. "Now get down on the ground or I'll blow your sister's head off."

Michael still didn't get it. He thought Tex was kidding. Unable to understand the joke, he decided to ignore it, and Tex as well. Words he must have been rehearsing for a couple of hours spilled out: "I got off the plane in Fort Lauderdale and drove right back so I could be the one to break the news. You've got a big brother! And that means I've got a little sister, right? Which is just so incredible. There *was* a reason why I had this overpowering urge to be near you, to be part of your life. I mean it all makes *sense*."

"Michael, you better leave," Carla said, enunciating each syllable, as if her mouth wasn't quite working.

"I know, I know," he babbled. "I said some dumb things, I *did* some dumb things. This is going to sound weird, but right now, at this time in my life I'd rather have a sister than a girlfriend. I mean—does that sound weird?"

"Michael, please. . ."

"It's just I've always thought I was alone in the world. And now I'm not."

The cowboy, demonstrating his talent for improvisation, decided to jog Michael back to reality by grabbing a fistful of Carla's hair. She grimaced but did not scream as he jammed the gun into the soft part of her neck.

"On the ground or I'll kill her. Right now. Do it."

I was trying to stay out of the scene long enough to free my hands from the tightened belt. Not an easy thing to do when your circulation has been cut off and your fingers feel like recently thawed link sausages. If I could get free there was the chance, small as it was, of grabbing my revolver from where the cowboy had shoved it into his jeans.

The belt was starting to give when another actor entered the scene, stage left.

"Hey! Hey you phony bastard, wait up!"

Jogging into the glare of the headlights, wearing his trademark, moth-eaten trenchcoat and little else, was Georgie Bates. Pockets.

"You sadistic son of a bitch, you beat up Wendy! Go on, take a swing at me, you think you're such a tough guy!"

112

Pockets wasn't exactly the cavalry, but he'd do for a diversion. I yanked harder at the belt, worked it down to my knuckles. Meanwhile the cowboy let go of Carla's hair and lashed out with a left that caught Michael square in the jaw. He moaned and sank to his knees.

One distraction down and one to go.

"Not him," Pockets sneered. "Me! What the hell did Wendy ever do to you, huh?"

When the guitarist was about ten feet away he shrugged off the trenchcoat and put up his fists. A tall, scrawny welterweight with a lot of heart. And no chance at all.

They say that when important things happen fast, you see it in slow motion. They lie. What happens is you don't see it at all. Only later can you reconstruct a sequence of events and give it shape in your mind, maybe slow things down so it makes sense.

So I can't say that I actually saw Michael lurch forward and grab Tex around his knees, although I'm pretty sure that's what happened. A couple of things I can swear to, though.

A shot was fired and Carla screamed.

Then Pockets leaped on the cowboy.

Somehow my hands came free and I was trying to make a grab for my gun. Missed it and tried for the Beretta instead. Came away with just the pillowcase, which had caught fire. Dropped it.

There was another gunshot, possibly two. The cowboy sighed and turned to rubber. I went a little crazy then, trying to sort through the heap of entangled limbs.

At first I thought Michael was merely unconscious, knocked cold in the ruckus. Then I touched the back of his head and it wasn't there and someone else was screaming. It may or may not have been me.

The next thing I'm really sure about is that Pockets had his arms around Carla, holding her back from Michael's body, and that's when I saw the gun in her hand.

My gun.

I'm not sure she was even aware of what was going on when I took it away.

There were sirens approaching by then. Blue lights flashing in the concrete canyon of Miami goddamn Beach. "Get her out of here," I urged Pockets. "Just walk away."

"Are you okay, man?"

"I'm dandy. Now beat it. You were never here. Carla was never here. Got it? Cut back along the boardwalk, they'll never see you."

The cop cars circled warily through the parking lot. Eventually they found me with my hands on top of my head, the .38 lying harmless on the asphalt, smeared with my prints.

I'm still not sure if I did the wrong thing for the right reason, or the reverse. Maybe Sal Carlucci has figured it out. If you see him, ask. And tell him Tony Mack is in trouble again.

Something tells me he won't be surprised.

Souls Burning
A "Nameless Detective" Story

by Bill Pronzini

Hotel Majestic, Sixth Street, downtown San Francisco. A hell of an address—a hell of a place for an ex-con not long out of Folsom to set up housekeeping. Sixth Street, south of Market—South of the Slot, it used to be called—is the heart of the city's Skid Road and have been for more than half a century.

Eddie Quinlan. A name and a voice out of the past, neither of which I'd recognized when he called that morning. Close to seven years since I had seen or spoken to him, six years since I'd even thought of him. Eddie Quinlan. Edgewalker, shadow-man with no real substance or purpose, drifting along the narrow catwalk that separates conventional society from the underworld. Information seller, gofer, small-time bagman, doer of any insignificant job, legitimate or otherwise, that would help keep him in food and shelter, liquor and cigarettes. The kind of man you looked at but never really saw: a modern-day Yehudi, the little man who wasn't there. Eddie Quinlan. Nobody, loser—fall guy. Drug bust in the Tenderloin one night six and a half years ago; one dealer setting up another, and Eddie Quinlan, small-time bagman, caught in the middle; hard-assed judge, five years in Folsom, goodbye Eddie

Quinlan. And the drug dealers? They walked, of course. Both of them.

And now Eddie was out, had been out for six months. And after six months of freedom, he'd called me. Would I come to his room at the Hotel Majestic tonight around eight? He'd tell me why when he saw me. It was real important—would I come? All right, Eddie. But I couldn't figure it. I had bought information from him in the old days, bits and pieces for five or ten dollars; maybe he had something to sell now. Only I wasn't looking for anything and I hadn't put the word out, so why pick me to call?

If you're smart you don't park your car on the street at night, South of the Slot. I put mine in the Fifth and Mission Garage at 7:45 and walked over to Sixth. It had rained most of the day and the streets were still wet, but now the sky was cold and clear. The kind of night that is as hard as black glass, so that light seems to bounce off the dark instead of shining through it; lights and their colors so bright and sharp reflecting off the night and the wet surfaces that the glare is like splinters against your eyes.

Friday night, and Sixth Street was teeming. Sidewalks jammed—old men, young men, bag ladies, painted ladies, blacks, whites, Asians, addicts, pushers, muttering mental cases, drunks leaning against walls in tight little clusters while they shared paper-bagged bottles of sweet wine and cans of malt liquor; men and women in filthy rags, in smart new outfits topped off with sunglasses, carrying ghetto blasters and red-and-white canes, some of the canes in the hands of individuals who could see as well as I could, and a hidden array of guns and knives and other lethal instruments. Cheap hotels, greasy spoons, seedy taverns, and liquor stores complete with barred windows and cynical proprietors that stayed open well past midnight. Laughter, shouts, curses, threats; bickering and dickering. The stenches of urine and vomit and unwashed bodies and rotgut liquor, and over those like an umbrella, the subtle effluvium of despair. Predators and prey, half hidden in shadow, half revealed in the bright, sharp dazzle of fluorescent lights and bloody neon.

It was a mean street, Sixth, one of the meanest, and I walked it warily. I may be fifty-eight but I'm a big man and I walk hard too; and I look like what I am. Two winos tried to panhandle me and a fat hooker in an orange wig tried to sell me a piece of her tired body, but no one gave me any trouble.

The Majestic was five stories of old wood and plaster and dirty brick, just off Howard Street. In front of its narrow entrance, a crack dealer and one of his customers were haggling over the price of a baggie of rock cocaine; neither of them paid any attention to me as I moved past them. Drug deals go down in the open here, day and night. It's not that the cops don't care, or that they don't patrol Sixth regularly; it's just that the dealers outnumber them ten to one. On Skid Road any crime less severe than aggravated assault is strictly low priority.

Small, barren lobby: no furniture of any kind. The smell of ammonia hung in the air like swamp gas. Behind the cubbyhole desk was an old man with dead eyes that would never see anything they didn't want to see. I said, "Eddie Quinlan," and he said, "Two-oh-two" without moving his lips. There was an elevator but it had an *Out of Order* sign on it; dust speckled the sign. I went up the adjacent stairs.

The disinfectant smell permeated the second floor hallway as well. Room 202 was just off the stairs, fronting on Sixth; one of the metal 2s on the door had lost a screw and was hanging upside down. I used my knuckles just below it. Scraping noise inside, and a voice said, "Yeah?" I identified myself. A lock clicked, a chain rattled, the door wobbled open, and for the first time in nearly seven years I was looking at Eddie Quinlan.

He hadn't changed much. Little guy, about five-eight, and past forty now. Thin, nondescript features, pale eyes, hair the color of sand. The hair was thinner and the lines in his face were longer and deeper, almost like incisions where they bracketed his nose. Otherwise he was the same Eddie Quinlan.

"Hey," he said, "thanks for coming. I mean it, thanks."

"Sure, Eddie."

"Come on in."

The room made me think of a box—the inside of a huge rotting packing crate. Four bare walls with the scaly remnants of paper on them like psoriatic skin, bare uncarpeted floor, unshaded bulb hanging from the center of a bare ceiling. The bulb was dark; what light there was came from a low-wattage reading lamp and a wash of red-and-green neon from the hotel's sign that spilled in through a single window. Old iron-framed bed, unpainted nightstand, scarred dresser, straight-backed chair next to the bed and in front of the window, alcove with a sink and toilet and no door, closet that wouldn't be much larger than a coffin.

"Not much, is it," Eddie said.

I didn't say anything.

He shut the hall door, locked it. "Only place to sit is that chair there. Unless you want to sit on the bed? Sheets are clean. I try to keep things clean as I can."

"Chair's fine."

117

I went across to it; Eddie put himself on the bed. A room with a view, he'd said on the phone. Some view. Sitting here you could look down past Howard and up across Mission—almost two full blocks of the worst street in the city. It was so close you could hear the beat of its pulse, the ugly sounds of its living and its dying.

"So why did you ask me here, Eddie? If it's information for sale, I'm not buying right now."

"No, no, nothing like that. I ain't in the business any more."

"Is that right?"

"Prison taught me a lesson. I got rehabilitated." There was no sarcasm or irony in the words; he said them matter-of-factly.

"I'm glad to hear it."

"I been a good citizen ever since I got out. No lie. I haven't had a drink, ain't even been in a bar."

"What are you doing for money?"

"I got a job," he said. "Shipping department at a wholesale sporting goods outfit on Brannan. It don't pay much but it's honest work."

I nodded. "What is it you want, Eddie?"

"Somebody I can talk to, somebody who'll understand— that's all I want. You always treated me decent. Most of 'em, no matter who they were, they treated me like I wasn't even human. Like I was a turd or something."

"Understand what?"

"About what's happening down there."

"Where? Sixth Street?"

"Look at it," he said. He reached over and tapped the window; stared through it. "Look at the people. . . there, you see that guy in the wheelchair and the one pushing him? Across the street there?"

I leaned closer to the glass. The man in the wheelchair wore a military camouflage jacket, had a heavy wool blanket across his lap; the black man manipulating him along the crowded sidewalk was thick-bodied, with a shiny bald head. "I see them."

"White guy's name is Baxter," Eddie said. "Grenade blew up under him in 'Nam and now he's a paraplegic. Lives right here in the Majestic, on this floor down at the end. Deals crack and smack out of his room. Elroy, the black dude, is his bodyguard and roommate. Mean, both of 'em. Couple of months ago, Elroy killed a guy over on Minna that tried to stiff them. Busted his head with a brick. You believe it?"

"I believe it."

"And they ain't the worst on the street. Not the worst."

"I believe that too."

"Before I went to prison I lived and worked with people like that and I never saw what they were. I mean I just never saw it. Now I do, I see it clear—every day walking back and forth to work, every night from up here. It makes you sick after a while, the things you see when you see 'em clear."

"Why don't you move?"

"Where to? I can't afford no place better than this."

"No better room, maybe, but why not another neighborhood? You don't have to live on Sixth Street."

"Wouldn't be much better, any other neighborhood I could buy into. They're all over the city now, the ones like Baxter and Elroy. Used to be it was just Skid Road and the Tenderloin and the ghettos. Now they're everywhere, more and more every day. You know?"

"I know."

"Why? It don't have to be this way, does it?"

Hard times, bad times: alienation, poverty, corruption, too much government, not enough government, lack of social services, lack of caring, drugs like a cancer destroying society. Simplistic explanations that were no explanations at all and as dehumanizing as the ills they described. I was tired of hearing them and I didn't want to repeat them, to Eddie Quinlan or anybody else. So I said nothing.

He shook his head. "Souls burning everywhere you go," he said, and it was as if the words hurt his mouth coming out.

Souls burning. "You find religion at Folsom, Eddie?"

"Religion? I don't know, maybe a little. Chaplain we had there, I talked to him sometimes. He used to say that about the hard-timers, that their souls were burning and there wasn't nothing he could do to put out the fire. They were doomed, he said, and they'd doom others to burn with 'em."

I had nothing to say to that either. In the small silence a voice from outside said distinctly, "Dirty bastard, what you doin' with my pipe?" It was cold in there, with the hard bright night pressing against the window. Next to the door was a rusty steam radiator but it was cold too; the heat would not be on more than a few hours a day, even in the dead of winter, in the Hotel Majestic.

"That's the way it is in the city," Eddie said. "Souls burning. All day long, all night long, souls on fire."

"Don't let it get to you."

"Don't it get to *you*?"

". . .Yes. Sometimes."

119

He bobbed his head up and down. "You want to do something, you know? You want to try to fix it somehow, put out the fires. There has to be a way."

"I can't tell you what it is," I said.

He said, "If we all just did *something*. It ain't too late. You don't think it's too late?"

"No."

"Me neither. There's still hope."

"Hope, faith, blind optimism—sure."

"You got to believe," he said, nodding. "That's all, you just got to believe."

Angry voices rose suddenly from outside; a woman screamed, thin and brittle. Eddie came off the bed, hauled up the window sash. Chill damp air and street noises came pouring in: shouts, cries, horns honking, cars whispering on the wet pavement, a Muni bus clattering along Mission; more shrieks. He leaned out, peering downward.

"Look," he said, "look."

I stretched forward and looked. On the sidewalk below, a hooker in a leopard-skin coat was running wildly toward Howard; she was the one doing the yelling. Chasing behind her, tight black skirt hiked up over the tops of net stockings and hairy thighs, was a hideously rouged transvestite waving a pocket knife. A group of winos began laughing and chanting "Rape! Rape!" as the hooker and the transvestite ran zig-zagging out of sight on Howard.

Eddie pulled his head back in. The flickery neon wash made his face seem surreal, like a hallucinogenic vision. "That's the way it is," he said sadly. "Night after night, day after day."

With the window open, the cold was intense; it penetrated my clothing and crawled on my skin. I'd had enough of it, and of this room and Eddie Quinlan and Sixth Street.

"Eddie, just what is it you want from me?"

"I already told you. Talk to somebody who understands how it is down there."

"Is that the only reason you asked me here?"

"Ain't it enough?"

"For you, maybe." I got to my feet. "I'll be going now."

He didn't argue. "Sure, you go ahead."

"Nothing else you want to say?"

"Nothing else." He walked to the door with me, unlocked it, and then put out his hand. "Thanks for coming. I appreciate it, I really do."

"Yeah. Good luck, Eddie."

"You too," he said. "Keep the faith."

I went out into the hall, and the door shut gently and the lock clicked behind me.

Downstairs, out of the Majestic, along the mean street and back to the garage where I'd left my car. And all the way I kept thinking: There's something else, something more he wanted from me. . . and I gave it to him by going there and listening to him. But what? What did he really want?

I found out later that night. It was all over the TV—special bulletins and then the eleven o'clock news.

Twenty minutes after I left him, Eddie Quinlan stood at the window of his room-with-a-view, and in less than a minute, using a high-powered semiautomatic rifle he'd taken from the sporting goods outfit where he worked, he shot down fourteen people on the street below. Nine dead, five wounded, one of the wounded in critical condition and not expected to live. Six of the victims were known drug dealers; all of the others also had arrest records, for crimes ranging from prostitution to burglary. Two of the dead were Baxter, the paraplegic ex-Vietnam vet, and his bodyguard, Elroy.

By the time the cops showed up, Sixth Street was empty except for the dead and the dying. No more targets. And up in his room, Eddie Quinlan had sat on the bed and put the rifle's muzzle in his mouth and used his big toe to pull the trigger.

My first reaction was to blame myself. But how could I have known or even guessed? Eddie Quinlan. Nobody, loser, shadow-man without substance or purpose. How could anyone have figured him for a thing like that?

Somebody I can talk to, somebody who'll understand— that's all I want.

No. What he'd wanted was somebody to help him justify to himself what he was about to do. Somebody to record his verbal suicide note. Somebody he could trust to pass it on afterward, tell it right and true to the world.

You want to do something, you know? You want to try to fix it somehow, put out the fires. There has to be a way.

Nine dead, five wounded, one of the wounded in critical condition and not expected to live. Not that way.

Souls burning. All day long, all night long, souls on fire.

The soul that had burned tonight was Eddie Quinlan's.

Dry Run

by Gary Lovisi

I couldn't get the thought of all that cash out of my head. Not for a moment. It had to be more money than I'd ever see in a whole life of driving a stinking cab.

I drive for Able Taxi, around the city, out to the 'burbs and airports, into the ghetto to get rich white kids their drug toys. I usually make $27,000 a year with the tips. Not bad really, but I wanted more. If I worked until I dropped dead I'd never make as much money as I thought I was going to make on the deal Fuentes was bragging to me about that day in the cab.

He said it was big money. I believed him. I knew he was some kind of mob guy, kissed the butts of the Italians that ran Red Hook. I saw it as a wild, one-time score that would set me up pretty for the rest of my life. Hell, man, I was pushing 40 hard, a chance like this wouldn't come along again. So I'd do the sure-fire smart thing—I'd knock off Fuentes and take the upfront money for myself.

"I've got a big deal going," Fuentes told me yesterday. "I hear you work cheap and ask no questions. That's good. I gotta make a delivery. I've got some heavy cash and I'm supposed to bring it to the back room of the Hermoso Bodega on 5th Street. You drive me there tomorrow. Just you and me. You park your cab outside the place, then take a walk with me inside."

I said, "Sure, whatever you want. What's my cut?"

122

"Oh, say $1,000. Cash. Not bad for an hour's work."
"Sure, man, not bad at all." I was drooling.
"Then you pick me up at 10 A.M. tomorrow morning, sharp."
"Sure, Fuentes. I'll be there."

You can bet your ass the next day I was there. Five minutes early. Fuentes was there early himself so he liked that. He got in the back seat of the cab. I sped off to 5th Street.

The city was quiet that time of day. The streets looking deserted in the mid-morning chill. It was a frigid March day, unusually cold considering the recent mild weather, so it kept the people off the street. That was fine by me.

I saw the small briefcase Fuentes carried, resting so delicately upon his knees where he was sitting in the back seat of the cab. He looked nervous. Sure, with that much cash anyone would be nervous, I thought. That briefcase had to be filled with big money. Maybe all twenties. Maybe all hundreds!

Soon all that money would be mine.

There was an alley back of 6th Street tailor-made for the job I had in mind. I'd drive down 5th Street, making it look like everything was going according to plan. Drive right up to the bodega. Then I'd turn around and slug Fuentes when he least expected it, then keep right on going into the alley back of 6th Street. I'd take the briefcase full of money and drop Fuentes back there with a welt on his head that he'd never forget. And that would be the end of that. By late afternoon I'd be on a nice beach in Bermuda with the best babe I could find and no worries.

I drove past 4th Street. The city was quiet. No one on the street but there was a lot of traffic. The bodega was on the next block, but when I stopped at a red light on 4th Street Fuentes got my attention—by pulling out a damn gun.

"Keep the brake on, Amigo. This is where I get out. You stay here and don't move." Then Fuentes was out of my cab like a flash, running through the traffic, down one of the side streets to be lost in the city.

It had all been so unexpected I hardly knew what to do. I watched him go, astounded by his actions. None of it made any sense to me then. He couldn't have known I was going to mug him. His actions really didn't indicate that, they indicated something however, but I just wasn't sure what it all meant.

Then I noticed he'd left the attaché case. My eyes riveted to the back seat where the case sat so innocuously. Not like Fuentes to leave behind a briefcase full of money—no matter how much in a hurry or frantic he was—unless the suitcase wasn't full of money at all!

My mind screamed, "Set-up!"

I flew out of the cab, rolling across the curb, managing to get under a nearby parked car just as my cab blew up in the biggest damn explosion I'd seen since a Nam napalming twenty years before.

When the smoke cleared and the screams of the people quieted down I saw what was left of my cab. It wasn't much, just a mass of melted metal, while glass of every store on the block littered the street. My head rang like one of those giant Chinese gongs—but as far as I could tell I was still in one piece and I didn't see any blood.

I was alive and that's what was important then. Once I was assured of that basic fact my mind later focused on other items of interest. Like, where was the money? Where was Fuentes? Why the double-cross?

When you're planning to do someone dirty you never figure he'll do you dirty first, but it seems that's exactly what happened to me. It sure messed up my plans.

Fuentes had disappeared into the muck of the city. No one I asked knew anything. I had a few contacts, but I guess Fuentes had better ones. It seemed to me he had gone deep and wasn't moving.

At first I was just happy to be alive after what I'd been through. Then it began to get to me. The thing was, I felt like I was *supposed* to have died in that explosion. Like it was actually meant for me. I just couldn't figure out why.

I took a drastic revaluation of my life up to that point. Enemies. People I'd offended. Jealous or envious types. Not many of these. It just didn't jive. I've always kept to myself since I came back from 'Nam. I've never been in jail, never arrested, never caused any trouble. Had an amicable divorce years ago, no money owed the sharks, and didn't use drugs. I was a 39 year old working drudge, honest (relatively) and clean, you could tell because I was such a damn failure. I even paid my taxes.

Then why the set-up?

I began to do my own investigating when the cops couldn't get me any action. What did I really know about Emileo Fuentes? He was an up and coming hood, into loan-sharking and gambling, dabbling in drugs and women. Just a guy out to make a buck—any way that he could. The word said he was moving up.

I asked around. I didn't get much. Nothing concrete. No one seemed to know anything, they were shut as tight as a clam at a fish fry. There were a couple of Puerto Rican guys I knew down in Sunset Park. I went over to see them. One didn't know a thing. Told me to move on out. Right away. I moved.

The other guy was a small-time gangster named Pedro. He'd been an old time buddy. He said he knew all about it.

"Okay man, come on, spill it."

"You're not going to like it, amigo. I heard it from a very reliable source, a woman I'm doing." He laughed, a smile crossing his handsome face as he remembered his latest trophy. "It's Fuentes' wife, my man! Seems she'd be a good source, don't you think? She gets lonely for a real man. So we get together sometimes. Usually when Fuentes isn't around. Sometimes when he is. She is a very nice lady. Very tasty."

"What'd she say?"

Pedro shook his head, took a deep breath, "You're right, amigo, it was a set-up."

"But why? I've never done anything to Fuentes. Why does he have it in for me?"

"That's the thing, it's not what you think."

"Then what the hell is it, Pedro!"

"Easy, amigo. This is the story I heard from Rosa. See, Fuentes is a small player, but he's been climbing the ladder to success. He wants to be one of the big boys real bad, have a lot of fancy cars and hot young putas. Maybe he's been seeing too many gangster movies. He's on his way up but the spaghetti benders are in his way. They run things here and in Red Hook and extract a price for what's called 'upward Mobility.'"

"Get to the point, Pedro."

"So, amigo, you were the price. Or part of it. See, Rosa told me about this hit Fuentes has to do for his guinea bosses. A dangerous job. It's against a made man. So it's not 'legal' and has to be done just right. Fuentes is the only one to do it. It involves a big cash payoff. Fuentes is scared shit but has to go through with it. The plan is for him to meet with this big capo. They'll drive up to a corner in a limo somewhere in Brooklyn, Fuentes gets in and gives the capo an attache case that's supposed to be filled with money. Then Fuentes jumps out of the limo and B-O-O-M! No more capo. Get it? It seems that you were the training, amigo. You're no one. A cabby without a family. Fuentes just wanted to see if he could perform the contract according to specifications. So he had to practice. You were the practice. The dry run. You screwed it all up though. You weren't supposed to have lived through it. Fuentes knows you're after him. He's in hiding for now, but he's still got the contract on that capo, so he'll have to come out pretty soon."

I didn't know what to say. All kinds of emotions were boiling over inside me, anger uppermost of all. Then that drifted off into a kind of numb apathy. Fuentes was right, I was a nobody. No friends. No family. No contributor to society at all. Nothing! I wouldn't be missed. No one even knew I was there! The reality sobered my thoughts. I didn't know what to do anymore. I couldn't even think about it.

Then the door burst open and two of the biggest guys I'd ever seen rushed in, guns leveled into our faces before we knew what was happening.

They pushed me to the floor and told me not to move. I didn't. My lips kissed the floor, I shivered. Then they started to rough up Pedro. It was obvious he was the one they were after. I figured Pedro had sold them some bad dope or something. It got intense. Pedro cursed them in super-quick Spanish. The goons roughed him up more. Harder. I saw drops of blood hit the floor around me. Land on my arms and face. It was warm and wet. I couldn't bring myself to look up at what was happening.

Then I heard another voice. Rough but commanding. It was Fuentes! I kept my face to the floor so he wouldn't see who I was, so far he hadn't noticed or cared who I was. He had more personal matters to attend to at the moment.

I guess the news about Pedro fooling around with Rosa finally got to Fuentes. People just love to talk and Pedro had a dick for brains when it came to women. And the one thing everyone without money talks about is sex and who's doing who. That talk gets around. It must of got around to Fuentes too.

I heard them mention me, the gringo. They glanced my way. Fuentes never guessed it was me. I made sure my face was hidden from them as I shook for dear life. One of the goons saw this and laughed. Fuentes said it would be a shame to kill such a fine coward. I just couldn't stop shaking.

Fuentes left the apartment, his two goons dragging the unconscious body of Pedro between them. I knew Pedro was going for a one-way, I'd never see him again.

They were gone almost as quickly as they had appeared and left me on the floor alone sweating rivers. I counted my lucky stars that Fuentes hadn't recognized me. I guess I looked like just another gringo buying drugs from Pedro. I'm sure he never would have guessed the guy looking for him knew Pedro, was in fact, in his rooms at the exact time he went after Pedro. Neither could I.

I can be a gutless wonder when I'm scared, but when someone tries to kill me—and for no reason—it's amazing how that will stiffen even my backbone. I wanted revenge. I wanted to kick Fuentes' ass. Who the hell did he think he was anyway?

I knew Fuentes had to move on the capo soon. I figured to follow him and make my move when the time was right.

It didn't take long. The days moved fast, the time shooting by. I followed Fuentes. Stayed clear of his two goons. Watched and waited.

By the third day I could feel the time drawing near. Early that morning Fuentes left his house. He was alone. Not the usual routine, and he carried a small attaché case tightly in his hand. He looked at it constantly. Carefully. I knew this was it.

Fuentes took a cab to Foster and 11th Street. I followed in an old beat-up hack I borrowed from a friend who used to drive nights, but was shot two weeks ago in the Bronx.

Fuentes looked nervous. Or maybe it was just my imagination and I was the nervous one. The cab let him off at the corner of 11th Street. He walked to the corner of 12th Street. A big black limo waited there. The chauffeur, decked out in uniform, and showing a noticeable bulge under the armpit, opened the door for Fuentes to enter the back of the limo.

Fuentes put one foot down on the velvet carpet. Hunkered down and slowly moved forward. I watched him move in. Saw him say hello to the capo, who was sitting there like a big Italian Buddha at the opposite end of the seat. They shook hands. Fuentes sweated. I could see it running down his face through the sites of the scope.

I pulled the trigger fast, twice, and Fuentes ate two in the back of the head near the stub of the neck.

The spray drenched the capo in blood and gray matter. He shouted in panic, tried to move Fuentes body off of him, tried to get out of the limo but then thought better of it.

The chauffeur/bodyguard was taken by surprise but responded quickly, drawing his piece, guarding the car, looking for me but unable to pick me out. The capo yelled for him to get Fuentes out of the car. The bodyguard helped him dump the Puerto Rican in the gutter. Then the capo saw the attaché case.

The bodyguard handed the attaché case to his boss, closed the door of the limo and ran to the driver side of the big car. He jumped in and gunned the car out into the traffic.

I watched them drive away. They'd gone about five blocks when the capo's curiosity got the better of him.

The explosion blew the doors and sunroof right off the limo. It mulched the capo and the bodyguard into a hundred red beefy pieces.

I watched the EMS workers gather Fuentes out of the gutter and place him onto a gurney, then roll him into the back of a truck. The head guy gave the thumbs down sign over the body. The EMS workers put down their equipment and lit up cigarettes. That's all I wanted to see. Maybe I lost all that upfront money, maybe it never was there to begin with, but Fuentes lost a whole lot more. He's one bastard who won't be messing with me again.

See, I didn't mess up on my dry run. I don't practice.

Death in the Ditch

by Del Marston

T he sun went down but the night was as hot as the day had been,
and besides, who could tell the difference once you were inside
O'Hara's saloon? The streetlamps on Halsted would have
given more light than the incandescents in O'Hara's, but Seamus
O'Hara was like that, too cheap to put in anything brighter.

"You want another one, Marston?"

Marston pressed his belly up to the mahogany and tilted his shot
glass back to get the last drop of bourbon down his gullet. "Yeah,
Billy, sure. And don't use the watered bottle this time. O'Hara's not
watching."

Billy smirked.

The atmosphere in the saloon was close enough to get in your ears
and wet enough to wring out. The Philco in the corner was tuned
to the Cubs' game, covered by telegraph from St. Louis. Borowy
had carried a two-run lead into the ninth. He'd been struggling all
night.

The barkeep poured another shot and put the glass on the bar.
When Marston reached for it Billy hung onto the glass. "Lemme see
your money, Del."

Marston grumbled and threw a coin on the bar. "I ain't *that* low.
Not yet."

"Didn't say you was." Billy released the glass and picked up the coin with one sweep of his hand. It was the only hand he owned. He'd left the other one with the arm it was attached to, on Tarawa. There was a picture of him and his buddies, grinning in their Marine uniforms, on the mirror behind the bar. In the picture, Billy had both hands.

Now he wore a ruptured duck on the lapel of his jacket.

Marston knew him, though. He'd even been to Billy's house up on Bellevue a couple of times. Met Billy's wife and kids. He said, "How's the family, Billy?"

Billy said, "They're down in Indiana, visiting my in-laws."

There was a screech of brakes from Halsted.

Marston uttered an oath.

The Philco said that Schoendienst and Marion had led off the bottom of the ninth with back-to-back bingles.

Billy said, "Why don't that moron Grimm lift that bum? Borowy ain't got it."

Marston lifted his shot glass and studied the bourbon. He dipped the tip of his tongue in it like he wasn't sure if it was whiskey or poison. Knowing O'Hara's stock, it was probably both.

The front door of the saloon swung open and a blonde shot in, running at top speed. She stumbled over a wad of Wrigley's and landed in Marston's arms. He managed to save the bourbon.

The blonde was wearing a white blouse that was pulled off both shoulders to show a chest that Howard Hughes would have paid a million to photograph. She had a little beret pinned to her hair and a skirt that would have showed her knees and then some if there'd been any more light in the joint.

"Don't let 'em get me," she gasped. Her voice sounded like a mother's recipe for the croup: two parts honey and one part whiskey. Or maybe the other way around.

"Let who get you?"

The blonde ducked around Marston, clambered onto a bar stool and tumbled over the bar.

The front door swung open again and a galoot in pinstripes and tommygun slammed into the joint. He pointed the gun around. There were only a couple of customers beside Marston and only Billy serving up the hooch.

The only sound in the room was the Philco. Dyer of the Cards had ordered a hit-and-run and Don Lang had grounded into a round-the-horn twin killing, Pafko to Schenz to Waitkus. Schoendienst scored all the way from second on the play. The Cubs were up by one with two gone.

Billy muttered, "Lift 'im, lift 'im."

130

The gangster pointed his typewriter at Billy. "What's that?" he gritted.

Billy said, "The darned ballgame."

The gangster said, "Youse seen a blonde bimbo bounce in here?"

Billy shook his head.

The gangster said, "Knuckles is mad. You got a back way out?"

Billy nodded toward the back of the bar.

The gangster swung his typewriter around the room. "Anybody sees the bimbo, you tell her that Knuckles wants her, and if she don't show up she's going for a real long swim in Lake Michigan." He headed for the back of the bar.

The Philco said that Slaughter had worked Borowy for a walk and Terry Moore was at bat. Sheffing went out to the mound to talk to Borowy.

Billy said, "For gosh sake, lift 'im."

Marston said, "Borowy can handle it. Moore don't hit him."

There was a lot of crashing and thumping around in the back. The thug reappeared, brushing dust from his suit with his free hand. The typewriter hung from the other. "Where's that darn alley go?"

"Adams."

"She's gone, then. She shows again, tell her what I told you."

Billy nodded. "You bet."

The thug slammed out of the saloon. Marston slid off his stool and swayed across the room. He pressed his face to the glass. "Looks like a Capone job."

Billy hawked. "Capone's dead two years."

"His boys ain't."

Marston swayed back to his stool. He was wearing a brown suit with no crease at all in the trousers. He had on scuffed wingtips. He was wearing a brown hand-painted tie with slashes of orange and purple on it. He was wearing a soft gray hat with some dark patches from old sweat.

The blonde slid her head back up from underneath the bar. "Thanks," she said. She straightened out her beret.

Billy said, "You get the heck out of here. I never seen you. I never want ta see you. You got me?"

"I got you." To Marston, "Stink still out there?"

"What?"

"I said—"

"I heard you. That was Stink Calhoun. Good thing he didn't recognize me. I guess a guy looking for you wouldn't notice another guy. Not unless there was something wrong with him."

Marston drank half of his bourbon and carried the shot glass with him. He grunted when he put his weight back on his feet. "Can't keep climbing on and off stools like that." He went over to the glass again to look for Calhoun's car.

The announcer on the Philco was yelling his lungs out. The whole thing took place while Moore was at bat. Two outs and the catcher at bat and Dyer had him bunt. It was a dumb call. So dumb the Cubs were caught with their thumbs in their ears. Moore wound up on first, Slaughter on second, and Musial was coming up.

Billy said, "Pull Borowy."

Marston came back from the glass. The brim of his hat was getting wet and dirty from the steamy grime on the glass. There was a place that was almost clean from Marston leaning against it with his hat on. "Car's gone."

The blonde said, "There might be another."

Marston said, "Stink's the bottom of the heap. Knuckles Florio mustn't want you so bad. What do they call you?"

The blonde found the wooden flap and came out from behind the bar. "Depends. Who's calling?"

Marston said, "Your mother."

The blonde said, "Sweetheart."

Marston said, "Yeah. Your mother and half of the Seventh Fleet."

The blonde said, "You got a car? Fifty bucks if you take me home."

"I thought it worked the other way around."

The blonde said something impolite.

The crowd noise on the Philco got loud. The announcer was going nuts but he was a Cubs announcer so he was going nuts in a most unhappy way. It took Marston a while to figure out what had happened while he was bantering with the blonde.

"Musial," Billy said. "I told ya Grimm oughtta pull Borowy. Friggin' Musial."

The blonde said, "How about it?"

Marston said, "Where's your digs?"

"Evanston."

"Evanston? Why don't we got to the North Pole while we're at it? Evanston!"

"It's where I live, darn it! How long will it take to drive me there? I don't want to be on the street after that visit from Stink."

"Yeah? You must spend most of your time on the street, though."

Billy reached over and changed stations on the radio. Ginny Simms started singing something about love.

132

The blonde turned away from Marston. She had a purse with her. She bent over it, like she was looking for her lipstick. When she straightened up and turned back she was pointing a little blue automatic at Marston. It couldn't have been bigger than a .22 but at a few feet it could make a little hole in his heart and he'd still be dead.

"Evanston," Marston said. "That's a nice town. Once met a kid who went to Northwestern, wanted a drink and said she couldn't find one in Evanston."

"It's a dry town," the blonde said.

"Right. Okay, sweetheart, let's go."

She put the gun back in her purse but she kept her hand on it. Marston figured her finger was still on the trigger. "You first," the blonde said. "Any of Knuckles Florio's gunsels out there, you get it before I do."

Marston finished his drink and slapped the glass back on the mahogany. "Borowy's losing it," he said.

Billy said, "Hurry back. We appreciate your rewarding trade."

Marston pushed the door open. There were still a couple of customer's in O'Hara's. They hadn't said a word or made a move during the episode. Dedicated men.

There were a few people on the sidewalk but nobody who looked like Florio's men. Marston looked over his shoulder. The blonde was there, pointing her purse at his back. Marston said, "You don't believe in ladies' entrances."

"I don't believe in ladies. Where's your heap?"

Marston led the way to his DeSoto.

The blonde said, "Jeebers, maybe I should of went with Stink."

Marston opened the door on the passenger side of the coupé and helped the blonde in. Then he walked around the car and climbed in behind the wheel.

The blonde said, "You're a real gentleman."

Marston said, "You wouldn't know." He turned the key and pressed down on the starter. The DeSoto heaved a couple of times and then started. He put it in gear and pulled away from the curb. As they moved toward Evanston the air got a little cooler and a lot cleaner.

The blonde said, "Right there. The brick one."

Marston parked the car. "How about my fifty?"

The blonde said, "Upstairs." She made him go inside first. The building was a few stories high. There was a streetlamp outside and a couple of trees. There was even a little lawn. It looked like a nice building. Evanston was a nice town.

133

She had an apartment on the second floor, up a flight of marble steps with an iron hand railing. The place even smelled clean. Marston was getting impressed.

Outside her door she said, "Step away. Get out of arm's reach." She put her other hand in her purse and came up with a bunch of keys. She had to juggle the purse and the keys and gun but she got the door open.

Marston said, "I don't know what you're so scared of, baby. You brought me here, I didn't bring you."

She jerked her head. "Inside."

He looked around. A nice place. Big couch, a Victrola, couple of lamps and overstuffed chairs.

"Sit down."

"You want to give me that kale, I'll be on my way."

"You're in no hurry."

"I guess not." She put her purse down but she was still holding the gun. "If I put this down," she said.

He raised his eyebrows.

"You can make a lot more than fifty out of this," the blonde said.

Marston said, "How? You want me to tangle with Florio, not a chance."

The blonde said, "You're Del Marston, right?"

"Yeah."

"Okay. You might as well know my name. It's Mildred Trendler. I share this place with another girl. Gladys Hendricks. She's a real sweet kid. Doesn't know from nothing. Came from out of town and I'm trying to take care of her. I don't know why."

Marston said, "You got a bottle here?"

Mildred jerked her head toward a cabinet. "Help yourself. Pour a glass for me, too. Look at this, I'm shaking."

She was.

Marston opened the cabinet, found a bottle of scotch. He picked it up and looked at the label. He said, "This is good stuff."

"I know."

He found the kitchen and brought back two glasses. You don't want it diluted, do you, Mildred?"

She shook her head. She said, again, "I'm shaking."

He poured them each a glass of scotch. He walked over and stood in front of her and held out one glass.

She took the glass and took a big swallow of it.

He was standing very close to her.

She put her arms around him and put the little automatic against the back of his head and pushed his face down toward her own. She turned her face up toward his and they exchanged a long kiss. Her mouth tasted of scotch. The gun on the back of his head was cold and hard.

Mildred said, "Thanks. That was okay." She stepped away from him. "I got to go in the other room. Wait for a minute."

She opened a door and walked into another room. He watched her go. She looked great from the back. He saw a corner of a bed with a pink chenille bedspread before she kicked the door closed behind her. He tossed his hat onto one of the overstuffed chairs and took a big drink of his scotch.

From the bedroom he heard the sound of a single shot.

2

Marston dropped his glass. It hit the floor without breaking and scotch splashed all over the cuffs of his trousers. He ran to the bedroom door and opened it.

Mildred Trendler was standing over the bed. She had the little blue automatic in her hand and there was smoke rising like a sinister snake from its muzzle.

There was a body on the bed.

Marston took a couple of steps toward the bed and looked down at the body. "What the heck!" he exclaimed. "I know that guy. Is he dead?"

Mildred said, "As a mackerel."

"What happened? I thought—was he waiting for you? What was he—I thought you were—"

"I know what you thought."

"That's Cockeye Johnson."

"I know who he is."

"He's—was—Florio's number two guy."

"I know who he is."

"Jeebers! We better get out of here!"

Mildred said, "Right." She skipped past him, put her hand on the doorknob. She spun around and tossed the little blue automatic at him. He caught it in mid-air. She slammed the door behind her. Before Marston could move he heard her fumble with the latch.

He worked the slide on the automatic. The chamber was empty. He popped the magazine. The bullet Mildred had fired into Cockeye Johnson must have been the last one in the gun.

From the living room came the sound of the Victrola. Mildred must have put on a record. It was an old song. The Ted Weems orchestra with Elmo Tanner whistling "Heartaches."

Marston rattled the doorknob but it was no good. He turned back to the bed and put his hand on Cockeye Johnson's face. The skin was cold. Johnson must have been dead for hours. How could that be? Mildred Trendler had just shot him a minute ago. Marston had heard the shot. The smoke had still been coming out of the pea-shooter when he came through the door.

He felt the barrel. It was warm. He sniffed it. Just fired, no question.

He shoved the pea-shooter into his jacket pocket and grabbed Cockeye Johnson by the shoulder to turn him over. Cockeye was stiff. Rigor mortis. That meant he must have been dead for hours. Marston turned him back.

The record ended and started over again.

Marston looked at the pillow where Cockeye Johnson's head had been. There was a deep impression there but there was no bullet hole. Two thicknesses of skull could probably stop a .22 round. Probably the bullet was still somewhere inside Cockeye's head.

Next, Marston turned Cockeye back over. He looked closely at the hole in the middle of Cockeye's forehead. The edges were blackened. Marston ran his finger around the edges of the hole and looked at it. Black. Powder marks. Mildred Trendler had held the gun right up against Cockeye's forehead and fired.

Maybe there was already a bullet hole there. Or maybe Cockeye was dead from some other cause.

The record ended and started again.

Marston sat down on the edge of the bed to think for a minute. Then he got up and looked around the room. It was an ordinary bedroom. There was a night table with a lamp and a book on it. He pulled open the drawer in the night table and found an address book. He flipped through it once and then slipped it into his pocket.

The dresser contained nothing but the expected blouses and stockings and other women's garb. There was a closet and he looked inside it.

He found a couple of ordinary dresses, a light spring coat and a heavy winter one. Behind these were some very strange things. They looked like tight outfits, form-fitting in fact. They were black, and they were made of leather. They looked almost like those frogman suits that the UDTs had used in the war. But the frogman suits had been rubber.

There was a rack and some masks on it, too.

Marston looked at the stuff and whistled.

In the back of the closet was a cardboard box. He opened it and looked inside. It was full of photos of shapely women dressed in one of the leather frogman suits. In most of the photos the women were wearing masks, but in a few of them their face was exposed.

One of the women was Mildred Trendler. Short, voluptuous. Her figure was wild. Sometimes it looked as if there were flaps in the leather that were opened to show pale flesh and dark bits. In the photos where Mildred was unmasked her blonde hair flowed over her shoulders in soft waves. She looked a little like Susan Hayward, or maybe Gloria Graham.

The second woman was taller than Mildred. She had sharp features and straight, black hair. She had a peculiar smile. Marston tried to figure out what looked odd about her. Maybe it was her teeth. Yeah. The top canines were longer than any he'd ever seen. Jeebers, she was a vampire.

Marston closed his eyes. This was probably the roomie. Gladys Hendricks. The innocent kid from out of town. Sure she was.

In some of the photos Mildred or Gladys appeared alone, but in others you could see one of the women holding a whip, standing over naked men who were kneeling in submission. In some of the pictures the men were actually being whipped. In others they were licking the women's boots.

Then there were the ones of Mildred and Gladys together, with parts of their leather costumes opened. Marston squeezed his eyes shut again for a minute.

Marston looked more closely at the pictures, then he stopped and whistled. He peered even more closely at the faces of naked, humiliated men, whistled softly and slipped a couple of the photos into his pocket. Then he closed up the box and made his way back into the bedroom.

He heard the needle scratch across the face of the disk as someone knocked it over. He turned and headed for the window. Mildred Trendler's flat was on the second story of the building. There were trees outside. Marston might be able to leap from the window sill, catch onto a branch and climb to the ground.

He threw open the window sash and was climbing onto the sill when the bedroom door crashed open and a pair of blue-jacketed toughs poured into the room, guns pointing every way. He was onto the sill and halfway out when the guns boomed and bullets whacked into the wall and smashed into the glass panes in the window.

He was halfway out the window already and there was no turning back into that hail of lead. He had to leap blindly. There was no time to aim for a tree. For a moment it looked like he might make it, but something smashed against his head as hard as a sledgehammer against an anvil. He had time to wonder if he was dead but he didn't have time to realize that he was alive before he hit the ground and everything went black.

There was a roaring in his ears and a red sheet in front of his eyes. Strong hands had seized him by the arms and turned him over onto his back, not at all gently. He must be alive. There was a flashlight shining into his face and he heard voices, especially a growling, gravelly voice giving orders to the men who crouched over him and circled around him.

They heaved him to his feet and half-shoved, half-dragged him to a sedan. Somebody opened the back door and Marston was hustled inside. Blue uniforms sat on either side of him. One of the cops reached across then slapped a pair of heavy bracelets on his wrists.

The driver threw in the gears and the car roared down the quiet street. Evanston might be a peaceful town but the peace had been disturbed.

Marston's head hung onto his chest. He tried to reach up and feel it but the cops wouldn't let him lift his cuffed mitts. He turned to the cop beside him and tried to say something but his mouth was full of cotton and when he managed to get a couple of words out the cop slugged him in the mouth.

"Shut up."

Marston could see out the window. The car was headed back to Chicago. There wasn't much traffic, and nobody paid any attention. The atmosphere in the car was hot and close, and somebody stunk of cigar smoke and Marston knew that he had bourbon in his belly and scotch in his trousers.

When they got to the cop station they drove into the garage and dragged him out of the car and downstairs. They couldn't be going to kill him, anyhow. If they were, they wouldn't have bothered to bring him here. They'd have taken him somewhere else and got rid of him before this.

A couple of cops threw him in a cell and walked out. They jerked the door shut as they left and Marston heard the heavy lock clatter into place. He turned around. The cuffs were still on his wrists and he was still wearing his brown suit and his hand-painted tie. The cops had even thrown his soft hat into the cell after him. Considerate of them.

He put the hat on his head, feeling the place where he'd been injured. It felt like a bullet had creased his skull just above one ear. It must have happened as he jumped from Mildred Trendler's window.

There was one light bulb in the cell. It was screwed into a receptacle in the ceiling. It was protected by a wire-mesh gadget that looked

138

something like a catcher's mask. It was turned on and it gave about as much light as a refrigerator bulb.

"Hey, sweetie, got a fag?"

Marston looked at the other man in the cell. He was as big as a horse and had a broken nose and long dirty hair. He was wearing coveralls with dried vomit on them. The stench hit Marston like a wave of sea water. He dry-retched and shook his head. "Nope."

"Too bad."

He sank slowly onto the bench that ran along one wall.

Broken-nose said, "Plain drunk?"

Marston ignore him.

Broken-nose said, "I puked on a cop's shoes."

Marston ignored him.

Broken-nose grunted. He was stretched out on the cell's single cot. "Stuck-up princess, ain't ya?"

Marston felt his pockets. The little blue automatic was gone. So was the address book. So were the photos. "Hot spit," he grumbled.

A cop with sergeant's stripes opened the cell door and stood outside the cell with keys in his hand. "Get out here," he growled.

Broken-nose shoved himself upright. "Hallelujah! So long, princess, look me up sometime."

The cop slapped Broken-nose with his billy. "Not you, prettikins, him." He pointed at Marston.

Marston straightened his hat and marched out of the cell, keeping as steady a stride as he could manage. He head was throbbing and his stomach was sending up sour waves. Outside the cell he turned back and said, "Don't call me princess, princess."

The cop grabbed him by the elbow and steered him down the corridor. It was lined with cells. The cop didn't say a word. Neither did Marston.

They passed through a doorway and into another corridor. The cop steered Marston into a room the size of a closet and slammed the door behind him. There was a table in the middle of the room. There were three chairs. They were wooden and hard and had been painted during the Warren G. Harding administration. There was a cracked pitcher on the table, and a filthy glass. The pitcher looked like it was full of stale water. There was a dead fly floating in it.

Marston still had his hat and he still had his handcuffs. Win some, lose some. There were no windows in the room.

The door thunked open and a uniform sergeant and a plain-clothes dick slaunched into the room. The sergeant put a hand like a Christmas ham on Marston's chest and shoved. The back of Marston's knees hit the edge of one of the chairs and he thumped into the chair.

He noticed the cop's uniform for the first time. "Wait a minute. You're a Chicago bull. How come this ain't Evanston?"

The bull looked at the plainclothes dick. The dick nodded. The bull grinned at Marston, all sweetness and good will, like William Bendix grinning at Alan Ladd in *The Glass Key*. He backhanded Marston across the chops, hard. The bull said, "I'll explain that to you. The explanation is, *shut up*!" He backhanded Marston the other way with his other hand. "What else would you like explained, Marston?"

Marston shook his head, half to try and clear it and half to tell the bull that he didn't want any more explanations. He tried to say something but he slumped onto the table. He wasn't out but he was completely limp.

The bull walked around behind Marston and grabbed him by the shoulders and hoisted him up and held him in his chair.

The dick turned one of the other chairs around and sat on it with his arms folded across the back. He looked at Marston. "Want to make a statement? I'll get a stenographer in here."

Marston shook his head.

"Why not? Give it a break, Marston. Jeebers, we found you with the corpse, you had the murder weapon, you tried to flee. The door was even locked. Just like in the murder mysteries. Calling Philo Vance." He gave out an ugly guffaw.

Marston tried to talk but he only managed a dry heave.

The dick pulled away, as if he was scared to get puke on his suit. It was a nice suit, in fact. Almost as nice as Stink Calhoun's was.

Marston managed to grunt in the direction of the water jug.

The dick nodded to the uniform bull.

The bull let go of Marston and Marston slumped in his chair. The bull picked up the pitcher and poured about a quarter of a shot of water into the glass and handed it to Marston.

Marston took the glass and lifted it gingerly toward his mouth. He opened his lips and poured the water in. He realized that the fly was in it and spewed the water out. It ran down the plainclothes dick's face, onto his white collar, his dark repp-striped tie, onto his double-breasted dark-gray suit.

The dick jumped up and leaped across the table. "You gosh-darned blankety-blank!" he screamed. "You no-good louse!" He dragged Marston out of his chair and threw him onto the floor. The uniform bull stepped back. The dick let out a shrill yell and jumped onto Marston's chest.

Marston heaved and the dick tumbled off and stumbled backwards until he hit the wall. Marston climbed to his feet and staggered across the room toward the dick. He brought his cuffed fists upward together and hit the dick on the bottom of the jaw.

140

The dick yelped like a dog that just got whacked by a car and slid sideways along the wall.

Marston went after him, hit him with his shoulder.

The dick screamed again and ran across the room.

Marston turned around and saw that the uniform bull was watching the proceeding. He had an amused look on his face.

The dick screamed at the bull and the bull shrugged, smiled again like Bendix, and lumbered across the room toward Marston. He patted Marston gently on the cheek then picked him up bodily and threw him across the room. Marston slammed into the table and it collapsed into a heap of kindling wood with him in the middle of it.

He started to get up again but the plainclothes dick had advanced and delivered a hard kick with the toe of a pointed shoe, into Marston's ribs. Marston grunted and the dick delivered another kick. Marston's ribs and his insides were a burning agony. Every time he thought they couldn't hurt any worse the dick delivered another kick and Marston's pain climbed to a new level of agony. He thought that only unconsciousness or death could save him, and he didn't care which one did.

Then the uniform bull lifted him up again, actually holding him in his arms like a kid, and crooning little words into his ear. The dick had gone over to the door. Somebody else was standing in the door. He was talking to the dick with an urgent look on his face and chopping his hands in the air for emphasis like Harry Truman.

The bull was pacing back and forth like a father, rocking Marston in his arms.

The plainclothes dick came back into the center of the room and said, "Put him down. Get him in shape. Get the bracelets off him. Bring him out." He left the room and slammed the door behind him.

The uniform bull found a bandanna in his pocket and dipped it in what was left of the water and wiped Marston's face off. The cop kept muttering something over and over. Marston couldn't figure out what it was. Finally he got it. The cop was muttering, "Poor baby! Poor baby!"

He got Marston back onto his feet and gave him a little water to drink. He found a bunch of keys in his pocket and tried them, one after another, until he found the right one for Marston's handcuffs. He took off the cuffs and dropped them into his pocket. "You okay now? Did that basket case hurt you? I hope you're okay."

Marston couldn't figure it out.

The cop steered him out of the room, back to the front of the station. His knees were wobbly as Jell-O.

The plainclothes dick was waiting. He'd changed his outfit completely. He had on a hound's tooth checked jacket, a maize button-down shirt with a paisley tie of the same color, a pair of butternut-brown flannel slacks and polished tassel loafers.

"Get out of here, you disgusting filth."

Marston shook his head. "What?"

"I said, get out of here. We don't want you. Get the heck out of here before I lose control."

Marston staggered to the front door. He shoved it open. It took all his strength to do it. He stood at the top of a flight of steps leading down to the sidewalk. He looked around. There was some moonlight coming down. The night was still hot.

He started down the steps.

3

When he was halfway down the steps the doors of the big sedan swung open and dark figures climbed out. Marston turned around and ran back up the steps. He grabbed the handles on the cop station doors and yanked.

The doors wouldn't budge. They had been locked from the inside.

Marston turned around. There were a couple of toughs with blasters in their mitts pointing up at him. One tough was holding a tommygun, the other was holding a big automatic.

Marston dove sideways over the railing on the side of the stoop. There were bushes on the ground and he landed shoulders first in the bushes. They broke his fall enough to keep him from getting kayoed but the breath went out of him with a loud whoosh.

He shook his head and got to his knees.

There were voices yelling.

Marston managed to stumble a couple of steps on wobbly legs then he saw the tough with the tommygun swing the gun around. The wooden butt of the tommy crashed into the side of Marston's head. His skull exploded into a million stars and rockets. He went back to his hands and knees and waited for the second clout of the tommy butt or maybe for the lead that would tear into him and end the one-sided fight.

All of this for fifty fish and he never even got to see the kale.

"Get up, Marston."

Why the heck didn't they just finish him and get it over with? He felt a fresh pain in his ribs. The big thug was prodding him with the tommygun. He was holding it by the stock and prodding Marston with the front blade sight. It felt like a knife going into him.

"Get over here. Get in the car."

The thug prodded him, shoved him with his shoe. It wasn't a real kick, just a hard shove. Marston went down flat on the ground.

"In the car!"

The thug let go a yammering blast of tommygun rounds into the ground next to Marston. One of the slugs hit a rock the size of an Idaho potato and a sliver of rock whizzed across Marston's bicep slicing a strip out of his jacket and etching a burning furrow into his arm.

"In the car," the gorilla growled again.

Marston tried to get up but he couldn't make it. But he didn't want to die or let the gorilla let loose another volley maybe into his body so he dragged himself across the cop station lawn toward the big sedan.

The thugs stood by and let him crawl to the car. He crossed the sidewalk like a slug the day after a rainstorm. The back door of the sedan was open and they stood back and watched him climb in. He collapsed onto the backseat of the sedan.

Somebody slammed the door behind him and the driver threw in the gears and the car screamed away from the curb, its lights off. Half a block away the driver turned the lights on.

Marston lay on the backseat, half-conscious. The thugs were talking about something and he couldn't make it out. They didn't blindfold him and he could see the streets going past. He tried to figure out what time it was but he couldn't do it. It was still dark outside but it might be ten or eleven o'clock at night or it might be three or four o'clock in the morning. He didn't see any traffic or lights on in any of the houses.

When the car pulled to the curb again Marston saw they were in front of a hotel in one of the suburbs, maybe Skokie or maybe even Cicero. Somebody came out of the hotel and talked to the driver for a minute and the driver threw the car into reverse and backed up a few yards and turned across the sidewalk and down a ramp into the hotel garage in the basement.

The thugs dragged Marston out of the sedan and into an elevator. One of the thugs gave the uniformed operator a look and the operator threw over the handle and Marston felt his stomach sink as the elevator rose.

Upstairs they took him across the hall and knocked on a door. After a minute Marston heard the door click open and it swung back and the thugs shoved him inside.

Knuckles Florio sat behind a desk the size of Butler Field. He had a cigar in his mouth and a carnation in his lapel. A woman was standing behind his chair with her hands on the sides of his head massaging his temples.

Florio looked at Marston and whispered something to the woman. The woman said something to a thug sitting in a chair near the wall. The thug said something to the gorillas standing at Marston's sides.

The gorilla with the tommygun sat down. The one with the automatic in his mitt shoved it into Marston's ribs. He said, "Into the washroom. Mr. Florio don't want ta talk ta you till you get cleaned up."

With the automatic in his ribs Marston managed to wobble out of the sitting room and through a bedroom into the washroom and slump over the sink. The gorilla threw a towel at him. "Here." Marston looked into the mirror. He was a mess. His hat was gone. His face was filthy and puffed. Blood from the scalp wound he'd got coming out the window of Mildred Trendler's apartment in Evanston had soaked through his hair and twigs and leafs had stuck in the gooey blood when he hit the lawn at the cop station.

His shirt was torn and soaked with blood.

"Jeebers," the gorilla growled, "you're a mess." He reached past Marston and turned on the water.

Marston dropped the towel into the sink and let it get soaked and then he cleaned off his face the best he could. There wasn't much more he could do. It made him feel a little less rotten.

He said, "Okay, buster. Let's go see your boss."

They managed to get back through the bedroom, Marston wobbling and staggering along, the gorilla plodding along behind him with the automatic still shoved into Marston's ribs. The bedroom looked like something out of *The Thief of Baghdad*. There was a mirror on the ceiling over the bed and there were red satin sheets on the bed. The only thing missing was June Duprez in a transparent veil and a pair of baggy trousers.

There was a sixteen millimeter movie projector and a screen across from the bed. Marston wondered if there was a movie camera and some rolls of sixteen millimeter film in the Evanston apartment, too.

He managed to get back into the sitting room. The gorilla shoved him into a chair opposite Knuckles Florio's. The woman behind Florio was wearing a tight dress that covered her from her neck

144

down. It was dead black and made out of some kind of shiny material. She wasn't wearing anything under it. She was wearing lipstick the color of fresh blood and long fingernails with sharp points and glossy polish of the same color. Except for those spots of blood-red everything about her was dead black or dead white.

Knuckles Florio blew a cloud of cigar smoke at the ceiling. There was a cut-glass decanter on the desk in front of him and a highball glass filled halfway with golden brown liquid. He laid his cigar on the rim of a cut-glass ashtray and took a sip from the highball glass.

The woman who had been standing behind him leaned across his shoulder, rubbing her torso against him. She picked up the cut-glass decanter and poured a little more liquid into his highball glass, bringing it up to the exact level it had been before Florio took his sip of it.

Florio folded his hands in front of his chest, his elbows on top of his desk. His shirt cuffs came a couple of inches past his suitcoat sleeves. He was wearing gold cufflinks with diamonds in them. He nodded at Marston like a friendly old priest. He smiled and it made him look like Edward Arnold.

Marston didn't say anything to Florio. He just looked at the woman behind Florio. She looked familiar to him, and he tried to figure out if she was somebody he'd ever known. When she leaned forward and pressed against Florio, Marston recognized her. She was Gladys Hendricks, the innocent kid from out of town.

"Where's Mildred?" Florio asked. His voice wasn't much more than a whisper, even when he spoke directly to Marston.

Marston said, "I don't know."

Florio raised his eyebrows.

Gladys Hendricks leaned over him, her arms folded across his shoulders. Her hands covered Florio's. The scarlet polish on her pointed fingernails looked like blobs of luminous blood. Her long hair brushed against Florio's face.

She put her red mouth to his ear and said something.

Florio nodded.

Gladys Hendricks stood up again.

Florio turned around and said something to her in his whispery voice.

Gladys Hendricks crossed the room. Marston could see that she was wearing black boots with long spiky heels. She sat down on a couch underneath a painting. Marston watched her settle onto the couch. The picture over the couch was in a fancy gold frame. It was a big painting of Franklin Roosevelt. There was a piece of black bunting hanging from the frame, covering up a lot of the gold.

Florio took another puff of his cigar and blew out the smoke. He whispered, "You know me, don't you, Marston?"

"Never had the pleasure before but I know who you are."

"Really. And who am I?"

"You've got a great future in modelling."

The smile on Florio's face turned to a snarl, the way it did in a movie like *Meet John Doe* when boss Arnold was crossed. But Gladys Hendricks didn't look like Barbara Stanwyck and Del Marston sure as heck wasn't any Gary Cooper.

"Where is Mildred Trendler?"

"Jeebers, Mr. Florio, I'm afraid I can't give you anything about a client. I'm on retainer to Mildred."

"You are, are you? Says who?"

"She hired me." He could see part of one window in the room and he could see that the sun was coming up over Lake Michigan and the Chicago suburbs between the hotel and the lake. "Last night. At O'Hara's saloon on Halsted. I thought you knew about that. Your boy Stink Calhoun was there."

"All right. And then?"

"Then we went to her place in Evanston. She set me up. There was a stiff there and she set me up with it for the cops."

Florio smiled. "Yeah. I hear they caught you red handed."

Marston shrugged. "If you want to call it that. She locked me in with the stiff and left. I have no idea where she went. Maybe back to O'Hara's. I don't know. She must have called the cops from a pay phone. Is that why the Chicago cops showed up even though it was Evanston?"

Florio grinned. "You're very observant, Marston. Now, what am I going to do with you?"

"I can't tell you what to do." He shot a glance at Gladys Hendricks. She had a drink in one hand and a cigarette in the other. Smoke from the cigarette was drifting up past the portrait of FDR.

"Maybe I'll just get rid of you." Florio reached into a desk drawer. He came out with Mildred Trendler's blue automatic. He played with the gat. "Ain't this a cute pea shooter? It's like a toy. Watch this, Marston."

He pointed the blue automatic at Gladys Hendricks. Marston shot a glance at her. She got whiter than ever. Florio squeezed the trigger of the blue automatic. The hammer clicked. Gladys jumped, then settled back on the couch, her face sagging from an expression of alarm into an angry pout.

Innocent kid from out of town.

"You really like that sick stuff, Florio?" Marston knew that Florio could do anything he wanted to him. He might as well go for broke. "Whips and boots? Then what are you ashamed of? You don't think you'd be laughed out of town if those photos came out? You have some movies of yourself getting your kicks with the leather broads? I bet they'd be popular at cop headquarters and in the newspapers. I can just see it, maybe stills in the *Sun* or the *Trib*."

Florio came to his feet with a rasping sound coming from his throat. "You son of a sea cook! I ought to kill you! I ought to kill you right now!" He pointed the blue automatic at Marston and pulled the trigger and the hammer went *click, click, click*.

He collapsed back into his chair and dropped the blue automatic back into the drawer and slammed it shut. He reached inside his jacket and pulled a nickel plated .45 and pointed it at Marston. "No more games. You got one hour to find Mildred for me or you're fish food." He gestured with the .45. "Go on. Your car's downstairs. I had my boys bring it in from Evanston. Get out of here."

Marston rose slowly to his feet. He smiled at Florio, at the thugs who guarded the room, at Gladys Hendricks. "I can only find Mildred if I have help. Come on, Gladys." He held out his hand to her.

Gladys Hendricks shrunk away from Marston, but Florio whispered, "Go on, Gladys. Help him find Mildred." She shook her head and pulled even farther away. Florio whispered, "Go on. Do what I tell you, you witch!"

Shaking, Gladys got to her feet. She stared into Marston's face, shot him a look of murderous hatred. He smiled back at her.

Florio made a gesture toward one of his thugs. "Give him his car keys," he whispered. The thug reached into his pocket and pulled Marston's car keys and threw them at Marston.

4

The DeSoto was standing in front of the hotel and Marston could see that it had even been washed off and polished. Marston shook his head. Gladys Hendricks gave him one final smoldering look and climbed into the car.

Marston turned the key and mashed down on the starter and the DeSoto's engine roared to life. "Innocent kid from out of town," he husked at Gladys.

"Fusser," Gladys answered. She had a good voice.

"How'd you get into that filthy racket? Mildred get you into it? How old are you anyhow? You couldn't be much more than twenty. You ought to be going to the movies with your boyfriend and planning for your wedding and babies."

"Don't hand me that guff. That's for suckers. You know how much this pays? What do you make a year, you cheap two-bit gumshoe?"

"Not enough, Gladys." Marston chewed on his lip. "But at least I can look in the mirror when I shave."

Gladys changed her tone. "Listen, you fool, you don't know what you've gotten into. Florio is dead serious. If we don't find Mildred for him he'll kill you." She drew a breath and let out something like a sob. "And probably me," she added.

Innocent kid from out of town.

"Right, kiddo. You're in this with me, right up to your neck. So you better help me out whether you like me or not."

"What do you want? Where are we going?"

They were headed back toward Chicago. It was full morning by now. Marston pulled the car to the curb in front of a hash house. The joint was full of workers stoking up on ham and eggs before they reported to their jobs. There were a few night owls scattered among them, nibbling at pastries and trying to swig enough coffee to get them home without running their flivvers up elm trees.

Marston guided Gladys Hendricks toward a vacant booth and signalled to the waitress. Practically every head in the place swivelled as Gladys Hendricks swayed past them in her black outfit. It was not designed for this kind of joint half an hour after dawn but it would have to do.

The waitress brought over their menus. She gave Gladys Hendricks a quick eyeballing then poked Marston in the shoulder. "Got a new cookie, Otto? Don't think you ought to put on a fresh shirt for a classy dish like her?" To Gladys Hendricks she said, "Don't take no guff from Otto, kid. He's an okay guy but sometimes you got to watch him."

They ordered some food.

Gladys Hendricks said, "How come she called you Otto? I thought your name was Del Marston."

"It is. Keep a lid on it. Around here I'm Otto Schultz."

"All right. You're a deep one, ain't you? We got to have a plan. God, you look awful, Del."

Marston said, "I've had a rotten night. I don't suppose you have any weapons with you." He ran his eyes over her form-fitting costume. "Other than the ones Mother Nature gave you. They all grow like that in Iowa or wherever the heck you came from?"

"Nebraska. You ought to see my sister." She was almost grinning and Marston found himself thinking that this kid might not have turned out so bad if she'd only had half a break. What happened, what went wrong? he wondered. Maybe a brother or a boyfriend who went off to fight the Axis and never came back. Heck, Billy the bartender had left an arm on Tarawa. Maybe Gladys Hendricks' sweetie was still there. Maybe that was what had turned her wrong. It was a darn shame, but there wasn't anything Marston could do about it. Not now.

"Get down to earth. You don't have a purse or anything, do you?"

"Not the way that basket case threw me out of the hotel. Everything's still up there."

"Okay, then. First thing we need to do is pick up a little ordnance. Knuckles' boys go heeled everywhere. We got to have some artillery of our own." He started to get up.

The waitress smacked their plates down on the table. The food looked kind of greasy but at least it was something to stick in their bellies. Marston reached over and stuck a piece of toast in the middle of an egg. He added a slice or bacon and shoved the mess in his mouth. Around it he said, "You eat up. I'll be back in a little while."

He disappeared through the swinging doors into the kitchen. In about fifteen minutes he was back with a hatbox under his arm. He sat down at the table and looked at his food. The grease was starting to congeal on the eggs and the bacon and the coffee had turned cold and there was a little film of rancid gunk on the top of it. He sighed and picked up a glass of orange juice and drained it in one gulp.

"Better than nothing," he gasped. "Not much better, though." He threw a bill down on the table and grabbed Gladys Hendricks by the arm and steered her toward the door. There was a fresh batch of customers in the booths by now and they did the same neck-swivelling act that they had when Gladys Hendricks arrived.

Marston handed Gladys Hendricks into the DeSoto's passenger seat and walked around the car and climbed in behind the wheel. She could of run away while he was doing it but she didn't. He was pleased by that but also puzzled.

He got onto Kingsbury and drove down it to Bellevue and turned and drove to a neat little bungalow with roses growing outside it. He pulled the DeSoto over to the curb and set the handbrake. He reached behind him and got the hatbox and opened it up. Inside were two gats. One was an automatic in a shoulder holster. The other was a revolver in a pistol belt.

Neither of these gats was a popgun like Mildred Trendler's little blue .22 automatic. The automatic was an Army .45, some GI's war souvenir, probably, listed on a military manifest as lost in combat at Anzio or Normandy or Iwo Jima, smuggled home in a duffel bag and sold for rotgut or reefer to ease the pain of memory. The revolver was a Colt Peacemaker, who knows how old, maybe the very gun that Doc Holiday used at the OK Corral.

Marston checked both gats to make sure they were fully loaded. He saw that the automatic had a full magazine and he slammed it home into the pistol grip. He worked the slide once to load a round into the chamber. He slipped six cartridges into the Peacemaker's cylinder. They glittered beneath the hot morning sun. He snapped the cylinder into place and handed the Peacemaker to Gladys Hendricks. "You know how to use this thing? Never mind, I know you do. Come on." He opened the door and climbed out of the car.

By the time they reached the front door of the house Del Marston had the shoulder holster in place under his suit coat and with the filth and bagginess of the suit you couldn't tell the difference. Gladys Hendricks had the pistol belt strapped on over her hip-clinging black dress and you could sure as shooting tell that she had something on.

Marston pounded his fist against the front door and when it opened a crack he shoved it the rest of the way and stepped into the house, pulling Gladys Hendricks behind him.

"Hello, Billy," Del Marston said.

"I didn't think you'd figure it out so fast," Billy said. Behind him Mildred sat on the couch nursing a cup filled with black liquid. There was a bottle on the low table in front of her and she poured something from it into the coffee while she watched Marston's arrival. The bottle was full of Irish whiskey.

Mildred Trendler said, "Gladys. What a treat. I'm really surprised to see you here."

Gladys Hendricks pulled the revolver from her holster and pointed it at the others. To Del Marston she said, "Get over there by the mantle. Keep your hands up. Don't try and get that rod out of your jacket or you're a goner."

Marston looked from Gladys Hendricks to Mildred Trendler to Billy. "What the heck's going on?"

Mildred said, "It was a frameup, Del. It's a good thing I got back to O'Hara's before he locked up the joint for the night and got Billy to help me out."

Marston said, "Frameup? I know that. You tried to frame me for the murder of Cockeye Johnson. You left me with the stiff and called the cops."

"No, I didn't!"

"You lying witch! You put a slug in that cold fish, locked me in the bedroom with him and went and called the Chicago cops. You must have known somebody there to get them to come up to Evanston like they did."

"I didn't, Del. I found Cockeye there before I ever came to O'Hara's the first time. That was why I tried to hire you for fifty smackers. I guess I kind of panicked. I locked you in there. I was scared to call the cops because I didn't know who chilled Cockeye."

"Then why'd you hire me? What were you doing at O'Hara's?"

"I ran away from the apartment and the stiff the first time because I didn't know what to do. Then I saw Stink Calhoun following me and I really panicked. That was when I ran into O'Hara's. I figured maybe I could get away from Stink. Then I got an idea. I'd hire some sucker and frame him for killing Cockeye."

"That's what I thought."

"But I didn't call the cops! I couldn't! After I left you with Cockeye's corpse I couldn't do it. I ran away again, back to O'Hara's. I told Billy that I needed help and he said that his family were down in Indiana and he could hide me at his house 'til we could figure out what to do next."

"And you've been here ever since," Marston said.

Billy said, "That's right, Del."

"Then who killed Cockeye Johnson? And who called the cops?"

There was a crash. Gladys Hendricks had picked up a vase and hurled it against the wall. She waved the big revolver at the others. "Who killed Cockeye? I did! Cockeye and I had a sweet blackmail racket going, threatening to send those photos to the press. You know who those men were, Mildred, don't you?"

"Big-time politicians. Leaders of industry. A couple of famous athletes. And some gangsters."

"That's right," Gladys Hendricks sneered. "You thought there was money in servicing those sick creeps' fantasies. That was nothing compared to what I was making off the photos. And I didn't even have to do the dirty work of blackmailing. Cockeye Johnson took care of all that. But he got too greedy. He tried to blackmail *me* by threatening to tell Knuckles Florio."

"You witch," Mildred Trendler hissed.

Gladys Hendricks grinned, waving the Peacemaker around like Kay Kyser waving his baton at his band. "I took care of Cockeye Johnson. I used your popgun, Mildred. And I didn't call the cops. I called Knuckles. He sent his pet cops to find you. But you double-crossed us. You ran away too fast. That was why Stink Calhoun chased you into O'Hara's. But you made everything all the better when you brought this fool Del Marston in. And now—"

Marston reached inside his brown jacket for the .45 automatic in his shoulder holster. He seemed to move with an odd slowness, as if he could draw the .45 before Gladys Hendricks could fire the Peacemaker.

A strange look came over Gladys Hendricks' face. She pointed the revolver at Marston, also moving with a peculiar apparent lack of urgency. She squeezed the trigger. The hammer slammed down on the bright brass cartridge.

Nothing else happened.

"Sorry, sweetie-pie," Marston said. "I'm afraid I never quite trusted you. I never quite believed that innocent kid from out-of-town story. You looked pretty familiar to me from the first. In fact you look a lot like a gun moll I once ran across in Detroit, so I put live ammunition in this Colt and dummy rounds in that Peacemaker of yours. So if you'll just—"

A series of thundering crashes blasted across the room.

"Hit the dirt!" It was Billy's voice shouting out, as he dove for the carpet, dragging Mildred Trendler with him with his one arm. They hit the floor together as a row of holes appeared in the little room's picture window.

Red splattered over Billy and Mildred Trendler. Mildred* screamed and rolled away from Billy. Billy didn't move. The top of his head was gone and red gore spattered the carpet.

Marston was crouched by the window, poking his head up every so often, just long enough to get off a round from the heavy automatic.

The door slammed as Gladys Hendricks raced out.

Marston shouted, "Don't, you'll be—" But then he stopped as he saw what was going on. Knuckles Florio's big sedan had pulled to the curb not five feet from Marston's DeSoto. The windows of the big sedan were rolled down and Marston recognized Stink Calhoun and the two thugs from Florio's hotel suite.

They had their gats blazing—a tommygun and no less than three automatics among them.

Gladys Hendricks was weaving and dodging in a crouching run down the path from Billy's house, headed for the big sedan. The three gunmen were careful to avoid hitting her, keeping their hail of deadly bees screaming their song of hate only at the house.

The passenger door swung open and Gladys Hendricks was pulled into the car. With a final blaze of lead that covered up the clash of gears the sedan roared away from the curb.

Del Marston struggled to his feet and turned to survey the carnage. Mildred Trendler lay huddled on the carpet, sobbing, her blonde hair and provocative clothes spattered with blood and brains. Billy, whose gore it was, lay unmoving, his single arm outstretched as if he'd tried to grab something in the final convulsive moment of his life.

Marston looked to see what Billy had been reaching for. It was a photo of his wife and two little girls sitting on the mantelpiece. The little girls were wearing their best party dresses. They were holding up a big hand-lettered sign that said, WE LOVE YOU DADDY. Billy's wife and kids would be back from Indiana in a day or two. Marston would have to give them the news.

Knuckles Florio's trap had failed. Marston and Mildred Trendler were alive. But Gladys Hendricks had got away, and had returned to Florio's side.

The battle was over but the war had only barely started.

"The Monk's Tale"

by P.C. Doherty

The Feast of the Assumption 1376
(15th August)

I have begun this journal because my Prior has asked me. I received his letter and, I say this in the spirit of obedience, his remarks about my past cut like barbs. I know I have sinned before God and man but here in the parish of St. Erkonwald in Southwark I daily atone for my sins. I observe most strictly the rule of St. Dominic and spend both day and night in the care of souls. God knows, the harvest here is great; the filthy alleyways, piss-strewn runnels and poor hovels shelter broken people whose minds and souls have been bruised and poisoned by grinding poverty. The great fat ones of the land do not care but hide behind empty words, false promises and a lack of compassion which even Dives would have blushed at.

My house is no more than a white-washed shed with two rooms and a wooden door and casement which do not fit. My horse, an aged destrier, whom I call Philomel, eats as if there is no tomorrow but can go no faster than a shuffling cat. He drains my purse of money. I simply mention these matters to remind myself of my present state and to advise my Prior that his strictures are not necessary. As I have said, my purse is empty, shrivelled up and tight as a usurer's soul. My collection boxes have been stolen, the chancel screen is in disrepair, the altar is marked and stained and the nave of the church is often covered with huge pools of water, for our roof serves as more of a colander than a covering.

God knows I atone for my sins. I seem to be steeped in murder, bloody and awful, it taxes my mind and reminds me of my own great crime. I have served the people here six months now. I have also taken on those duties assigned by my Prior as clerk and scrivener to Sir John Cranston, coroner of the city. Time and again he takes me with him to sit over the body of some man, woman or child pitifully slain. "Is it murder, suicide or an accident?" he asks. And so the dreadful stories begin. Of stupidity, a woman who forgets how dangerous it is for a child to play out on the cobbled streets, dancing between the hooves of iron-shod horses or the creaking wheels of huge carts as they bring their produce up from the river. Still, a child is slain, the little body flung bruised and marked while the young soul goes out to meet its Christ. But there are more dreadful deaths. Men drunk in taverns, their bellies awash with cheap ale; their souls dead and black as the deepest night as they lurch at each other with sword, dagger or club. When the wound is made and the soul fled, Cranston and I arrive. I mean no offence for Sir John, despite his portly frame, plum red face, balding pate and watery eyes is, I think, in heart a good man. An honest official. A rare man indeed, who does not take bribes, searches for the truth, ever patient before declaring the true cause of death and I am always with him. I and my writing trays, my pens and inkpots, transcribing the lies, the deceits, the stories which flourish like weeds about any death.

I always keep a faithful record and every word I hear, every sentence I write, every time I visit the scene of the murder, I am back on that bloody field fighting for Edward, the Black Prince. I, a novice monk who has broken his vows and taken his younger brother off to war. Every night I dream of that battle: the press of steel men, the lowered pikes, the screams and shouts. Each time the nightmare goes like a mist clearing above the river, leaving only me kneeling beside the corpse of my dead brother, screaming into the darkness for his soul to return, I know it never will.

However, I beg Christ's pardon for I wander from the story. I was in my church long before dawn on the eve of the feast of St. John saying my office, quietly kneeling before the chancel screen, the only light being that of a taper lit before the statue of the Madonna. I confess I had not slept that night. Instead, I had climbed to the top of the church tower to observe the stars for I do admit that the movements of the heavens still have the same fascination for me as they did when I studied at Oxford in

Friar Bacon's observatory on Folly Bridge. I was tired and slightly fearful for Godric, a well known murderer and assassin, had begged for sanctuary in the church and while I prayed he lay, curled up like a dog, in the corner. He had eaten my supper, pronounced himself well satisfied and settled down to a good night's sleep. How is it, I ask, that such men can sleep so well? Godric had slain a man, struck him down in the market place, taken his purse and fled. He hoped to escape but had the misfortune to encounter a group of city officials and their retainers, who raised the hue and cry and pursued him here. I was attempting to repair the chancel screen and let him in after he hammered on the door. Godric brushed by me, gasping, waving the dagger, still bloody from his crime, and ran up the nave breathlessly shouting,

"Sanctuary! Sanctuary!"

The officials did not come into church though they expected me, as clerk to Sir John Cranston, to have handed him over but I could not.

"This is God's house!" I shouted, "Protected by Holy Mother Church and the King's decree!"

So they left him alone though they placed a guard on the door and swore they would kill him if he attempted to escape. Godric will either have to give himself up or abjure the realm.

Anyway, I digress, my prayers were again disturbed by a commotion outside the church and I thought the city authorities had sent armed retainers to take Godric, for we live in turbulent times. Our present King, Edward III, God bless him, is past his prime and the mighty men of war have their own way in most matters. I took the taper and hurried down the church, splashing through the puddles as there had been a violent thunderstorm, you may remember it, two days previously. Outside, the city guards had been disturbed from their sleep and were locked in fierce argument with Sir John Cranston, who bellowed as soon as he saw me,

"For God's sake, Father, tell these oafs who I am!" He patted the neck of his horse and glared around. "We have work to do, priest, another death murder at Bermondsey, one of the great ones of the land. Come! Ignore these dolts!"

"They did not know who you are, Sir John." I replied, "Because you are muffled in robe and hood worse than any monk."

I then explained to the men that Sir John Cranston was coroner of the City of London and had business with me. They backed off like beaten mastiffs, their dark faces glowering with a mixture of anger and fear.

"Leave Godric be!" I warned. "You are not to enter the church!"

They nodded, I locked the church door and went over to my own house. I stuffed my panniers with parchment, quills and ink, saddled Philomel and rejoined Sir John. The coroner was in good spirits, thoroughly enjoying his altercation with the city guard for Sir John hates officialdom, damns them loudly along with goldsmiths, priests and even, he looked slyly at me and grinned, Dominican monks who study the stars!

"Ever heavenwards," I quipped in reply, "We must look up at the sky and study the stars."

Why?" Cranston replied brusquely. "Surely you do not believe in that nonsense about planets and heavenly bodies governing our lives? Even the church fathers condemn it."

"In which case," I answered. "They condemn the Star of Bethlehem."

Sir John belched, grabbed the wineskin slung over his saddle horn, took one deep gulp and, raising his bottom, farted as loudly as he could. I decided to ignore Sir John's sentiments, verbal or otherwise. He means well and his wine is always the best that Gascony can grow.

"What business takes us to Bermondsey?" I asked.

"Abbot Hugo," he replied. "Or rather Hugo who was once Abbot. Now he is as dead as that cat over there." He pointed to a pile of refuse, a mixture of animal and human excrement, broken pots and, lying on top, a mangy cat, its white and russet body now swollen with corruption.

"So, an Abbot has died?"

"No, murdered! Apparently Abbot Hugo was not beloved by his brethren. After Prime this morning he had his customary daily meeting with the leading officials of the Abbey and, as usual, infringed the rule of St. Benedict by breaking his fast in his own private chamber, a jug of Malmesy wine and the best bread the abbey ovens can bake. His door was locked. Some time later, when he did not attend Divine Service, the brothers came and found his door still barred. When they forced it open, Hugo was lying dead at his table. At first they thought it was apoplexy, a stroke or the falling sickness but the Infirmarian, a Brother Stephen, smelt the wine cup and said it contained Belladonna. So," Sir John looked sideways at me, "We hunt murder in a monastery. Priests who kill. Tut! Tut! What is the world coming to?"

"God only knows!" I replied. "When coroners drink and fart, and make cutting remarks about men who are still men with all their failings, be they priest or prelate!" Sir John laughed, pushing his horse near mine, slapping me affectionately on the shoulder.

"I like you, Brother Athelstan!" he bellowed. "But God knows," he mimicked my words, "Though God knows why your order sent you to Southwark and your Prior ordered you to be a coroner's clerk."

We have had this conversation before. Sir John probing whilst I defended. Some day I will tell him the full truth though I think he surmises it already.

"Is it reparation?" he queried.

"Curiosity," I replied, "Can be a grave sin, Sir John." But the coroner laughed and deftly turned the conversation to other matters.

We rode along the river bank arriving at Bermondsey shortly before noon. I was glad to be free of the city, the stinking streets, the shoving and pushing in the market place, the houses which rear up and block the sun. The great swaggering lords who ride through on their fierce, iron-shod destriers in a blaze of silks and furs, their heads held high, proud, arrogant and as ruthless as the hawks they carry. The women are no better with their plucked eyebrows and white pasted faces: their soft, sensuous bodies are clothed in lawn and samite, their heads covered by a profusion of lacy veils; while only a coin's throw away a woman, pale and skeletal, sits crooning over her dying baby, begging for a crust to eat. God should send fire on the city or a leader to raise up the poor, but there again I preach sedition and remember my vow to keep silent.

At Bermondsey the great door to the abbey was kept fast. Sir John had to clang the bell as if raising the "Hue and Cry", before the gates squeaked open and we were led into the abbey forecourt by a most anxious-looking lay brother. The abbey was a great facade of stone, carved and sculptured, soaring up into the heavens, man's ladder to God. The place was subdued and quiet. The cloisters were empty, the hollowed stone passageways ghostly, even menacing. I felt I was entering a house of shadows. The lay brother took us to the Prior's office, a large comfortable room, the floor, so polished it could serve as a mirror, was covered here and there by thick woollen rugs. The black granite walls were draped and decorated with cloths of gold. The Prior was waiting for us; like all his kind, a tall, severe man, completely bald, with features as sharp as any knife and grey eyes as hard as flint. He greeted Sir John Cranston with forced warmth but, when I introduced myself and described my office, he smiled chillingly, dismissing me with a flicker of his eyes.

"Most uncommon," he murmured, "For a friar to be free of his order and serving in such a lowly office." Sir John snorted rudely and would have intervened if I had not.

"Prior Wakefield," I replied. "My business is my own. Like you, I am a priest, a man as learned as yourself, who now wonders why murder should be committed in a Benedictine monastery."

"Who said it was murder?"

"The Infirmarian who sent the message," Sir John interrupted. "He told us the abbot had been poisoned, even naming the substance found in the cup." The Prior shrugged.

"You are correct." he murmured. "Evil news seems to have wings of its own."

"We are here to see the body!" Cranston bluntly reminded him.

The Prior led us out into the cloisters which lay to the south side of the abbey church. Its centre or garth had been carefully cultivated, laid out with raised vegetable beds, herb gardens and the sweet-smelling roses now in full bloom under a hot mid-day sun. As the rule of Benedict laid down, there was silence, except for the scratching of pens from carrels where monks studied or pored over painted manuscripts. The doors of their cells were wide open because of the oppressive heat.

The Prior led us down more passageways and out to the Abbot's personal residence, a large, spacious, two-storied building. The ground floor was the Abbot's own refectory. We passed through it, up some wooden stairs into what the Prior termed the Abbot's private chambers: a large study sumptuously decorated, the walls painted red with golden stars, thick rugs on the floor and a huge oaken desk and table. There were cupboards full of books, the rich, leather coverings exuding their own special perfume so my fingers itched to open them. Behind this lay the Abbot's bedroom and I was struck by its austerity, no glazed or coloured windows here and the walls were just white, freshly painted with lime. The only furniture were a stool, a small table and a huge four-poster bed now stripped of any coverings, it bore the Abbot's corpse, rigid, silent, accusing under its linen sheet.

Cranston did not wait for the Prior but pulled back the linen cloth to expose a skull-like head and skeletal features made even uglier by the rictus of death. Abbot Hugo had been an old man, well past his sixtieth summer. Cranston pulled the sheet down further, revealing how the Abbot had been laid out for burial in the thick, brown smock of his order with coarse sandals strapped round the bare feet. The Abbot's face, like the features of any murdered victim, fascinated me; the slight purplish tinge in his face and sunken cheeks. The monks had attempted to close his eyes in death and, unable to, had placed a coin over each of his eyes, one of these had slipped off and the Abbot glared sightlessly at the ceiling. Cranston indicated I should examine the body more closely, not that he is squeamish, I just think he enjoys making me pore over some corpse, the more revolting the better.

"I must open the robe." I said turning to the Prior. The fellow nodded angrily.

"Get on with it!"

Taking the hem of the Abbot's robe, I lifted it and pushed it right up to his neck to expose a thin, emaciated body, a dirty white, like the underbelly of a rat. There were no contusions or bruises and the same was true of the neck and chest; the only marks were the ink stains on two fingers of his left hand.

"Nothing unusual about that," the Prior remarked, "Abbot Hugo was a great writer." I nodded and looked closer. The ink seemed to be stained permanently but there was no cut on the fingers and, when I raised the cold hand, I detected nothing untoward. I re-arranged the Abbot's robe and, muttering the Requiem, pulled the linen sheet back up to his chin before examining the half-open mouth. The Infirmarian was right, even the most stupid of physicians would have detected poison. I gently prised open the lips, still not yet fully rigid in death, revealing yellow stumps of teeth. The gums, tongue and palate, however, were now stained black and, when I leant down and smelt, detected the sour sweet tang of a powerful poison.

"How do we know," I asked, "that the Abbot died alone?"

Wakefield shrugged.

"Quite easily. Two lay brothers always stayed at the foot of the stairs leading to his chambers. They would sit there, pray, meditate or be on call when the Abbot rang a small bell on his desk."

"That could be heard at the foot of the stairs?"

"Yes."

"And these two lay brothers maintain no one went up?" The Prior smiled thinly.

"I didn't say that. They did allow the servant through with a tray bearing wine and bread, as well as the Abbot's Secretarius, Brother Christopher."

"Ah, yes, Brother Christopher." I replied. "And how long was he in there?"

"A very short while."

Cranston slumped on the foot of the bed.

"Abbot Hugo, you liked him?" he barked.

The Prior nodded.

"I respected him deeply."

"And your brethren?"

"Abbot Hugo was a hard man but a holy one. He was a zealot who upheld the rule but could be capable of great compassion."

"When was the meal served?" I asked him.

"I asked the servant. He said the cellarer had laid the bread and wine out during the fourth hour after midnight. That was customary. Abbot Hugo's instructions were always to bring it when the hour candle had burnt mid-way between five and six."

The Prior looked down at the floor. He was embarrassed, uneasy.

"There is something else?" I asked.

"What do you mean?"

"Oh, you know full well what I mean." I said curtly.

The Prior coughed nervously.

"You are right," he answered after a while. "The Infirmarian, he has kept the Abbot's wine and bread locked away but he went down to the kitchen to inspect the jug of wine which the Cellarer had used. He found a large stain on the table. It smelt of Belladonna."

"Ah!" Cranston let out a long sigh.

I watched the Prior closely.

"Did anything happen in the days leading up to Abbot Hugo's death?" The Prior was silent.

"Answer the question!" Cranston snapped.

The Prior rubbed his eyes with the back of his hand and glanced up. He looked grey and exhausted.

"Yes, today is. . . ."

"Wednesday!" Cranston interjected.

"On Sunday evening after Compline, the Abbot met us here in his own quarters. He announced he was going to resign, retire."

"Why?"

"He claimed he was too old to continue as Abbot and wished to go into retreat. Go to another house, revert to being a simple monk and so prepare for his death."

"What was the reaction to this?"

"We were all horror-struck. We had our differences with the Abbot. That is only natural in an enclosed community but we did revere him."

There was a pause as Cranston and I eyed each other. We both knew what question we would like to ask next.

"If the Abbot had retired," I began slowly. "Who would have been elected as his successor?"

The Prior's face softened as if he was preparing me for what came next.

"I think I would have been." His face flushed as he looked at both of us. "I know what you're thinking, what you're hinting at." He got up. "To slay someone is an abominable act, a mortal sin.

To be guilty of the murder of a man like Abbot Hugo would be nothing more than blasphemous sacrilege."

"Tush, Prior Wakefield," Cranston said softly. "We did not say that."

The Prior flung a look of hate at me.

"He did!" he said.

"My Lord Prior," I replied. "I did not. Before God I did not!" I looked at Cranston. "Sir John, we must interview the lay brothers. My Lord Prior, Sir John will use the Abbot's study. First, we would like to question the lay brothers; the servant who brought the bread and wine as well as the two who stood guard at the foot of the stairs."

The Prior nodded and, giving a hasty bow to Sir John Cranston, stalked out of the room. Once he was gone I closed the door, opened one of my panniers and, bringing out a sharp needle which I use to sew parchment together, went over to the corpse and pulled back the shroud. Abbot Hugo's face, still stared, transfixed by death. I pressed the lower jaw down and, using the needle, scraped between the yellow teeth.

"What is it?" Cranston asked.

I went over to the casement window and opened the wooden shutter to look more carefully at what the needle had dug out for me. A soft, greyish, pulpy mass. Cranston came over to stand by me, a look of disgust on his face.

"What do you think it is?" he asked.

I grimaced.

"The remains of a meal the night before or even the bread. God knows!"

Cranston, apparently bored by my mysterious attitude, pulled the shroud back over Abbot Hugo and told me to join him in the Abbot's study where he slumped unceremoniously into the great chair behind the table. He waved me to a small stool which stood alongside, gripping the side of the desk as he studied it carefully. A book of hours in one corner, the clasp broken, allowing us a glimpse of the golds and blues of the illuminated writing. Rolls of parchment, a writing tray similar to the one I used, bearing an ink pot, a long quill pen and a small battered, wooden cross which the abbot must have used when meditating. Nothing remarkable but Cranston told me to list it. After all, it is quite common after such inquisitions for the coroner to be accused of filching the dead man's goods.

After this, the Prior returned with the lay brothers whom Cranston wished to question. They were all old, rather venerable men, who had been taken into the abbey for good services performed in the King's wars or in some nobleman's household. Cranston questioned them carefully, tolerating their garrulous replies but dismissed them, for what they said corroborated the Prior's story.

During the afternoon Cranston and I pieced together the events leading up to the Abbot's sudden death, only the distant booming of the abbey bell or the soft patter of sandalled feet in the corridor outside interrupted our deliberations. For once in his long, hard-drinking life, Sir John refrained from downing goblet after goblet of rich red wine. Perhaps it was his concentration and sober attitude which made me guess that Sir John had been directed here by some powerful personage at court.

"Look, Athelstan," he said, using his fat, stubby fingers to list events. "Abbot Hugo was a holy but strict man; he rises and sings the morning office with his brethren. He then returns to his room. In the kitchen the cellarer pours a goblet of wine and lays out a dish of freshly baked bread. These are brought up by a lay brother who leaves it outside the room on a bench: the staircase is guarded by two lay brothers: the Abbot's Secretarius brings the bread and wine in and leaves. No one else comes up but later Abbot Hugo cannot be roused. The next thing is that the Abbot's door has been broken down and the Prior, who had been talking to the sub-prior, Brother Paul, at the time, comes into the room. The sub-prior is with him." Cranston paused and looked at me. "What then?"

I sighed and shrugged.

"According to Prior Wakefield and the lay brothers," I replied, "Wakefield and Brother Paul found the Abbot slouched back in his chair. The Prior removes the body himself and lays it on the ground. A few minutes later the Infirmarian arrives. It is he who smells the wine and detects the poison."

"Had the Abbot eaten or drunk anything?" Cranston queried.

"According to Prior Wakefield," I replied, "He had, a little. They found this when they removed the cup of wine and bread. They have kept it under lock and key as evidence." Cranston shook his head and sighed in exasperation.

"I see," he said despondently, "no solution in this."

"Who wants a solution?" I asked Sir John abruptly. The coroner looked at me slyly.

"News was sent immediately to the court and, within an hour, the order to come here had arrived at my house." He chewed his lip thoughtfully. "But what answer can I give? Was the bread and wine poisoned in the kitchen and, if so, by whom? Or did Brother Christopher or one of the lay servants perpetrate the crime?"

I shook my head, unable to offer Cranston any solution.

The day drew on. Cranston asked for food and this was brought; a jug of ale, some small white loaves and two bowls of rich broth stew, garnished with onions and leeks and heavily seasoned. Cranston, eating noisily, slurped from his bowl, using the special pewter spoon he always carried with him. As he ate he summarised what we knew.

"We have an old Abbot who intends to resign. He attends the first part of the Divine Office just after midnight and retires here to his chamber, though he is expected back in the abbey church about six to sing Prime. He locks himself in his room, the only visitor is his Secretarius, Brother Christopher, who brings in the bread and wine brought up by one of the servants. Brother Christopher," he continued, "is only there for a few minutes. But the cup he has brought in is poisoned." Cranston rose and, after stretching himself, walked round the room. "The solution is quite simple. The murderer either must be one of the following: the Cellarer, for there was a poison stain found in the kitchen, the old servant who brought it up or, more likely, Brother Christopher. No one else could have done it for the stairs were guarded."

I agreed and was about to make my own suggestion when the great bell of the abbey began to toll for Vespers.

"Sir John," I asked, "What shall we do now?"

"What do you mean?"

"Are we to return to the city or to stay here?"

"We have come so far we might as well see the matter through." he replied.

"Then, if you don't mind," I retorted. "I would like to join my brothers in Christ in church." Cranston shrugged.

"Do what you like."

I left Cranston in the Abbot's study and went quickly down to the church. The great west door was open. I went inside. Torches had been lit which only increased the sense of watchful silence, making the shadows dance and slither across the great pillars. The sunlight still streamed through the coloured glass windows but I thought the church must always be dark. I went up through the heavily ornamented rood screen, past the pulpit and into the sanctuary, a small chapel in itself with choir stalls of carved wood on either side. Each stall had a richly decorated canopy at the back with a desk in front. The monks were now filing in from another door; ghostly figures with their hoods pulled up. They looked indistinguishable, despite the fire of the torches and the light of the huge beeswax candles placed on the altar. A dark figure loomed over me, pulling his cowl back. I recognised Prior Wakefield.

"You wish to join us?" he whispered.

"Yes, Father."

He waved me to an empty stool.

"Brother Anselm is sick, we would be only too pleased for you to help us with our singing."

I could not decide if he was being helpful or sarcastic but I murmured my thanks and took my place, waiting for the other monks to join us. I caught the faint, fragrant smell of incense but my soul sensed something else. The figures lining up in their stalls were quiet, calm, possessed of one intent, to use all their energy in the praise of God. Nevertheless, I caught the awful smell of fear and knew that each man must be wondering which of their brethren had committed the horrible crime of murder. The Abbot's empty seat, which stood at the west end of the choir, dominated the gathering, its very emptiness turning it into an accusatory finger as if the Abbot was stretching his hand out beyond death, seeking his killer here, at the very foot of God's throne.

I leaned against the stall seat and waited until the leading cantor moved up to the lectern, a huge brass stand in the shape of an eagle with outstretched wings. In a clear angelic voice he began the chant.

"Oh, Lord, arise in haste to help me!"

The monks thundered their reply, answering each verse with the response. I joined in, forgetful of sin, blasphemy and sacrilege, only too pleased to be back amongst my fellow priests, singing the beautiful plain chant of the church.

After the service I joined the monks as they filed back across the darkening cloister into the refectory or frater, a long, well lit room roofed in timber and generously served by huge windows; some filled with horn, others with beautiful decorated glass. The high table on the dais at the end was empty except for the Prior who stood there intoning the "Benedicite". The monks sat down, pulling back their cowls, sitting patiently while the lay brothers served them and a young monk, standing at a pulpit built in the refectory wall, read from the writings of Jerome. Apart from the reading, the meal was ate in complete silence. No one seemed concerned by my presence, though I sensed an atmosphere of menace and I knew their very detachment masked close scrutiny, indeed resentment at my presence. So intense was this feeling that I gulped my food and, forgetting all etiquette, hastily rose, bowed to the great crucifix which hung above the dais and gratefully fled back to the cloisters.

Cranston was waiting for me in the Abbot's chamber, noisily eating a better meal than I had been served in the refectory and taking great gulps of wine from a shallow bowl.

"Did you enjoy yourself, Brother?" he asked his mouth full.

"An interesting experience," I replied. "Though one I would not like to repeat."

Whilst Cranston gobbled his meal I went over and picked up the book of hours, trying to calm myself by studying the beautiful paintings, a feast of colour and light. Cranston announced he had finished eating by noisily smacking his lips, slouching back in the abbot's great chair and belching as loudly as a trumpet blast.

"And what has my Lord Coroner decided to do now?" I said sarcastically.

Cranston shrugged.

"I have told that whey-faced Prior I wish to see the following: himself, the Sub-Prior, the Infirmarian, the Cellarer and, of course, dear Brother Christopher. We shall question these to throw some light on our dark mystery."

He had hardly finished speaking when there was a knock at the door and Prior Wakefield entered, a file of monks behind him. Cranston, now full of his own importance as well as good wine, made no attempt at welcome. He imperiously waved them in front of the desk and, after instructing me to light candles, ordered me to take careful note of what was said.

The young man who had been the leading cantor in the church helped me find a tinder and light the branched candlestick bringing the room to life.

"Good" murmured Sir John, revelling in his authority. "Those things that were done in the dark," he added, misquoting scripture, "shall be examined on the mountain top."

"There is no need to treat us like errant scholars, Sir John." Prior Wakefield insisted.

"I am not," Cranston replied brusquely. "But I am the King's Coroner."

"You have no jurisdiction in this abbey." Wakefield interrupted.

"I have every jurisdiction. The King's writ rules here as it does anywhere else. So, my Lord Prior, please introduce me to your brethren."

Wakefield, swallowing his pride, gestured towards his fellow monks. The Sub-Prior Brother Paul small, chubby-faced and great bellied, he could have taken the part in any mummer's play as Robin Hood's Friar Tuck. The Infirmarian, Brother Stephen, tall, scholarly looking, a man full of his own importance with a great nose and arrogant eyes. If I had not known better I would have sworn he was the Prior. Brother Ambrose, the Cellarer, surprisingly lean, sallow-faced, a look of constant worry souring his mouth. Finally, Brother Christopher the Secretarius, the young man with the voice of an angel.

Once the introductions were over, Cranston went through what we had learnt so far and no one demurred.

"Right!" Sir John barked, using his stubby fingers to score points. "We know you, the Cellarer, poured the drink and prepared the bread during the fourth hour after midnight. It stood in the monastery kitchens until taken up by the lay brother, who placed it outside the Abbot's lodging on the same bench later used to break the door down. The only visitor was you, Brother Christopher." The young man nodded, a look of intense fear in his eyes as he nervously ran his fingers through his close cropped, blond hair. "You did take the wine in?" Again Brother Christopher nodded. "Speak up, man." Prior Wakefield was about to intervene but Cranston stopped him with a warning glance. "You have a tongue, Brother Christopher?"

"Yes, I have a tongue," he answered softly. "I took the tray in, as usual Abbot Hugo was kneeling on his prie dieu." He nodded towards the far corner before pointing to the book of hours on the table. "I placed the tray on the table."

"Did the Abbot say anything?"

"He whispered 'Gratias'"

"What then?" I interrupted. "After you left, what would Abbot Hugo do?"

The young man spread his hands.

"As customary, he would sit where you are and write letters whilst breaking his fast. A few minutes before Prime he would leave his chamber and join us in the abbey church."

"Did the Abbot write anything the night he died?" I asked.

"No," the Cellarer, interrupted, "He simply checked my accounts. The roll was found on his desk."

"Who has it now?"

"Brother Christopher later gave it over to me," the Prior answered. "I have looked at it. There's nothing untoward."

Sir John grimaced.

"Are you hinting that Brother Christopher did anything wrong?" Wakefield asked peevishly.

"Oh, no, Brother Christopher would not do anything untoward!" Cranston and I looked in surprise at Brother Paul's clever mimicry of the Prior's words. Wakefield, his face flushed with anger, turned on the Sub-Prior.

"Brother Paul, I suggest you keep your mouth shut!" Wakefield smiled at the Secretarius. "Do not worry, Christopher, we know you did nothing wrong."

"How do you know?" the Sub-Prior interrupted, "He was the last man to see the Abbot alive. He did carry the wine in."

Brother Christopher fell to his knees, sobbing into his upraised hands. Cranston and I were both transfixed by this tableau. The calm composure of these monks now broken by the child-like weeping of Brother Christopher and the look of hatred exchanged between the Prior and Brother Paul. I was about to intervene but Cranston waved me to silence.

"We both know how you looked after your darling Christopher!" the Sub-Prior spat spitefully.

"What are you hinting at, Brother?"

Wakefield drew himself up to his full height and I was surprised at the way that the small Sub-Prior, his smiling face now hard and impassive, stood his ground.

"Oh, we know how you interceded with the Abbot," he commented, throwing a knowing look at Cranston, "To beg for mercy when this young man was found stealing from the monastery at night, dressed in multi-coloured hose, red shoes and velvet jacket, to enjoy the pleasures of the city."

"That was years ago" Brother Christopher sobbed.

"We are forgetting one thing," Brother Stephen, the Infirmarian interrupted. "Traces of the Belladonna poison were found in the kitchen."

"What are you implying?" the Cellarer shouted. "You are the Infirmarian, you had access to poisons!"

The Infirmarian was about to yell back when Cranston clapped his hands.

"Enough is enough is enough!" he bellowed. "Prior Wakefield," he continued evenly as the brothers regained some composure. "I suggest we interview each of you separately and I will begin with you. The rest should wait outside."

He was about to continue when he was interrupted by a knock on the door and the lay brother who had earlier admitted to bringing the wine and bread from the kitchen, shuffled in, head down, hands hanging dejectedly on either side of him. He went over to Prior Wakefield and knelt at his feet.

"Peccavi," the old man whispered, "I have sinned."

"What is it, Brother Wulfstan?"

"It is true," the old man whispered in a now still room. "I brought up the wine as usual and, as usual, I drank from it." There was a few moments silence, shattered by the uproar the lay brother's words caused.

"See!" the Cellarer shouted. "I am innocent!"

"It must have been poisoned later," the Infirmarian added gleefully, "And the only person who touched it was our darling Brother Christopher."

The young monk, unable to accept this, howled in protest and, before anyone could stop him, fled from the room.

Cranston rose to his feet.

"Prior Wakefield, you will wait on me now. Brother Ambrose," he indicated to where the lay brother still lay sobbing at the Prior's feet. "Take this man away and, Brother Stephen," he turned to the Infirmarian, "Bring back the Secretarius. Now! Go, all of you!"

Once the room was cleared, Cranston sat down and turned to me, a look of complete surprise on his face.

"So, my dear Athelstan, Chaucer's words are true, the cowl doesn't make the monk."

"No more than the robe makes the judge or armour the knight." I replied, "Though I agree, we have uncovered a filthy plot of passions here."

Cranston grimaced.

"The murderer must be Christopher. We must find out why."

I shook my head.

"Too easy," I replied.

But Cranston just shrugged, shouting for Prior Wakefield to come back into the room.

The Prior had regained his composure and, not waiting for Cranston's invitation, pushed across a small stool to sit opposite him. He did not even bother to stare at me but sat fingering the tassel of his cord, waiting for Cranston to begin. The coroner smiled.

"Prior Wakefield, your relations with Brother Paul, the Sub-Prior, are not what they should be?"

"What do you mean?"

"There is very little charity between two brother priests."

"I do not like Brother Paul." Wakefield replied evenly. "Read your Aquinas, Sir John, one can draw distinctions between loving and liking. I do not like Brother Paul because he is arrogant, with great ambition but not the talent to match."

"Nor," continued Cranston drily, "Does he like your protégé, Brother Christopher."

"Brother Christopher is a weak vessel, he fell from grace some years ago. I recommended him to the post of Secretarius so both I and Father Abbot could keep an eye on him."

"Your Sub-Prior is hinting at something else."

Wakefield's sallow face flushed.

"Brother Paul will have to atone for his sin," he answered. "He hints at an unnatural love between Brother Christopher and myself. That is not true."

"Who sent the messenger to me?" Cranston interrupted.

"I believe it was the Infirmarian, Brother Stephen." Cranston nodded.

"Then we will see him next."

"He has brought the Abbot's wine and bread with him."

"Good." Cranston replied.

Brother Stephen entered the room as soon as Wakefield left, placing the bread and wine triumphantly on the table before Cranston as if laying an altar for Mass. Cranston sniffed at both before handing them to me. There was a tinge of mould on the bread so I snapped it in two and held it close against my nose but I could detect nothing. The wine cup was a different matter. A silver chased goblet, it was still half-full of wine but reeked of that sour-sweet stench I detected from Abbot Hugo's lips. Cranston watched me pull a face.

"What made you think of poison?" he asked Brother Stephen abruptly.

"What do you mean?" the Infirmarian snapped back.

"Well," Cranston smiled. "Abbot Hugo was an old man. You found him dead over his desk?"

"I did not find him."

"Agreed, your prior did, but you came into the room and immediately checked the cup. Was it spilled?"

"Of course not."

"So why examine it?"

"I do not know," Brother Stephen replied crossly. "Perhaps I am naturally suspicious. I looked around, everything was in order."

"Everything?" I interjected. A slow doubt began to form in my mind. "You are sure about that, Brother Stephen?"

"Yes. I simply picked up the cup out of curiosity. But the smell of Belladonna was so strong I knew immediately it was drugged."

"Are you so proficient in poisons?" Cranston asked, "That you can detect it even when it's laced with wine?" Brother Stephen looked at him arrogantly.

"Of course. I am a specialist in poisons: Nightshade, Belladonna, the juice of the foxglove. Not that," he looked at us both in one sweeping glance, "Not that I am the only person with access to them. We use poison in keeping our beehives, to get rid of rats and mice and in the garden. Indeed, any of the brothers could mix poisons from the herbs we grow."

"So, why did you send for Sir John?" I asked. "Why the King's coroner?"

"Sir John knows that himself," Brother Stephen replied artfully and, before I could intervene, Cranston smoothly dismissed the Infirmarian, telling him to send Brother Christopher in.

After a short while the young monk entered, escorted by Prior Wakefield. He was white-faced, red-eyed, his cheeks stained by tears.

"Sit down," Cranston said kindly. "We have no need for you, Prior Wakefield."

The Prior seemed reluctant to move.

"I repeat myself, my Lord Prior, there is no need for you to stay."

Once Wakefield was gone, Cranston leaned across the table.

"Brother Christopher, let us be brief. We know when the wine left the kitchen it was not poisoned or the lay brother who drank from it would have died. We have also learnt that no one approached the wine whilst it was outside Abbot Hugo's study. The only conclusion we can draw is that you must have poisoned the cup before bringing it in and stained the kitchen table to spread confusion. Well, what do you have to say?"

The young monk, looking totally crestfallen, shook his head.

"I am innocent!" he stuttered, "Completely in this matter!"

"Oh, no, you're not!" Cranston snapped. "My Lord Prior!" he bellowed.

Wakefield, waiting outside, re-entered immediately.

"I would be grateful," Cranston declared and broke off yawning, "If Brother Christopher could be taken and locked in some cell. I believe you have armed retainers?"

The Prior nodded and, before he could object, Cranston rose.

"By the King's authority, I order this and I do not wish my orders questioned."

Wakefield took the young Secretarius by the arm as if he was some small boy and led him out of the room. Cranston stretched and turned.

"I would like to be civil, Brother Athelstan but, with all due respect to yourself, I have had enough of monks for one day. So I bid you goodnight."

Cranston nodded his head and scurried off whilst I stayed in the Abbot's study and sent for the Infirmarian.

After some time, Brother Stephen arrived, cross-faced and sleep laden.

"What is it, Friar?" he brusquely asked.

171

"One question, monk!" I snapped back. "And one question only. If you gave me Belladonna in wine, how long would it take for me to die?"

The fellow seemed to find that a pleasant thought.

"No more than a few seconds," he replied.

I gave out a great sigh and grinned.

"Then Brother Stephen, I demand this on the King's authority; you are to rouse Prior Wakefield and tell him to take Brother Christopher from custody and bring him here. Now!" I shouted, seeing the arrogant obstinacy in his face. The monk shrugged, dismissed me with a supercilious glance and padded out of the room. Well over half an hour passed before I heard footfalls in the corridor outside.

"Come in!" I shouted. "Do not let us wait on idle ceremony!" Wakefield entered, holding up a now distraught Christopher, white-faced, wild eyed. I momentarily wondered if he had lost his wits. "Brother Christopher," I began kindly, "Sit on the stool. Prior Wakefield, please stay outside." I leaned across the table. "Brother Christopher, I do not think you are the murderer." I was pleased to see the look of relief in the young man's eyes. "But you must gather your wits. You put the tray bearing the wine down on the table?"

The young monk nodded.

"Then come!" I rose. "Come here, Brother Christopher, and sit in the Abbot's chair."

The young man did so, slowly like a dream walker, his eyes staring fixedly at the table top.

"Now, Brother, you are the Abbot. You have drunk your wine. What would you do next?"

The young man picked up the quill, dipped it in the inkhorn and, taking a piece of paper, began scratching words upon it. I went round and noted ruefully that the young monk had written the words of the Chief Priest from Christ's trial in the Gospel—"What need of we of proof?"

"I need proof," I said quietly. "Now please pretend you are the Abbot, imitate his every mannerism."

I sat on the stool and watched Brother Christopher play-act. As I urged him on, my suspicions firmed into certainty. I asked him a few questions about what had happened on the day before. He answered that he had worked in his office, he told me who had visited him. When he mentioned one name, I remembered something said earlier in the day.

"Thank you, Brother," I said. "Just one final question. You brought the wine and bread into Father Abbot? When did you see him previously? I mean, by yourself?"

172

"Oh," the young monk answered. "I brought him a letter, sealed by the Prior." He stopped and gazed into the air. "That was the previous evening. Then, just before retiring, I came back with the writing tray."

"The one that is on the desk now?" I asked.

Brother Christopher nodded.

"Yes, it is. Why?"

I shrugged.

"It's of little matter. I thank you, Brother. You may join Prior Wakefield and inform him, on my authority, as well as that of Sir John Cranston, that you may return to your cell on one condition, you are to stay there until we leave."

Early next morning, woken from my sleep in the Abbot's chair by the booming of the bells for Prime, I stretched my aching body and went down to rouse Sir John Cranston. The old coroner was snoring like a pig and I confess I took great joy in waking him. I told him of my conclusions. At first he argued vehemently against me, angry that I had ordered Brother Christopher's release, so I went through my arguments again. Sir John, sitting up in bed, still dressed in the clothes he wore the previous day, reluctantly agreed to what I asked. Cranston rose, washed himself at the Lavararium and followed me round the cloisters back to the Abbot's lodgings. An old lay brother sat dozing on the low cloister wall, half listening to the dawn chant of the monks in the abbey choir. I gently roused him and told him to bring Prior Wakefield and the Sub-Prior to us as soon as the service was over. This time Cranston did not sit in the Abbot's chair but dramatically waved me into it, as if his own presence was no longer necessary. Playing the role he had assigned me, I placed two stools before the table and we waited quietly until Prior Wakefield and Brother Paul entered. I gestured at them to sit.

"Prior Wakefield," I said. "Tell me what you were doing when the news of Abbot Hugo's death was brought to you?"

The Prior, his eyes still red from lack of sleep, yawned as he rubbed his brow, trying to remember.

"Yes, I have told you," he snapped peevishly. "I was in my office talking to Brother Paul. He had asked to see me on some matter. I forget now." Brother Paul nodded in agreement.

"Then what?" I asked.

"The lay brother came down, saying something was wrong, Brother Paul and I ran up here and, once the door was forced, we both entered the room."

"What then?" I asked.

"Abbot Hugo was lying back in his chair. Brother Paul pulled the chair back, I picked the Abbot up. He was no weight and laid him gently on the floor. I checked his breath and felt for the blood beat in his neck but there was nothing."

"Is that when you changed the pens, Brother Paul?" I asked abruptly. Never have I seen a monk's face go so ashen.

"What do you mean?" he asked hoarsely.

"You know what I mean," I replied. "Like Brother Christopher, you know how the Abbot often sucked the end of a quill whilst writing or preparing to write. So you coated it with poison and, the previous evening, went into Brother Christopher's office and placed the poisoned quill on the Abbot's writing tray. You knew when Abbot Hugo would pick it up and I suggest you kept very close to the Prior, hence your request for a meeting just before Prime on that fatal day. You had no reason to doubt anything would go wrong. Abbot Hugo's routine was established. He was a creature of habit."

"This is. . . ."

"I would be grateful if you did not interrupt me!" I snapped, "and let me finish. You had to be with the Prior so when the body was discovered you gained immediate access to the room. After that it was simple. While Prior Wakefield moved Abbot Hugo's body you poured the poison into the cup and replaced the poisoned quill with an untainted one. A few seconds, the phial of poison and the quill already hidden in the voluminous sleeves of your robe. No one would dream of examining where the writing tray was placed. I am sure if we check the Cellarer's account, we would find places where the Abbot used the quill to tally amounts. He would have then leaned back in the chair, unwittingly drinking the poison as he licked the quill. He would feel ill, place it down and fall back into death." I paused. "Later on, a little poison was dropped on the table down in the kitchen and you successfully spread the seeds of suspicion. Any one of your brothers could have poisoned the Abbot's wine, even when the old lay brother admitted to sipping from the cup, you thought you were safe. For the only possible culprit could be Brother Christopher."

"That is ridiculous!" the Sub-Prior muttered. "You have no proof!"

"Oh, yes I do" I replied. "First, you did visit Brother Christopher's office the night beforehand on some petty errand which engaged the young Secretarius' attention. Secondly, the fresh pen, you used to replace the poisoned one. You made sure that it had been dipped in ink and certainly used by yourself. Now you are a right-handed man, when you use a quill the tip is worn away on the right side but Abbot Hugo was left-handed, his quill should have been worn down on the left." I picked up the quill from the writing tray. "This is the untainted quill you brought in." I pointed to the tip. "Look, it is worn down on the right side. When I checked Abbot Hugo's corpse I noticed the ink stain on his left hand. This quill could never have been used by him. Finally, Belladonna is a quick-acting, powerful poison. If the Abbot had raised the cup to his lips he would never have had time to place it back on the table. It would either have fallen on the table or the floor.

"Why?" Prior Wakefield asked, glaring at the Sub-Prior.

"Oh, I think I can answer that" Cranston interrupted. "There is no love lost between you two. If Abbot Hugo had retired; you, Prior Wakefield, could well have replaced him. That's the last thing Brother Paul wanted. So Abbot Hugo dies in mysterious circumstances. A feeling of suspicion is created and your superiors may well have been tempted to place someone else, an outsider in charge."

"A mummer's tale!" Brother Paul sneered. "A fable, nothing else."

"In which case," I remarked, digging into the pocket of my own robe, "You will not object to placing the tip of this quill in your mouth?" I drew out a battered quill and held it up. "Look, Brother Paul, it's worn on the left side and is still stained with ink. I ask you to put it into your mouth."

"That's not the quill that Abbot Hugo used," Brother Paul snapped back and immediately raised his hand to his lips to bite back his words.

"You are correct! How do you know that, Brother Paul?"

"I don't! I don't!" the Sub-Prior murmured. "I will say no more."

"What are you going to do?" Prior Wakefield asked for the first time ever looking at me squarely in the face. "I ask you, Brother Athelstan, not Sir John Cranston, for you too are a disgraced monk aren't you?" he smiled thinly. "Oh, I made a few enquiries, a little digging amongst the gossip, Brother Athelstan, who fled his novitiate to join the King's army and took his own younger brother, only to get him killed. A man who not only broke his monastic vows but the hearts of his parents."

God forgive me, I could not stop the tears welling up in my eyes. Wakefield's words stirred my memory and I recalled the tragic, tear-stained faces of my mother and father.

"I have sinned," I replied. "And my sin is always before me and let that be Brother Paul's sentence. You, Prior Wakefield, will be elected Abbot. Brother Paul will resign as Sub-Prior and stay in this monastery for the rest of his life being ruled by a man he hates. I could not think of a worse form of hell. That is," I added crisply, "If Sir John agrees."

Cranston, who had been watching me closely, nodded and rose, not bothering to give the still seated Brother Paul a glance.

"I would be grateful, Lord Prior, if you would ensure that this malignant was locked away until we leave. Of course, he may object to Brother Athelstan's sentence, in which case he can take his chances before the King's Justices in the Guildhall. I suggest he does not do that."

Prior Wakefield nodded and patted Brother Paul on the shoulder, who followed him as meekly as a lamb out of the room.

Once they had left, Cranston came up and nudged me gently on the chest.

"They are bailiffs in cowls," he said, quoting a current proverb about monks. "I don't like monks" he continued evenly. "I am not too sure whether I like you but I do respect you Athelstan. Now let's be gone from this hell pit!"

Our journey back into London was uneventful but, before we parted, Cranston pulled back his hood and leaned closer to me.

"I agree with your sentence, Athelstan" he said, "But the Infirmarian sent for me because Abbot Hugo had once been spiritual confessor to our dread King, Edward III. I will let the court know what happened. I am sure Brother Paul will meet with an accident before Michaelmas Day."

I left Cranston to go back to my own church. The pools of water were still on the floor and the church door hung loose. Someone had stolen the small statue of the Virgin from its niche. Godric the murderer had been taken, snatched by officials of the Mayor, or so Ranulf the rat-catcher told me when I found him sleeping on the steps of the sanctuary. I gave him a coin and dismissed him. I knelt before the crucifix and said the "De Profundis" for Godric's soul and for that of Abbot Hugo and for my own brother, Francis. Souls sent before their time to stand before the throne of God. So now I have related this story, perhaps I will look once more at the stars, say my Office and go merrily to bed. Pray God Cranston gives me peace.

What Goes Around. . .

by Mark Schorr

I owe it all to the most vile, despicable, heartless editor in New York. If you know the publishing business, you know I'm speaking of Luther Coyne. When he had his heart attack and went into the hospital for a cardiac operation, wags quipped it was exploratory surgery. Others said it had to be microsurgery. No one sent him flowers.

Coyne is known for his rejection letters, masterpieces that can convince a writer with a dozen bestsellers that he is an illiterate, inarticulate lout. Coyne is notorious for lying, cheating, and stealing. He bullies the editorial board, intimidates agents, abuses his staffers. He is a very successful man.

I was the victim of one of his letters. I had published several novels pseudonymously. They were well-received popular fiction, full of sex, violence, and exotic locales. I wrote under a pen name because the New England college where I taught would never condone a professor churning out potboilers. Two literary works had been printed under my own name—not by Coyne—to generally negative reviews and minimal sales.

Coyne brutally rejected my last novel. His note began, "This is particularly miserable writing, even for you" and got progressively nastier. We had a confrontation and I responded to his venom

177

in kind. Someone subsequently divulged my pseudonym to the chairman of the English department. I was just short of tenure. I was called into the chairman's office, and with a great deal of harrumphing, told it would be best if I found other employment. Coyne never openly admitted that he was my Judas, but I subsequently learned of his actions through a gossipy secretary.

The fall from grace devastated me. I won't bore you with the details, but within six months I was living in a shabby apartment on the Lower East Side, supporting myself by writing books for "The Urban Avenger" series. He's the ex-Green Beret who goes around battling urban blight by killing slumlords, muggers, and assorted human vermin. It's low-paying junk, but pays the bills. Barely.

I also teach part time at Kings County Community College, a decidedly inferior facility which offers miniscule pay, overcrowded facilities, and a faculty whose incompetence is exceeded only by their arrogance. My students are either young louts convinced they will be the next F. Scott Fitzgerald or bored punks who are forced to take my introductory composition class. I despise them as much as they despise me.

One night, deep in the depressive funk that has hovered around me since my firing, I found myself outside of the midtown skyscraper where Coyne works. It was nearly nine p.m. and the only ones visible inside were the cleaning crews, those faceless minions who keep the steel and glass towers gleaming.

The Great Man himself was exiting. Whatever you say about Coyne, he worked long and hard. He enjoyed his job. Crushing hopes and ruining dreams. For months I had fantasized about confronting him. Perhaps that would provide a catharsis, relieve this bleak misery. Force him to admit he had told the dean about my pseudonym. Demand an apology, or a book contract.

He tried to hail a cab, but it was pouring, and New York cabs are not allowed to stop for passengers when it rains. I gleefully watched as one Yellow Cab swerved as if to pick him up, only to send a tsunami of water on his trenchcoat. The taxi sped away, leaving Coyne waving his fist and shouting uneducated words at the cabbie's muffler.

Coyne stomped off, heading west, toward Penn Station. He lived outside of the city proper, and no doubt feared he'd miss his train to Westchester. Hunched beneath his umbrella, clutching his alligator skin attaché case, he moved assuredly down the deserted streets. Cars hissed by on the rain slick pavement. No one else walked in the downpour.

I longed to confront him in front of an audience, verbally humiliate him. Perhaps at the editorial board meeting, in front of those he had cowed for years. Throw hot coffee into that smug smile, spit in that critical eye.

I was about to call to him when he turned down a still darker street. I wished I had the Urban Avenger to keep me safe. Coyne feared no one. What would he do to repel a mugger, slash him with his cutting wit?

I was a few feet behind him when a gust of wind folded his umbrella. Again, Attila the Editor launched into a stream of invective that a high school football coach would be ashamed of. He fumbled with his umbrella, trying to straighten the ribs. I reached to tap his shoulder, startle him, seize the upper hand.

Without a conscious thought, as my hand neared his shoulder it turned into a fist, picked up momentum, and slammed into his temple.

The Great Man crumpled like so much paper. I froze, glanced around nervously. Cars passed but his body was hidden by a parked car. I dragged him into a deep doorway. I felt for a pulse. Strong. He did have a heart, I guess. I didn't know whether to wait until he recovered, and apologize, or just leave him.

His fancy attaché case lay on the sidewalk, a dozen or so feet away. What ideas were inside, what future bestsellers or memos displaying his cruel wit?

A young man scurried by, picked it up, and casually hurried on. One of those New York predators who prowl the city. Like vultures, at the first sign of weakness, vulnerability, inattention, their talons are unsheathed.

Had he seen my encounter, or thought the case was accidentally dropped from somewhere? I was about to yell, "Stop thief," when I realized how awkward my position was. I gazed down at the unconscious Coyne. In a way it was fitting justice for this corporate predator to lose something to a lower class citizen with similar morals.

I thought back to a lunch I'd had with Coyne, back when he was still offering charm to keep the advances low. He'd paid cash in the restaurant, with some offhand comment about credit cards being a nuisance. I presumed that he had run up too large a debt somewhere. The sign of apparent mortality on the part of the Great Man had warmed me then.

Rent was due on the apartment where I lived. My slumlord charges five hundred dollars a month for a studio apartment with one window looking out on an air shaft. No extra charge for the hundreds of cockroaches. I owed a month's rent and this month's blood money was coming due. I knew that if I didn't pay, I would get a visit from the super. The building superintendent—a Golden

Gloves boxer gone to seed—never visited for problems with plumbing, electricity, vermin, cracked plaster, broken windows. But if the rent was overdue, his smirking face was at the door, mumbling words that could be interpreted as a threat.

I looked down on Coyne, his Burberry trenchcoat gaped open to reveal a designer gray three-piece suit. I felt the urge to kick that smug face, but I am not the sort to hit a man when he's down. Instead, I reached into his pocket and took his wallet.

What was one more robbery on the mean streets of New York, a city with a homicide rate twice that of West Beirut?

Eight hundred dollars. A few crisp hundreds and the rest twenties. Who needed it more, him or I? He had a gold pinkie ring on his left hand and a Rolex on his wrist. But if I tried to sell them, it would be my luck that I'd be caught. A regular junkie, the kind my Urban Avenger eliminated, would of course take anything of value. So I popped the ring off his finger and pulled the watch off.

A few hairs by his wrist caught in the strap and he stirred. I struck him again. Lightly, just enough to ensure my own safety. It was much easier hitting him the second time around.

I was soaking wet as I hurried away, but felt better than I had since I was booted out of the hallowed ivy-covered halls of academe. I went down into the subway and, after wiping the ring clean of prints, left it on a seat. Then I boarded a train, not the one I usually rode, and, when no one was looking, set the Rolex on the seat. I felt like Robin Hood. People riding the subway generally weren't the sort to wear Rolexes. I hoped that some hardworking blue collar person was rewarded for a life of drudgery by sitting on the Rolex.

Perhaps it would've ended there, if not for another fortuitous circumstance a few weeks later. While walking in Greenwich Village one evening, I spotted a critic who had villified one of my mainstream novels. The critic was a plump little man with a self-satisfied air. He himself wrote books laden with embarassing purple prose, cardboard characters, and banalities so trite that if one of my students handed it in I would vigorously ridicule him in front of the whole class.

My feet began to follow him even before my mind knew it. My fists clenched and unclenched. I beamed him brainwaves, urging him to walk down more and more deserted streets. But his foul little mind refused to obey.

I thumped him just as he was putting the key in the lock of his loft and pushed in behind him. As he lay unconscious on the floor, I rifled his pockets and was disappointed to find a mere seventy-five dollars. His watch was a cheap electronic import. It confirmed my assessment of him as a man with poor taste.

Once a week in the months that followed I targeted a deserving individual from my past, and exacted a tariff for his abuse. My least profitable haul came from an editor at a second-rate publisher who had rejected one of my mainstream books with a note that read, "This is underserving of my, or any other reader's, attention." He had a paltry twelve dollars in his wallet. I struck him a couple of times while he was unconscious to make up for his inadequacies. I'm not proud of it.

Two weeks after that, I balanced accounts with a bi-coastal film producer who had finagled me into writing a free treatment for him. The producer had close to a thousand dollars in his wallet and several thick gold chains around his neck. I left the chains in the mail slot of a shelter for abused children.

Fortunately, I had kept every rejection letter I had ever received. What was a list of shame and pain now became a source of hours, indeed days, of pleasure. Other suitable victims included rude editorial assistants, former agents, a few obnoxious fellow authors. I would choose my target, investigate his habits, and plot my attack. The foreplay was as much fun as the act.

But soon my list began to thin. Some of the cruelest individuals had been women, but I am too much of a gentleman to waylay a female. No matter how deserving.

Was it time for repeat attacks on the truly loathsome? No. Better to expand beyond the literary world. I considered others who had added misery to my life. The department chairman who fired me. My landlord. The creature above me who loves disco played at airplane engine sound levels. Fellow community college teachers who huddle in cliques and talk about me behind my back. The rude clerk at the grocery store. I replenished my list.

Why am I confessing this all now? The statute of limitations has passed. Why did I stop?

I had submitted my latest mainstream novel to a small publisher and got a snotty rejection, written by the Harvard-educated twit who had been made editor because of family connections. He rose to a top spot on my list.

It was one of those humid New York days where the fabric bonds to your skin and you pray for a stronger air conditioner. I followed my quarry down into the hellhole that masquerades as mass transit, the Lexington Avenue line. The subway rumbled into the station.

Because of my time tracking I had honed my street smarts. At a certain point I became convinced I was being watched. Not by the Harvard editor. He was reading *Barron's* and was oblivious to his surroundings.

I covertly scanned the faces around me. About halfway down the car I saw a young man who looked vaguely familiar. He turned away before I could completely register who he was.

I followed my prey up to the street. I knew the brownstone where he lived. On the block before his, there was a construction site. The perfect spot for justice to be enacted.

Again I had that feeling of being watched. I debated calling off the mission, but it was too perfect. I knew my prey would be heading out to the Hamptons for the rest of the summer. If I didn't get him tonight, I would have to wait a month.

But that eerie feeling of being watched threw me off. The editor was past the construction site before I could reach him.

The feeling was stronger, almost palpable. In the second before the darkness struck, I remembered the young man from the train. One of my students, a particularly talentless lout who was too egotistical to realize it. I had vigorously pointed out his inadequacies in front of the class, provoking gales of laughter from his fellow untalented troglodytes.

I woke in the mud of the construction site. My wallet was gone.

Star

by Molly Brown

When Leslie woke up, John was just leaving. It was one of those tiny New York flats without internal doors, where you had to walk through the bedroom to get to the kitchen, and the bedroom was in full sight of the front door. "Where you goin'?" she asked sleepily.

He paused in the doorway and walked back to the bed. "To get some food," he said. "I've just looked in the kitchen, and the cupboard is bare!" He indicated the kitchen with a sweeping, dramatic gesture. Typical actor, never off-stage for a moment.

"That's all right. I'm not hungry, anyway."

"But I am," he said. "There's a deli on the corner. It'll just take me a minute to pick up some eggs and bread and stuff, and then I'll come flying back to you." He leant over to kiss her, and she giggled. "Make yourself at home. I'll be right back."

"Aren't you afraid to leave me here alone? How do you know I won't steal the family silver?"

His face hardened. "You couldn't if you wanted to," he said, sounding *serious*. Geez, she thought, didn't he know I was kidding? "There's a pot of coffee in the kitchen, help yourself. I want you awake." The front door closed and he was gone.

I want you awake. What was that supposed to mean? She shrugged and stretched, and then she hopped out of bed and walked through the kitchen into the bathroom. She had a quick shower, and went back into the bedroom. She rummaged through his closet until she found a shirt to suit her, a pale blue to complement her eyes, nicely over-sized, very sixties' movie. She went back in the kitchen and poured herself a cup of coffee. One swig and she spat it into the sink. God, it was strong! No wonder the guy was so hyper.

She opened the refrigerator. There was one small carton of half-and-half, nothing else. She checked the freezer section, empty as well. He hadn't been kidding about bare cupboards. She sighed and held her cup under the hot water tap. Once she'd watered the coffee down enough so that she could drink it, she added a bit of the half-and-half and went back into the bedroom to wait.

John was sure taking his time. Maybe the deli was busy; it was a Saturday morning after all. She wandered into the living room, still sipping her coffee, and looked around. He didn't have much. A sofa, two metal folding chairs, a wooden table. Plain white walls. No pictures, no books, no stereo, nothing. The bedroom furnishings consisted of one double bed, one television set, and one video. About a dozen cassettes were piled on the floor beside it. No sign of anything else.

The lack of pictures surprised her—she'd never known an actor who didn't have loads of pictures of himself. Her apartment, down in the village, was positively *buried* in pictures of herself. Publicity stills of her as Helena in *A Midsummer Night's Dream* in Central Park, Frenchie in a touring company of *Grease*, the wife in a dinner-theatre production of *Deathtrap*, and the time she'd been a background singer in one of the "I Love New York" TV ads.

But then he'd told her he didn't do much stage work, he worked mostly in film. Cheap videos, he'd told her, ones that never make the cinema. But it was regular work, and it paid the rent.

They met at an audition for an off-off-Broadway revival of *Streetcar*. She read Stella to his Stanley, and they had a cup of coffee afterwards. He phoned her a few days later to find out if she'd made the call-backs, but she hadn't. He hadn't either. He suggested they met for a drink and some mutual consolation. That's when he told her about the videos.

"In a way, it's an actor's worst nightmare," he told her. "I've been completely typecast. I play the same role, over and over. But there's a huge demand for the damn things, so they keep churning them out, and I keep working."

"So what's the role you keep playing?"

He took a sip of his drink and looked around the bar. No one was within hearing distance. "Oh," he said casually, "I'm usually a mad slasher. Though sometimes I get to shoot someone."

Leslie giggled. "You're making video nasties!"

"Do you disapprove?"

"Nah! In this biz, you gotta take work where you can find it. You know what I did last year?" She leaned forward, lowering her voice to a confidential tone. "I did the voice for a porno flick. They got this big-chested bimbo to play the lead, right? But she couldn't talk! I mean, she had a voice like Minnie Mouse. So my agent phoned me up and asked me if I'd do it, just record her lines so they could dub them in. Well, all my right-on friends would have *killed* me if they knew, but it was anonymous, and I was broke. Mostly, all I had to do was moan and say stuff like, 'Ooh, don't stop!' Besides, if I didn't do it, someone else would."

"That's exactly how I feel," he said, nodding. "If I didn't do it, somebody else would."

He phoned her the next day. "I'm doing another video," he said, "and they need someone like you. Are you interested?"

"Sure. What do I have to do, send them a photo, go to a casting, what?"

"Why don't I tell you all about it over dinner?"

Across a candlelit table in an Italian restaurant, he told her he'd fixed everything. Not only was she going to be in the next film, she was going to be the star. I wonder if Katharine Hepburn started like this, she thought ironically. But what did she care? Work was work.

They went back to his apartment after dinner. "You're going to be a star, Leslie," he told her. "You're going to be a star."

He'd been gone a long time now. She was getting hungry. She went through all the drawers and cupboards in the kitchen. Empty. Except for one box of cereal, way at the back of a shelf. That would do. She poured some into a bowl and screamed. It was crawling with worms. "Damn," she said, tossing it in the bin.

She watered down some more coffee and took it into the bedroom. She turned on the television and flicked from channel to channel, but there was nothing she wanted to watch. She reached down and looked through the video cassettes; none of them were labelled.

She put one in the machine and pressed "play". For a moment she thought the tape must be blank, then a title appeared: "To Slash A Brunette". She laughed out loud. So he had copies of every video he was in! He was a typically egotistical actor after all. She figured she ought to watch it, it would give her an idea of the sort of thing she was getting herself into.

A woman was sitting on a bed in her underwear, reading a magazine. The setting looked familiar. It was the room she was in now. God, she thought, these must be really low-budget. Nothing happened for a minute, then the woman looked up. "Oh, it's you," she said. "Where the hell have you been?" Then she frowned. "What's that supposed to be?" She started moving backwards. "Look," she said. "This isn't funny, so stop it!"

Leslie rolled her eyes. That woman couldn't act her way out of a paper bag. She pressed "pause" and mentally went over the way *she* would have said those lines. With meaning. With *feeling*. She pressed "play" again.

The woman was screaming, "Stay away from me! Stay away from me!"

Leslie didn't think much of the script; surely they could have given her something more interesting to say.

A figure moved into the shot, a man wearing a long coat, leather gloves, and a tight-fitting black leather hood that zipped up one side and had holes for the eyes and mouth. He was holding a long knife.

That must be John, he told her he always played the slasher.

The woman tried to run, but he caught her. She screamed and screamed. The man held her from behind, so that she was facing the camera.

This is so unrealistic, Leslie thought.

He wielded the knife, and began to cut.

"OH YUCK!" Leslie said out loud. This was disgusting. They'd really gone overboard with the cheap special effects. She fast-forwarded through the disemboweling sequence, trying to find the obligatory scene where the hero (usually a hard-boiled private eye or a tough cop) is introduced. There wasn't one. There was a long shot of the woman lying dead and mutilated, followed by blank tape.

Leslie's forehead wrinkled in consternation. This couldn't be the whole film—maybe he just kept copies of his own scenes. Though he didn't seem to have any lines.

She put another tape in the machine. The title appeared: "To Kill A Call Boy". The same room, the same bed. A young man, about twenty years old, with bleached blonde hair and one earring leaned back stretching his arms. "I've been waiting for you," he said. What followed was a repeat of the first film, despite some minor variations.

She ejected the tape and put in another. A woman again, only this time in the kitchen.

It was finally dawning on her. These were real. Real people. Real deaths.

Her stage experience came in handy; she was dressed in less than twenty seconds. She ran for the door. It wouldn't open. She picked up the telephone; it was dead. She went back to the door and pounded and screamed. The door was soft to the touch. So were the walls. The place was sound-proofed.

She ran to the window. She was fifteen floors up, but she could throw something down to the street to get attention. The windows were sealed shut. She picked up one of the metal chairs and swung it against the glass. The chair broke. The glass didn't.

"Help me!" she screamed. "Get me out of here! Get me out of here!"

There was a click and then a whirring. She spun around and looked where the sound was coming from. A panel in the wall slid back, revealing the lens of a camera.

The front door opened, and a black-gloved hand reached inside. *She was going to be a star.*

The Persian Apothecary

by Cay Van Ash

T here is always, I suppose, an element of drama in the life of a doctor and, in the confused post-war years of Cairo in the nineteen-twenties, it was never far below the surface. God knows, I had had my share, but nothing was farther from my mind on that hot August afternoon when I came out on the terrace of Shepheard's Hotel and sat down at the nearest vacant table.

My round of house calls had just ended with a visit to an American lady confined painfully to her room by a failure to realise that eating fruit in Egypt is as risky as drinking the water it is washed in. At the tables surrounding me, tea was being served and a twinge of nostalgia tempted me. I summoned a white-robed waiter and ordered. Nothing warned me that, thereby, I was to involve myself in a dark and dangerous business.

The terrace was busy and noisy with a younger crowd of visitors who chose the off-season period, when temperatures were high and prices low. Beyond the railings, the street was noisier with a cacophony of motor horns and engines. Though camels had long since been banned from the Shâria' Kamel, the stream of vehicles still threaded an erratic path through a swarm of handcarts and pedestrians, passing to left or right as the occasion offered.

I reached inside my jacket for my cigarette case, then felt a light touch on my shoulder and looked up to see a girl standing at my side, seemingly no more than twenty-two or three, stockingless, with her hair cut short in the currently graceless fashion and likewise her flimsy summer dress, which barely covered her knees. Her eyes, which were dark and lustrous, bore an expression bordering on panic.

"Please! I do not know how to say this," she began tremulously. "I need your help desperately."

"Sit down," I said, startled, "and tell me what I may do."

"You are kind. Thank you."

With a pathetic attempt at a smile, she sat on the edge of the chair facing me, resting her elbows on the table. Her clothes and her shoes suggested one of the less expensive stores in Oxford Street, but her olive-skinned complexion and accented English prompted me to think that she might be Spanish or Italian.

"You do not know me," she went on, "but I know you. I often saw you, during the war, when you came to the hospital where I was working as a nurse. My name is Halîmah. . . ."

"Good Heavens! I thought—"

She shook her head. "No. I was born here, but now I am a medical student in London. My mother was French, perhaps, but I do not remember her."

"I see! So you are making a holiday visit home."

"That is more or less it. I came on a tourist ship, but I am not a tourist." Again she hesitated. "Somehow I must make you understand. There is a man upstairs, one of your countrymen, who is ill—dying, I believe—because of me. . . . I have done what I can, but I do not know enough and I have no drugs. I was going out to try to buy something when I saw you and came back—"

I stood up abruptly. "Then, if the matter is urgent, there is no time to be lost. Take me to him."

I saw the waiter approaching with my order, but I waved him away, picked up my bag, and followed Halîmah inside. We did not speak again till we were in a part of the hotel where some of the cheaper rooms were situated—though nothing at Shepheard's was cheap. She halted before a door and fumbled with a key.

"Who is he?" I asked curiously. "Your husband?"

She flushed slightly. "So it says in the book downstairs. But it is untrue. We met on the boat, the first day out from Tilbury."

We entered a room dimly illuminated and relatively cool. The window was open, but the shutters were closed against the sun, casting a barred pattern of shadows obliquely across the form of a man who lay stretched upon the bed, clad only in his underpants.

189

I strode quickly to his side and peered down. He was little older than she, with the muscular physique of a football player. Though neither unconscious nor delirious, when he tried to speak the words were incoherent. His body was shaken by convulsions and, from wrist to shoulder, the whole of his left arm was hideously swollen and discoloured.

"His name is Clive Anderson," said Halîmah distractedly. "He is a student, like me—but a law student."

"It looks like some kind of neuro-toxic poisoning," I muttered. "How long has he been like this?"

"Since early this morning." She licked her lips nervously. "I—I know what it is. It is scorpion venom."

"What! A scorpion? Has he been out in the desert?"

"No, but. . ."

I straightened up impatiently, making no further attempt at examination.

"I can do nothing here," I snapped. "He must be got to hospital immediately. If we act swiftly, his life may be saved. But he'll be lucky if he doesn't lose that arm." Taking up the telephone, I asked for a number which I knew without needing to consult my notebook and, while waiting for the connection, added: "You should have done this hours ago, or at least called a doctor."

"I do not trust Egyptian doctors," she replied, "and we cannot afford hospitals."

"That can be worried about later—" I broke off, talked rapidly on the telephone, and put it down. "The ambulance will be here in a few minutes."

I glanced around the room, frowning slightly as it occurred to me that not only would my fees go unpaid but I might end up by paying the patient's hospital bills out of my own pocket.

"If you are low on funds," I said severely, "your choice of a hotel was, surely, somewhat extravagant?"

"I—I know," she whispered. "But, here, I thought we might be safe. . . ."

Safe? Safe from whom, or from what?

The man on the bed uttered a low groan. Halîmah spun around, fell on her knees, and threw her arms around him.

"I love him!" she cried hysterically. "I love him! Jesus! Don't let him die!"

I thought it a little odd that she should call upon Jesus rather than Allah—though she probably believed in neither. Taking her by the shoulders, I drew her gently upright.

"Easy!" I warned. "Don't lose your nerve now." I shook my head dubiously. "A scorpion? Are you sure? A man as strong and as

190

healthy as he appears should not have been so seriously affected by a scorpion sting."

"But—but what if it were five or six?"

"What! You mean that he was stung several times?"

"I—I did not say that he was stung." She stared up at me with curiously frightened eyes. "You will not understand, but I will try to explain. Last night, we were walking back here through the Ezbekîyeh Gardens. We had been listening to the band. It was dark, and under the pergola it was darker, because of the leaves overhead. There, suddenly, we were attacked by three men. One seized me by the arms. The other two hurled Clive to the ground and fell on top of him. I saw something flash—a knife, I thought—and I screamed. Then people came running, and the three men raced away. . . ."

"Good God! Didn't you go to the police?"

She gave me a tired smile. "Why? We had not been robbed and, so far as we knew, not much harm had been done. Clive's shirtsleeve was torn, and there was a small cut on his arm but, by the time we reached the hotel, it had stopped bleeding. Then, during the night, he became ill."

I regarded her incredulously, with a question on my lips and a hundred more seething in my mind. But this was not the time.

"The ambulance will be here any minute," I said. "I will go with it and do what is necessary. But I have guests to dinner and I cannot talk to you again tonight. Tomorrow I have surgery and patients to visit. I will help you if I can, but I must know more of this matter. Meet me here on the terrace at the same time as today."

After dinner that night, I telephoned the hospital and was thankful to discover Anderson considered out of danger. But the extraordinary circumstances of his injury still troubled me. Seemingly, he had been poisoned by a crude form of injection. By whom? And why?

These questions disturbed my sleep and interfered with my work next day till, at length, I found myself on the terrace at Shepheard's and, by coincidence, at the same table. But I postponed ordering, conscious of an uncomfortable possibility that Halîmah might not show up—leaving my curiosity unsatisfied and Clive Anderson on my hands.

However, no more than ten minutes had elapsed when I saw her ascending the steps from outside, with the sunlight silhouetting her figure through her dress in a manner once regarded as disgraceful.

I stood up politely and set a chair for her.

"You have been to the hospital?" I inquired.

"Yes. Clive is much better, and they let me spend some time with him."

Today she was more composed and, as she talked, I found her English quaint—fluent, but curiously literary, marred by a London accent and occasionally startling idioms.

"Now," I said, "tell me what this is all about."

She nodded gravely. "Yes, I will tell you all. May I have a cigarette?" I gave her one, lit it for her, and she began like an Arab storyteller: "First, you must know that here, in Cairo, there is a terrible man called Hassim el-'Ajâmi. . . ."

"Meaning that he is a Persian?"

"Yes. Many years ago, he came from Isfahan. Some call him Hassim the Apothecary. He has a tiny shop in the Souk el-Attarîn, where he sells perfumes, simple remedies, and cosmetics—*kohl*, henna, and antimony for the eyes. But he has also a secret store of poisons, extracted from strange plants and the crawling things of the desert. He is an evil bugger. He—he *arranges* things. . . ."

She paused, waiting for my reaction, but I displayed none and she continued:

"When one has a relative who has lived too long, a girl child, or a troublesome husband, one goes to Hassim el-'Ajâmi. And, if the price is right, he will even arrange how it be done—for he knows many wicked bastards who will do anything for money."

A waiter appeared beside us.

"Tea?" I proposed.

"Yes, please!" I gave the order, and she smiled as the waiter departed. "In England, I have learned to put milk and sugar in my tea, instead of cinnamon and lemon, to smoke cigarettes, to show my legs, and to swear like a lady. . . ."

It was midway between noon and nightfall. Faintly above the noise of the traffic, the voices of the *mueddinîn* chanted the Call to Prayer, relayed from mosque to mosque.

Halîmah drew deeply on her cigarette and exhaled smoke through her nostrils like a dragon. "But I have started in the wrong place, so I must start again. I have told you how I worked at the hospital, during the war. Do you remember a certain Dr. Forsyth?"

"Yes," I said. "I remember him very well."

"He praised my work, and was good to me, telling me that even I might be a doctor. Then, when the war was over, he pulled the strings for me, so that I might enter the medical school in London. My father complained that he could not afford it—though, in truth, he is quite well off. He believes that daughters are only to be sold like cattle to the highest bidder, and he let me be a nurse only

192

because I could bring him money. But I persuaded him that, as a doctor, I could bring him much more, and so he agreed. Thus I went to London. . . ."

I smiled abstractedly. London, just then, was more remote to me than to her. Out in the Shâria' Kamel, a ragged band of hawkers clustered about the railings which excluded them from the terrace, thrusting their arms through and exhorting me to purchase worthless trinkets, spurious antiques, and bunches of sweet-smelling jasmine for my companion.

"For two years, I worked hard and did well in my exams," said Halîmah. "Then, earlier this year, there came yet again a delegation from Egypt to argue about our independence—which, they say, is no true independence while the British are here. Of course, they got nowhere but, to keep them happy, an informal party was held for them, and some like myself, who could speak Arabic and needed to earn a little money, were engaged to wait upon them and serve them the drinks forbidden by the Prophet." She gave me a sly smile. "It was also required that we should wear very little! One among the guests was named Rashîd Hamâdi. . . ."

"Rashîd Hamâdi! Isn't he the Minister of—"

Again she nodded. "Yes, he is. He is also stinking rich. I pleased him, and he wished to have intercourse with me in a very disgusting manner. This I would not permit, and he was angered—which was bad. One does not offend such a man. But, in England, he could do nothing to me and, soon after that, the delegation left."

Halîmah laughed shortly but without mirth.

"A few weeks before the summer term ended," she went on, "I received a letter from my father, telling me that he was ill and begging me to come home. With it, he sent money for the fare. What else could I do? But, knowing my father, I knew that, once in Egypt, he might not allow me to leave again. Therefore, I used the money to buy a cheap return ticket on a ship for tourists. And it was on that ship that I met Clive. . . ."

She hesitated, stubbed out her cigarette in an ashtray, and resumed:

"As soon as we reached Cairo, I went to my father's house, where I found—as I had half suspected—that I had been deceived. He was not ill. Rashîd Hamâdi had been to see him. I had hurt his pride, and he meant to be revenged. He did not care what it cost. So he offered money to my father, asking him to bring me home, and my father had sold me to him."

"How?" I objected. "Under our present laws, he could not sell you as a slave!"

"No—but he could sell me as a wife, which, in Egypt, is the same thing!" Halîmah glared at me. "To Rashîd Hamâdi, what was a so-called marriage, which he could dissolve when he pleased? Naturally, I refused and there was a dreadful scene. My father was angry—and frightened because he had already taken money which, he said, he could not repay. But still I refused. Then my father flew into a rage, snatched up a stick, and ordered me to take my knickers off. But I told him he should go to bloody hell and ran out of his house."

"So what do you intend to do now?" I asked.

"When Clive recovers, we will go back to London together and complete our studies."

"But, without your father's support, how will you live? How will you pay your tuition fees?"

She shrugged. "We shall manage. Clive will help me, though he has little more than I have. If necessary, I will work as a waitress or as a prostitute." She laughed harshly. "You look shocked. Why? Should a woman not be ready to do anything to be with the man she loves?"

I could find no immediate answer.

"Tell me what happened after you left your father's house," I said.

"I picked up Clive from the pension where he was staying, and brought him here to Shepheard's, knowing that we were both in danger. What would Rashîd Hamâdi do? He could easily have me kidnapped, and who would look for me?—certainly not my father. But there was Clive. So Rashîd Hamâdi has put the matter into the hands of Hassim el-'Ajâmi, the poisoner. . . ."

"You should complain to the police!"

"The police?" she retorted contemptuously. "Your police are here to protect you against us, not to protect us against each other. They would not listen to me—"

"But they will listen to *me!*" I said grimly. "I have friends. . ."

I ceased speaking as our conversation was interrupted by the return of our waiter. Setting out cups and saucers, a milk jug, a sugar bowl and a teapot, he bowed and retired. Halîmah, assuming the role of hostess, and demonstrating that she knew how to do it, filled her cup first, then mine.

"Sugar?" she asked formally, and pushed the bowl towards me.

"Please!" I replied, and lifted off the lid—then, with a hoarse cry, leapt up, overthrowing my chair, as I found the vessel to contain

194

not only some knobs of sugar but the largest scorpion I had ever seen!

Halîmah's chair went flying, as she too sprang to her feet and, for an instant, we stood on opposite sides of the table, staring wild-eyed at the repulsive creature scrabbling at the edge of the sugar bowl, furious at its confinement, and striking viciously over its back with its venomous tail. But Halîmah's response was the quicker. Snatching up the teapot, she upended it, drenching the scorpion with a scalding mixture of hot water and tea leaves.

People behind us were jumping up from their tables and we were soon surrounded by a vociferous throng. Waiters pushed their way through, shouting at one another and demanding how it could have happened—then a red-faced assistant manager, breathless but profuse with apologies.

"Probably the lid was left off somewhere," I suggested, "and it crawled in."

But I did not believe it and, so far as I knew, scorpions did not like sugar. I turned to Halîmah, my mind made up.

"You are not safe, even here," I said. "Go and pack your things and come home with me. We have a spare room for guests, and my wife will welcome you."

It was past midnight, and the two women had long since retired, but still I sat in my study, struggling to cope with the paperwork which is a doctor's worst affliction—for the end of the month was near. I was not proceeding very well with it, which was hardly surprising, after what I had seen and heard that day.

But the chances that I might have been stung were slight—the bizarre incident at Shepheard's had been no more than an arrogant warning that Halîmah and all who befriended her were the targets of a formidable opponent. One who could introduce a scorpion into a sugar bowl at Shepheard's Hotel was not to be lightly discounted!

Hassim el-'Ajâmi. . . I had often heard tales of infanticide in India by means of snakebite, and of fiends who caught and sold snakes. But I had never before heard of one who prepared and stored organic poisons for the same and similar purposes.

All his fellow shopkeepers in the teeming narrow alleyways of the Mûski must know about him. Yet none denounced him—thinking, perhaps, that they too might someday need his services, or that, if they spoke, they too might become his victims.

Making an honest effort to thrust such thoughts aside, I picked up my pen and gave renewed attention to the column of figures which I had three times added up with different results. But, ere I had achieved a fourth, I was again interrupted, this time by a sound from below—a faint but unmistakable sound of breaking glass.

I stiffened in my chair and listened. No one should be down there, and we had no cat in the house. Had a window been broken? Were we, already, under attack?

No further sound followed, but I was too old a hand at such games to let it pass. Sliding open a drawer, I took out an automatic pistol—not an item of daily use. It took me some minutes to find the cartridges and to load it. Then, standing up carefully, so as to avoid even the creak of my chair as I pushed it back, I moved out silently into the passage.

Out there it was dark and I could perceive no light below till, reaching the stairhead, I saw a dim glow emmanating from the open door of my consulting room, which told me that the light was on in the dispensary. With the pistol ready in my hand, I tiptoed down. But, just as I reached the door, the light went out.

I peered cautiously around the frame. The room was faintly lit by starlight through the shuttered window and by which I could just make out the formless shape of one who stole across towards me, feeling a way round the furniture. I waited, then stepped smartly in front and jabbed the muzzle of the weapon hard into the intruder's stomach.

A sharp intake of breath and a squeal answered.

"Good God!" I burst out. "Is it you?"

I reached out, turned on the light, and saw Halîmah, with her hands clutched to her midriff and clad in a man's pyjama jacket.

"What on earth are you doing, creeping about here in the dark?" I demanded. "Have I hurt you?"

"You—haven't done me much good!" she gasped. "I—I woke up. I was dreadfully thirsty, and—and I needed a glass of water. So I came down. . . ."

"Why?" I asked. "There was ice water in the thermos flask beside your bed."

"Was there? I thought it was tea or coffee." Halîmah recovered her breath and, with it, her composure. "I didn't want to disturb anybody. I didn't know where the kitchen was, but I knew you'd have water in your dispensary. But, till I got there, I couldn't find any of the switches."

"Not surprising," I said, smiling. "They were all installed by some madman who put them on the hinge side of the doors!"

"While I was groping around, I knocked down a flask and broke it. But it was empty and I've picked up the pieces."

"Then there's no harm done," I assured her.

For a moment too long, I stared at her slender legs and the incongruous pyjama jacket, and she laughed.

"Yes, it's Clive's—and no, I don't have anything on underneath!" She regarded me with round eyes and an expression of mock gravity. "All right! You've caught me! You've done a lot for me, and now I've got to pay, haven't I? In the only way I can. . . ." She started to unbutton the jacket, and glanced sideways at the black leather couch. "You can put me down on that. . . ."

I really did not know whether to laugh or to be angry.

"The sacrifice is unnecessary," I said tactfully. "You are in love with your—your fiancé, and I love my wife, who is asleep upstairs."

"Yes, of course!" Halîmah looked surprised. "But what has that to do with it?"

"It has everything to do with it!" I said sternly. "Fasten yourself up, and go back to bed!"

She obeyed, glancing at me curiously, and we went outside. I switched on the light at the foot of the stair and waited for her to ascend. We had not yet reached the era of double switches.

"The light at the top is controlled by the switch on your left," I informed her.

Halîmah, saying nothing, climbed the steps, casually displaying shapely thighs and a well-rounded rear. Halfway up, she paused and looked back over her shoulder.

"You are a very kind man," she said, "but very strange . . . ."

Nothing more occurred that night and, needless to say, the episode was not mentioned over breakfast. Halîmah could not go out unescorted, so, while I held surgery, I lent her some of my medical books, telling her to use the time usefully and get on with her studies.

After lunch, when I went out on my rounds, I took her with me to the hospital, where she was permitted to stay till the evening. I learned on inquiry that young Anderson was better, though still exhausted. But I did not go up to see him.

I had a full afternoon's work ahead of me, for at that time of year we were always beset by minor cases of sunstroke and amoebic dysentery among the foreign community. But while I journeyed about the city—as usual, employing taxis, since I hated to drive my own car in those chaotic streets—I thought often of Halîmah and wondered how soon I might get rid of her. Even after Clive Anderson was discharged from hospital, they could not leave Egypt till the ship which had brought them sailed once more for England.

The girl had a naïve honesty and candour which I found refreshing. But she made me feel old. The war had changed too much, and I could not yet get used to these new youngsters, to whom the most intimate of human relations was a triviality, reflecting, with a wry smile, that Halîmah had indignantly rejected the advances of Rashîd Hamâdi from no sense of moral outrage, but simply because she disliked him!

Time slipped into the past, till I heard the Call to Prayer an hour before sunset and again an hour after. The stars spangled the night and a soft, warm breeze came up from the Nile, gently stirring the fernlike branches of the palm trees. I hailed my last taxi and made for the hospital, telling the man to wait while I went inside to collect my embarrassing house guest.

But there was no sign of her in the foyer and when I approached the desk I learned, to my astonishment, that Halîmah was no longer in the building.

"She left ten minutes ago, with two men," said the white-uniformed receptionist, raising neatly trimmed eyebrows at my startled response. "But she wrote a note for you, gave it to the night sister, and asked her to bring it down here."

Taking the folded sheet of paper, I smoothed it out and saw three sentences pencilled in a feminine hand:

"They are waiting for me downstairs.
I do not want to make trouble here,
so I will go with them. But I know
where they are taking me."

A name followed, and the location of a house near the Pyramids.

"She has been abducted!" I said, and threw the note back across the desk. "Call the police and send them to that address."

If Halîmah felt any qualms about involving the Egyptian police, I certainly did not. But I could not wait for them to do the job alone.

Leaving the smart young receptionist open-mouthed, I hurried out to the taxi and leapt in.

"Take me to Gizeh!" I directed.

Out past the Kasr en-Nil bridge, there was little traffic on the road as we sped westward through darkness till we saw the bright lights of Mena House Hotel up ahead and turned off to the left. A few minutes more and we were passing alongside the wall of the old Moslem cemetery to a cluster of nondescript houses, where neighbours sat on chairs by open doors, smoking, and drinking coffee.

Here we paused briefly to ask directions. The name written on Halîmah's note meant nothing to me, but the first man we accosted nodded vigorously, pointed, and, a hundred yards farther on, we halted finally before a house much like the rest. In the background, the silhouette shapes of the First and Second Pyramids loomed up, stark and sinister, against the sky, like two-dimensional images painted on a backdrop.

My driver—who clearly did not like the look of things— refused to wait. I paid him and, as he drove off, gazed up at the house—a square, ugly structure, three-storied and flat roofed, with plaster peeling from the walls, shuttered windows projecting on the street, and a massive wooden door.

Obviously, the affluent Rashîd Hamâdi did not live there, but he might own the place or control the owner. Halîmah, if she were inside, would probably be brought to him when and where he found it convenient.

Still I was not quite sure what I intended to do. Any attempt to force my way in was out of the question. I was unarmed, having felt unwilling to go about my professional duties with a pistol in my pocket. It would be best, I thought, to wait for the official force from Bab el-Khalk—who, surely, could not be far behind—and, in the meantime, keep watch in case Halîmah were taken elsewhere. I glanced back at the tail light of my taxi receding citywards and, at that moment, heard a dry, cracked voice speaking in a hoarse whisper.

"Ya Inglîsi! Effendîm!"

I turned, saw the door open and, lined in the light from within, the phantomesque figure of a woman shrouded in a shapeless black garment, drawn up over her head like a cowl, and holding a fold of it up before her face with one hand, while beckoning to me with the other.

"You have come for her!" she hissed. "She said you would. . . ."

"Halîmah?" I asked sharply. "She is here?"

"Yes, yes, *effendîm!* Come quickly inside, but make no sound. I am Madîhah—*his* servant, but *her* friend. . . . Come!"

Following, I found myself in a large, stone-floored room, lit by a crude oil lamp hung from the ceiling, redolent with aromatic odours, and which looked like the workshop of Abu Sîna, the alchemist. Everywhere, there were bottles and oddly shaped vessels—glass jars in which things crawled, ancient alembics and a small furnace.

I started, realising that I was in the house of Hassim el-'Ajâmi. Of course! For an adequate reward, he had agreed not only to contrive the assassination of Clive Anderson, but also the kidnapping. I could hear a man's voice speaking loudly and volubly in an adjoining room, but could not distinguish the words.

"The police will be here soon," I said.

"The police?" Madîhah dropped the fold from her face, disclosing wizened features which she did well to keep covered. "No, no, *effendîm!* The police must not come here!"

"Too late," I replied shortly. "They are on their way."

She stared at me uncertainly, then shrugged. "*Ma'alesh!* So it cannot be helped. Come!–I will show you. But, whatever you see or hear, be silent."

Grasping my arm with bony fingers like talons, she led me to an arched opening closed by a curtain, and held it fractionally aside, allowing me to peer through into a traditionally furnished room, with a raised *dîwan* at one end, upholstered and strewn with cushions. Upon this, sat Hassim el-'Ajâmi—a big, powerfully built man in his fifties, wearing a loose, grease-stained *gallabieh* and an untidily tied turban. He was bearded and hawk-faced, and his eyes blazed like those of a fanatic.

Halîmah knelt on the floor, facing him, sitting on her heels, with her hands behind her back, her clothes pulled down to the waist, and her breasts bare.

Hassim el-'Ajâmi was shouting at her furiously—an impassioned tirade in Persian, which I did not understand. Neither, I supposed, did Halîmah—a detail which had apparently escaped him—but, when he paused for breath, she answered with equal vehemence, in Arabic or English. But, in either language, her replies were the same.

"No!. . . Never!. . . I will not!"

Madîhah closed the curtain. "He is telling her that she must submit when they come for her." (Possibly, I thought, to sign some form of marriage contract?) "If she does not, he will give her something made from the bark of a tree to take away her mind and make her stupid like a sheep. But, if he tries to do this, you must prevent him—for she would never recover."

I hoped fervently that no such eventuality would arise. Having seen him, I did not fancy a bout of fisticuffs with Hassim el-'Ajâmi. Once more, I applied my eye to the gap in the curtain.

For a while longer, the one-sided argument went on. Then suddenly, losing all patience, Hassim el-'Ajâmi leapt up, bore down upon Halîmah, and dealt her two resounding slaps, left and right. Halîmah jerked back her head and spat in his face.

Instinctively, I started forward, but Madîhah clawed at my arm, restraining me.

"Not yet!" she insisted. "Wait!"

Hassim el-'Ajâmi towered over the girl menacingly, but he did not strike her again. Instead, falling silent, he slumped down upon the *dîwan* and sat there sullenly, cupping his chin in one hand and glowering at the floor. Then he raised his head and shouted an order.

"Ya Madîhah! Ta'ala hêna!"

"That is for me!" whispered the old woman at my side. "Wait—and do nothing."

Slipping quickly past the curtain, she approached the *dîwan*, ignoring Halîmah, and prostrated herself before her employer, who spoke a few curt words. She rose, crossed to a stone *suffeh* supported on three marble arches, where various utensils were placed, and returned carrying a tall brass *narghîleh* with a large, lemon-shaped reservoir at the base, which she set down at the foot of the *dîwan*. Detaching the baked clay pipe bowl, she went back to the *suffeh*, to fill it with the sticky black substance which the Egyptians call tobacco, and piled glowing scraps of corncob charcoal on top. Then, re-fitting the pipe bowl to the *narghîleh*, she uncoiled the snakelike tube, handed the end to Hassim el-'Ajâmi, bowed, and retreated to join me on the other side of the curtain.

She looked up at me and, in the dim light of the lantern overhead, her old eyes flashed like onyx beads.

"Inshallah!" she whispered. "Let it be His will!"

Clasping the long wooden mouthpiece in his fist, Hassim el-'Ajâmi put it to his lips and inhaled deeply, so that the perfumed water bubbled audibly in the bulbous container, as the smoke was drawn through it. In the same instant, his face changed—his mouth gaped open and his eyes bulged horribly. Uttering strangled, inarticulate sounds, he clutched at his throat and fell sideways, knocking over the *narghîleh*, so that the burning tobacco was scattered and the water flooded out to extinguish it.

Rarely have I seen anyone struck down so dramatically. Could it be that his insensate rage had brought on an apoplectic fit? Tearing aside the curtain, and remembering only that I was a doctor, I burst into the room and ran to the man sprawled half on and half off the cushioned *dîwan*. But even before I reached him, the spasmodic twitching of his limbs ceased and he lay staring up at me with sightless eyes.

Halîmah arose from her kneeling position and, to my surprise, I saw that her hands were not tied but merely clasped behind her.

"Elhamdu'lillah!" she ground out viciously between her teeth. "He is dead. Praise be to God!"

Madîhah grabbed my arms, dragging me upright.

"Go!" she urged. "Go swiftly, both of you! When the police come, I will say that you left before he died."

Halîmah drew the thin silk straps of her camisole up over her shoulders and fastened her dress, wincing as she did so.

"Christ!" she said. "My tits hurt like hell!"

The business ended as mysteriously as it had begun. Halîmah was arrested next day and carted off to an Egyptian prison, where, I thought, she might be roughly treated—the native officers did not take kindly to girls of their race who consorted with foreigners and behaved as she did—but at least she would be safe. Though his villainous accomplice was dead, Rashîd Hamâdi—against whom no action could be taken—might well employ others.

As for myself, though my participation in the affair must be known, no one came near me till some three weeks later, when my friend Frazer, of the Cairo police, invited himself over for a drink and a chat after dinner.

"Well—they've gone," he announced, sitting down in my most comfortable chair and accepting a cigar. "The ship sailed this morning. Halîmah? We kept her locked up for a few days, till her boy-friend was out of hospital, and then sent both of them off to a handy place we've got in Alexandria."

Inserting a matchstick carefully into the rounded end of the cigar, he continued:

"Hassim el-'Ajâmi *could* have committed suicide—though it was a queer way to do it. It wasn't in the tobacco, you know, but in the water—something which vaporised and killed him stone dead at the first whiff. Who put it there? I'm not sure we want to know. Whoever it was did a public service. Perhaps it was the old woman—who, incidentally, has disappeared—or even the girl herself."

"Hardly," I objected. "Since she was abducted and taken there by force, what opportunity did she have?"

"We've only her word for it that she was abducted." Frazer struck a match and rotated the cigar expertly over the flame. "She might have planned it all in advance and called you in to back her up if her plans misfired."

I shook my head. "No. More likely it was old Madîhah. She must have known where her master kept his store of poisons."

"True!" he admitted. "But the odd thing is that it wasn't the kind of stuff he had in stock—something less exotic and more sophisticated, like prussic acid."

I thought suddenly of Halîmah's midnight visit to my dispensary and said nothing.

Frazer looked at me and shrugged. "Anyway—no matter. They're on their way to England, where, I suppose, they'll marry and live happily ever after. The girl will presumably inherit quite a lot of money from her father."

"But maybe not for some years," I said, "since he is still alive—"

I broke off abruptly, aware that my official friend was staring at me in a peculiar fashion.

"I'm afraid you still don't get it," he said sorrowfully. "Hassim el-'Ajâmi *was* her father!"

Too Late Blues

by Mark Timlin

I f Ronnie hadn't forgotten his cigarettes it would have been all
right.

I don't smoke, and Derek only smokes spliff, so Ronnie
couldn't even ponce one off either of us. All the way from his
place into town, he was going on about it, and he was beginning
to get right on my nerves. When we got close to the centre he said:
"We've got time. Pull over, and I'll get some fags in that shop. I
won't be a minute."

Except it's just past nine in the morning, and the shop's full
of schoolkids, and people buying papers, and Ronnie takes
considerably longer, and I'm parked on a bus lane. I never even
saw the copper. He must have come through the buildings. First
thing I know Derek looks round for Ronnie and says: "Filth."

I nearly shit myself. I look round too, and there he is. I can only
see his middle through the back window. But I can see well enough
to know he's a cozzer, and he's writing in his notebook. Then I see
Ronnie behind him, and the next thing is the back door's open and
they're both in the car, and Ronnie's torn off the copper's radio and
tossed it in the front, and he's got his gun stuck in the copper's face.
It was unreal because the copper was just a kid, see. He looked like
he didn't even shave yet, and before Ronnie knocked it off I saw
that his helmet was too big for him. That made it worse somehow,
him the fact that his bleeding hat didn't even fit. They should have
given one that did before they let him out on the street.

So now we're on the way to a blag, and we've got a bleeding copper as a passenger. I mean, I ask you. And what's even worse is that the local CID are waiting for us to arrive.

You've got to understand I didn't want to grass. I hate grasses. I'd string the bleeders up if I had my way. But Ronnie and Derek were well mental, always armed. A menace to society, and it was only a matter of time before they were back inside with my help or without it. And I'd been captured pulling a stroke of my own a couple of weeks previous. Nothing serious, but with my form I was for the high jump, and that little sod of a DI who nicked me knew it. I told him that Ronnie and Derek had asked me to drive for them on a little over the pavement tickle. But I'd turned them down flat. I mean I hate shooters, worse than grasses, worse than nonces even.

The DI worked out that if I went back to the pair of them and told them I'd changed my mind, and went out on the job and filled in the DI in plenty of time, all would be sweet. He'd get a result. Ronnie and Derek would get their just deserts and I'd get another chance, and maybe a few quid for my trouble out of the informant's fund.

And now what I've got is some young copper lying on the floor in the back of the Granada and a big load of trouble.

"Drive, for Christ's sake," says Ronnie. "Before someone susses us out."

I remembered what I was supposed to be doing then, and I slapped the motor into gear and takes off smartish. Too smartish, as I nearly take the side off a Telecom van, and get well tooted up and a mouthful of abuse for my trouble. If the fat ponce driving had known we had two guns on board, and two nutters carrying them, he would have kept his gob shut. "Take it easy," says Ronnie.

"Do what?" I said to him. "Don't you tell me to take it easy. You're the one who's kidnapped a copper. What the bloody hell did you do that for?"

"What was I supposed to do, shoot him in the bloody street?"

"You weren't supposed to shoot him at all. You were supposed to take the ticket like a punter, and let him get on with his life."

"Yeah, and if he'd radioed through for a registration check on the car, what then?"

"The car hasn't even been missed yet." I said. I knew that for a fact. I'd been checking the railway station car park for a week. The geezer who belonged to the Granada parked it up at 7.30am, and picked it up again at 6pm. He was as regular as a cat fed on goose grease.

"But you can't prove it's yours can you?" said Ronnie.

"But he can't prove it ain't. Look at the state of him, he's just a boy. He'd've given me a form to produce my license within five days, and we'd've been on our bloody way."

And then the poxy radio does start performing, and I nearly jump out of my skin, and Derek stamps on it until it's quiet, and in little pieces all over the rubber mat in the front.

"Do you think anyone saw?" I asked.

"No," said Ronnie. "It was too quick."

But how the hell would he know?

"Well, what are we going to do with him now?" I asked.

"I don't know," says Ronnie. Not a great thinker, Ronnie. A great doer, but not a great thinker.

"Let him go." I said.

"How can we? He's got the number of the car and we're off to knock over a Securicor truck."

"He didn't know that, did he?" I said.

"Well he knows now for sure," said Derek.

"So we can't let him go," said Ronnie.

I knew what he meant, but I pretended I didn't and said, "We can't take him with us. Let's forget the whole thing."

Which wasn't going to please the DI and DS and four DC's waiting outside Barclays in the high street, all tooled up, expecting two armed black men in balaclava helmets to rob the truck delivering cash for the weekend rush.

I was meant to get away in all the excitement. That was the deal.

"Sling him out," I said. "And let's go home."

"Bollocks," said Ronnie. "He's clocked us."

"He'll never recognise you," I said.

"Why 'cos we all look the same to you lot?" Ronnie said, and he was right nasty with it.

"You know I don't mean that." I said. Christ, we'd shared a cell together long enough. When you've heard someone doing a shit in the middle of the night it stops mattering what colour their skin is. What I'd meant was, that as he was wearing the balaclava rolled down to just above his eyes, like a woollen cap, and as the collar of his jacket was turned right up, even his own mother would have had trouble recognising him. Besides he didn't even look like Ronnie, not the Ronnie I knew anyway. Not with that excited look in his eyes and his nostrils flared and the pistol in his hand. All I could see was that pistol in his hand, and I was willing to bet that it was all the young copper could see too.

"He'll recognise you though," said Derek to me, and he was right.

"So that's it." Said Ronnie. "He goes."

"Goes where?" I asked.

"Policeman's heaven," said Ronnie.

"You can't do that," I said.

"Shut up you," says Ronnie, and I can see he's beginning to lose his rag. "What are you going to do about it? You're not even carrying, raas. The next time I go away, I go away hard. They'd chuck away the key, just for me having this." He lifted the gun slightly. "Conspiracy to rob on top and I'm fucked. I ain't going away again I'm telling you. I'll kill this bastard first."

"No," said the young copper. It was the first time he'd said anything, and it shut the rest of us up for a minute.

"I won't tell," he went on.

Ronnie and Derek had a right chuckle at that. I didn't think it was all that funny.

"It's my first day," said the copper.

"Do what?" Says Ronnie.

"My first day out on my own."

"Your bad luck son," says Ronnie. "It's not exactly going to be a long career, is it?" And him and Derek have another good old laugh. "Drive down by the river," Ronnie says to me.

"What about the job?" says Derek.

"We'll nish it for now. There's always another week. If it wasn't for you, you bastard," says Ronnie and hits the copper with the barrel of the gun, like it was his fault, which in a small way it was.

So I did what I was told and drove down to the river, and we found a bit of waste ground, and Ronnie drags the copper out of the car. He makes him take off his tunic and wrap it round his head. The poor kid was crying by then. I felt sick and could hardly look, and even Derek wasn't happy. But Ronnie didn't care. He's right cold-blooded when he gets started is Ronnie. If I'd tried to stop him he'd have done for me too. Ronnie takes the copper down by the river and does the business. I hardly heard the shot. Maybe he wrapped something around the pistol too. But even so, the noise frightened a flock of gulls away from whatever they were doing.

I cleared the bits of broken radio out of the front of the car, and put them in the kid's helmet and threw it down a hole, between the foundations of some old building that had been knocked down years ago.

Ronnie came back holding the gun down by his side, but like it wasn't there, or he wished it wasn't, if you know what I mean. He was about as pale as any lemonade was ever going to be. I think even he'd realised he'd gone too far that time.

"He's dead," he said. "Let's go. Forget this ever happened, both of you."

I wish I could. I really do. But pretty soon that bastard of a DI's going to come and find me.

Christ knows what I'm going to do then.

Until I Do

by Robert Lopresti

Y ou can't solve them all.

   If you're smart and lucky you learn to recognize the losers before they can get to you. You work on them, sure. Sweat and strain, put in the overtime.

But you don't let them work on *you*. Not the ones that won't get solved.

Because if you let yourself care you're in big trouble. You can retire, move somewhere warm, spend your days wearing goofy shirts and watching the beach girls, looking to the whole world like just another old duffer.

But you'll wake up one night with a dead man's name on your lips and a head full of questions. The ones you asked, the ones you should have asked.

You can't solve them all. But some of them won't go away. . .

Sergeant Dewey Price looked at the man across his desk and sighed. Tomorrow he was starting on a six-month leave of absence— advanced training and a well-earned rest—so he was trying hard to stay out of anything that would leave loose ends behind.

That was why the desk clerk had sent the old guy to him. "A visiting fireman," the clerk had explained. "Retired cop who wants a tour. Figure you had nothing else to do."

George Masur wanted more than a tour. He was white-haired, close to seventy, thinning out the way some old men do, yet Price

209

would have spotted him as a cop anywhere. A face patient as a stakeout; eyes restless as a rookie.

"How long have you been in Florida, George?" Price asked after they shook hands.

"Four years. The wife and I have a cottage up in Clearwater. Moved here after I retired from the Wriggs Canyon police force. That's in Northern California."

Price was tempted to see how long Masur was willing to keep making small talk, but he was sure the old man would turn out to have more patience than he did. "So, George. What brings you here today?"

Masur accepted the change of subject with a nod and said: "Katherine Anne Segrist."

"And who is she?"

"She was a teenage girl from Wriggs Canyon. Age eighteen. Freshman at the county college." He leaned back, telling a story he knew by heart. "She was pretty and smart. Could have gone to Stanford if she wanted, but she picked the local school, cause her mama was sick, and she was the only child."

Price nodded. He could be patient too.

"June twenty-eight, 1968. Two hikers found her body in the woods. She had been raped and then stabbed to death."

Masur ran a big hand through his hair. "Slashed up real bad, even before the animals got to her."

"A shame," said Price.

"A stinking tragedy. Fortunately there were witnesses. Two teenagers had seen Kathy go into the woods with a man."

"You got a description?"

"Oh, yeah. For once, the eyewitnesses even agreed with each other. He was tan, six foot tall, wore sunglasses. Hair blond and short, almost a crewcut. Wore a T-shirt from San Francisco University."

Price raised his eyebrows. "That's a heck of a good description."

"I'll say. But there's a reason. The couple knew Kathy Segrist, and they were amazed to see her sneaking off to the town's favorite necking spot with a fella. She was what they used to call a nice girl, back when nice girls weren't supposed to do stuff like that."

"So they took a real good look at the man," said Dewey Price. "Yeah, I can see that. How long did it take to find him?"

Masur grinned again. "So far? Twenty years. The son of a gun walked out of the woods a few hours later, within ten yards of another couple—whose description matches the first, by the way—and walked off into never-never-land. We never found a trace."

"That's a tough one," Price said.

"No one in town saw the guy before or after. If Kathy had a boyfriend no one knew it. We sent two cops down to San Francisco University for a week. We had the witnesses going through the U's yearbooks like they were mug books."

"No results?"

"Zip. The case wouldn't close." Masur sat back, scowling out the window at a distant memory. "Mrs. Segrist—the invalid mother, remember? She took a turn for the worse and died a week after the killing. The father had a car wreck two months later. Probably suicide, but everybody called it an accident."

"Rotten shame," said Price, wondering where this was leading.

"Meanwhile the officer in charge of the case was making a jackass of himself. Those wonderful descriptions made him so confident he told the press it would be a matter of days or even hours."

"But months went by," said Price.

"Right. So the cop looked like a moron, which is exactly what he was. It finished his career, more or less. He stayed a Lieutenant until he retired."

Price raised an eyebrow, and Masur nodded. "Yeah, I was the jackass cop."

"Like I said, George, a rotten deal all around. But there's only one thing to do with a case like that: forget it. Otherwise—"

"Don't you think I know that?" the old man snapped. "When I retired I put it out of my mind. At least I thought I had."

He shrugged. "Then last week I saw a man in a T-shirt from San Francisco University. Down here in Florida."

Dewey Price began to wonder whether the old cop just might be a nut case. "The same guy?"

"Of course not. But I did a doubletake all the same. How did an SFU shirt get all the way to the east coast?"

"Oh, I get it. Southern Florida University."

"Right. When the guy told me his SFU shirt was from a school here in your town I spent three days on the phone, tracking down those witnesses. Two of them remembered distinctly: the killer's T-shirt read SFU. Everyone just assumed it meant Frisco."

"Pretty clever," Price admitted.

"Better yet, one witness remembered the colors of the shirt. Frisco doesn't use 'em. Southern Florida does."

"That's good work. But where do you go from here? And what do you want from me?"

211

Masur shrugged. "What I'd really like is for you to tell me you caught a tall blond man attacking a woman in 1968 and he's still in prison someplace."

"Sure. But in the real world what do you want?"

"I'd like to check your files, especially for the late sixties. Check for unsolved crimes. See if the blond man came back here when he vanished from Wriggs Canyon. Or who knows? Maybe he came to Wriggs because the heat was on in Florida."

"Or maybe," said Price. "Maybe he was a native Californian who picked up the T-shirt at a garage sale."

"Could be," said Masur. "But this is one step better than nowhere, and that's where I've been for twenty years of looking for this guy." He raised his eyebrows. "So what do you say?"

The cop sighed. "You know you have no official standing. Even if you weren't retired, you wouldn't have any swing in Florida."

"I know that. But I'm not looking to arrest anybody. I don't want a gun permit. What's wrong with checking historical records?"

Price looked at him doubtfully. "If you find anything—"

"I'll hightail back to you," said the old man, nodding for emphasis.

"You'd better." Price stood up. "I'll go talk to the Captain, get his okay."

"Terrific. Thanks, Sergeant Price. You don't know how much it means to me."

The younger man looked at him and shrugged. "I wouldn't want your chances, but I hope you get the guy."

"Thanks. Until I do—" He coughed. "Until I do I can't really feel retired, you know? I realize that now. I'm just on special assignment."

Dr. Rosa Aguirrez looked skeptically at George Masur, who was sitting patiently on a hard chair beyond her desk. "I don't really see how I can help you, Lieutenant. Sergeant Price suggested you talk to me?"

"Yes ma'am. Before he left on his vacation. He said your files might be more complete than the police logs or the newspaper morgue. I've tried both of those already."

"Tracking a killer," said Dr. Aguirrez thoughtfully.

"I know you're a professor in women's studies, not criminology, but a couple of people have mentioned. . ."

He faded away because she was gazing out the window, deep in her own thoughts. It was a beautiful spring morning at Southern Florida University and students were walking by, enjoying the sunshine.

Finally, the professor seemed to make up her mind. "My research area is the study of violence against women. I've collected extensive records on rape here in Florida."

"Hey," said Masur, his eyes wide. "That sounds like just what I need."

"I doubt it. You see, I'm interested in statistics. Patterns. You're looking for a particular case."

"A pattern is just what I'm looking for. Something to tie a crime in California with a crime here." He leaned forward. "Please, Professor. Let me take a look. What harm can it do?"

Arnold Salt was a good-looking man. He was the Dean of Students at SFU, but he looked more like a politician or a newscaster.

He sat at his desk, and gave George Masur a dreamy smile. "Northern California . . . that's beautiful country. My uncle used to have a farm out there."

"Yeah, I always liked it, but when I retired the wife wanted more sunshine." The old man shrugged.

Salt turned to his desk, getting politely back to business. "These old cases you're bringing up, Mr. Masur. They happened a long time before I became Dean, of course. You said the late sixties?"

Masur nodded and tossed a folder onto the desk. "The first was March, 1967. Cassie Oliver, a student here at Southern Florida. Found raped and murdered in the swamp."

"Mmm hmm. And if I read this correctly they found the killer the next morning."

"A group of students volunteered for a kind of a manhunt. One of them found a drunk sleeping in an alley in town. He had blood on his shirt and the knife was at his feet."

"Well, that seems pretty clear cut." Salt said and then shuddered. "Pardon the expression."

"November 1970," Masur went on. "Margeret Rosen, again a student here. Raped and murdered in the woods."

"Tragic, tragic. But if these notes are right that case was even more obvious."

Masur nodded. "The boyfriend she had been necking with threw himself in front of a train an hour after it happened." He paused. "I didn't think anyone still killed themself that way."

The Dean of Students nodded sadly. "Unfortunately it is not unknown among college students. They like the melodrama of it, I suppose."

"Live and learn," said Masur.

"But I don't see what these cases have in common with the tragedy you mentioned back in—Wriggs Canyon, was it? Both of

213

these crimes were solved."

"It wasn't easy to find the connection," Masur admitted. "It wasn't until I put records together from half a dozen sources that I saw the match." He smiled. "My whole bungalow is filled with clippings and photocopies. The wife finally went to visit her sister cause she couldn't find a place to sit down."

"Fascinating," murmured Salt. "But the connection?"

"The same man was involved in both of the murders here in your town. He was the volunteer who found the bum in the alley, and he was part of the crowd who went hunting for Margaret when she was missing."

Salt shook his head. "Coincidence."

Masur grinned. "You should know. It was you, wasn't it?"

The Dean blinked. "Ah. Yes, of course it was. I wasn't going to deny it."

"Just as well. I checked the yearbooks, too. You were a handsome young man. Blond and tan, with a crewcut."

"So?"

"Just like the guy who killed Katherine Anne Segrist. Did you spend the summer of sixty-eight at your uncle's farm, by any chance?"

Salt was sitting very still, his hands pressing hard against the desk top. "I admit I was a student here when those two women died, but damn it, those cases are solved. They found both the killers."

"Right," said Masur. "In fact, *you* found the first one. But did that bum have the knife in his hand before you got there?"

"Why don't you ask him?"

"I can't. He died in prison. The police here asked him at the time, but his recollection was too blurry to amount to much."

Salt shook his head. "And what about the other one? The boyfriend who jumped in front of a train?"

"Did he jump, or was he thrown? Let's say somebody found the couple necking in the woods. He knocked the boy out, did his thing with the girl and then dragged the guy to the railroad track. All the engineers saw was the fellow landing on the tracks; they don't know how he got there."

"Rubbish," said Salt. "Absolute rubbish. And let me point out that your case in California was nothing like these two, even in the fairy tale way you describe them."

"No? Why not?"

"Because your killer out there didn't try to set up someone to take the blame, as you say he did here. That's where your analogy falls apart."

"Not a bit," said Masur. "It was different only because he didn't have a chance to make it the same. He was spotted with the Segrist girl, remember? He didn't dare stick around to try and set up somebody else, especially when he was a stranger who would be instantly noticed."

The old man stretched comfortably. "So he left town fast. We thought he went south toward Frisco, but actually he went north. To your uncle's ranch, right?"

"This is rubbish," Salt muttered.

"So you said."

"You can't prove any of this."

"I don't have to, thank God." Masur stood up. "I just have to convince the cops it's worth looking into. Then we'll see how long it takes them."

"Takes them? To do what?"

Masur shrugged. "How many business trips do you take every year, Dean? The police will start checking the towns you visited, and I'll bet a year's pension they'll find some crazy coincidences. Unsolved killings, or frame-ups like the two in town. Don't bother answering; your face says it all."

"Now wait a minute," said Salt. His voice was hoarse. "You haven't talked to the police yet?"

"Not about you, no. I suppose it was ego, but I wanted to see you once before they took over. I've been looking for you for a very long time."

Salt stood up. "Listen, we can talk—"

Masur held up a warning hand. "Stay behind your desk. I'm not stupid. You come near me and I'll run into the hall and scream my head off."

"I'll stay right here. But don't be hasty. I mean, maybe we can work something out. You mentioned your pension—"

Masur grinned and shook his head. "We have nothing to discuss, Salt. You're a dangerous man, and I'm gonna let the cops deal with you."

He turned to the door, feeling better than he had in twenty years. This was the moment of triumph and there was nothing on earth Salt could say that would make him stop now.

"Did you ever wonder," the Dean said softly behind him. "Ever wonder why Kathy Segrist went into the woods with me? Would you like me to tell you?"

George Masur hesitated. Slowly, he took his hand away from the door.

Sergeant Carl Bolle smiled at Dewey Price. "Well, it's good to see you, pal. How was the leave of absence?"

215

"Too long," said Price. "Too short. I don't know." He slumped into a chair across from Bolle.

The leave hadn't agreed with him, Bolle decided. He looked older, worried.

"What have you got on the Masur case, Carl?"

So that was it. "Now Dewey, we kept you informed—"

"For god's sake, Carl. You must know more than you've told me on the phone. I want to hear it all."

Bolle waved his hands. "Wish there was more to tell you. Masur's house in Clearwater burned to the ground one night. Arson for sure.

"No bodies were found. The Clearwater cops found his wife at a relative's house, but she had no idea where George had gotten to. She told them that her husband had been researching a murder here in town so they called us.

"Two days later we found his corpse in the swamp. Coroners say he was hit on the back of the head. Lucky the crocodiles started at his feet or we might never have identified him."

Price made a face. "Do we know who he talked to at the U?"

"Hah. Let's find out who he didn't talk to and save time. He spent a very busy month, interrogating everyone from campus security to the freshman cheerleaders to the university president. Anyone who might know anything."

Price ran his hands through his hair. "Damn it, Carl. He was on to something. Somebody he talked to is a rapist and a killer."

"Maybe," Bolle agreed. "Or maybe he stumbled into a completely different can of worms. Peek into enough corners. . ."

"And what have you done about it?"

"Me? I've talked to everybody on that damned campus, plus the board of trustees. Everybody is sick to death of me and if I go back there without a warrant someone'll be having a word with the Chief."

Bolle sighed. "Look, Dewey. Whatever he knew died with him. If he had any evidence, it burned with the house. He should have come to us."

"Evidence," said Dewey. "What about that professor? Dr. Aguirrez? Does she know what he was working on?"

"Yeah. She's mad as hell. Says some of the papers that burned up in Masur's house were research that will take her six months to replace. She's not exactly eager to get more involved."

Bolle looked across at the other man, trying to gauge his mood. "So, how does it look to you?"

Price grimaced as if he had a bad taste in his mouth. "I want in on this, Carl. I want to be part of the investigation."

"Sure, Dewey, sure. Only—"

"Only what?"

"Just don't get too worked up, okay? I got a bad feeling this case just ain't gonna close."

You can't solve them all. But some of them won't go away. . .

Lord Peter and
the Butterboy

by Mike Ripley

"I had that Lord Peter Wimsey in the back of a cab once."

"What?"

I hadn't meant to snap at the old man, but he'd caught me on the raw. "Lord Peter, the detective. And Gent. Oh yes, he was a Gent."

What was the old fool on about? "Er. . . t'riffic. Excuse me, pal, but I'd like to get home before the monsoon lets up."

It was raining so hard you could actually see the Islington streets getting cleaner. If it kept up, they'd be privatising the Highways Department. "Twice, actually, if the troof were known. Once when I were a Butterboy."

Just my luck. Halfway home on a Saturday evening having carefully plotted a route to Hackney to avoid the football grounds where there were home matches. The plan was get home, get changed, get fed and get out to meet an old flame called Fly as I was on a promise down in Ponder's End after her film club's latest offering in its Warren Oates Retrospective season. No hassle, no problems. Then it started to rain, and rain hard, and then I had the flat in the rear nearside tyre.

One of the benefits of driving round London in a delicensed FX4S Austin black cab is that, normally, nobody notices you. One of the disadvantages is that when it rains, especially on a Saturday, they not only notice you, they follow like wild dogs tracking wounded prey. I had been a good boy and turned down all the hailed offers I'd had from women loaded down with shopping and men staggering out of the pubs having decided they'd missed the football anyway. All those good intentions and I get a flat tyre.

And it was slating it down, the rain seeping inside the collar of my bomber jacket and running down the arms and inside my gloves as I struggled to get the jack set up.

And I had an ancient onlooker, an old wrinklie with an umbrella and a long raincoat and galoshes.

And I just knew he would start giving me advice.

"I remember these things coming in in 1958," he said, leaning over me so that more rain dripped off his umbrella and on to my head. "'Course, the FX3 was introduced before that."

"Yeah," I said under my breath, "that would make sense."

Oh God, I had a taxi nut.

"'Course, I'm talking about long before this FX model, yer know."

Where do they come from? Why do I attract them?

"That's nice," I said, ignoring him. He ignored me ignoring him.

"Beardmores," he said.

"Naturally," I agreed, adopting the well-tried policy of keeping smiling and not turning your back.

"Beardmore Motors," the old geezer went on, "that's who used to make cabs, the old black cabs before this lot."

He flicked his umbrella at Armstrong, my trusty cab, and showered me with even more water. My hair was already plastered to my skull and I was standing on the wheelbrace having learned long ago that the best way to undo wheelnuts on a flat is before you jack it off the ground.

From my vantage point, a foot in the air, I gave him my killer look. Like the rain, it bounced off.

"I had a Beardmore Mark 1 De Luxe when I first picked him up," he droned.

"That'd be the one before the Mark 2," I grunted, shifting one of the nuts.

"First new cab after the Great War. Came in in 1919. Four cylinder, 16-horsepower engine, interior light and starter motor. Pretty good shmutter in them days. Six hundred and ninety quid new. 'Course, I got mine from an uncle, second-hand. He was too bleedin' lazy to work the West End but I always said that was where the money was."

"Some things haven't changed then," I had the last of the nuts loose now and started to fumble the brace into the jack, cursing as my wet gloves slipped on all the sharp edges I'd never noticed before.

"That was how I come to meet him, cabbing for him. Twice; like on two different occasions."

"What? Who?" I asked before I could stop myself.

"Lord Peter Wimsey, the great detective, like I said."

"Oh yeah, him."

I didn't say any more, honest. I didn't encourage the old man; I didn't even look at him.

I just went on changing the wheel and cursing as I got wetter and really only took about half of it in.

Like I said, it was a Beardmore Mark 1. That was my first cab, and the first one that became known as the Black Cab or the London cab. There were still horse-drawn ones before the War, you know.

Anyway, I picked him up outside the Savile Club and he asks me to take him to Brocklebury's where there's a second-hand book sale on or something. We only get as far as Piccadilly Circus and, blow me, he says he's left his catalogue and can't go to this shop without it.

I hadn't put him down as a travelling salesman, mind you. No, he was obviously a real Toff, so I didn't know why he was carrying a catalogue but mine's not to reason why, so I says "Back to the Savile Club?" and he says no, make it 110A Piccadilly instead. We get there and he dives inside and I wait. After a while, another Gent comes out and gets in.

This is a Gent's Gent if you know what I mean, but very well spoken and he says he's going to Brocklebury's instead of 'is Lordship. And he tells me I've just driven Lord Peter Wimsey.

Of course, all us mushers got to know Lord Peter in the Twenties. Familiar sight he was and more than once one of us would get him out of a scrape—out of a fountain or down from a lamp post sometimes—and get him home safe. He was always very generous, mind, and if he didn't have company with him in the back of the cab, he'd always have a word or two for the driver.

And then there was the time he looked after Harry Hill. That became famous in cabby circles. It would be about 1925, 'cos Harry was driving a Beardmore Mark II and Lord Peter was already calling us "Butterboys" then.

There'd been this big trial at the House of Lords involving Lord Peter and as it broke up when the jury got a result, there was 'undreds of people—if not farsends—milling about outside the Houses of Parliament. Then this big bearded geezer, who had it in for Lord Peter's brother, pulls out a gun and starts taking potshots at all and sundry. He does a runner and poor old Harry Hill, who's comin' over Westminster Bridge looking for a fare, is heading straight for him. He panics and shoots out one of Harry's front tyres. The cab throws a wobbler, out of control, and Harry careers into the bloke with the gun and pins him up against a tram then crashes into the end of the bridge.

There was nothing he could have done about it—an honest accident. But there was an inquest and suchlike and it worried Harry sick so he couldn't work for months. It was Lord Peter who sought him out and told him not to worry and stood by him. He looked after Harry's family as well. Dead generous he was.

So we all kept an eye-out for Lord Peter after that.

He called us cabbies "Butterboys" because of the Yellow Cabs brought in in America in 1924. Yellow Cab mushers were called butterboys because of the colour, you see, and Lord Peter spread the 'abit. All newly licensed drivers after that were "Butterboys". Of course, if you'd been around a bit, or done "the knowledge" like you have to today, you were a "musher" but only cabbies call each other mushers.

I didn't actually get to give him another ride, though I saw him round town often enough, until—it'd be 1936.

By then I had a new Beardmore Mark V, the Paramount Ace it was called, from Beardmore Motors of Paisley up in Scotland. Wonderful machines. They'd be worth their weight in gold nowadays.

I was working lates—10 p.m. until morning—and cruising Shaftesbury Avenue, though the theatres had long-since chucked out. Still, there were plenty of punters floating up and down the streets.

I spotted Lord Peter in full theatre rig, top hat, the lot. He was standing with another bloke on the corner of Rupert Street, like they'd just come out of a Stage Door. The bloke with him was a younger chap, dead good looking, wearing a tweedie cap and an overcoat with the collar turned up almost like he didn't want to be recognised.

Lord Peter waved his cane in the air and I cuts across to pick 'em up. As he opened the door I heard 'im say something like:

". . .don't be such an ass. A faithful Butterboy will see you home."

I knew straight off it was him, but I couldn't place the other fella.

Anyway, Lord Peter gives me an address off Lisson Grove and then proceeds to give this fella he's with a right good talking to. All very polite, mind you, 'cos his Lordship always did speak well and never resorted to effin' and blindin' however much he was provoked. But nevertheless, this was serious GBH of the lugholes. I mean, he was giving the young bloke some rotten stick.

I only caught parts of it, through the screen, and naturally I wouldn't listen in if it was a really private conversation, but he was going on about some letters—from a woman, of course.

"No, I will not return them, you young idiot," he was saying to the other chap.

"Children really shouldn't play with matches. Do you realise just how close to a major scandal you've come?"

The young chap went wild at that and ranted about how he didn't care what Society thought. It was his life, wasn't it?

"Not exclusively, my dear chap," Lord P. said. I remember that.

"Your dalliance must rate as the second-worst-kept secret in England this year and you are in line to be the second biggest scandal if we are not all very careful. You are equally destined for greatness, but you will not be allowed to abdicate your responsibilities. You will be expelled and shunned, socially and artistically."

Then the other bloke starts really shouting: "What gives you the right? How dare you play God?"

"Calm down, old chap," Lord Peter said. "It's not a question of playing God. Look on me only as a safe-deposit box for your conscience. A reluctant one at that, I have to add, but certain influential people—people who recognise your genius just as much as you do—have asked me to act as honest broker in this, frankly, squalid little affair. Consequently, I appoint myself the guardian of the knowledge of this particular piece of your past. But past is the operative word. The affair is history."

Well, the younger chap came out with some ripe language then and even started jumping up and down, almost trying to get up and walk around in the back of the cab. He was flinging his arms about and yelling, but Lord Peter keeps his head.

"No, no and thrice no. I have explained. Your letters to her and her letters to you will both remain in my charge and should anything happen to me, I have left instructions for them to be destroyed unread. In the meantime, they are a safeguard. You will no longer moon sorrowfully after her and she, in turn, will not be tempted to risk her marriage and her position by approaching you when your fame increases, as it surely will. The matter is ended; the case is not altered, but closed."

It was then the young bloke snapped and he went for Lord Peter like a real street brawler. I could feel the cab swaying as they crashed about but all I could see in the mirror was this chap on top of Lord Peter, pummelling away for all he was worth.

Naturally, I couldn't have any of this, so I pulls over on to the pavement. We were cutting through Portman Square at the time and it was quite quiet, fortunate for all concerned.

So I'm out and round the side just as their door pops open and they fall out at my feet, at it like tigers. I grabs the young bloke by the scruff of his overcoat and yanks him to his feet. He's like an eel, and strong with it. He whips round, kicks me in the shins and elbows me in the face.

I go down, slumped against the cab, me head spinning.

Lord Peter's standing up by this time, his hat missing and his shirt front all torn. Dead calm, he slips off his cloak and throws it in the back of the cab, then he pulls his gloves tight and then gently dusts down his jacket.

The young bloke's turned on him by now but Lord P just stands there and takes up a boxer's stance. Doesn't say a word. The young bloke gives a big grin and peels off his coat, then they go at it. Right there on the pavement in Portman Square. If it hadn't been after midnight, I could've sold tickets.

But it don't last long. The young guy has some very fancy footwork, I'll give him that. Moves like a ballet dancer and tries to nip in under with a few jabs but I don't think one of them connected. No killer instinct, you see.

Lord Peter picked his shots, two jabs to the face then a one-two-one combination to the stomach and jaw and young Lochinvar is out for the count.

First thing Lord P does, of course, is come over to help me up, telling me how awfully sorry he was about it all. Then I helps him pick up the young chap and we put him in the cab where his Lordship gives him a handkerchief to put on his nose and mutters "No lasting damage, thank goodness." And then he says something about "his face is his fortune" which I don't understand.

Anyway, we get to Lisson Grove and we stop and by this time the young tearaway's cooled off and is seeing sense.

He shakes Lord Peter's hand and his Lordship says something about "You really should take up that Hollywood offer, you know. Out of sight and all that."

The young chap slinks off and then Lord Peter turns to me and slips me two tenners—twenty quid, no word of a lie—and says he fancies a long walk home to take the blood off the boil. There's no need for him to tell me to keep my mouth shut, you'll note.

That was taken as read. After all, I was one of his faithful Butterboys.

"And do you know sumfink?"

Was the old man *still* rabbitting on?

"You're gonna tell me."

"That young bloke went on to become a household name and people recognised him the world over. Some would say he became more famous than Lord Peter hisself."

"Really," I said, deadpan, throwing the jack into Armstrong's boot, then peeling off my soddened gloves. They were leather and would never dry properly. And I was now running late.

"And another thing."

"Yeah?"

"The next day, I'm cleaning out the cab and I finds this on the floor in the back."

He held something small and shiny in the forefinger and thumb of his left hand.

"What is it?" I asked wearily, squinting through the rain.

"A cufflink. One of his. See the design? Three mice and a cat ready to jump. I don't think he'd mind me hanging on to it for a souvenir, do you?"

"Probably not," I agreed, reaching for the driver's door.

He came up to my window and I lowered it a fraction.

"My grand-daughter's always on at me," he shouted as if I was deaf. "She says I should write it up."

"I think you'll find somebody has," I said, starting the engine.

But a couple of weeks later, while waiting in Marylebone Library for Loraine (the big blonde one in the music section) to knock off work, I did a bit of snooping and found nobody had.

I've been trying to find that boring old bugger ever since.

Squeezer

By Steve Rasnic Tem

"You look like you deserve a hug," Anita said, again, as she had said every time Jefferson ran into her. Only this time they were alone, late at night in the park across the street from the movie theater. There wasn't the crowd of people around she had always seemed to require. The crowd whose individual members looked so fondly at Anita's heartfelt expressions of her humanity. "I think you *do*! I think you *do* deserve a hug today!" When there was a crowd Jefferson could avoid her; he could fade into that large and unmanageable, unhuggable crowd.

But here there were no witnesses. The last show at the theatre had been an hour ago; Jefferson had hung around in the park because he liked the dark and the relative emptiness of late night. He had not expected to see Anita here—he supposed she was returning from some late night hugging session.

She looked at him intently, and seemed disturbed by what she saw. But then she had never seen Jefferson late at night, with no one else around. She started to pass him, confirming finally for him that these offers of hugs had become merely formal, required greeting for her, and had no conviction behind them at all.

Tonight Jefferson would have none of that. It was dark and there was no one else around, and he had not touched, much less held, anyone in months. His skin felt dead, a brittle carapace for his nerves. His bones ached as if riddled with holes. He had a need to touch someone else's life, and if not their life at least their desperation, which for him was much the same thing.

He stepped forward into her body and offered himself up to her embrace. She hesitated at first, stiffened as if there were something wrong with his skin, as if she had found something repulsive in the feel of him, but then she whispered "Oh, sweetie. . ." with a heavy exhalation, as if a hope had at last been realized, and wrapped her arms around him, her legs and hips seeming to stretch, as if she would envelope him completely if she could.

Jefferson held fast to her, at first in a familiar desperation, using her to anchor himself to the remaining tatters of his sense of reality. Then he increased the firmness of this embrace as he felt more and more in control of himself and of his situation. This young woman said she believed in touching, had in fact made hugging a credo, an entire belief system. But he sincerely doubted she understood touching at all. He believed a true touch between human beings to be impossible. But it was that impossibility which made it seem so essential. In fact, his embrace became so strong that the surface area of his arms and hands seemed to increase dramatically, impossibly, so that his grip covered every inch of her flesh, every square inch of her life, so that he could feel her increasingly harsh breathing beneath his touch, her pores opening in panic beneath his touch, releasing the oils and toxins all lives give off as they are winding down, as he squeezed and squeezed in an attempt to touch the life within her, to know that life at the level of his fingertips.

When at last he felt the spasms beneath his hands, the last swift jerks of her body, he looked down at her steady gaze, her lips sheened with a red froth as they dropped back as if to take his mouth in a final kiss, and he wondered at what he had done.

Jefferson would think of Anita many times after that. She became more to him than merely a first love, more like his first encounter with the sweet pulse which drove life itself. She was his first bride, and although even then he knew there would be many others, surely there could never be another to surpass the feel or the taste of his sweet Anita.

She became the standard by which he judged other women, by which he imagined them. And during the months which followed he would imagine many women in his arms.

Marie was someone he followed for weeks before finally arranging their "accidental" meeting. She cleaned several of the larger houses in the neighborhood, arriving at the corner by bus each morning around nine, and normally departing the same way about two p.m. She was short, slight, brunette; some might have called her "ethereal." It was easy for him to imagine her dissolving completely under the persistent press of his arms.

She ate lunch every day at the Blue Ribbon Diner. After several days of watching her, Jefferson adopted the same habit, choosing a table to the side, only a few feet away.

She ate a great deal for such a small person. He wondered where she put it all.

He dreamed of squeezing the food back out of her, years of it unused and simply waiting for him to empty her with his embrace. All that untapped energy, all that unused life.

Once or twice she glanced in his direction and smiled. He felt his arm muscles tense, his chest suddenly swelling with an emptiness.

At last came a day he chose to come late, after the lunch rush was well under way. As always, there was the empty chair at her table.

"May I?" He smiled widely, and he could feel a strain in his empty belly.

"Sure. . . I don't mind," she said, as if it mattered. "I see you here all the time."

"You always make the food taste better," he said. He made himself say it without blushing. Anita had given him just that kind of confidence.

She looked at him with a slightly startled expression, then laughed out loud, presumably at the audacity of his compliment. But she still smiled at him. She nodded and hid her eyes. Obviously he had pleased her.

Over the next few weeks Jefferson was careful when and where and how he touched her. He was courting her embrace, in fact, and had to make his moves cautiously, despite his sometimes overwhelming desire to bury her under his hands. She seemed anxious for more as well, and now and then he had to stop her from moving his hand to where he was not yet ready to be.

"Kiss me," she whispered late one afternoon, long after her regular bus had left. She had led him to a quiet corner of the park, surrounded by broad shrubbery. "Please. . . don't be shy." Her breath was full and warm against his face. His fingers itched to enter her lips and meet that breath at its source.

"Not now. Patience. . ." he whispered back at her. Her back stiffened under his hand. He wanted badly to press into these hardened muscles—how firm she had become through her labors, so wonderfully fit that he could have written testimonials to the physical efficacy of housework for the modern woman's figure—but he had to pull his hand away instead.

"Just. . . *forget* it!" She stood up and started away.

He was afraid he had waited too long. He leaped up and ran behind her, grabbing her around the waist and turning her, and holding on with eyes squeezed shut as his lips suddenly opened and he said, in a voice that sounded so much like Anita, whom he had squeezed into the empty spaces inside himself that long ago night, "You look like you need a hug."

He was surprised to find that the tighter he squeezed her, the tighter she squeezed back.

"Hold me," she whispered with ragged breath. "Hold me tight."

And he did. He held her because she wanted him to hold her—that was always the best way. Like everyone else in the world she needed to be held. The flesh of the human body clung all too tightly to its solitary bones. The mixing of flesh, the joining of individual bodies, was illusory, and always promised far more than was delivered. Make love for hours with even remarkable talent and passion and you still finished the evening spent and alone within your own sweat-slicked, shivering hide, your own thoughts hidden and untouchable from the other beside you in your bed. All you could do was hold, and squeeze, and imagine a bonding of skin to skin which could not happen no matter how desperately you squeezed.

"Too tight, honey. Too tight," she said between clenched teeth trying to resemble a smile. But Jefferson could see the fear and confusion in her eyes. He moved his hands to her neck and her face and squeezed some more, and was amazed at the relaxation forced into her muscles, the redness and then the pallor that came to her cheeks, and as he squeezed he imagined her moving into the too-rigid outlines of *his* body, and he could almost hear the endless conversations they might have inside himself.

Blue shaded her eyes as in his mind his body opened lengthwise, like a huge vertical mouth, and took her in, and swallowed her up, and used her to assuage its loneliness.

Carol came into his life with a small child, Jenny, who was as beautiful as Carol herself, perhaps more so. At first Jefferson thought that the existence of this child must necessarily preclude his having any sort of relationship with Carol. For children frightened him. They always had. In part, he knew, this was because of the great delicacy of their bodies. It was hard for Jefferson to accept that such delicate bodies could survive. You couldn't help loving small children, certainly—their physical vulnerability made it inevitable. But that just made them all the more threatening, actually. They looked up at you with eyes filled with trust, and a mock-intelligence which suggested that they *knew* how you

228

felt, that they were human beings as well, but their freakish vulnerability made that a lie. Their dwarfed, frail bodies were a joke, a hideous satire of the solitary death we each must face.

And yet for all his understanding, Jefferson was completely seduced by this little girl.

"Buy me a doll, *please*, Uncle Jeff?"

He wanted to ask her what she wanted it for, perhaps for companionship—she looked so much the doll herself, but he knew better than to say something others might think strange. "Your momma's going to think I spoil you." He made himself grin.

"Oh, spoil me, spoil me!" She laughed and gave him a hug.

"So you want a hug, huh?" he said into her blonde curls smelling of soap.

She pushed away and looked at him solemnly. Then nodded slowly, her eyes fixed on his.

He bent over and wrapped himself around her. But formally, with little pressure. It wasn't a real hug at all, the way he defined the word, but it appeared to satisfy her. She laid her small, all-too-crushable skull on his shoulder.

"Hugs are nice," she said softly.

"Hugs are all that really mean anything," he said. "Don't ever forget that."

"Well, I'd certainly agree with that," Carol said from the doorway. Jefferson looked through the yellow nimbus of Jenny's hair into Carol's smiling face.

"Jealous?" he asked, and made himself grin.

Carol strolled across the room toward them, the lines of her body flowing down and curving around him as she gathered him to her. "Oh, you bet," she breathed into his ear, and he wanted to pull away, so tightly she pulled on him, and so firmly her little girl still held on to his waist, a desperation with which he was so intimately familiar.

But he did not pull back, instead squeezing her in return, although not as tightly as he was ultimately capable of squeezing.

The day was to be spent at a roadside carnival, a place where they could scream and fear for their lives without fully believing in that fear. It was one of Jefferson's favorite spots. Carol had been hesitant to go but Jenny was eager, typically with more enthusiasm than understanding. "You'll think you're going to die," he whispered to the little girl. "But then you don't. It's quite a surprise, really. I hope you won't be disappointed."

She nodded and watched his eyes solemnly.

The roadside carnival had been set up alongside Wildcat Wrecks, the oldest auto salvage yard in the region. This seemed so appropriate to Jefferson it practically took his breath away. The county commissioners had condemned it several times but at the last minute the owners always came up with some measure to avoid the action. Twisted wrecks and crushed cars were stacked into occasional mountains a dozen feet high, waiting for years sometimes until the price of scrap reached levels the owners thought acceptable, the sides of these precipices buttressed with piles of stone and miscellaneous rusted steel debris.

Jefferson thought of these automobiles as "people cans", a private little joke he had never shared with anyone. It was a wonder anyone ever survived their trips down the highway. The rides at the carnival pretended to be people cans as well, but he supposed they were in fact much safer.

On the roller coaster, in mock fear but in a truthfully passionate embrace, he almost squeezed Carol to death. Jenny obviously had no idea what was happening—she thought her mother had passed out from the thrill.

Jefferson could not believe he had lost control in public that way—perhaps it was having both females together in combination with the pretended danger, perhaps it was the proximity of the junk yard—he spent the last half of the ride arousing Carol, helping her get her breath back, apologizing sincerely (although he didn't think she was aware of what he was saying), until she was at least able to stagger from the ride with his and Jenny's well-meaning but ineffectual assistance. Several people tittered, obviously thinking she'd had too much beer before the ride. Jefferson relaxed a little—she did, indeed, appear drunk.

He found a place out of view of the crowd, behind some tents at the back of the carnival, where he let her down into soft grass and stretched her out. He gave Jenny a dollar and sent her off for a coke for her mom.

Jefferson slapped Carol's face several times, vaguely excited that he had a good excuse for it, and marvelled at the alternating patterns of pallor and redness made when he struck her soft skin.

Suddenly her hand reached up and grabbed his wrist. Her head jerked up and she started choking. "You tried to. . .you *tried*. . ." Her eyes popped open from the force of her choking, and Jefferson could see the sudden shock of knowledge in them. It seemed as if she had recognized him for the very first time.

"*You*. . ." she began again, and he threw himself on her, pressing his right shoulder hard into her mouth so that she could not speak and wrapping his arms, his legs around the thrashing, desperate life of her, admiring the energy and will of her, wishing that he had some of that life and will for himself. With alarm, he became aware that he had a growing erection prodding at her lower belly, and anxious to stop this erection he squeezed her head more tightly, he squeezed her neck, needing to consume her before she could consume any part of him.

At last she sighed and rattled and he clamped his mouth over hers to capture this final bit of her breath. And then he heard the soft crying behind him.

He jerked around as Jenny screamed and started through the flimsy wire fence that separated the carnival from the salvage yard. Jefferson rose to go after her but Carol's hand had clutched his left wrist so tightly he could not escape her. He bent over her again and screaming smashed his right fist into her face and arms until at last she released him. He leaped up and ran through the fence, which scratched and clawed him and which he had to kick and smash against until it too would release him. Now he could see Jenny some distance away, running into the valley made between two mountains of ravaged cars, smashed and burned containers for the soft, sickly, all-too-brittle bodies of people.

He quickly closed the gap on the little girl but there were so many twists and turns between the ranks of cars that she was always able to remain just out of his reach. The longer she stayed away from his touch the more he needed to touch her.

Although he pushed himself as hard as he could to catch her, and the vigor of this effort engendered an anger that heightened almost with every step, Jefferson was also rapidly considering how he might prevent himself from killing her. Would it be possible for him to *keep* her rather than kill her?

If he kept her he could take her out whenever he liked and hug her, squeeze her to his heart's content but of course he'd have to be careful that he didn't do it too often and too hard, perhaps just until she passed out or until she was so afraid she fouled herself or her skin released the toxins preparatory to death. She was a small child, after all, and wouldn't cost that much to feed and surely he could keep such a small child quiet enough for his purposes. Perhaps he could experiment with varying amounts of food and drugs in order to find just the right level to maintain her in a pliable, maximally squeezable, yet still living state.

He rounded the burned-out husk of an ancient DeSoto in time to see Jenny climbing a rust-red mountain of cars directly ahead of him. She was screaming, she had probably been screaming for some time now, but the junkyard was technically closed and the blended screams from the carnival behind him effectively covered all individual sound.

231

Jefferson leaped to the back of the first car, reached up and grabbed the antique door handle of another and used this to pull himself to the hood of a woody stationwagon. Jenny looked back and screamed again, her mouth distorting as if her face were in the process of ripping open and flapping in the breeze. She scrambled over a collapsed Buick and then to the top-most boulder in a pile of stones supporting one side of the stack of cars. Jefferson could see that her knees and shins were badly skinned, bright blood sheeting down as if her small stick-like legs were being peeled. He hoped that she would not injure herself further. Any more damage to her delicate skin and he might not feel so compelled to hold her.

Jenny disappeared from the top of the mountain of cars.

A door panel shifted under Jefferson's foot. A side mirror in his hand broke off and he dropped it to the ground. Glass began to crack softly like ice thawing as more metal moved and slipped and the contours of the rusted mountain underwent a subtle change. He struggled slowly to the summit and looked over. Jenny stared up at him from an empty aisle just beyond the mountain. She turned and ran.

"Jenny!" he screamed, and reached out his hands.

The mountain trembled as the topmost stones which buttressed it slipped from their perch and crashed onto rusted brittle hoods and quarter panels, slamming through partial windshields and changing the perspective of the overlapping vehicles stacked beneath Jefferson's uneasy feet. He looked once again at Jenny's distant running form and thought to hug himself instead as he fell back off the summit and was folded again and again as the mountain unravelled and seven decades worth of cars descended with him.

For a brief sliver of time he thought how he might embrace himself fully, his skin bonding to his own skin and the heart of him becoming so compressed that it was hard and invulnerable to even the strongest touch, and then all the stones and wrecks of time came down upon him and his thought was squeezed to nothing.

Surrogate

by Robert B. Parker

B renda Loring sat in my office with her knees together and her hands clasped in her lap and told me that last night a man had broken into her home and raped her for the second time in two weeks.

With my instinct for the *bon mot*, I said, "Jesus Christ."

"It was the same man as before," she said. Her voice was still and clear and uninflected.

I said, "Last night?"

"About ten hours ago," she said. "I've just now left the police." Her face was blank and, without makeup, it looked unprotected.

"You want to talk about the rapes?" I said.

She shook her head slightly and looked down at her clasped hands.

"That's okay," I said. "I can get it all from the cops. You still living in Cambridge?"

She nodded. "My husband's involved," she said, "my ex-husband."

I said *Jesus Christ* again, but only to myself. I don't like to overwork a phrase. "You want to talk about that?" I said.

She was still looking at her hands, folded motionless in her lap. "The police don't believe me about my husband."

Her stillness was profound. But it was stillness of tension, like a drawn bowstring. I said, "Brenda, whatever this is, I can fix it."

233

She looked up at me for the first time since she'd started speaking. "Two rapes too late," she said in her lucid monotone.

"Yes," I said.

She looked back down at her hands.

"Tell me a little more about your husband," I said.

"Northrop," she said. "Mrs. Northrop May."

"I was at your wedding," I said.

"The day after I was raped the first time," she said, "Northrop came to see me. He came in and sat down and I gave him a cup of coffee and he said with a. . . not a smile. . . a. . . a smirk," she nodded her head decisively in approval of the word's rightness, "and he said to me 'so, how's your love life?' and I said 'my God don't you know I was raped?' and he said no and asked me about it. And. . ." she thought a minute, concentrating on her hands. "He wanted details: 'what did he do? what did I do? did he make me undress?' " she shivered slightly, "and all the time he had that smirk and he was. . ." again she paused and looked for the right word. "Avid," she said. "He was avid, listening. And then he said 'did you like it?' "

I could feel the muscles across my shoulders bunch a little. She was quiet, still examining her hands. I said.

"Then what?"

"I asked him to leave," she said. She raised her head. "I know he's involved."

"But he didn't do it?"

"No. I saw the man's face. It wasn't Northrop. Besides this man was able to do it."

"You mean erect?"

She nodded.

"And Northrop couldn't?"

"Not very often and, before the divorce, getting worse," she said.

"You think Northrop knows who did it?" I said.

"As he left last week, he looked at me from the doorway with that hot smirky look on his face and said, 'maybe he'll be back.'"

"Cops check on him?"

"He was with three other people having late supper at the Ritz Café," she said. "After theater."

"The cops figure you for a vindictive divorcee," I said.

"Probably."

Two stories down on Berkeley Street a car horn honked impatiently. Brenda rummaged in her bag and found a pack of cigarettes. She took one out and lit it and inhaled a long lungful.

"Faulkner," I said. "Novel called *Sanctuary*. You ever read it?"

234

She shook her head. The long inhale began to seep out.

"Character in there called Popeye," I said. "He was impotent, had other people do it for him."

"Yes," Brenda said. She was looking right at me now and her voice was richer. "That's what I think," she said.

"What time of day did he come around to smirk last time?" I said.

"After lunch."

I looked at my watch. "Let's go over to your place and see if he comes around this time."

"So you'll be there if he comes?"

I nodded. Two spots of color appeared on Brenda's cheekbones. She got abruptly to her feet. "Yes," she said, "let's go."

Brenda lived on the fifth floor of a wedge shaped brick building at the Watertown end of Mt. Auburn Street. We were on the second cup of coffee, and almost no conversation, when Northrop May showed up. He rang, Brenda spoke to him on the intercom and buzzed him in. I went into the kitchen. In maybe thirty seconds I heard Brenda open the apartment door.

May said, "How've you been Brenda?" His voice sounded vaguely British. Half the people in Cambridge sounded vaguely British. The other half sounded like me.

"What do you care?"

"I worry about you, Brenda, you know that. Just because our marriage has ended doesn't mean I no longer care for you. I want to know that you're happy. That you're dating and things."

"I'm fine," Brenda said.

"Good," May said. "Good. How about last night, did you have a good time last night?"

I heard a sudden movement and the sound of a slap and I came around the corner in time to see May holding both Brenda's wrists down. I shifted my weight slightly onto my left foot, did a small pivot and kicked May in the middle of the back with the bottom of my right foot. He let go of Brenda and sprawled forward face first on the floor. When he hit he scrambled on all fours toward the couch and behind it before he used it to help him to his feet. His face was the color of skimmed milk when he looked at me.

"Hiho, Northrop," I said.

"What are you doing?" he said. "She was hitting me. You had no reason to do that. I was just defending myself."

Brenda moved toward May. "You son of a bitch," she said. Her voice hissed between her teeth. "You lousy dickless bastard." He edged away, keeping the couch between him and me. Brenda went after him, swinging at him with both fists closed. He put his arms up and edged away some more. But he was edging toward me and he didn't like that.

"Keep her away," he said. Brenda kicked at his shins.

I reached out and caught Brenda's arm. "Stop a minute," I said. "Let's talk."

Brenda leaned steadily against my restraint. May began edging the other way, toward the door. "I'm not talking," he said. "I'm going to leave right now."

I shook my head, still holding Brenda's steady weight with my left hand. Northrop looked at me. He was about my height but much lighter, angular and narrow with round gold glasses and blond hair combed straight back.

"I'm not going to fight with a pug like you," he said.

"A wise choice," I said. "Sit down. We'll talk."

His face tightened and his eyes moved around the room. I was between him and the only door. He went to the couch and sat down. With his legs crossed and his hands folded precisely in his lap he said, "Very well, what is it? why are you here? why are you detaining me? and why on earth is that woman acting even more insane than usual?"

"Your wife has been raped," I said, "and you're responsible."

He shook his head once, brusquely. "That's absurd," he said. "There are half a dozen people who can testify that I was with them, far from here, both times."

"How do you know it was both?" I said.

"You just. . ."

I shook my head, slowly. May was quiet, and I knew he was running back in his mind what I had said. Then he shrugged impatiently.

"I don't know—once, twice, whatever. I have not raped my wife."

"Ex-wife," Brenda said. "But you had it done." Her voice was clotted with intensity. "You had somebody do it and then you came smirking around afterwards like some kind of peeping Tom."

She was arched toward him, her face thrust close to his.

"You can't prove that," he said. His voice was as pale as his face.

"We don't need to prove it," I said. "We only have to know it. We're not the law. We don't have to sweat the rules of evidence, Northrop."

"To do what?" he said. He stayed stiffly in his legs-crossed-I'm-completely-at-my-ease pose.

"I'm perfectly willing to kill you," I said. "I can do it easy and I'd feel no guilt."

236

He didn't move.

"I have killed people before," I said. "I know how. I could float you out that window like a paper airplane, right now. You deserve to go. Brenda would swear you jumped mad with remorse. That would even the score, Brenda would be safe. I can't see any reason not to do it."

"Do it," Brenda hissed. She went to the window and opened it wide. "Do it."

May's composure went. He looked rapidly around the room. He uncrossed his legs and put both feet on the floor and leaned forward as if to get up. He looked at the door. Looked at me. I could see him give up inside, his body tension changed.

"My God, Spenser," he said. "You. . .my God you can't . . . Please."

It was late October and rainy. The breeze from the open window was cold.

"Who'd you hire to do it?" I said.

He looked at everything: me, Brenda, the window, a brass candlestick on the end table. He was in way over his head. And he was caught. He'd thought about staving off the law, and provided means. But he hadn't thought about me. He had no way to stave me off.

"Some things you gotta do yourself, Northrop. You can't hire someone for this."

"I'll hire you," he said. "You're a detective. I'll hire you to investigate, to investigate everything. My family has money. I can pay you very well, a lot."

I took a quick step forward, got him by the shirt front, yanked him off the sofa and spun him toward the window. Then I shifted my grip to the back of his collar and the seat of his pants and ran him toward the window.

His head was out in the rain when he screamed. "Hanson. Richie Hanson."

I held him there, his head out the window, his feet off the ground.

"Where's he live," I said.

"South End, Clarendon Street, down by the Ballet." May's voice was thin with panic. I pulled him back in and sat him on the couch. He sat shivering. I always hated to see fear. It made me feel lousy, especially when I'd caused it. "What number Clarendon?" I said.

"Nineteen."

I picked up Brenda's phone and punched out a number. On the second ring a voice said, "Harbor Health Club."

"Henry? Spenser. Hawk there?"

"He don't usually come in this early, Kid. You know Hawk, probably having breakfast now."

"Yeah. Get hold of him, Henry, and have him call me." I gave him Brenda's number.

"In a hurry?"

"Yes."

"It'll be quick," Henry said.

We hung up and I went and stood against the door. Probably no need to. May sat on the couch without form, limp against the brocade.

"What are you going to do?" he said.

"I'm going to have Hawk bring Richie Hanson over here."

"No," Brenda said.

"It's a way to clean this up," I said. "Might be good, too, for you to get by facing him."

"I don't want to," Brenda said. "I'm afraid."

"No need," I said.

"I don't know this Hawk," Brenda said. "Can he get Richie whatsis?"

"Hawk will bring you Nama the killer whale if he feels like it," I said. "If we get them together we'll know everything. Maybe even understand some of it."

"I understand it," Brenda said softly. She turned back toward May and the angles of her body sharpened. "I understand that he isn't man enough to do it himself. He isn't man enough to do anything." Her voice was hissing again. "Did you ask this guy what it was like? Did you get it up when he told you? Is that what it takes?"

Northrop's face took on some definition as if hatred had disciplined it. "It takes response," he said. "I can feel passion when it's returned."

"Frigid? You have always tried to say that. That's bull-shit. I always liked sex. It was you that turned me off you creepy bastard." A very nasty smile distorted her mouth. "Ask Spenser. Was I cold when we were together?"

I made a small noncommittal gesture with my head.

"I never understood it," May said. "Before we were married. . ." he shook his head and made a helpless measuring motion with his hands. "And afterwards it was gone. Now and then you seemed to like it, but mostly it was gone."

"I never turned you down."

"No, you never did. You lay back and gritted your teeth and did your duty like a soldier." May's voice was full of defeat. It had gotten toneless and small as he talked, as if it came from some small recess inside him, out of the light.

Brenda was walking back and forth in front of him, arching toward him as she spoke. "And you, you weird bastard, you always wanted to hear about who else I'd done it with, and what I'd done, and what I'd let them do. It was creepy."

"I wanted all of you," May said. "I wanted to share everything, to have no secrets. Sure, maybe it turned me on a little. That's human isn't it? But mostly I just wanted us to be closer, and you kept telling me different things, and not telling me anything, and I just wanted the truth. You kept part of you away from me."

"I'm not a goddamned peep show, North. Part of me is mine."

The nickname had crept in. They weren't victim and violator anymore. They were domestic adversaries again, tripping the same old grim fantastic over the same old painful ground.

"I never knew you," he said.

The phone rang. It was Hawk.

I said, "There's a guy named Richie Hanson, 19 Clarendon Street. I need him here as quick as you can get him." I gave him Brenda's address.

Hawk said, "Okay."

I said, "I don't know this guy. It's possible he's dangerous."

Hawk's laugh was liquid. "Me too, Babe. I bring him along."

He hung up. While I'd been on the phone the argument had paused like a stop action replay. When I put down the phone they began again as if in mid-sentence.

"There was that central part of you," Northrop said, "that was remote and arrogant." He spoke smoothly, almost as if he were speaking a part he'd rehearsed.

"Don't you understand that it is my pride to keep part of me private? To have a part of me intact? You're weird, North. You're sick."

May's eyes filled and tears came down his face.

"Sick," he said, and his voice, despite the tears, was still atonal and remote. "Why is that sick? All I ever wanted. . ." his voice shook a little. "All I ever, ever wanted was so simple, so ordinary. . . I just wanted affection. I wanted you to act like you loved me. . . that's all I wanted. . . is that sick? Is that some sort of weird thing to want, simply, gestures of affection?"

"Your definitions," Brenda said. They were so caught up in the argument that they might have been alone. I was watching a marriage that had been driven into the corner. Its meanness was being reported. *Hurry up, Hawk.*

"Anyone's definitions," May said. He looked at me, almost startled, realizing suddenly that for the first time in all the times they'd had this argument there was a third opinion handy. "If you're making love, do you want response?" he said. I made my noncommittal head gesture. "Do you like your partner to lie quiet and still?" I varied the previous head motion. "She lie quiet and still with you, Spenser?"

Brenda's voice scraped out between her tightened teeth. "You bet your ass I didn't." I thought about blushing. May put his head in his hands.

"The simplest thing in the world," he murmured. "Just love and get it back. Not sick. Not weird. The simplest thing in the world."

The rain spattered against the window, driven by a shifted wind. Somewhere, probably in the kitchen, I could hear a faucet drip.

"Tell me about Richie Hanson," I said.

"Hanson?"

"Richie Hanson. Is he a hood? How's a Brattle Street smartie like you know someone who'd hire out to rape someone?"

"I met him at Concord Correctional Institute," May said. "Isn't that a joke, Correctional Institute. I was giving a poetry and criticism workshop there, part of the University outreach."

"And Hanson was doing time?"

"Yes, when he got out he got in touch with me. Wanted a letter of recommendation."

"Poetry workshop," Brenda snorted. "What the hell do you know about it. You never published a poem in your life, except those things that are mimeographed in Harvard Square."

"You needn't be a cook to judge a soufflé," he said.

Brenda made a spitting sound. "I've heard you say that so often," she said. "Isn't that typical? Always able to describe it; never able to do it. A legless man that teaches running."

Her voice was low, but easy to hear, articulated by her intensity.

The intercom rang, and I heard Hawk's voice when I picked it up, "Mistah Hanson to see Marse Spensah, bawse."

I said, "Considering the years of practice, that's the worst darkie dialect I've ever heard." I pressed the button to let them in and went to the apartment door. In less than a minute Hanson appeared at the door with Hawk behind him. Hanson was a blocky blond guy with scraggly hair, thin on top and long over the ears. There was a slight rim of blood inside one nostril and a darkening bruise under his right eye. In his neighbourhood he was probably tough. Compared to Hawk he was butterscotch candy.

Hawk pushed him gently into the room, shut the door and leaned against it. He was Ralph Lauren western this week, snakeskin

240

boots, jeans, denim shirt, western jacket, big hat. He was the only other guy I knew who had an 18-inch neck and looked good in clothes. The angular planes of his face gleamed like carved obsidian when he smiled.

"Afternoon, boss," he said.

"Jesus," I said, "Midnight cowboy. Hanson give you any trouble?"

"Nothing that counts," Hawk said.

"Richie," I said, "you know these folks?"

Hanson looked at Brenda. She was motionless, standing near May, hugging herself without seeming to realize it, rubbing her upper arms as if she were cold. He looked at May sitting on the couch. He looked at me and opened his mouth, then shut it and glanced over his shoulder at Hawk. Hawk smiled his glistening pleasant smile.

"Mr. May here on the couch tells us you raped his wife," I said.

"Ex-wife," Brenda said without affect.

Hanson looked at May again, and, half turning his head, out of the corner of his eye, again at Hawk.

"We'd like to know why you did that," I said.

Hanson said, "I don't know what's going on here. Who the hell are you?"

Hawk leaned effortlessly forward from the door and hit Hanson a six inch punch over the left kidney. Hanson gasped and went to his knees. Hawk leaned back against the door.

"He paid me," Hanson said. He got slowly to his feet and moved a little away from Hawk. "The professor paid me. He came to my place and give me five C's. Said not to hurt her bad, just do it and I'd get the other five when I give him the pictures."

I said, "Pictures?"

Brenda looked at the floor. I glanced at May. He was staring at the fist his two hands made between his knees.

"He wanted pictures of her. . .ah. . .you know, disrobed. Said it would be proof that I done it."

There was no sound for a moment in the room except that rattle of the fall rain against the window.

"We'll want those," I said.

"I give them all to the professor."

I looked at Hawk. He shook his head. I nodded. "Creep like you would keep a couple," I said. "We'll toss your place later. How about you Northrop. Where's your copies?"

"I burned them," he said.

Hawk grinned broadly. I nodded again. "Yeah. We'll look through your desk too, Northrop."

Brenda had not changed position. She was still rubbing her upper arms, looking at Hanson the way she had been looking at May.

"How could you do it?" she said.

Hanson looked at her blankly, "Huh?"

"How could you rape someone like that, for money?"

Hanson looked puzzled. "Hey," he said, "you're a nice looking broad."

Brenda's face was bunched in concentration. "But what about me? What about how I felt? It's like I was a. . . a mechanism and you were a mechanic. Didn't you ever think about how I might feel?"

Hanson looked even more confused. "A grand," he said. "A grand's a lot of dough, lady."

Brenda stared at him. Her breathing was getting more rapid.

Hanson looked at May. "How about you, you pansy bastard, what'd you do get lovey dovey and feel bad and confess?"

May didn't look up.

"I should never have hooked up with a goddamned pansy like you. You don't know how to act."

Without moving from the door Hawk said, "Shh." Hanson stopped as if a lock had clicked.

"Jail," Brenda said, her breathing was heavy, like she'd been running. "You are both going to jail forever, don't you care?"

Neither man looked at her.

"Don't you care? Doesn't either of you care how I felt?"

She looked at me and Hawk, a woman alone in a roomful of men. "How would you like it," she said. "How would you like this pig to walk into your house and strip you naked and rape you. How would you like to be lying on the floor, the floor for crissake, with his sweat all over you, and have him take your picture?"

Hawk's face was impassive and pleasant. For all you could tell he might have been listening to the beat of a different drummer.

"Doesn't anyone care about that?" Brenda said.

"Hanson can't," I said. "Lot of guys like him in the joint. Sometimes, I suppose, it's the joint makes them like that. Sometimes being like that gets them into the joint in the first place. He doesn't care about you; he doesn't even care about himself. Hell, he doesn't understand the question."

"How about you, North. Do you understand the question?" Brenda had turned, still hugging herself and leaned toward May again.

May pressed his clasped hands against his forehead, his body bent forward. His voice was very small. "I'm sorry Brenda. I was crazy. It's just that I wanted so little. It seemed so little to ask. I guess it drove me a little crazy."

"What you wanted 'North' was total possession," Brenda said.

He nodded. His face against his hands.

"I couldn't give you that," Brenda said, almost gently.

"I know," May said. "I guess, I loved not wisely but too well."

Tears suddenly appeared in Brenda's eyes.

I said "May, you're not Othello nor were meant to be. It's not her fault that she got raped."

Brenda straightened, turned away from May and said quite briskly to me, "How long will they be in jail?"

"Hard to say, depends on the sentence, and that depends on judges and lawyers and jurors," I shrugged.

"If they go," Hawk said.

"What's he mean?" Brenda said.

"It's an imperfect system," I said. "Hanson will fall. He's done time. They'll mail him right back, express. But Northrop. . . he's a professor; he's got money. He might not go. If he does he might get out soon."

"You mean he could do this to me and get away with it?"

"Not everyone who's bad gets punished," I said.

"I still walking around," Hawk murmured.

Brenda stared at me. "He might not even be punished," she said. She didn't seem to be talking to me. "And they're not even sorry." She didn't seem to be talking to anyone.

"I could whack them out for you, if you'd like," Hawk said.

Brenda looked at him a little startled. She smiled. "No," she said. "No thank you."

The room was quiet again. Brenda closed her eyes, put her palms together, and placed the tips of her pressed fingers against her lips. She stood that way for maybe twenty seconds. Then she went to the sideboard and took a small silver automatic pistol from her purse. Holding the gun in both hands as I'd taught her to a long time ago, she began to shoot. The first two rounds got Northrop in the face. The third shattered the lamp behind him on the end table. The fourth thudded into a big gold pillow in the wing chair and the fifth, after she steadied and aimed, drilled Richie Hanson through the upper lip just below his left nostril. The 25 caliber Colt had made small snapping noises as she fired, like an angry poodle. But in the silence that settled behind the shots, May and Hanson were exactly as dead as if she'd used a bazooka.

Hawk was still leaning against the door. "Dyn-o-mite," he said.

Brenda put the gun down on the sideboard, got a package of Merit Cigarettes out of her purse, lit one with a butane lighter, and dragged a third of it in. She looked at the just created corpses and let the smoke drift slowly out through barely parted lips.

"If they had been sorry," she said.

I looked at Hawk. "Yeah," he said. "I can take care of it."

"Good," I said. "Come on babe, we're going to go visit Susan Silverman."

Brenda frowned. She spoke slowly now, tiredly. "We're going to. . . cover this up?"

"Yes."

"But what will you do with. . ." she gestured at the dead men.

Hawk said, "I know a man with a salvage yard."

"You came to me for protection," I said. "Directly from the cops this morning. We went straight to Susan's and have been there ever since. It'll be a few days before they even know Northrop's gone. Nobody'll look for Hanson."

Brenda looked at the apartment.

"Brenda, one of the things Hawk is best at in all the world is covering up a death. You wish you hadn't shot them?"

"No," she said. Her voice was very firm.

I picked up the small silver gun and slipped it in my pocket. I offered her my arm. She took it and we left. As I closed the door behind us I could hear Hawk whistling softly to himself, "Moody's Mood For Love," as he punched out a number on the phone.

In a half an hour we were in Smithfield, and Susan was helping Brenda feel better. Me too.

Jukebox Jungle

by John D. MacDonald

Margaret Street Blues

The first night he was back he went to Morry's Golden Slipper. Dusk had changed to night in such a stealthy way that the flavor of it still hung in the air. He stood on the sidewalk for a few minutes. Sometimes when the weather is cold, you get an ache between your shoulder blades because of the way you hold yourself. It was a warm night but Cate felt that muscle-knot in his back.

He stood with the hot airlessness against his face. A small girl roller-skated solemnly by, the skate clacking over the sidewalk cracks. The cars lined up abreast and panted patiently, then roared off as the light changed. Cate smelled spilled beer, the lidless garbage cans behind the Russell Café next door, a distant trace of a woman's musky perfume.

The street was the same. Margaret Street never changed. In the daytime the old women, as shapeless as their market bags, possessed it, along with five thousand smudged children, with the number peddlers, the horse players, the broken-down fighters, the cokeys, the bums, the sneak thieves squinting at the sunshine.

But when the neon buzzed Margaret Street awoke with the thump-stomp of the jukes as shrill and endless as a cry of pain, an arm locked around a throat and heels drumming the alley asphalt as a quick hand rifles the pockets. Then most of the children slept, some of them on broken leather couches in the back rooms of the beer joints. The old women talked and laughed toothlessly across the high air shafts. At night, on Margaret Street, you felt the cool of the gun steel where you had it tucked under your belt. Your palms sweated. You moved carefully and you kept your mouth shut, and if you were alone you stayed out of the shadows. Because this was the new jungle. And beasts walk in the jungle.

Cate pulled the screen door open and stepped in. It flapped shut and they looked at him. Rossen, the bartender, froze with his hand on the tap, his eyes slightly narrowed, his face carefully blank. Two customers, strangers, thickset men in work shirts, turned to stare and then returned to their amiable argument.

Gina was sitting in the far side of one of the booths. He saw her stare at him. He could see a man's elbow extending beyond the edge of the near side of the booth. He wondered who it was.

Gina's eyes were hot and interested. Life was a storm that constantly twisted through Gina, shaking her and tearing her. She had a compact figure and a sallow complexion. If she had a placid temperament few men would have found her attractive. But with the great hot eyes and the restless lips and the sense of urgency about her, she was as elemental and moving as the first taste of spring.

Cate moved slowly into the room. He saw Gina lean toward the man opposite her and saw her lips form the words, "Paul Cate!"

The man looked around the edge of the booth. Cate had thought a thousand times about seeing Hank Olaf again, and each time the roil of nausea had stirred inside him. Big Olaf with the corn-tassle hair and the face like a clenched fist and the tiny blue eyes through which you could look into an emptiness where once there might have been a soul.

Rossen pulled the tap lever toward himself, filled the small beer glass and wiped the head flat with the bar stick.

"Welcome to our city," Hank Olaf said.

"You're crazy, Paulie," Gina said. "Why did you—"

"Shut up, Gina," Olaf said. "Shut your silly mouth. Paulie isn't crazy. He's just what you call stubborn. He's the type of guy you got to tell twice. Got to admire him a little."

"You better kill me this time, Hank," Cate said, almost gently.

"I'll take that as a suggestion, Paulie," Hank Olaf said.

Cate looked at Olaf's tailored summer-weight suit, white mesh shirt, the collar open at the brown oak-neck, the star sapphire

gleaming in the heavy gold setting on the little finger of his right
hand.

"You're doing well, aren't you, Hank?" he said.

Hank grinned. "Take a look at him, Gina. Runover heels and
worn out cuffs and a dirty shirt and a two-day beard. Look at the
bum, Gina. He used to look pretty sharp when he run around with
you, eh?"

Paul forced himself to smile at Gina. There was a hard satisfaction in him that came from not showing the fear, from not
turning and running. He walked casually over to the bar, turning
his back on them in the booth.

Rossen said, not moving his lips, "Be a good guy, Cate. Go
someplace else."

Paul put a dime on the bar top. "A small draft, Rossen."

Rossen looked over Paul's shoulder toward the booth. He drew
the beer. That meant Hank Olaf had given him the nod to go
ahead.

Gina walked over to the juke. Paul watched her with the beer
glass at his lips. She bent over the selections and punched the bars
for five numbers. She looked at him and through him on her way
back to the booth. Just as she sat down the first number started.
A plonk-plonk of a guitar and a nasal twang, "Thet little ole gal
down by the Rio Grande. Sed she'd wait for me while I traveled
cross the land. . . ."

Gina, to whom heaven was a double-feature horse opera, and
the sweetest singing was adenoidal.

The screen door flapped again, a meaningless, empty sound.

Cate turned and nodded at Dizzy Mary and the strange man
with her. No one on Margaret Street knew her last name. It
was doubtful as to whether Dizzy Mary remembered it. Her IQ
was probably somewhere in the sixties or low seventies. She was
blonde and she was impossibly beautiful with a soft wholesomeness
about her that always made Cate think of milk maids and sleepy
summer mornings. Her eyes were wide and empty and her voice
was little and thin and high. Each night of her life she drank
herself into meaningless, sodden helplessness, awaking the next
morning with no memories, no regrets, no hangovers, no flaw in
her beauty.

"Gee, Paulie," she squeaked. "Paulie Cate. You been away,
Paulie."

The date was inclined to be stuffy about it, until he took in Paul
Cate's shabby appearance.

"Hello, Diz," Paul replied.

"Kid, ya look awful! Ya been sick?" Mary asked.

"Come on, come on," the date said impatiently. He pried Mary loose and steered her for one of the dark booths in the back. Mary waved back at Paul and giggled her way into the shadows.

Rossen came out from behind the bar and went back to take their order. The second cowhand lyric was on. Hank Olaf got up and went to the end of the bar and pushed open the door into the back room.

Paul looked into the mirror behind the bar and saw Gina staring at his back. Her mouth had a twisted look and she beat time absently with her foot. He went over to her. Ghosts crawled across the hot dark lenses of her eyes.

"Go now, Paulie. Get out now," she said tonelessly.

"What possible difference could it make to you?"

"You know Gina. I feed stray dogs. I set out milk for the alley cats. Get on your horse, Paulie. Ride off into the sunset. You know what he's doing, don't you?"

"Making a phone call."

Her voice rose husky-clear over the music. "Then why are you waiting for it?"

"You wouldn't get it, Gina. You'd never in a million years get it through your head. On this subject you're as stupid as Diz. There's only one answer to running. If you've run once, you'll run the rest of your life unless you come back and face what you ran away from."

"You sound like a revival meeting, Paulie."

He smiled without humor. "So it's a revival meeting. We're reviving one Paul Cate. He's been dead for a little over a year."

"Have you been hit on the head lately?"

Hank came back toward the booth, scowling as he came. "Cast off, mate," he said. He pushed by Paul and sat down.

"How does it feel, Hank?" Paul asked.

"How does what feel?"

"Running into something you can't understand. Sitting there trying to think what angle I'd have coming back here."

"Go on over to the bar and have a beer on me, Paulie. You can't have any angle."

It unfolded like a play. He was one of the actors and the scenes and lines were inevitable. It took them ten minutes to arrive. Sipe and Anderson. They came in, cheery and hearty, nodding at Hank and Gina, yelling something back at Dizzy Mary, grinning at Rossen, shouldering in close on either side of Paul Cate.

Sipe slapped his shoulder. "Old Paulie. Good old Paulie. What you drinking, Paulie? The horses been unkind to you lately?"

Anderson spoke across him to Sipe. "I always liked old Cate. It's real nice when punks like us get a chance to 'sociate with a guy with an education. You learn something every day."

"Sure," said Sipe. "Looks a little thin, don't he?"

"You can't go by that. He's always been rugged. Say, who's that joe the Diz has got on the string? I've seen him some place."

"He's on delivery for Pritch. He's the new guy. Took Al's place. Al drew a two to five and Pritch figured he wasn't worth the bite to buy him off."

"Paulie's finished his dime beer. Let's take him to that new place. He'll like the new place, won't he?"

"He'll be nuts about it," Anderson said. "Come on, old pal."

As they moved away from the bar, Cate felt the delicate tap of fingers across his body. Sipe and Anderson were workmen. No foolish chances.

The barroom suddenly had a bright nightmare look as they moved him toward the door. All colors were intensified. Details were fixed and frozen. Rossen's hairy hand on the bar rag. The gleam, in the shadows, of Dizzy Mary's pale hair. Gina's mouth, like broken fruit. Olaf's smile, like a grimace of pain.

"You'll like this place," Sipe said as they pushed him gently through the door. Cate guessed, wrongly, that it would be at some distance from the Golden Slipper.

There was a narrow sidewalk between the Golden Slipper and Russell's Café. "It's right back here," Anderson said, giving him a hard thrust with his stone shoulder. Paul staggered down the sidewalk, caught himself when he was in the heavy shadows beyond the angled beam of the nearest streetlight.

They came in after him. Sipe was first, Paul swung with all his strength. Sipe blocked it easily with an upraised arm. Inside, through the wall of the building, Paul could hear the juke. He guessed with some small objective portion of his mind that he was opposite the booth where Gina sat, that she could not be more than five feet away from him. Someone turned the juke up very loud in the middle of a line. The same record that Gina had first played. "Sed she'd WAIT FOR ME. . ." it sang.

Anderson slid by him in the narrow space and got behind him. His big hands touched Paul's shoulders lightly, slid like a caress down to the elbows and then locked tight.

Sipe, in front of him, was silhouetted against the lights of the street. He wrapped a handkerchief around the knuckles of his right hand. He said, "Yeah, Al's woman was sore as hell at Pritch. She give him a bad time there. Couldn't understand why Pritch would let Al do time. Bend him a little, Andy."

Anderson interlocked his arms with Cate's, drawing Paul's arms closer together behind him. "Better?"

"Fine. Funny he don't yell or anything."

Anderson laughed. "It's his education. What did Pritch tell Al's woman?"

Paul Cate didn't hear the answer. Sipe came in with his knee first, and a flower of pain blossomed up through Cate's body and exploded with a roar in his ears. He strained upward with each blow, pressing hard with his heels against the concrete and then felt himself sagging heavily in Anderson's grasp.

Each blow seemed to add a felt-like thickness between the hard hands and his unprotected body, and gradually the pain lessened until each thud against him was a distant, heavy vibration.

One thin slice of his brain retained acuteness. "Al's woman is a looker. . . DOWN BY THE RIO GRANDE. . .hold him up a little, dammit. . .CROSS THE LAND. . .that Pritch is a shrewd guy. . ." Sipe stinks of the nearby garbage. Squeal of brake bands. Another shadow that stood solidly, watching. That would be Hank Olaf.

He felt the teeth along the left side of his jaw turn to gravel in his mouth. There was a thin nerve-scream to a broken tooth, oddly like the high note of a violin.

"Steady him now for the kiss-off."

The blow drove through his face and out the back of his skull, tearing it like wet cardboard. It spun him over and over and over and over, and then he knew he couldn't still be spinning because his face was in the angle of the wall of Russell's and the warm concrete. He heard the clink-clack-clink-clack of footsteps receding, merging with the traffic sound. The juke number ended. Dizzy Mary giggled thinly at the other end of a long black tunnel. The concrete vibrated against his cheek as a heavy truck went by.

He worked his fingers so that his hand crept like a big spider up to his face. He fingered his mouth and was mildly and distantly surprised to find it was open. He pushed up with his thumb and closed his mouth but as he took his hand away it sagged open again. There was wetness on his face and an odd jagged spur on his cheek.

It took a long time to work around so that his head was toward the light. He put his palms flat against the concrete and pulled his way, a few inches at a time, toward the light. A new number started on the juke. They had turned the volume down.

Just below the sidewalk, just under the surface of it, was a vast black velvet blanket stretched taut. As he moved toward the light, he felt the concrete growing increasingly brittle under his fingers, like the shale ice on a winter pond. He had to move carefully now. If he broke through the concrete he would land down in the black velvet and never find his way out again. He reached forward and caught the corner of the building in his fingertips. . . .

"How long have I been here?" he asked the nurse. His teeth were wired together in front and the tip of his tongue kept returning to the wire no matter how hard he tried to keep it away. It gave his voice a funny, muffled, hissing quality.

"Three days." She was heavy, with a sheen of perspiration on her face.

"Is it night?"

"No, it's about noon. This place fools you. It's in the basement. That's why the lights got to be on all the time. You got somebody who'll pay the shot, we'll move you upstairs out of this ward. This is the charity ward for males. We couldn't find any address on you when they brought you in."

"How bad am I?"

"The doctor'll be around the ward tomorrow morning. You ask him."

"I'd just like to know."

She stared at him. "Somebody didn't like you a little bit. Broken cheek bone and jaw. There was some internal bleeding, but it stopped yesterday. Funny, but they missed your nose. Almost always the nose is flattened when anybody gets worked over."

"How long'll I be here, nurse?"

"Brother, as soon as you can walk fifty feet, you're out. I told you this is a charity ward."

The walls were battleship gray. He counted thirty beds. No bed was empty. The smell of antiseptic was so heavy that he imagined he could taste it, yet underneath were other smells.

Delahay came an hour after Cate had sucked his luncheon gruel through his wired teeth. He pulled a chair over and sat down. He looked at Cate contemptuously as he pulled out his notebook and pencil stub.

"You should have known better than come back to town, Cate. You damn well knew something like this would happen. Let's have the story."

"It was Sipe and Anderson."

"Sure, sure. Sipe and Anderson. I won't even write that down. They'll prove that they were seventy miles away when it happened. And I suppose Olaf told them to do it."

"If you know, why ask me?"

251

"I hoped you fell down some stairs. Wasn't that it? A flight of stairs, eh?"

Delahay, the cop, knew Margaret Street. He'd been born there, had fought in its gutters, splitting his knuckles on the rock-hard jaws of people named Zarendowsek, Tomaselli, Rourke, Krdzak, Cohen. He'd fought his way, using other rules, up to lieutenant of police, but then the machine had broken his back to patrolman. Once they made certain his spirit was gone, they rewarded him with his sergeancy. Nothing was left of Delahay but soft gray fat, an acid contemptuousness and bored resignation.

"No," said Cate. "If you want a report you've got to put in it that I was beaten up by Sipe and Anderson because Hank Olaf told them to do it."

"And I suppose you wanna press charges, eh?" Delahay asked ironically.

"No charges. You asked me and I told you."

"You disappoint me, Cate. For a long time I figured you as smart. You traveled with a rough outfit, Hank and his crowd, but you were legitimate. How many other kids off Margaret Street get to be a C.P.A.? With his own office? The first thing I know you start drinking a little heavy and then Hank's boys smash your office and wreck your apartment and roll your car into the reservoir. Hank cuffs you around and you blow town. He brags he chases you the hell and gone away. Nobody knows for what. I listen here and there. Now I know what happened. Hank had a gimmick to chisel the syndicate on their end of the local slot machine take and you told him you'd play along and then you flubbed it for him, didn't you?"

"That's none of your business."

"So he scared you out of town and you wait over a year and come back looking like a bum. Why, Cate? I don't get it. Why go right down there and ask for it? You must have known that every time Hank looks at you he thinks of the two or three hundred grand a year you bobbled right out of his hands. Hank Olaf doesn't forget easy. He's a man holds a grudge."

"Just put this down in your book, Delahay. Write it all down. Sipe and Anderson came in and took me out. Dizzy Mary was there. So was Gina Ferraine. Dizzy Mary's date was a dark stocky man who started working for Pritchard recently. Rossen saw it too. Put it all down because as soon as they let me out I'm going right down and laugh in Olaf's face."

"You poor damn fool! The next time might kill you!"

"That's just the point. Hank's fix is strong enough so that he can laugh off a thing like this. But he can't laugh off murder.

252

That brings Captain Moley and his homicide boys in, and the fix doesn't cover Moley. I know that much. And if it's in your book, it'll give Moley the right lead."

Delahay stared at him. "Lemme get this, kid. You *want* him to kill you?"

Cate shifted his sore body on the bed. "What do you think? Hank Olaf got me in over my head. He got me in debt. He knew I was honest and he knew I was smart. He made me agree to rig the books he keeps for the syndicate. I owed him two thousand bucks. At the last minute I came out of the fog. The books went in rigged all right, but the summary statement was on the level. He took my business and my bank account and my girl and my car and. . .my pride and any guts I had." Cate shut his eyes tightly, despising the tears of weakness that squeezed out of the corners.

"Easy, kid. Easy," Delahay said.

"I tried living with what he'd done to me for a year. A man can't live that way. So I came back. He might as well finish the job, Delahay. I'm going to keep on giving him that chance to finish the job as long as I can crawl."

"What then, kid? What then?"

"He'll kill me, or he'll give up. And when he gives up I'm going to open up again, right back in the office where I started at the corner of Front and Margaret. I'm going to get back the little accounts I started with. Fergesson's Market and the Palace Diner and Bel-Mer Frocks and all the rest of them. I can get them back because they'd rather give the business to somebody who came out of the neighborhood. And every time I see Hank Olaf on the street I'm going to spit on his shoes and there isn't going to be a damn thing he'll do about because by then he'll know he's got to take it or kill me."

"Why don't you pick an easy way, kid? Go right down Front to the tracks and jump in front of the first freight that comes along."

"Put it all in your book, Delahay. Write it all down."

2
Die, Die Again

The afternoon sun was bright and hot as Paul Cate walked down Margaret Street. The bandage on his cheek was white and fresh. He walked slowly because there was a weakness in his legs, and his clothes, against his body, had the strange scratchy feeling of convalescence.

Mert Steen of Bel-Mer Frocks stood in the doorway of his shop. His eyes widened.

"Paulie-boy! Hell, I heard about it. Them monkeys! Come in and sit."

Paul allowed himself to be led in. He sat in a wooden armchair placed beside a dress rack. Mert produced a cigarette for him and lit it with a flourish. "You look like hell," he said.

"I'll be all right. Mert, how's business?"

The little man shrugged. "Who can tell? Paulie, you should be back in business. These boys I got handling my books now, a big outfit. Who is Mert Steen to them? Poo! A nothing. I ask them. I say do you think I should maybe cut down the size of the storeroom to give me more sales space? With you, I could get advice. With them I get the cold eye."

"Maybe they won't let me go back into business, Mert."

"That Olaf! All the time you're away he gets bigger. Maybe he's too big, Paulie. Top heavy. A thousand angles he has. All the dirty kinds of business there is. On this street he's king. He gives money to the kids. My money. Archer Fergesson's money. He comes in and he says to me, 'Mert, I'm a little short and fifty would tide me over.' I give him the fifty. I got to. You ever see a rack of dresses after some woman comes in like a customer and sprays with just a little tiny bit of acid? Such a thing can cost me five, six hundred. But always he is in for his fifty. Once every month. Always a loan. And I can't even take it off the tax as a business expense."

"You could keep a record and take it to the Bureau and try to get permission to take it off as a legitimate expense. Then they might wonder whether Hank reports it for tax purposes."

"Before I do that I order me a nice stone for the cemetery. I could even have both dates carved on it."

"If I do start in again, Mert, I'm going to have to keep my office in my pocket until I get set."

"No, Paulie. A little loan to friends. How much would it be? Can it kill me? Rent on one room, and then a desk, two chairs, a file cabinet and supplies. And a little extra to make you look good, Paulie. A good pin stripe you should have. For me it is a selfish thing. If you're working I make more."

Cate felt the sting at the corners of his eyes. He looked away from Mert's face for a moment, ground the cigarette out in the ash stand.

"I may take you up on that," he said.

"Paulie!"

"Yes?"

"Paulie, be careful. That Olaf, he hates you. People who take what you got always hate you because maybe inside they feel dirty when they look at you. That is one thing I have always seen happening. So be careful."

A half block further along Margaret toward Front, Cate turned into Pritchard's Smoke Shop for some cigarettes. He could hear the clack of the pool balls overhead and a distant blur of voices coming from the horse room in the rear.

Sipe was leaning on the counter studying a punch board. He looked at Cate and his eyes widened. "Paulie! How the hell do you feel?"

"Rough."

"Kid, the orders were to mark you. I laid off the nose. Once you really bust the nose flat, the guy looks like an ex-pug the rest of his life."

"Thanks, Sipe."

"Lemme see how they got them teeth wired. Bad break?"

"No, it was clean. Right here."

"From the way it felt," Sipe said with the satisfaction of a man who knows his trade, "I thought it would be clean. Soon as that wire comes off I'll buy you a steak, hey? Just to show it was nothing personal."

"You had to do it, Sipe. I knew that. But just for the record, if you were on the floor right now I'd kick you in the mouth. You know that."

Sipe nodded wisely. "The old psychology. I don't blame you feeling sore. Kid, why haven't you hit the road? You better be out of town by dark."

"I'm staying," Paul said. "If you want me tonight I'll be at the Golden Slipper."

Sipe looked troubled. "Paulie, if you do that he's going to give us a ring to come around. Rossen'll tell him, you know."

"Then come around and get your exercise, Sipe."

"I don't get it. Hell, I don't want to bust that face again before it knits. It wouldn't be—I just wouldn't want to do it. Like kicking a kid out of a baby buggy."

Cate left him and went out. He crossed Front Street and continued down Margaret to the corner of Sandstrom. He went into the small, grubby, dusty lobby of the Regency Hotel, asked a desk clerk he didn't know for Sam Aigo, the owner. Then a wave of weakness hit him, and he wavered over and sat in one of the greasy tapestried chairs to wait for Sam.

Sam appeared in his shirt sleeves. He looked stolidly down at Cate. "What do you want? I hear you're poison, Paul. I don't want trouble with Olaf."

"A proposition, Sam. I've got to have a place to live. I want a small room with a bath. I'll get your books back in shape for you."

"What makes you think the books need it?"

"Sam, Sam. Look! This is Paul Cate. Remember? I kept my thumb on the back of your neck and you made good dough. We licked the pilferage problem and started to make money on the sandwiches you serve in the grill, and we straightened out the crooked bartenders. When I'm not around everybody chisels you, Sam. You're a soft touch. So don't give me that glare."

The grin came at last, transforming the sullen heavy face. "Kid, you come around just at the right time. I need what you got. Me, I got help that takes money out of the poor box even. I give you a room like a king. A room almost as good as mine." The grin faded. "But you got to work fast Paul. I hear Olaf is going to run you out of town again. I hear the tale along the street."

"He did it once, Sam. I won't run again."

"You hungry?"

"All I can eat is something soft enough so I can suck it past all this wire."

"Come to the kitchen, Paul. With my own hands I'll fix you some of that onion soup. Remember? Sam Aigo. Best cook in the world."

The box came at five o'clock and was delivered up to the room Sam had given him. It bore the label of Rufe Tomasoni's Men's Shoppe on Front Street. There was a note inside, on top of the folded suit, the shirts, socks and ties.

So you think we can let an old customer look like a bum? Mert says you are going to maybe help him a little with the books. Paul, I got a tax problem and I don't like the answer I get from downtown on it. Come around and give me the answer, kid, and this box is for free. If I don't like your answer either, you're going to pay through the nose, believe me.

He took a hot bath and put on the new clothes. The weight he had lost made the shirt a trifle loose around the collar, and he had to pull the belt so tight on the trousers that they gathered at the waist. But the jacket sat well on his angular shoulders.

He went down to the grill room. The new clothes gave him a feeling of assurance.

Sam came in and bought him a drink and told him that a special dish would be coming out of the kitchen soon. "Like cooking for a baby, it is," Sam Aigo said, "or like in the old country for the old men without the teeth."

After he finished the concoction, Cate walked over to the cash register. Sam had temporarily relieved the buxom young redhead.

"Sam," said Paul, "now don't blow your top because that isn't the way to handle it. The young bartender, the dark-haired one, has a friend. A blonde. She left fifteen minutes ago. She came in with a shopping bag and sat down around the corner of the bar."

"Is that bad?"

"Only when she comes in with a bag as light as a feather and goes out with a bag that's almost pulling her shoulder out of joint. I bet she walked out with six fifths."

Sam turned pale and then brick red. He cursed in his own language. He said, "I'll yank that punk into the storage cellar and I'll—"

"No, Sam," Paul said gently. "Not like that. I'll get hold of a friend and have him tail the blonde. Then there's a chance for a recovery. Maybe they're stashing it away with the idea the bartender'll quit at inventory time. I've got to run along."

"Where are you going?"

"To the Golden Slipper."

"No, Paul. Stay here. Don't go down there. Down there you haven't got a chance."

Cate smiled. "It's funny, but I know that if I don't go down there tonight, I haven't got a chance."

"You're talking crazy!" Sam Aigo bellowed.

Paul smiled and left. He stood outside and lit a cigarette. Margaret Street had come to life with the darkness. He squared his shoulders and began walking steadily toward Morry's Golden Slipper.

He glanced idly at a tall girl. She stopped and said, "Paul! Paul Cate!" Her voice had a soft breathless quality. "Oh, Paul, don't you even know me?"

"Fran!" he said. "Fran Fergesson. It's been—"

"Two years, Paul. I was away for the last year you were here and when I came back I heard. . .that there'd been trouble. Then I heard about. . . last week." She reached her fingertips out, touched his face and then yanked her hand back as though her boldness had startled her. "What did they do to you, Paul?"

"The usual efficient job. Fran, you've changed. You were. . ."

"All knobbly bones and joints and snarly hair. I know."

The eyes, he saw, were the same. Wide and blue under a bold arch of brow. The mouth was soft, vulnerable. But the greatest change was in the maturity of her figure. She seemed to wear the surprisingly ripe femininity like a costume but recently donned so that the wearer was not yet accustomed to it.

"You were a child," he said.

"Hardly. It was just delayed adolescence. I was eighteen, you know, and I'm twenty now. Paul, you're in trouble. Bad trouble."

"It's hardly a new situation, Fran. How's your father?"

"Fretting about the market again. He bought some new display bins and things and he doesn't think they're paying for themselves like the salesman said. He wants to talk to you, Paul. He's always thought you were the only one to give him good advice."

A drunk suddenly lurched into her. He backed away and peered at her owlishly. "Honey, lambie," he said, "I couldn' fine a prettier girl to bunk into."

Her voice hardened and she thrust her chin out at him. "On your way, chum, or I'll have you thrown in the tank. My old man's a cop on this beat."

"Parn me; Parn *me!*" the drunk said and wavered off.

Fran turned back to her conversation with Paul as though nothing had happened. The girls of Margaret Street learn all the knacks of self-protection at a tender age.

"Can I help, Paul?" She looked away suddenly as though she had said too much. "Can we help, Dad and I?"

"I don't think so. This is my baby. Fran, if—"

"Yes?" she said eagerly.

"Fran, if things should work out all right, maybe one of these days we can take in a movie."

"I'd love it," she said, as though he had offered her a cruise to the south seas.

He watched her walk away. She smiled back over her shoulder at him.

Cate nearly walked by the Golden Slipper. He had to stop and force himself to pull the screen door open. Once inside he felt dizzy. When his vision cleared, he saw Rossen favoring him with a hard, glassy stare.

"On your way, punk," Rossen said. "On your way."

"Charlie," Paul said, "you've been tending bar for the hard boys so long you seem to be getting illusions about yourself. I've got a gun in my pocket and I'm going to blow three neat little holes in that big belly of yours."

Rossen glared and said, "Yeah?" Cate watched him steadily. A greasy film suddenly appeared on Rossen's wide forehead. He licked his lips. He looked away from Paul. "I just work here. If you want to be a damn fool, that's your lookout."

"Now ask me to have a beer on the house," Paul said quietly.

"Now look, I—"

"Charlie!"

"Can I buy you a beer?"

"Try again. And say Mr. Cate?"

"Can I buy you a beer, Mr. Cate?"

"Thank you, Charlie. That will be nice. I just didn't want you getting too many illusions, Charlie. I'm afraid I'm not carrying a gun."

"Nice!" Gina's voice came softly to his ears. She was in the same booth. Alone. He looked beyond her, through the wall into the darkness of the passageway where the pain had been a thing born of the jungle. "You look better, Paulie, than you did before the treatment. Come and sit with me."

He took the beer off the bar, winking as he did so at a sour-faced Rossen. He carried it over to the booth.

Gina inspected him. "You can't get your mouth open, eh?" There was a sadistic pleasure in the glowing depths of the hot eyes. The cherry sundae lips curled.

"No," he said shortly.

"I can figure you, Paulie. Oh, how I know you. But you're making a bad guess. Hank won't let you suck around and talk him out of anything. He's going to run you out like he did before."

"Is he?" Cate asked politely.

Her eyes narrowed. "What kind of an angle have you got? You sound—as though the deck could be marked." There was a puzzled look on her face.

"Why should you worry?"

"You were good for laughs, Paulie. Until Hank came along. He's strong, Paulie. He's the strongest man I ever met. He keeps me in line, Paulie. And that's more than you ever did. So why am I worrying? There's nothing you can do to Hank Olaf."

Rossen went quickly into the back room.

"I suppose you're waiting for him?" Paul asked. She nodded. "With Rossen phoning him he'll be along sooner."

"If he didn't come until one in the morning, I'd still be here."

"A truly touching loyalty."

The screen door slapped shut. Gina looked beyond him. "Hi, Diz."

She came over to the booth. "Gosh, like old times," Mary said. "You'n Paulie. Gosh!"

"Knock it off, Diz," Gina said. "Go find your own booth, you damn lush. Go crawl into a shotglass."

Mary giggled vacantly. "Geez, you're funny, Gina. You're a scream." She went back into another booth.

"That one," Gina said with contempt. "All those damn looks. If we could trade brains I could blow this town for good."

Rossen came out of the back room looking smug. Paul made idle small talk with Gina and kept himself from betraying his nervousness.

Hank was along within ten minutes. He turned his bull shoulders as he came through the door and he walked with a muscle-bound swagger, setting his feet down hard. He smiled but his eyes were like little blue marbles tucked deep into the sockets of flesh.

"Well, well," he said, shoving Gina over with his hip as he wedged into the booth, "the bad penny. Ain't you tired of falling on your head, Paulie?"

"I'm getting used to it."

"What's your offer?"

"For what?"

"Talk sense. What's the deal? What have you got to say that'll keep me from handing you the next treatment? I like to see you run, Paulie. You run good."

Paul looked down at his fingertips. "You smell, Hank. You always have. I guess I didn't notice it much until I came back."

The room was so still that over the traffic growl Paul could hear the ticking of the cheap alarm clock set among the bottles on the back bar.

He looked at Gina. She had a white look around the lips. Hank Olaf stared directly at the knot of Paul's new necktie. He sucked his lips in against his teeth and exhaled through his nose with a faint whistling sound.

"I hate your guts, Cate," he whispered. "You and your line of chatter and all your Hunky friends. You crossed me and I broke you. Now you're going to learn what sweat means. Sipe and Andy are on their way over."

"Then I better hurry if I want to finish my beer, Hank."

"You got the crazies, Paulie," Gina whined.

"We'll beat on this monkey until they got him up at Marcy State in a wet sheet, Gina. Maybe that's where he should have been all along."

Sipe and Anderson came in. They came up to the booth.

"See if you can make him bounce," Hank Olaf said.

"I don't like it," Sipe said softly.

"Since when did anybody start caring what you like and what you don't like, Sipe? You want to go back to twenty buck prelims for a living?"

"Come on, kid," Anderson said tiredly. "On your feet."

Paul Cate didn't look back as they walked him to the door. He said, loud enough for Hank to hear, "Another concussion so soon, boys, and I could drop dead. But that's your problem, not Hank's."

3
Dizzy Mary

They walked him moodily to the narrow passageway. Sipe stuffed his hands in his pockets. "Go on, Cate Run. We'll go back in and tell him you got loose and ran for it."

"You heard your orders, boys. Let's get to work. This time, Sipe, just for variety, you hold me and let Anderson try his luck."

"Not me," Andy said softly. "Not me. I don't think I'll even hold you."

"Run, damn you!" Sipe cried bitterly.

Cate smiled woodenly. He turned away from them and went back to the screen door. Sipe muttered something to Anderson. They turned together and walked on down the street. Paul Cate pulled the screen door open and went back into the barroom.

Hank's tiny eyes widened and his mouth sagged open. "What the—"

"Don't get upset, Hank. They decided to wait until I was back on my feet."

"They did, eh? Tomorrow those two are going to be a couple of sad boys."

Paul went over to the booth. Hank had his legs crossed, his big foot in a highly polished cordovan shoe, swinging.

"Why don't you try your luck, Hank?" Paul asked. "Just like the time with that Chinese. Remember? Once you got slugging you forgot your name and who you were hitting. They pulled you off before you killed him. You were lucky. Murder would have put a crimp in your career."

Dizzy Mary had gone up to the bar. She sat on a wire-legged stool and watched them blankly.

Hank Olaf doubled his big fists. "I could—"

Gina put a restraining hand on his wrist. "No, honey. No!"

"Make your play or give up, Hank," Cate said harshly, the wired teeth giving his voice a phony theatrical quality.

"Cate, so help me—" Hank said.

But Paul gathered the spittle in front of the wired teeth. He spat awkwardly. He heard Rossen's sharp intake of breath. Dizzy Mary screamed with empty laughter.

"Right on his shoe! Spittin' right on his shoe!"

He could sense the anger draining out of Hank Olaf. The small eyes turned shrewd. He glanced toward Dizzy Mary.

"Charlie!" Hank snapped. "Shut the damn door and bolt it. Cut the lights."

Paul heard the door slam, the snick of the bolt, and then the room was in darkness. The car lights flickered through the dusty front windows, made patterns that slipped across the wall.

"How you supposed to drink in the dark?" Mary said, as though she were about to break into tears.

"What are you going to do, Hank?" Gina whispered.

"Shut up!" he said. "This wise guy is getting himself fixed. He got me so sore I couldn't think."

"I don't want no trouble," Rossen said warily.

Paul's eyes were used to the light by then. He saw the bulk of Hank Olaf, on his feet. A hard hand grasped the front of the new suit and slung Paul toward the back of the room.

"Gina!" Hank said. "Get the Diz into the back room. Hurry it up."

"What you doin'?" Mary complained. "What is this?"

"Come on, honey," Gina said soothingly. "Hank wants you to go into the back room for a drink. You know, on the house."

"I don't want no trouble!" Rossen said bitterly. His shadow merged for a moment with Hank's and there was the pistol-shot sound of a hard palm cracked off a cheek. "Okay," Rossen mumbled. "Okay."

"Just stay out here by the door and watch for trouble. Put some dough in that juke and turn it up loud. Pull the shade down on the door, you dummy."

The backroom light clicked on. The door was half open. Hank pushed Paul heavily. "Get in there, smart guy."

Hank shut the door behind him and leaned against it. A forty watt bulb hung from a ceiling cord. It made harsh shadows on the stacked cases of beer, the wall phone, the four faces.

262

Hank moved quickly to Paul, spun him around, grabbed him around the middle with his heavy left arm and tightened his right hand on Paul's right wrist. He trundled him over toward the back wall of naked cinderblock. He had the strength of an ape. Three times, as Paul winced and whimpered with the pain of it, Hank drove Paul's fist into the cinderblocks. The bruised knuckles split and puffed. The piece Rossen had punched in the darkness was a heavy boogiewoogie piano backed up by drums and a muted trumpet that cried like a lonely child.

Paul felt his body eel-wet with the cold sweat that the pain brought. The pain also brought weakness. Hank shifted his hold and jammed Paul's left fist against the concrete, striking with a downward motion that peeled the knuckles as though it had been done with a rasp.

Then he spun Paul around and thudded a booming right into the solar plexus. He caught Paul and eased him, gasping, onto a wide low stack of cardboard cartons of canned beer.

Paul was conscious but almost completely paralyzed.

Mary whined, "Where's the drink? Whyn't you stop horsing and give me the drink?"

"Get away from her, Gina," Hank said. "Get over there."

The pianist thumped out the rolling bass.

"What are you doing?" Gina asked. She moved into Paul's line of vision. Her mouth was working and her eyes were twin pools of dark fire.

Hank advanced on Mary. She said, "Hey!" in a startled voice and backed away.

"We can't get him one way, we can get him another way," Hank said. "You seen it all, Gina. Every bit of it. How Paulie makes a pass at Dizzy Mary and she isn't having any and he gets sore and he gets her back here in the back room with the door shut. Rossen hears some thumping and he goes in and finds that this crazy Cate is beating the hell out of Dizzy Mary. So he calls the cops. For an assault charge I got friends that can make sure Paulie goes away for five years."

"But Mary will—"

"Her? When she comes out of it, tell her that Cate did it. She's got enough liquor in her right now so she doesn't ever know what day it is."

Mary had backed as far as she could go

"Hold still, honey," Hank whispered.

"Lookit—" Mary started.

Paul strained until he could look back into the corner. Hank's broad back bulked high and wide. He could see the crown of

263

Mary's shining head over Hank's left shoulder. Hank's big fist cocked back. Mary gave a thin squeal of terror.

Gina stood over at the side, biting the back of her hand. "No, Hank!" she moaned. "Don't do it!"

"Who cares a damn about this dame?" Hank grunted. His fist shot out.

Paul managed to topple off the low stack of crates. He landed on his elbows and knees and fought his way to his feet. He staggered weakly.

Mary sobbed as Hank hit her again. Gina ran and pulled at Hank's shoulder. She screamed at him.

"No, Hank! Hank, you'll kill her! Hank! Stop it."

He turned. His face was an animal's face. He slapped Gina away with the back of his wet hand. She stumbled and fell, touched her face where Hank's blow had fallen.

Paul took two faltering steps toward Hank. He saw Gina get her feet under her. Her eyes were blank and bottomless pits with all the hot fire gone. Her mouth was pursed and puritan. She yanked her skirt up and her hand touched the lean leather scabbard tied to the outer roundness of the white thigh.

Her fingers seized the slender hilt, then came free bearing a sliver of silver flame. She sprung and thrust, and the flame, withdrawn, had turned from silver to red-black. She thrust again at the small of his back. She was hunched, stooped, implacable, and her breath came harsh with each thrust. Beyond Hank, the sobbing blonde slipped to the floor and lay on her side. Hank roared with pain and surprise.

He half turned and he pressed the back of his right hand against his kidney, arching his back. Surprise and shock slowed his movements.

"Gina!" Paul said. "No!"

As though his words had some other meaning, she shifted the stained knife in her grasp and struck high as he turned, struck at the wide strong place where the bull neck joined and merged with the ox-heavy shoulders.

He went down then, folding oddly as though the heavy bones had been instantaneously slipped from the flesh of arms and legs. He dropped with the suddenness of a puppet when the strings are slashed. He lay sprawled on the floor, his face frozen and vacuous with the horrid surprise of instantaneous death.

Gina backed four slow steps away from him, backed until her heels hit a three-high stack of wooden cases. She sat down and her face was as dead as Hank's as she pinched a fold of her skirt between thumb and forefinger and wiped the knife through it.

"He shouldn't have hit me," she said with dulled voice. "He knew that I told him never to hit me. He knew that." She turned her face toward Paul and she frowned with puzzlement. "I told him never to hit me. Why would he do that?"

Dizzy Mary sobbed quietly, not moving.

Somehow Paul found a nickel and got it into the phone slot. He held himself upright by grasping the upper edge of the phone box. He dialed zero.

Beyond the door, nightmare music had begun. Adenoidal twang. "Thet little ole gal. . . ."

"Police. Quick."

The door opened. "What's happening in. . .God! Dear God!"

"Yes. Sergeant Delahay. Yes. Delahay. Quickly."

". . . . while I traveled 'cross the land. Where the tumbleweed rolls wild and free. . . ."

"Why did he have to hit me? I told him he should never hit me."

"This is Cate. The Golden Slipper. Quick. An ambulance too. And homicide. Olaf's dead."

". . . Oh, thet little ole gal I leff behine. . ."

"I don't want no trouble," Rossen moaned.

She lived with her father over the market. Archer Fergesson was explaining and emphasizing each point by stabbing the palm of his left hand with a blunt forefinger.

"Dammit, Paul, it don't make sense. The fella I bought 'em from said six percent. I don't see how I'm paying fourteen percent on these cabinets."

"Look, Mr. Fergesson," said Paul, "you pay interest not on the unpaid balance, but on the whole cost of the cabinet. So the average outstanding debt over the life of the loan is one-half the purchase price. So you pay twelve percent. And their service charge makes up the other two. I say get a short term note from the bank and pay them off and get back onto a reasonable rate of interest."

Fran, leaning against the doorway, gave an elaborate sigh. "Does a girl ever get to the movies?"

Paul grinned at her and stood up.

Archer Fergesson shook his head. "I'm glad you're back in business, Paul. Dammit, nobody else explains things to me." He looked beyond Paul at his daughter. "Sure be nice if I could get the advice for free, too."

Fran flushed crimson. "Dad! Please!"

Paul nodded sagely. "Maybe we can arrange it."

265

"Both of you are awful!" she said hotly.

Fran pulled the door open and went halfway down the stairs. Paul winked at Archer Fergesson and followed her out. He pulled the apartment door shut. Fran waited in the semi-darkness, looking up at him.

"You two think you're very funny, don't you?"

He put his hands on her shoulders and turned her as he went down to the step below the one on which she stood. Their eyes were on a level. "Funny like a crutch," he whispered.

"Oh, Paul. Paul!"

"I want to kiss you but I can't yet. Not with a face-full of silver wire."

Her lips pressed hard against his as her arm went around his neck. "Wire, schmire," she said.

Then they went slowly down the rest of the stairs and out onto the sidewalks of Margaret Street. The neon flickered and buzzed and the jukes thomped their music into the snarling traffic.

Paul looked down into her eyes and said, "We belong here. On the street."

Secret amusement touched her eyes.

"Where else, Paulie? Where on earth else?"

"Another Glass, Watson!"

by John Dickson Carr

"He laid an envelope on the table, and we all bent over it.
It was of common quality, greyish in colour. The address,
'Sir Henry Baskerville, Northumberland Hotel', was printed
in rough characters. . ."

So writes Dr. Watson in the fourth chapter of *The Hound of
the Baskervilles*. The game is afoot. A great case is in full cry.
Mr. Sherlock Holmes and his colleague, not for the first time,
are about to meet some very rough characters indeed.

The Northumberland Hotel, presumably, was in Northumberland Avenue, and leading off the Avenue in Northumberland
Street you will today find an Inn named after the great detective.

And it is right that we should find it there, for it was also in a
Northumberland Avenue hotel that Holmes traced Francis Hay
Moulton, the energetic American who had spirited away Lord
St. Simon's bride in *The Noble Bachelor*. Northumberland Avenue
is close to Scotland Yard. It is also a stone's throw from Charing
Cross Station; Holmes and Watson, off for one of their sudden
dashes into the country, could always find a train leaving just
when they wanted it. Nobody else has ever been able to accomplish
this.

From *The Illustrious Client* we learn that both the detective and the doctor "had a weakness for the Turkish Bath". They liked to relax in the drying-room on the upper floor of the Northumberland Avenue establishment. The Baths came to an end a few years ago. But the building still remains, with its front door immediately outside the inn. Northumberland Avenue, heavy and lowering, is in fact as full of romance as Baker Street itself.

It is even more fitting that an inn, a tavern, a pub, a chop-house (call it what you will) should be named after the most famous character in English fiction. An enthusiast for Mr. Sherlock Holmes once suggested that there ought to be a statue to his memory. But this is all wrong. Statues are frozen, lifeless, exalted on their pedestals. There is nothing frozen about Sherlock Holmes. Even when he sits back in his chair, his eyes closed and his finger-tips together, he is as vibrant with life as when he crawls about a room in search of clues. A moment more, and he will leap from his chair; a moment more, and he will shed dressing-gown for frock-coat and top-hat, or the cloth cap which means war. In these matters the British have a sound, practical, romantic instinct. Statues are erected to those whom they admire or esteem. But inn-signs are reserved for those whom they both honour and love.

"The Sherlock Holmes!" Think, I beg of you, of that name and what it means.

It is as dreamlike as "The Treasure Island", yet as homely as "The Bull and Bush". It does not suggest blood and corpses, however much such things may lurk in the background. On the contrary, it suggests the snug sitting-room upstairs: the cigars in the coal-scuttle, the fire and gaslight aglow: in short, the height of comfort and cosiness.

For Sherlock Holmes, despite his surface austerity, was the soul of hospitality. Few detectives can ever have been so bedevilled by their clients. They rout him out before dawn, as Helen Stoner did in *The Speckled Band*. They arrive with the hop, skip, and jump of near-madness, after the fashion of Alexander Holder, the banker, in *The Beryl Coronet*. They burst into the room and faint on the hearthrug (Dr. Thorneycroft Huxtable in *The Priory School*). Or, like the ungrateful Inspector Lestrade, they creep in to scoff at his methods and pick his brains.

It does not matter. Unruffled, unfailing, Sherlock Holmes gives them whisky or brandy if they are men (brandy is Watson's prescription for almost anything), and hot coffee if they are women. His ear is always attentive. Food can be, and is, provided in abundance.

"Mrs. Hudson has risen to the occasion," said Holmes, uncovering a dish of curried chicken. "Her cuisine is a little limited, but she has as good an idea of breakfast as a Scotchwoman."

This cryptic statement is significant; the conservative Watson ate ham and eggs. But it was a special occasion. At the breakfast-table, under cover of a dish, Holmes returns the stolen Naval Treaty to that unfortunate Foreign Office official who for weeks has lived under suspicion of having stolen it. Holmes's sense of the dramatic, perhaps, is a little ill-timed. The luckless Percy Phelps is so overcome with relief that he dances, shrieks, and collapses. Once more they are compelled to revive a client with brandy.

On the other hand, in the story of *The Noble Bachelor*, to which reference has been made, Holmes's sheer kindness of heart sets out a feast for his guests. "A quite epicurean little cold supper," declares Watson, "began to be laid out upon our humble lodging-house mahogany. There were a couple of brace of cold woodcock, a pheasant, a *pâté-de-foie-gras* pie, with a group of ancient and cobwebby bottles."

No nonsense, here, about Vitamin C or a balanced diet. Sherlock Holmes rubs his hands with pleasure at the sight. His delight, Watson indicates, comes less from the sight of the supper-table than from the prospect of uniting in friendship an affronted English bridegroom and a wayward American bride. But careful consideration must show us that far too much has been made of Holmes's indifference to the pleasures of the table.

Holmes never scorned food and drink. There were times when he simply forgot them. Absorbed in a complex case, as in the affair of John Openshaw and *The Five Orange Pips*, he returns shaken to Baker Street at ten P.M. He looks pale and worn. Tearing a piece from a loaf of bread, he devours it voraciously with the cry that he is starving.

And yet he has had breakfast that morning; and both Holmes and Watson were tremendous breakfast-eaters at a late hour. Most of us, at a pinch, could go foodless for twelve hours without actually reeling. Holmes could do it, but it upset him.

The truth of his tastes may be seen with great clearness in *The Dying Detective*. Anguished, ghastly, he has gone for three days without food or drink to trap the murderer of poor Victor Savage. Belladonna and crusts of beeswax were hardly necessary as a disguise. That wild talk of oysters and half-crowns was not all pretended delirium. Then the gaslight brightens; Mr Culverton Smith snarls in the grip of the law. After dragging deeply at a cigarette, Holmes's first call is for biscuits and a glass of claret from his inexhaustible sideboard. But Mrs. Hudson's cuisine will no longer suffice; instead he carries away Watson for a dinner at Simpson's.

Holmes's maternal ancestors were French. He loved his food, and he needed it. Indeed, it would be possible to argue that the aroma of good cooking and the bouquet of good wine rise as pervasively through the stories as the tang of yellow fog or the reek of shag tobacco. Good novels, they say, are full of inns. Certainly good stories are full of plates and glasses; it is a part of the Victorian scene, entwined in curtained cosiness, and the adventures of Sherlock Holmes would be bleak without it.

He is very fond of dining in Italian restaurants: not only at such well-known places as Frascati's in Oxford Street, but at others which are more difficult to trace. There is Mancini's, mentioned in *The Hound of the Baskervilles*. There is still another, described as "garish", to which Watson is abruptly summoned during the quest for the Bruce-Partington plans.

"Am dining," writes Holmes, "at Goldini's Restaurant, Gloucester Road, Kensington. Please come at once and join me there. Bring with you a jemmy, a dark lantern, a chisel, and a revolver."

Watson has qualms, as well he may. The last time they burgled somebody's house, he may have recalled, they were obliged to leap on top of a six-foot wall and then run two miles, much of it across the switchback surface of Hampstead Heath in the dark.

"Have you had something to eat?" rather casually demands Sherlock Holmes, solicitous of everyone's comfort except Watson's, when his companion arrives laden with burglar's tools at Goldini's. "Then join me in a coffee and curaçao."

That occurred in the year '95, an *annus mirabilis*; Holmes has not hitherto shown much interest in liqueurs. On the other hand, his taste in drinks is as broad and catholic as Watson's own. In addition to the famous tantalus, forever flowing with spirits, Holmes has put in a good store of claret and Burgundy. Of the Burgundy we can be certain: a bottle of Beaune with lunch gives Watson courage to protest about Holmes's use of cocaine. And he is cured of that habit to indulge a taste for better things. Assuredly his close attention to wine-bottles and corkscrews enables him to solve the problem of *The Abbey Grange* in '97.

But these are later cases. At the very beginning, in '81, a depressed Watson haunts the Criterion Bar. If he hadn't, he would not have encountered young Stamford and he would never have met Sherlock Holmes. The thought is too appalling to pursue. We need not accuse Watson of over-conviviality, as did the late Monsignor Knox, or say he was extravagant on his half-pay. As late as the year '91, according to Holmes, you could lunch at the very best hotel for half a crown. You could occupy its finest rooms (rooms, distinctly plural) for ten bob a night. And, if eightpence was a very steep price to pay for a glass of sherry, then a whole shilling for a cocktail must have seemed really intolerable.

Nostalgia, nostalgia, nostalgia!

During a joyous Christmas interlude, not long after the good doctor's marriage, we find Holmes and Watson drinking beer at the Alpha Inn, Bloomsbury. The affair of *The Blue Carbuncle* ends, as it should, at the supper-table. Even in the last chronological adventure–on the terrible 2nd of August, 1914–their habits are unchanged.

Von Bork, the master-spy, has been foiled and outwitted. There is an east wind coming. "Another glass, Watson!" exclaims a familiar voice from a gaunt man of sixty. On the edge of a world in ruins, above the last twinkling lights, they drink Imperial Tokay from the cellars of Franz Joseph at the Schoenbrunn Palace.

Last adventure? Gaunt man of sixty? No; this won't do. Holmes is immortal, like D'Artagnan or Sam Weller; he does not age or grow infirm; he is still with us. Such a reflection alone must gladden the heart of any wayfarer in London who sees on the new hanging sign in Northumberland Street the familiar profile.

Above all it must gladden the heart of Mr. Holmes himself. "By Jove, Watson!" We can fancy the lean figure stiffening in the mist, the imperious gesture to Watson, the door eagerly pushed open. Now Sherlock Holmes, it is true, would never consent to visit openly a place named in his honour. Essentially a modest man, despite all his quirks of vanity, he would revolt through all his fastidious soul. But it would delight him to prowl there in disguise.

In the old days, we know, the perfection of his disguises was equalled only by their staggering variety. They ranged from a Tibetan Llama to a French *ouvrier*; from Sigerson, the Norwegian explorer, to Captain Basil, the swaggering sea-dog. As a clergyman he deceived Irene Adler. As an old bookseller he made Watson faint. As a plumber named Escott he wooed and won the housemaid of Charles Augustus Milverton. Imagination boggles at what disguise he would assume in "The Sherlock Holmes".

Yet how those deep-set eyes would glisten, those long and nervous fingers twitch, to revisit the scene of his glory among the criminal relics he loved! Climbing a staircase that might be that of 22IB Baker Street, he would find his own room little changed, his possessions and his effects just as he left them–the dressing-gown on its hook, tobacco in the Persian slipper, unanswered letters still affixed to the mantelpiece and his decoy bust still in the window to mislead Colonel Sebastian Moran. Downstairs in the bars are the relics of his famous cases. In *his* day the relics were not so neat or tidy. In *his* day they had a way of wandering into unlikely positions, and turning up in the butter-dish.

But they are nearly all here, from the great hound affrighting the air to John Straker's cataract-knife and the King of Bohemia's snuff-box.

And so, should you yourself be there one quiet night, be sure to look carefully if covertly about you. That stolid business-man by the barcounter, that Foreign Office official at the restaurant-table, may not be quite what they seem. As a train whistles from Charing Cross you may catch a flash from the keen eyes of Sherlock Holmes—or think you hear the great-hearted chuckle of Sir Arthur Conan Doyle.